"I NEVER LEARNED FANCY TALK—"

So John stopped talking, capturing Alexis's parted lips with his own. She felt the thrust of his tongue, the thrilling sweep of it.

"Alexis—" his blue, blue eyes bored into hers "— you know what might happen if we follow this . . . attraction to its end?"

"No. I'm only sure I want it," she argued softly. "I want you."

"I can't leave here again—ever."

"I know. . . ."

"And I could never ask you to stay. I did that with Caroline."

"I know."

"The day might come when you ask yourself what you're doing in this godforsaken neck of the woods—"

"Damn it, John, I know!" Only one thing could quiet him. Alexis pressed the length of her body against him, her finger across his lips in a gesture that said, "Be still and come hither. . . ."

Books by Lucy Snow

HARLEQUIN SUPERROMANCES
 83—SONG OF EDEN
115—A RED BIRD IN WINTER

These books may be available at your local bookseller.

Lucy Snow

A RED BIRD IN WINTER

Harlequin Books

TORONTO • NEW YORK • LONDON
AMSTERDAM • PARIS • SYDNEY • HAMBURG
STOCKHOLM • ATHENS • TOKYO • MILAN

Published May 1984

First printing March 1984

ISBN 0-373-70115-2

Grateful acknowledgment is extended to the following:

George C. Miller, Toronto, for the lines "there are countries
we . . . in the morning" by George C. Miller.
Copyright 1977 by George C. Miller. As quoted in the
anthology 30 (Some Odd) Poems. Used by permission.

Printed in Canada

This book is affectionately dedicated to
Sandra Rabinovitch
my colleague and crony

CHAPTER ONE

"Stick to your own kind."

Karl Hulst's voice was smooth, as smooth as his manner. He was lean, graceful and muscular with a thick swath of prematurely gray hair, and his physical attractiveness was at least partly responsible for the attention the press was always eager to give him. At forty-five, Karl was at the height of his career as conductor of the Chicago Festival Orchestra. The darling of audiences as well as journalists, he was sharing the last few minutes before his concert with a writer—the beautiful woman keeping him company in the elegant waiting room of the orchestra's downtown concert hall wasn't there on business.

"Come now, Karl," Alexis answered a bit playfully, though she knew he didn't relish levity right before a concert, especially not this concert. It was the orchestra's first after the Christmas-New Year's break. "Don't be a stick-in-the-mud. This is a big deal for me—a full page in the Sunday edition. Imagine it—a full page!"

She awaited his response, hoping his enthusiasm over this new success would match her own. The distinguished man glanced at himself in the gilt-framed mirror. Carefully, his long sensitive fingers reached for a tightly closed white rosebud and snapped it into the lapel of his jacket. "Would you, my dear?" was all he said as he turned to Alexis and handed her a narrow band of white silk.

Alexis took the tie with the ease of one long familiar with fine fabric. Deftly her perfectly manicured fingers tied the silk into exactly the sort of bow needed to complete Karl's outfit: full-dress tails. Stepping back, she took a long appraising glance at the man, and when she raised her eyes to his, she answered his silent question with a nod of approval. She had helped him dress for concerts more times than she could count. Four years. . . . She'd been his companion, his lover for four years, which was a good part of the reason she'd hoped his reaction to her good news would have been a little more enthusiastic.

They moved to one of the brocaded couches and sat down, both completely at ease despite their formal clothes. Neither was a stranger to opulence.

"A big deal, is it?" Karl asked, and Alexis sensed his distaste of her use of slang. It was a habit she'd picked up in her work, especially lately. The article she'd just sold, the one she was so excited about, had required research in a part of the city she'd never investigated before.

"Yes, Karl—a major step, a departure."

"Alexis," he said, turning to face the lovely woman at his side and looking at her pointedly to emphasize his words. "As I told you before, I can't understand why someone of your background needs to work for a living at all, let alone slumming down in the river wards for the squalid little items of no interest that one could expect to discover there. You're not a social worker, my dear."

"I'm a writer, Karl, and this is the first real story I've ever done."

"Don't be ridiculous, Alexis."

Perhaps he was right. It was ridiculous to think that in the five years since she'd left the University of Chicago, Alexis Juneau Smythe had never yet written a real story. As a matter of fact, she was a free-lance features writer for several large dailies and magazines, and this lengthy article was only one of many she'd had published in the past few years. It was just that those others had been so different.

Alexis had worked her way up, though no one would have called her method of climbing "the hard way." Her mother had got her her first job, right after she graduated. Margaret's wealthy friends had just established another of their charitable organizations, and they had needed a promotion manager. From there, Alexis had begun to do a little society reporting, her position as an "insider" making her popular with newspaper readers—and a little unpopular with her mother's friends. When she'd started writing profiles of prominent Chicago personalities in society, business and the arts, she'd moved in a direction that eventually established her as a competent journalist. She'd even gone back to school for a master's in journalism. But until she met Betty Welty, she'd never known just what kind of writer she could become.

Betty was a Chicago alderwoman, a black who was sensitive to the problems of her ward because she had been brought up under the same conditions she was working so hard to better for others. When Alexis had been assigned to do a profile on Alderwoman

Welty, she had been a little hesitant, a little afraid the official wouldn't take kindly to describing her work to a Smythe. But Betty Welty didn't care at all that Alexis was from one of Chicago's richest families. She opened up to the journalist's sincere interest and probing questions. The result was a profile of which Alexis was duly proud. And when Betty called her to thank her for the profile and to offer her a personal tour of her ward, Alexis readily agreed.

It was on that tour that she met Marilyn Bank and decided to do an article on her. At sixteen, Marilyn had already had two children, whom she was raising on her own. At seventeen, she'd decided to change her life and had managed to get to college. Now, at twenty-six, she was not only a Ph.D., but a professor at the university she herself had attended. Alexis's article about Marilyn Bank was the story of a struggle—the story of both a poor person's and a woman's struggle. When the assignment editor saw it, she jumped at the chance to publish the article, which Alexis had submitted without guarantee of payment. This afternoon Alexis had learned the article would appear in the next weekend edition of the paper. She was excited, and she had expected Karl to be excited, too.

Unlike the subject of her latest article, Alexis had grown up among the crème de la crème of Chicago society. Yet few people who knew her—including Karl—knew that she hadn't been born into the family that had raised her. She had never been able to bring herself to ask for details, but she had been aware since childhood that her real mother had given her up at birth. Her adoptive parents, Margaret MacIntyre

Smythe and the late Wallace Hamilton Smythe, were from very wealthy and distinguished families. Wallace's people had "come over on the May-flower"—some said literally—and it would have been hard to find an older, more well-bred family than the Smythes. Nor would it have been easy to find a richer family than the descendants of "Juneau" Sam MacIntyre, a crusty prospector who had made a fortune in gold in turn-of-the-century Alaska.

Wallace and Margaret had enjoyed a long and happy marriage, and they had treated Alexis exactly as though she'd been born to them. In fact, before his death two years previously, Wallace Hamilton Smythe had been a noted historian, a man with a highly regarded style of writing. Everyone just assumed Alexis had come by her journalistic talent "naturally."

At twenty-six Alexis looked like the woman she had been raised to be, a woman who had grown up in a fine—indeed exclusive—section of the Windy City. She'd spent her whole life in the area in which Kenwood meets Hyde Park, and breeding meets brains. In Kenwood were the stately mansions of the monied elite, in Hyde Park, the University of Chicago, where Wallace Smythe had held a distinguished chair in history. Like other young women she knew in her "neighborhood," Alexis had been properly introduced to polite society at a ball held in her honor, and in her family's own ballroom. Looking at her that evening as she sat beside Karl, both of them reclining with easy poise on the delicate Louis XIV settee in the green room, one wouldn't have had difficulty picturing Alexis ten years previously—a lovely sixteen-year-old dressed demurely in white silk for her "coming out."

She wasn't wearing white silk tonight—her strapless black *peau de soie* gown was from one of Chicago's finest stores. Generally, she was in the habit of choosing conservative, well-crafted ensembles. She preferred French designers, but shunned anything that was flamboyant, even in seasons in which flamboyance was fashionable. She went instead for quality fabrics, elegant lines, gentle beiges and dove grays—colors that did justice to her own rather delicate coloring. Like her clothes, her manner was almost always elegant, refined.

Alexis's hair was a smooth well-cut bell that fell just past her jaw, a style that set off the unusual honey shade that was her own, though the lighter and darker blond streaks running through had been her hairdresser's idea, interspersed so skillfully that they seemed but shimmering lights and shadows. For the concert, the same hairdresser had twisted Alexis's hair into an intricate chignon sweeping up from the back of her long neck, emphasizing the shapely slope of her shoulders.

Her deep blue-green eyes were her most striking feature, the only part of her not touched by some agent or unguent meant to improve or intensify her looks. For overall, her appearance was as polished as the appearance of a fine work of art. Her skin, for instance, glowed a little too golden for the northern January night. Because she had spent Christmas with her mother at a resort in the Caribbean. And because she could afford the most expensive lotions for tan-

ning, and later for softening the effects of too much
sun. Everything about Alexis—except for those startling eyes—was a tiny bit unnatural, though very lovely, the way a statue of flawless marble is unnatural,
though its beauty is capable of making the viewer
catch his breath in appreciation—almost in astonishment.

Perhaps Karl Hulst had lost his astonishment at
her beauty, for he seemed not even to notice how
lovely Alexis looked—not that that bothered her. She
had other things on her mind.

"The reason I'm so pleased about this article,"
Alexis said, wanting to continue their conversation
despite the fact that Karl was glancing at his watch in
a rather bored manner, "the reason I want your
opinion is that it *is* such a departure—so different
from the profiles of executives and socialites...."

"And what's wrong with executives and socialites?"

"Nothing, Karl. It's just that ...."

"I should think you'd be the last person in the
world to object to dealing with socialites."

"I haven't objected to anything I've done so far. I
just want to do something more. Something different."

"The point is, my dear," Karl commented, placing
his hand over hers where it lay in her lap, pale against
the dark silk of her gown. "You don't need to worry
about all this. What does it matter what you write
about? It's not as though you needed the money."

"Of course I don't write for the money." She kept
her voice even, hiding her emotions. Perhaps it was
her imagination, but it seemed to be getting difficult

to talk to Karl. He had been very interested in her work when they had first begun seeing each other. But since she'd been working with Marilyn Bank, he seemed not to want to talk about her projects. It was his right, of course, not to have to listen. Still, his lack of interest made her feel a little sad...perhaps a little lonely, or something else. The feeling that had been gnawing at her with growing persistence over the past few weeks felt very much like restlessness.

Karl yawned, then stretched his arms, loosening his muscles a bit before his performance. "I just find it hard to get excited about down-and-outers—"

"Down-and-outers?" Alexis asked, surprised at his use of that insensitive term. "I don't consider the people I write about as 'down-and-outers.' Marilyn Bank isn't what anybody would call—"

"Look, Alexis," Karl interrupted. "It's all very interesting the first hundred or so times you've heard it, but really, it's the oldest story in the book."

"What is? What are you talking about, Karl?"

"Horatio Alger—rags to riches—that's what I'm talking about." There was a contemptuous quality to his voice that he didn't make the least effort to mask. "Don't people ever get tired of hearing about other people who have pulled themselves up from impossible depths? Frankly, the whole thing bores me."

"Does it now?" Alexis replied, her well-bred tones hiding her deep disappointment at Karl's blasé and callous attitude.

"Oh, my dear, I'm sorry," he said suddenly. He knew her well enough to know when she was upset, Alexis reflected wryly, though he didn't seem to know her well enough to keep from upsetting her.

"I've offended you. Of course I'm pleased with your success as a writer. You mustn't think for a moment that I'm not."

The conductor reached across the small distance between them and planted a kiss on her cheek. Then he settled back with another glance at his watch. For her part, Alexis felt she had been wrong to bring up the subject of her article at such a time. Though Karl was never bothered in any way by stage fright, she usually tried to talk only of light matters when she waited backstage with him.

Karl, however, didn't let the current subject drop. "Why don't you reverse the process?" he asked.

"Reverse the process? I don't understand."

"Well, instead of telling the stories of people who've gone from rags to riches, why not do things the other way around? Riches to rags. I think you'd get more interesting results if you wrote stories about people who had tasted greatness, then toppled from the heights. At least," Karl said, drawing out the words, "decline is intriguing. . . ."

The boredom had crept back into his tone. In fact, he raised his lean hand to his lips to stifle another yawn that threatened.

But Alexis hadn't noticed his tone. His words had piqued her writer's curiosity. "Riches to rags?" she said thoughtfully. "What sort of idea did you have in mind?"

"Talk to any wino in the park," Karl answered abruptly, revealing his lack of real interest. "Everybody's got a story."

Alexis looked at him. She thought he'd been serious, that he was offering her an idea for new stories.

She turned away, her profile a perfect cameo against the backdrop of the green silk draperies of the room. Her sigh, a hopeless little exhalation, sent a whiff of her perfume into the air between her and her lover.

"Ah, Alexis," Karl said softly, "I've done it again, haven't I, my darling?"

"It's all right, Karl," she answered evenly, glancing at the slim gold band of her wristwatch. "We really shouldn't be discussing this now. It's only a few minutes until—"

"There's enough time for me to tell you one story—one real story," he said contritely, taking her hand in his own but staring off into the distance in the manner of one who is straining to remember exact details in their proper order. "Ah, yes," Karl said, nearly to himself, "Webber—that was the name. . . ." Then he turned to Alexis and, raising his voice, he began his tale.

"The story I'm about to tell you was told to me confidentially, so I must ask you to forget about it once it's passed your ears."

Alexis nodded.

"Very well, then. The story concerns the daughter of one of the matrons on our present board of directors, a widow of some influence. From an old Chicago family—but I won't say which. The lady had one child, a daughter who was her pride and joy, as they say. It seems the girl was quite a talented clarinetist, and when she had run the usual gamut of private teachers, our matron decided she was ready for bigger things and packed her off to New York."

"To study further?" Alexis asked, settling back as Karl continued.

"To study. To study at Juilliard."

At the mention of the world-famous music school, Alexis nodded in recognition and appreciation.

"Apparently, the girl was doing quite well in her studies—until she fell in love, or, as her mother put it, 'fell into bad company,' " Karl went on, smiling a little.

"Who was the man?"

"A regular Li'l Abner—that's who!" Karl laughed, but Alexis wasn't sure why.

"What do you mean?"

"The matron's daughter fell in love with a real country kid—you understand, my dear—what they call a 'ridge runner,' a hick, a hillbilly...."

"A hillbilly in New York?" She cringed a little when she repeated the term, unsure whether it was derogatory. "Where was he from? How did he get there? Was he at Juilliard?"

"Indeed he was at Juilliard," Karl replied. "How he got there, I couldn't say. Charity case of some sort, I suppose. He was from the hills of Arkansas, the Ozarks—the boy was a long way from home, that's certain. I don't know how much you know about the region, but areas of the Ozarks are pretty isolated, not exactly the bright lights of Broadway. I've guest conducted down there a number of times. It's .... Well, let's just say, that for a boy from the hills, New York would be quite an adjustment."

"He was just a boy?"

"He must have been seventeen or so when he arrived in the Big Apple. I heard the story a few years ago, so I can't say for sure. And I ought to tell you that all this happened ten or fifteen years ago."

"What? What exactly happened?" Alexis asked. She was beginning to wonder what this story had to do with Karl's suggestion that she should write about people who had failed after initial success. To go from the Ozark hills to a fine music school in New York sounded like rags to riches to her.

"Well," Karl continued, that small almost- condescending smile still curving his lips, "our hillbilly was some violinist, apparently one of the best to come along in years. He did brilliantly at Juilliard during his first year, but he got the reputation of being an oddball—bit of a hermit. I guess he never quite fit in with the Juilliard crowd. Maybe the big city was just too much for the kid. Anyway, it's not surprising that he had some difficulty getting along there, and perhaps that was why he welcomed a little assistance from...."

"The rich matron's daughter."

"Right."

"And they fell in love and ran back to the hills, and our rich matron never saw her child again?" Alexis smiled a little at her romantic conclusion to the tale, almost hoping it was the right conclusion. It wasn't.

"No," Karl said. "No, not exactly. The two of them stuck it out for another year or so, until they discovered that our rich matron was about to have a new heir to her fortune."

"The girl was expecting a baby?"

"Not only that, but worse as far as the matron was concerned. She discovered the couple was married— had been secretly married for a while. The thought of it nearly broke the dear lady's heart—her daughter married to a hillbilly. She did what she could to get the girl back to Chicago, or failing that, back to Juilliard. But to no avail. The minute they realized there was a baby coming, the kids ran back to the Ozarks, and by all accounts, Webber is there still.''

"Webber?"

"I think that was the kid's name—the violinist."

"And the matron's daughter?"

"Ah," Karl said, sighing a little too dramatically. "Here comes the sad part. It seems the girl died there in the hills—whether before or after the baby was born, I couldn't say. What's really tragic is that she was an excellent clarinetist. I myself heard her play a number of times. It's a shame, but I guess these things do happen."

"And what about Webber—the violinist? I suppose his career was ruined, as well?"

"I suppose so, though I don't know how much it mattered to him. Our matron seems to think he went back to country fiddling, which she feels is the proper sort of music for one of his persuasion."

"His persuasion?" Alexis asked, again sensing that Karl found something funny in the fate of the country musician.

"To each his own," Karl replied. "It's probably best for country folk to stick to country music."

The idea didn't make a lot of sense to Alexis. "But he was exceptionally talented...."

"So the story goes. Talented kids are a dime a dozen, Alexis. It takes more than talent; it takes guts."

"And you think it wouldn't take guts to come all

the way to New York from the Ozarks with nothing but your violin and your talent?''

"I'm sure I don't know, my dear," Karl answered. His tone indicated he was already tired of the story he'd told her. "I merely related this little tale so you could see that not only are there those who rise to greatness—there are those who fall. That girl could have had a brilliant career if she'd stuck to her studies instead of getting involved with someone whose upbringing was so different from her own. It was a real tragedy to lose such a musician, to have such a promising career fall into ruin.''

Alexis felt for the girl, but it seemed to her that this Webber person had suffered equally; after all, he, too, had once been considered promising.

She would have asked Karl more about Mr. Webber, but suddenly she heard applause and realized the concertmaster, the first violinist, had stepped on stage. The audience would be expecting Karl in seconds, and indeed, there was a knock on the door just then, before it was discreetly opened by the stage manager. He peered around it and motioned for Karl to come along.

"Stick to your own kind, my dear," Karl whispered as he brushed past Alexis. This repetition of his previous words startled her—as though he had read her thoughts and realized his tale of the two doomed musicians had aroused in her greater sympathy for the country kid.

Gathering her thoughts quickly, she followed the two men down the narrow backstage corridor that led to the wings of the theatre's large, brilliantly lit stage. Onstage, a full symphony orchestra awaited the leadership of Karl Hulst. Alexis was suddenly full of the pride she always felt when she watched Karl conduct. Each time she was privileged to be with him as he worked, she looked forward to the moment when he raised his baton for the first measure of music. From where she stood, she could see his face. She waited expectantly for him to look up, to raise his arms, to begin. Always at that moment, she liked to see his face, to see there the pride in his own talent, the confidence his long training and wide experience had given him.

He glanced up, and for the first time in the four years she had been his lover, Alexis was disappointed in Karl. For what she saw in his expression was not pride and confidence—it was haughtiness—perhaps even a hint of cruelty. For a breathless instant, she was shocked. And then she remembered the twinge of restlessness she had experienced earlier. More and more, she was beginning to feel there was something wrong with her life. And she also felt that that was silly. She was lucky to be leading this kind of life; part of that good luck was having Karl Hulst. She looked again, seeing that he was about to turn once more to the audience, to acknowledge their thundering applause. Enthusiastically, Alexis joined in their acclaim.

CHAPTER TWO

BUT ALEXIS'S DISSATISFACTION INTENSIFIED as January turned to February and winter deepened. When she set out one morning to do some shopping, she thought the expedition would do her good—lift her flagging spirits. Yet by the time she found herself walking north up Chicago's "Magnificent Mile," an area of fine stores, she realized she'd already lost interest in the shopping spree. The north wind assaulted the fine skin of her face. It felt as though it were blowing straight down from the north pole—right across the frozen expanses of Canada—across the American border—across her own cheeks like a slap. It was depressing.

She went into expensive stores full of lovely things, but somehow she found it hard to concentrate. She came back again and again to the same idea, a simple enough idea, to be sure, but one that had never occurred to her before. For the first time in her life, she was thinking of leaving Chicago.

Of course, she had left on vacation countless times. Her mother had a condominium in the Bahamas. Alexis and Karl took a house near Saint-Tropez on the Riviera each August. And there were always skiing trips to Innsbruck in the Austrian Alps when she needed a vacation. But this time Alexis wasn't thinking about a vacation. She was thinking about changing her life.

She took a seat in the elegant restaurant of one of the stores. A waitress dressed in a crisp white-aproned uniform took her order, but when the woman returned shortly with the beautifully garnished seafood salad, Alexis found she had lost her appetite. She sipped at a glass of Perrier with lime and feigned interest in the salad, but it was useless. She gave up trying to eat and let her thoughts stray.

It just seemed that nothing in her life was exciting anymore. She felt guilty when she thought about how ridiculous her dissatisfaction would seem in comparison to the problems of some people, and yet, she couldn't help being unhappy.

Part of the problem was Karl. She'd been thinking about him seriously lately, and she was finally ready to admit their relationship was less than ideal. Of course, she couldn't have asked for a more active social life than the one she shared with him. Receptions, luncheons, dinner parties—there was no end to them, no end of opportunities to shine and be shown. And Karl was generous, too. Quite without making the connection between her actions and her thoughts, Alexis absently twirled the pavé diamond watch that sparkled at her wrist. Karl had given it to her only days before, for Valentine Day.

But he wasn't passionate.

And he was nineteen years older than she. This fact in itself didn't bother Alexis. After all, age alone wasn't much of a determining factor in anything. The problem was that Karl had made good use of his years—almost too good, if that was possible. He had been everywhere, seen everything. It was hard to excite a man like that—hard to impress him. Why Alexis felt the need to impress Karl, she wasn't sure. But it disappointed her to think there was nothing she could show him or teach him—nothing they could discover together, each of them suddenly joyous with childlike delight. Anything childlike—including children themselves—almost disgusted Karl, who prided himself on being so "civilized." Alexis had always considered him wonderfully sophisticated. Yet lately, she wondered whether the more appropriate word might be "jaded."

Sighing, she finished her drink and left a generous tip for the woman who had served her uneaten lunch. Alexis gathered up her dove-gray leather handbag and her few parcels and left the restaurant, heading for the elevators. But before she reached them, a colorful display outside the store's travel department caught her eye. "See America," the poster read, and printed on it was a map of the country with stylized paintings depicting the attractions of various states. There was a picture of Niagara Falls up in one corner of New York State, and a jaunty Empire State Building down in the opposite corner. There were cotton blossoms, sailing ships, buffalo.... And toward the lower center of the map, there was a nicely executed picture of a log cabin surrounded by pines and nestled in the hills. It caught Alexis's attention for some reason that nagged at the back of her mind.

She entered the department and walked toward a rack of travel brochures, choosing several to slip into her bag for future reading. She very much doubted that seeing any part of her own country would be a sufficient diversion, considering her present state of mind, but she wasn't sure about that—or about anything. That was the problem.

Back on Michigan Avenue, Alexis hailed a taxicab. It never took her long to get one, so she had the time and the silence, as she rode, to think about another aspect of her life that was rapidly becoming less than wonderful—her work. Though she herself had been enormously pleased with the publication of her article on Marilyn Bank, she hadn't received nearly the feedback she'd hoped for. Ms Bank herself had been thrilled, and Alderwoman Welty had congratulated Alexis on her objectivity and thoroughness. But apart from that, there had been only one other comment on the piece, which had stung Alexis deeply.

One reader had written a letter to the paper's editor, saying he found it disgusting that a person from a family who had always lived in a mansion should dare to think she knew anything about what life was like in a tenement. When she read that, Alexis remembered Karl's warning. Perhaps he had been right. Her ego took quite a bruising as a result of that letter, and she didn't feel any better after a meeting with the editor who had purchased the article in the first place. Alexis had planned several other articles as follow-ups, but when she explained her ideas, the editor made it clear she wasn't interested in another item from Alexis at the moment, and probably wouldn't be for some time. As she explained it, what had made the article so appealing hadn't been so much Alexis's writing as her viewpoint. After all, everyone in Chicago could recognize the name Smythe. And a rich person writing in-depth articles

on poorer people was controversial and interesting—
for a while. . . .

Alexis had nearly slammed the door in fury as she
left the editor's office. Sometimes she was sorry that
her good manners prevented her from telling off a
person or two now and then—from giving a door a
good hard slam when she felt like it.

The cab entered the wrought-iron gates that stood
open at the circular drive in front of Alexis's home.
The house itself wasn't visible from the street, for a
tall, perfectly trimmed ornamental hedge surrounded
the grounds. But as the cabbie pulled up to the front
door he let out a low whistle, indicating his amazement at the size and the beauty of the building before
him.

Of modified Georgian style, the main part of the
house sported clean lines accentuated by its stone
construction. Black shutters graced row upon row of
windows in this five-story central portion, the wide
portico flanking a wooden door with a huge, shining
brass knocker. Off the central part of the building
were two wings, one on either side, both also several
stories high.

In one of these wings, Alexis maintained a suite of
rooms. She could easily have had a place of her own.
Her father's will had made her an heiress, and she
earned money from her work, as well. She'd considered taking an apartment downtown, but had decided to stay with her mother. Now that Wallace was
dead, there were only the two women in the large
house. To have left her mother alone wouldn't have
been at all right. At one time the mansion had been
full of people. Juneau Sam had built it himself—and

he'd let every relative who came calling live there as long as they liked. It must have been quite something in those days, Alexis often thought. It was something now, too, a beautiful, lonely, empty something.

Sighing, she paid the driver, nodding when he thanked her heartily, but refusing his offer to carry her parcels for her. She made her way up the stone staircase, considered fumbling in her purse for her key, gave up the idea and knocked once with the smooth brass knocker that stung her fingers in the piercing cold.

She was answered immediately by a middle-aged woman in a burgundy-colored business suit. In Juneau Sam's time, the maids had been Irish girls with coppery curls and lilting accents. He'd had dozens of them because he had an eye for a pretty face, and a pocket that never emptied. Now there was Ms Buckner, a "home-management consultant" from the best domestic agency in Chicago.

When she'd removed her coat and boots and put on gray kid slippers, Alexis glanced in the large, ornately framed mirror that stood in the spacious front hall of the house. Reflected there were the alternating black and white squares of the hall floor. As a child it had amused her to know that some people had floors that looked just the same but were made from linoleum or vinyl. In this home, each square was made of hand-cut Italian marble. The mirror caught and reflected a dark Rubenesque painting framed in gold, a potted palm, a swath of red wallpaper with a flocked design, the entrance to a room, and in front of that, the bottom stairs of a white marble staircase with a curved ebony banister. Against that backdrop of elegance and wealth, the mirror also showed Alexis, a tall figure in gray tweed and gray silk blouse that made her blue-green eyes look all the more intense, intense with a kind of sadness that seemed out of place amid so much comfort and luxury.

"Is that you, dear?" a soft voice called from the drawing room adjacent to the hall, and it was only then that Alexis noticed another voice had momentarily stopped—the grating tones could only belong to Evelyn Kain.

"Yes, mother," Alexis answered, moving toward the drawing room. The room was bright with the brittle light of the February afternoon. Ten-foot-high windows, bathed in sheer curtains and drawn-back pale blue draperies, allowed daylight to accentuate the delicate curves of French Provincial sofas and chairs.

In one chair sat Margaret MacIntyre Smythe, her legs crossed at the ankles, her hands folded in her lap. It seemed to Alexis that her mother's beauty never lessened, only changed to accommodate her age. Though her hair was completely silver, she still had the slender form of her youth, the fine eye for design and detail that made the rose-colored afternoon dress she wore look as beautiful as the flowing dresses of her girlhood. And her green eyes were as warm as they had ever been. And her soft smile was as sincere.

"Sit down, dear," Margaret said, motioning to a chair at her side. "Have some coffee. It's just been brought in, and—"

"Could be a little hotter." Alexis wasn't surprised at the interruption from the woman who sat in the chair on the other side of Margaret. Evelyn had been silent for the past three minutes, and for her that was probably some kind of record. The dowager Mrs. Kain came from a family so wealthy that it was said Evelyn collected banks the way her friends collected diamonds. Not that she lacked those, either. Even at this time, the middle of the afternoon, she fairly dripped with them. Her blue-white hair was topped with a hat several innocent birds had given their best feathers to decorate, and there was no doubt in Alexis's mind that the feathers had looked infinitely better on the birds.

"As I was saying, Margaret," Evelyn went on, as if she didn't want to waste any more time keeping silent, "I'm absolutely appalled. . . ."

"I don't see how the situation is any different now from what it's always been, Evelyn." Margaret's voice was even, though Alexis knew her mother was straining to be patient with this woman who had been her friend since childhood. "The girl has her own world, her own life. You mustn't expect her—"

"But how can she stand it—living with that barbarian?"

"Ev, I doubt very much that the man is a barbarian. He's a teacher, after all."

"He's a farmer. The man is a plain dirt farmer."

"He's your son-in-law."

"He is not!" Evelyn nearly shouted. Both Margaret and Alexis flinched at the volume of her voice, which had risen in pitch until it was almost a squeak. Margaret sighed in the manner of one who has been forced to participate in the same argument many times over, but Evelyn Kain was paying little attention to her hostess. "That hick is no son-in-law of mine. Caroline, rest her soul, had the good sense never to bring him to my home. He is not my family."

"But his daughter is? I don't understand you, Ev," Margaret said. "You're complaining because Caroline's daughter, your granddaughter, refused to visit you. And in the same breath, you're bragging that Caroline's husband has never set foot in your house."

"Ex-husband."

"All right, ex-husband. What do you want? Are they to be family or are they not?"

"You know very well what I mean, Margaret. Don't be obtuse."

"I'm not being. . . ."

Alexis tuned out. Her mother and Mrs. Kain had been arguing about one thing or another for as long as she could remember. Whatever they had to say to each other was of little interest to Alexis. If Margaret hadn't been so kind, she would have ended her friendship with Evelyn ages ago, for the woman was a gossip, a self-centered and selfish person with very definite ideas about everything—ideas definite enough to be called prejudice. Alexis sipped at her coffee and thought about the travel brochures in her bag. Perhaps she should take a look at them.

"Studied at Juilliard. I told her. Caroline, I said—"

"It's been more than a decade, Evelyn."

"I don't care how long it's been. What I care about is the fact that Caroline left Juilliard to run off with that heathen, and now, after all these years, he's turning my own grandchild against me. I don't want her to grow up in the hills. I don't want her to be a little savage just like her father—''

"I hardly think—''

"Who?'' The single word from Alexis startled the older women into embarrassed silence.

"I beg your pardon, dear?'' Margaret said, clearing her throat.

"Who is it that your daughter married, Mrs. Kain?'' Evelyn adjusted the pale mink collar of her suit coat with a nervous gesture, all the while staring at Alexis with her mouth open as though she were, as usual, ready to speak, but for some reason unwilling. "I. . . . I. . . .''

"Perhaps you'd let us continue in private?'' Margaret said to her daughter, reaching across and laying her hand on top of Alexis's. Alexis nodded, smiling at her mother's gentle tones. She regretted her sudden curiosity, not because it was impolite but because it had caused Margaret discomfort. Mrs. Kain's affairs were probably boring in the extreme, and Alexis felt she should be glad to be excused from hearing about them. She wondered what had prompted her own question. What did she care about whom Mrs. Kain's daughter had married? Despite her mother's friendship with the woman, Alexis herself had had little to do with Evelyn over the years.

She excused herself and left the drawing room, but Evelyn couldn't quite wait to resume her loud discussion. "Totally unsuitable that my only granddaughter. . . .''

In the bedroom of her suite, Alexis took off her suit and put on a pink silk robe whose folds fell softly around her long slender legs. She exchanged the gray kid slippers for matching satin mules. She was tired, though she didn't know why. Lately she hadn't been working very hard. While she'd been doing the Marilyn Bank article, there hadn't been enough hours in the day, enough days in the week. Now all she had to work on were two routine profiles: a bank executive, and an opera singer who was visiting from out of town. She'd already interviewed them; all that remained was to type the final drafts of both articles. There would be plenty of time to do it in the morning.

Which left the whole long evening to be filled. Normally she would have gone out with Karl on such an evening, but he was in San Francisco doing a guest tour. Sighing, Alexis sat down on the brocade coverlet of her canopied bed and pulled her purse toward her. The brochures were only a little creased from the way she had shoved them into the handbag, and she smoothed them out. She noticed that each one had on the cover a larger version of the symbolic paintings she'd seen in the display poster, the map of America. Thumbing through the pamphlets, she found the one showing the picture of the log cabin surrounded by trees. The brochure was about Missouri and Arkansas. The trees of Arkansas weren't only pine, the pamphlet explained. There were oak, hickory, gum, persimmon and sassafras in the Ozarks.

The Ozarks. Alexis thought for a moment. And then several quite separate ideas came together in a way that suddenly made a lot of sense. She remembered the conversation she'd had with Karl more than six weeks before. She remembered the nagging, almost subconscious feeling of familiarity she'd experienced looking at the travel poster. And she understood her curiosity about Evelyn Kain's totally unsuitable son-in-law.

"ALEXIS, IT'S A STORY that was told to me in the strictest confidence. . . ."

Margaret Smythe sat before the library fireplace, a novel open in her lap. The swelling flames cast a softening light on the older woman's face, but they only served to heighten her daughter's already high color. Margaret sat back in her wing chair, relaxed and at ease. Alexis sat at the very edge of a similiar chair on the other side of the fire. Her elbows balanced on her knees, her face resting in her hands, she looked so like the child she had once been, so uncharacteristically open and eager, that her mother relented a little. "You know, Alexis," she said, "you're a lot like your father."

Alexis knew Margaret meant Wallace, not her real father—whoever he had been. "When Wallace was after some bit of information," Margaret went on, "he would hunt night and day until he found it. He'd bury himself in books—absolutely surround himself. I. . . ." A look of sorrow passed over her face. Alexis understood and kept her peace. It wasn't easy for the widow to speak of the man she'd lost, not even after two years. She was silent for a bit, then continued. "I suppose when a person really wants to know something, they eventually find what they're seeking."

"It's part of being a good reporter, a good writer."

"And what could Evelyn Kain's son-in-law possibly have to do with your being a good writer?" Margaret asked with a smile.

"I don't know. Maybe I'll find out. If you give me some information."

"But why are you so curious?" Margaret stared into the fire for a moment, then raised her deep green eyes to the shaded eyes of her daughter. "All right, dear, if you insist. But I must keep the tale brief— and you must keep it confidential."

Alexis nodded. She had long ago been trained to consider the display of too much eagerness vulgar, so she didn't reveal her pleasure at her mother's acquiescence.

"It all happened about fifteen years or so ago. At the time, Evelyn's daughter, Caroline, was a headstrong but very talented seventeen-year-old. I don't suppose Evelyn relished the idea of her daughter's seeking a career as a musician. Nonetheless, the girl was shunted from teacher to teacher until there was literally no one left for her to study with. As I said, she was difficult, and I'm sure there were some teachers who rued the day they ever let Evelyn talk— or bribe—them into taking on her girl.

"But there were others who felt Caroline was exceptionally gifted as a musician. The last of these convinced the girl she should try to get into Juilliard, and her attempt was successful. Naturally, Caroline loved the idea of living in New York, or to be more frank, of living away from Evelyn. Anyway, off she went, apparently full of determination to be the best clarinetist to come from the state of Illinois. At the time I privately felt she was also full of determination

never to live in Illinois again. Though it grieves me
still to think about what happened to her, I must
admit I was not at all surprised.''

"And what did happen to her?" Alexis asked. The
warm glow of the fire danced off the satin finish of
her pink silk robe as she shifted her long legs and
leaned just a bit closer to where Margaret sat across
the small but perfect Turkish carpet before the fireplace.

"What happened eventually was that Caroline was
killed trying to execute a tricky turn on a mountain
road during a rainstorm.''

"A mountain road?"

"Yes. In the Ozarks." Alexis nodded imperceptibly, but Margaret noticed. "Is this story beginning
to ring a bell?" she asked, clearly wondering where
Alexis might have heard the confidential tale before.

"Yes," Alexis answered, "I think perhaps so. Go
on. How did Caroline Kain end up down there?"

"Well—" Margaret sighed a little "—the very first
year she was in New York, she met a young man who
was also at Juilliard as an out-of-town student. I
believe he was about her own age—both of them
were very young. But as sometimes happens, they fell
deeply in love, perhaps more in love than one might
have expected from youngsters of their tender
years.''

"How do you know they were so in love?"
Alexis's instinct for ferreting out information was
working in full force. Margaret smiled at the serious
look on her daughter's face.

"Because of subsequent events, my dear," she answered. "I must say, the tenacity with which Caro-

line stood by her husband against the opposition of
Evelyn was remarkable in the extreme—in fact, it
was admirable. You see, the girl chose to marry out
of her own class—well out of it. And though I personally feel one takes a great risk in ignoring one's
own background when choosing a mate, I'm not so
hardhearted as to insist love is without a certain very
potent power of its own.''

Alexis didn't respond immediately to her mother's
ideas about love. The only powerful love between
man and woman she had experienced was the love of
Margaret and Wallace. For herself, Alexis had what
she considered a constructive and comfortable relationship with Karl. As far as backgrounds went, they
were ideally suited. Most of Alexis's friends thought
she and Karl were lucky—and most of the time,
Alexis felt they must be right.

''Well,'' she said, choosing her words carefully,
''was it her son-in-law's background only that Evelyn
felt made him so unsuitable for Caroline? What
about his future? He must have had talent, too, if he
was studying at Juilliard.''

''Yes. The young man—whose name, by the way,
was Wright Webster—no Webber, Wright Webber—
was apparently quite a violinist. As things turned
out, he caused a sensation in New York. His early
training had been competent, nowhere near Caroline's, of course, but good enough that when he came
to the attention of a really fine teacher, he caught on
rapidly—so rapidly that he earned the distinction of
being asked to solo with the New York Philharmonic
during his very first year at school. I needn't tell you
how impossible that would be under most circum-

stances. Nonetheless, he acquitted himself magnificently. The reviewers were most enthusiastic, and—''

"How do you know these things?" Alexis interrupted, with the reporter's urge to uncover sources, but also with a deeper curiosity about Wright Webber, a curiosity that may have been more evident to Margaret than it was to Alexis herself.

"Why do you ask, dear?"

"Because it seems to me that Evelyn, who must have told you the story, wouldn't be all that keen to admit her son-in-law was so talented."

"You're quite right, Alexis. What I'm telling you was told to me not by Evelyn, but by Caroline herself. She was married to Webber for four years before she died, and she came home to Chicago a number of times during the course of her marriage. When she was with Evelyn she refused to speak about her husband, but when she came to see me, she seemed to want to speak of nothing else.

"She told me how she had met a boy unlike any other. That first year she was away, Caroline seemed to change from a headstrong and rebellious girl into a responsible young woman. She was really only a child, as I said, but I could see how she loved the young man. She told me he was from a world far different from her own, a world in which the worth of a person was measured by what they are, not by what they have. I explained to her that that was true of her own world, too, if she would only look around carefully. But there was no convincing her. To Caroline, Wright Webber came from the hills of heaven, and she was obviously just biding her time until she could escape with him back to that place. For all his talent and his success in New York, the boy was very uncomfortable most of the time. I think Caroline must have been his only friend.

"At any rate, my dear," Margaret said, glancing at her watch, "I said my tale would be brief.... During their first year at Juilliard, Caroline and Wright were what you might call sweethearts. At the end of that year Wright went home to Arkansas, and Caroline found innumerable ways of torturing Evelyn all summer long. The second year, the two youngsters had quite clearly become lovers, and at the end of that year Caroline went to spend the summer in the Ozarks. Evelyn threatened to disown her, but Caroline didn't care. In fact, it was during that summer, we later found out, that Caroline and Wright married. They returned to school in the fall, but remained only a month or so. As soon as they discovered Caroline was pregnant, they went back to Fayetteville."

"I remember Caroline," Alexis said thoughtfully, "but only vaguely."

"She was eight years older than you," Margaret replied, "and she boarded at school, so she wasn't around often. You would have been only nine when she went to New York. Poor Caroline. She died when her little girl was three. She had only five or so years with Wright, and though I would never want Evelyn to hear me say it, I honestly believe those five were infinitely happier than the seventeen years that had gone before."

There was a moment's reflective silence. In the sudden quiet, the slow ticking of a grandfather clock was audible, and occasionally the embers of the fire sounded softly as they shifted in their dying light.

"What was her name?" Alexis said.

"I beg your pardon, dear? Whose name?"

"Evelyn's granddaughter—the little girl. Is she still with her father?"

Margaret thought for a moment, then shook her head, a small ladylike gesture that sent the light shooting through the silver strands of her hair. "I don't know for sure," she answered. "I believe her name is Patricia. Caroline spoke often of the child. Evelyn refers to her only as 'my granddaughter.' Yes, to answer your other question. She is still with Wright down in Arkansas. Which fact drives Evelyn into paroxysms every once in a while. She can't bear the thought that Caroline has, as she sees it, managed to exercise her rebelliousness even beyond the grave. Evelyn would like nothing better than to bring the child up here and raise her as she thinks fit. The girl's father would never allow such a thing. I'm sure of that. Besides, she's a teenager now. I imagine she's already quite established in her life-style."

"Has the Webber man ever come up with her?"

"With his daughter? Oh, no, I should say not. I think he'd be as uncomfortable as he'd be unwelcome."

"Whatever happened with his career?"

"I'm sure I don't know, Alexis," Margaret said, raising her slender hand to her lips to hide a small yawn. "I'm going to retire now, my dear; it's rather late. If you don't mind, I'll go up. I'll see you in the morning."

"Good night, mother." Alexis rose and gave the

older woman a daughterly kiss on the cheek. Alexis settled back into the wing chair before the fire. Her imagination was aroused; dozens of questions were buzzing through her mind. As a writer, she was growing more and more familiar with the way an idea for an article would suddenly start percolating—but she wasn't growing used to the sensation of having more questions than she could hope to answer pop into her head all at the same time. She wanted never to get used to it, for she knew that kind of inquisitiveness was what gave the edge to good reporting.

Why, she wondered, would a man like Wright Webber leave the hills in the first place? What sort of man must be he be? And what about Caroline? How could she give up her own promising future—not to mention her own family—to follow a mere boy into the hills? Or was that overly dramatic? After all, Caroline and Wright lived in America in the twentieth century—surely these days one place was pretty much the same as another. Question after question occured to Alexis, and after an hour's thinking on the subject she decided to go up to the office adjacent to her bedroom and type the two articles she'd planned to type in the morning. For some reason she felt the necessity to clean the slate, to be finished with the old so she could start the new. Even though, at that moment, she had no idea what the new could possibly be.

OVER THE NEXT FEW DAYS, however, an idea began to form so clearly, so inevitably, in Alexis's mind that she wondered why she hadn't thought of something like it long before.

When she realized the country violinist her mother had told her about was the same man Karl had described so many weeks before, she remembered Karl's suggestion to do stories on people who had "fallen from the heights." The story of the violinist was a straw in the wind, but Alexis grabbed it. The very next day she went to the public library, and later to one of the university libraries to see what information was available on the Ozarks. During several hours of research, she began to see that there was a wealth of material worthy of magazine and newspaper articles.

After a few more days' thought, she decided it wouldn't be right—probably wouldn't be interesting to readers—to go into the personal material on the Webbers. But by that time Alexis had amassed a great deal of other material, and she was seriously considering what the newspaper editor had said about unusual viewpoints. Suppose she were to write a series of articles on rural America, told from the point of view of someone with an entirely different background? Alexis knew if she did things properly, she could make her articles as interesting as the tales of strangers who describe the magical lands they've traveled through. But there would have to be good hard thinking in the articles, too. Already she could see important issues that could use examination. And as a reporter, she knew the only way to write well about a place was to go there.

So quite without deliberately deciding to do so, Alexis Juneau Smythe began to formulate plans to abandon the fast-paced, slick life of the city and to bury herself, at least for a while, in the shaded hollows of southern hills.

"I KNOW IT MAY SOUND FARFETCHED, mother," Alexis began tentatively, choosing her words as one might choose diamonds to be set in a very special ring. "I know it doesn't sound like the sort of thing I might be expected to do, like the sort of place I might be expected to go, and yet...."

Margaret said nothing, merely sat quietly listening as Alexis began to detail her plan. They were in the sun-room at the rear of their huge house. The bright rays that slanted through the eastern windows were filtered somewhat by foliage, casting a softened light on the faces of the two women who spoke over a breakfast of imported fruit, croissants and freshly ground coffee brewed at the table.

"I don't know whether you've noticed, mother," Alexis went on slowly, "but I've been rather restless lately. I'm not pleased with my work. It's begun to seem stale to me. I—" She looked up then, somehow expecting her mother to disagree with her. Margaret, however, continued to stare thoughtfully into her fine china cup. It was a moment before either woman spoke, and when the elder began the younger wasn't immediately sure which direction the conversation would take.

"Wallace was a fine writer, Alexis. But his isn't the only fine writing in this family. As you well know, I've read every word you've ever had published—and then some. I've saved things you wrote when you were seven—imagine, seven years old! You have an exceptional talent, I'm sure of that. I haven't spoken before because I know a mother's opinion in such matters is suspect—"

Alexis made a move to interrupt, but Margaret

went on. "No, dear, no one expects her mother to be a decent critic. Nevertheless, I do have some criticism to offer—both positive and negative. As for the positive, I think you are as good a writer as Wallace was at your age, if not slightly better. But you are wasting your talent."

Alexis was surprised at this. She hadn't discussed her work with her mother very often, and it was a slight shock to find out Margaret had come to the same conclusion she herself had reached in the past few days.

"Mother, I—"

"Please let me finish, Alexis," Margaret said, her cultivated voice showing no sternness or reproof. "It is all very well to do nice polite articles on famous people, to go to their lovely clean offices, to sit in their finely upholstered chairs, to chat politely with them over coffee. But it is quite another thing to do real reporting, real writing. Wallace always said writing things down was the last—and sometimes even the least—task of the writer. Everything that goes before is important—enormously. I was impressed with the article you did on that woman who became a professor, impressed not by the fineness of your writing, which I've noticed many times before, but by the courage of your research, your interviews, your coming out and saying things that needed saying, regardless of the fact that the truth makes some people very uncomfortable indeed."

"But mother, I would think you'd want me to stick to the things I know—to...."

"To stick to your own kind? I think not, dear. Your society reporting was lovely, very tasteful.

Later, when you began the profiles, I thought you did a fine job of presenting portraits of some of our elite. But when I saw what you were really capable of, I hoped you'd finally come into your own. I must say also. . . ." And Margaret hesitated for a moment, whether to give impact to what she was about to say or because it was difficult for her to speak of such matters, Alexis wasn't sure. "I feel compelled to remind you that your adopted maternal ancestors, the MacIntyres, were not quite so elegant as the family of Wallace Hamilton Smythe. 'Your own kind' may be quite different from what some people think."

In the past, Margaret's understanding had often opened the floodgates of Alexis's heart, and it didn't fail Alexis this time. She revealed all to her mother—her plans to visit the Ozarks, to write about what she saw there. And more, she told Margaret about the gnawing restlessness that seemed to eat away at her even in her most contented hours. In the end Alexis felt Margaret accepted her need not only for a change of scenery but also a change of focus in her life.

TELLING HER PLANS TO KARL was harder than telling them to her mother. At first, he seemed to think she was joking. When he finally realized how serious Alexis was, he accused her of biting off more than she could chew, reminding her that she had no experience of rural life and was therefore foolish to think she could write about it in an intelligent, let alone interesting manner.

And then he became angry, insisted Alexis was wasting her time—almost implying she wasn't really a writer at all, was only playing at writing—a dilettante, an amateur. "But, then," he said, "Who am I to stop you from doing what you think you must? Go ahead. When you get back we'll talk about things. We'll see where we can go from there...."

"But Karl," she had said, distressed at the finality of his tone, "this is only temporary. I—"

"If it's so temporary, why can't you name a date for your return? Surely you don't expect me just to wait until you decide you're ready to resume our relationship?"

"I can't give you a date because I don't know when I'll be back. That's the only way I know of to do it. If I put a time limit on myself, I might leave before I've even got started. I need to relax, to look around a bit before I sink my teeth into—"

"By all means—whatever you think best." Karl squared his shoulders. He was a stubborn man, one not at all used to opposition.

"Karl," Alexis said, putting her hand on his shoulder, smoothing his well-cut gray hair away from his temple. "We won't have to resume anything because we won't be ending anything. This is just a pause, a break. The trip may come to nothing. I may not be away long at all. I may find I'm going on a wild-goose chase rather than tracking down real stories, real issues to write about. But I've got to see."

Eventually they settled their difference over a bottle of champagne in Karl's dressing room, and though Alexis couldn't say he was exactly happy to see her off, at least he was no longer petulant and resisting.

She decided on Fayetteville, Arkansas. It was the

largest urban centre in the northwest of the state—
right in the Ozark mountains. At thirty-six thousand,
its population was no match for the millions who
lived in Chicago, but it wasn't the middle of nowhere, either. In fact, it was the home of the University of Arkansas, and Alexis felt that would be a
logical place to begin learning about the area. She
might even interview some students and teachers,
looking for ideas and angles. So, as far as location
was concerned, her mind was made up.

Until Evelyn Kain inadvertintly changed it. The
afternoon Alexis was on her way to her travel agent
to book her ticket south, she descended the white
marble stairs to unexpectedly meet Mrs. Kain being
ushered into the entrance.

"Hello, dear," Mrs. Kain said in her habitually
too-loud voice. "Come down, come down. You're
the very person I'm here to see."

As she took the last few stairs and stepped onto the
black-and-white marble floor, Alexis composed herself. She had always found it hard to be patient with
Evelyn, and now that she knew the story of Caroline
Kain Webber, knew that Evelyn must have caused
her daughter considerable pain, she was feeling even
less kindly toward the matron. Nonetheless, she extended her hand politely and led the older woman
into the sitting room. Evelyn was resplendent in a
lavender outfit of some filmy fabric that gave her the
appearance of a large ship under full sail in the purple light of dusk.

"Mother is out, Mrs. Kain," Alexis said. "However, if you'd like some tea, I can have some
brought."

"Thank you, dear. That's kind of you, if you don't mind." The woman took a chair and sat back to make herself comfortable. Alexis cringed at the gesture. She wanted to complete the arrangements for her trip, not spend the next hour or so in idle gossip. She excused herself and went to the kitchen to ask Ms Buckner to bring them tea and some of the pastries Alexis had bought that morning. When she returned to the sitting room, Alexis found Evelyn deep in thought.

"Your mother tells me you're planning a trip," she stated after a few moments of silence.

"Yes," Alexis responded simply, not wanting to initiate a detailed conversation. "Yes, I am."

"Your mother says you'll be leaving for Arkansas soon. Is that so?"

"Yes, Mrs. Kain."

"She says you'll be staying down there for a while?"

"I'm not exactly sure how long. Perhaps a month or so. It depends on—"

"Then you'd have time to do me a little favor." The statement was not a question.

"I expect to be quite busy. I—"

"It won't take extra time—I mean, at least it won't take much time. I simply want you to check on something for me."

Evelyn was speaking slowly, but not because there was any hesitancy on her part to demand what she wanted. Alexis knew her intent was to slowly draw Alexis into agreeing to her demands, as though she could trick her into compliance if she moved step by step.

"I don't think I'd have time to—"

"All I want you to do is visit my son-in-law."

At the mention of that relative, Alexis thought she saw Evelyn Kain suppress a grimace. She herself allowed her expression to reveal nothing—neither her knowledge of Wright Webber, nor her curiosity as to what Evelyn now wanted from the man. She didn't trust the matron, didn't want to involve herself in any scheme of Evelyn's.

"Mrs. Kain, how can I visit a complete stranger? I'm not going south for visits. I'm going to work." Her assertiveness didn't please her visitor.

"You know, my dear, you may be a woman on your own, but that's no reason to forget your place." By the tone of Evelyn's voice, Alexis could tell the woman was about to drop all pretense of being nice, was about to "pull rank" on her. "I'm your mother's oldest and closest friend. I wouldn't hesitate to help her in any way I could think of, and I must say I find it unseemly that you're unwilling even to listen to what I propose. I'm sure that if Margaret were here, she'd be most annoyed at your curt and—and belligerent manner."

Though she knew full well she had been neither curt nor belligerent, Alexis decided to accommodate Mrs. Kain. As far as she was concerned, the woman was a manipulative bore, but good manners required that Alexis remain polite. She decided simply to play along with Evelyn—then to forget about the incident once she'd left. "Where would I find this man, your son-in-law? I assume you know I'm going to Fayette-ville? Is he there?"

"Uh, no. No, my dear, he's not. But he's not far.

It won't take you long to get out to Mountain View."

"But I'm not going to—"

"It's only a hundred miles or so. It might be a nice drive through the hills." The dowager said the words as though she herself couldn't possibly imagine such a thing as a nice drive through the territory of the heathen.

"And just what would you like me to do in Mountain View, Mrs. Kain?"

Now Alexis really was curt, but Mrs. Kain didn't notice because she thought Alexis's question indicated her willingness to do what the woman wanted her to do.

"Well, now," she began, drawing in her breath. "My son-in-law is called Webber. J. Wright Webber. I must admit I don't know what the J. stands for— Jeremias or something like that. They all have strange names down there. Anyway, he teaches at the Ozark Folk Center. It shouldn't be hard to find him. Everybody knows everybody else in places like that."

Alexis knew about the Ozark Folk Center. It was a large complex outside the town of Mountain View devoted to country crafts and country music. It attracted top musical artists and tourists from all over. She guessed it was extremely unlikely that everyone there would "know" this J. Wright Webber. It didn't matter. It didn't matter to Alexis whether there wasn't a soul in the whole state of Arkansas who knew the man or could lead her to him. She had no intention of seeking him out—and she especially didn't intend to "check on" him in any way whatsoever.

She was thinking just that when she realized that

Mrs. Kain had been rambling on. Alexis drew her attention back to the woman.

"Is her name. All I want you to do is to get Webber to invite you into his home—I know they live rather, well, rather roughly, according to our standards, but you won't have to stay long. All I want you to do is get a look, a good look, as to how he's raising her. Write down everything—the kind of room she has, the sort of clothes. I want to know exactly what my granddaughter has to put up with. I want my lawyers to do all they can to get her away from that barbarian and. . . ."

Alexis was appalled. Apparently, she wanted her granddaughter to be taken from her father and brought up to Chicago to live in the Kain mansion. If Evelyn hadn't been who she was, and if Alexis hadn't been who she was, she would have told the old lady what to do with her manipulative ideas. As it was, Alexis stuck to her resolve to ignore Evelyn's request. It was too ridiculous to contemplate, anyway. She was saved from even answering the woman because Margaret came in, and Alexis slipped out during the exchanged greetings between the two old friends.

YES, ALEXIS HAD BEEN SURPRISED, to put it mildly, by Evelyn Kain's request. So she was also surprised to find herself asking her travel agent about the best flight to take, not to Fayetteville, but to Mountain View. She reasoned that the folk center would be a far more convenient location for her foray into the hills. She reasoned that interviews with native musicians and craftspeople would make exciting reading. She reasoned that this town of two thousand would be more of a change, a more healthy change, than the city of thirty-six thousand. She reasoned that she'd have more to learn and more to write about if she just went ahead and buried herself in the rural mountain community—just dived right in, so to speak.

And she completely ignored the fact that during the whole of her research, during the whole of February while she'd been making up her mind, and through all her conversations with Margaret, Karl and Evelyn, there was growing in her a compulsion. Separate from her need to get away. Her need to improve her work.

The truth was, Alexis had to meet Webber, Jeremias Webber. Wright Webber. J. Wright Webber—she wasn't even sure of his name. But she *was* sure he must be a remarkable man. All her life she had lived in the glittering world of the social elite. Success was a byword in her world. Yet here was a man who had given up success to run back to the hills of home. And more, a man for whom the daughter of Chicago's richest matron had abandoned her comfortable home—ultimately, her life. Alexis didn't know what kind of man Wright Webber might be. But she knew for a fact she wanted to find out.

CHAPTER THREE

FOR THE TRIP she chose a pale green wool ensemble. It was March and not particularly warm, so Alexis was glad the dress had long sleeves and a high neck, glad also that the matching coat was lined. With beige and green accessories, the effect was one of understated but unmistakable elegance—expensive elegance.

Alexis was entirely relaxed as she glanced out the window of the plane. Beneath her spread a panorama whose beauty nearly brought tears to her eyes, for as she flew over Middle America she could see clearly, though from a great distance, the patchwork farms of Illinois and Missouri. They seemed tiny from the air, but the individual farms must have been quite large. It was easy to pick out which fields had been plowed in the fall and which had been left covered with stubble. In fact, there was such a variety of color even in late winter that Alexis could easily imagine how lovely the farms must look when the green of true spring began to color the fields in their myriad shades. She imagined the farmers who had cleared those fields, the men and women whose hard patient work had carved out a civilization from the wilderness. She sighed. There were a lot of things she had never stopped to think about before, but at the moment felt were worthy of her attention.

The plane crossed the winding Missouri River, which glinted like a huge but benign snake lounging in the sun. It was an old river full of bends, full of legend, beautiful in the serene way of things whose existence seems to defy time.

And they crossed the Mississippi, too. Though she had flown south before, Alexis had never really bothered to study the terrain. Always before, she had been napping or reading. This time she sensed a change was coming over her, a new hunger for knowledge, a new awareness—almost it seemed, a new sense of being alive. She wasn't sure exactly how the change had come about, but she rather hoped it was because she had made the right decision in taking steps to change her life, at least for a while.

The patterned farmlands beneath her were nothing like the skyscrapered streets she was temporarily abandoning—nor were they exactly like the area to which she was headed, land not as suitable for farming as the plains of the great rivers. The closer she came to Little Rock, Arkansas, the destination of her flight, the more she felt she, like a snake, was shedding her old skin and taking on a new one, which might, after all, glitter like the Missouri in the sun. She laughed at the thought. *Perhaps I should be a poet instead of a journalist!*

She had decided on Little Rock because it was easy to fly to. Also, it was only eighty miles from Mountain View. She had arranged with her Chicago travel agent to have a rental car ready for her when her plane landed, and the arrangements went without a hitch.

It took her a few turns to get used to driving the

car. She'd had a car of her own since her late teens, but Alexis didn't drive often when she was in Chicago, depending instead on taxis, or on Margaret's driver—or Karl's. She liked the feeling of the car's power responding to her touch, liked the feeling of new freedom that filled her as she turned onto Highway 65, headed north.

Arkansas. From her reading she knew it was the twenty-fifth state of the Union, admitted in 1836. She knew its entire fifty-two-thousand square-mile area was home to fewer people than lived in Chicago. Its bird was the mockingbird, its tree the pine, which she saw a lot of in passing. The state flower was the apple blossom, and as she thought about that the lines of a poem she had read, by a man named George C. Miller, popped into her head.

> there are countries we
> have not seen which will taste
> like crisp apples
> when we go to them
> in the morning

The lines expressed exactly how she felt, that there was something new and wonderful waiting for her. The Land of Opportunity, that's what Arkansas had been nicknamed, and winging her way north toward Mountain View, she hoped it would prove to be so.

East of where Alexis traveled was the Grand Prairie, where rice was grown. In every part of the state, agriculture of one sort or another thrived, and as she drove she saw humorous bumper stickers that reminded her she was in farm country. "Crime doesn't pay, and neither does farming,'' read one. "If you complain about farmers, don't talk with your mouth full!'' quipped another.

She followed 65 until she reached 16, turning northeast toward Stone County. Already she was close to the heart of the Ozark region, a treed plateau broken into gently sloping hills covered with hardwood forest that was bare at this time of year, but that promised a richness of green in the months to come. Often she saw meandering streams running alongside the road or flowing under it. The hills rose to meet her as she went, until she began to feel as if she was sailing, as if the gray afternoon sky was the ocean sky and the hills the waves of the sea. Her tires sang on the road; the promise of the future sang in her heart.

Here and there a hidden valley opened to view. Sometimes a cabin, nestled in the woods, revealed itself. Sometimes a cow or a horse raised its head to see her pass. There were farms along the road, though she couldn't see any people around. The land itself was scenery enough, and the sight of dark hollows shrouded in mist gave her the uncanny feeling that the things she had read about the Ozark landscape were suddenly coming to life.

Alexis wasn't used to reading maps, so when it came time to turn onto Highway 9 she was a little unsure of herself. Nonetheless, she made the turn. Ten minutes later, when the road seemed about to peter into nothing, she wasn't quite so sure. She came to a halt where the paved road forked into two narrower gravel roads, which then disappeared into the woods a short distance away.

Perplexed, Alexis merely sat still for a moment, then rolled down the car window to get a breath of air. Remarkably fresh air, it turned out. She realized then that the Chicago air was heavy, even hard to breathe, compared to the pure earth-scented air that filled her lungs. So engrossed was she in the exhilarating experience that it took her a moment to realize the insistent sound she was hearing wasn't her imagination. Somewhere not far from where she sat, something or someone was making a slow rhythmical noise that sounded like metal being scraped against metal. A little frightened, yet curious, Alexis gingerly opened the car door.

She stepped onto the roadway and walked a short distance ahead. The sound was coming from behind a clump of trees off to the right. Looking down, Alexis saw that the ground between her and the trees seemed quite wet. In fact, it was probably very soft beneath the newly green grass. She hesitated, but decided she really did need help in finding her way. There was only one chance of getting that help. She took a step and felt her fine leather boots sink up to the ankles in the equally fine black soil of the state of Arkansas.

By the time she reached the clump of trees, not twenty yards away, she was already used to lifting her feet the ridiculous height necessary to pull them out of the mud with each step. She was certain that a person was making the sound, for as she moved closer she heard a voice, the voice of an old man softly cursing now and then, as though whatever he was working on wasn't cooperating.

Reaching the trees, Alexis entered the wood. In the

shaded recess she stopped, dumbfounded. For she suddenly had the strange sensation of witnessing a scene from a childhood story she hadn't thought about in years.

Not ten feet away was a perfect gnome of a man. His long gray beard straggled down the front of his faded red flannel shirt. From the soft mound of his much-worn brimmed and peaked hat streamed more gray hair—long, ragged and uneven. One could believe a mad barber had once had his way with the man. Faded trousers, hiked up by an old necktie knotted at his waist, didn't quite make it all the way to his scuffed and battered shoes. Thin ankles, innocent of socks, showed whitely beneath his pants. And like the elves of the children's story, the old man was so engrossed in his mysterious task that he didn't see or hear Alexis, who now stood breathing rapidly from the exertion of her mud-impeded walk, and from pure surprise.

The man was attempting to fix a piece of machinery that had seen better days. In the silence of the wood, only his scraping and the occasional curse sounded. So Alexis was totally shocked when, without even turning his head, the old man suddenly said, "What the hell are you starin' at?"

"I—it—well—" She couldn't think of a word to say. With exaggerated patience, as though he had all the time in the world to listen to a stranger make a fool of herself, the old man turned his head. He had rugged features and sparking eyes of deep blue, like cut sapphires. There was wisdom in those eyes and a teasing kindness, too, but both were lost on Alexis. Nor was she aware of the fact that her appearance in her designer clothes was probably as strange to the old man as his appearance was to her.

"Wander off the beaten path?" he asked.

"Yes, yes, I seem to have."

"Where you tryin' to get to?"

"Stone County."

"Stone County, Illinois; Stone County, Missouri; Stone County, Oklahoma; Stone County, Georgia or Stone County, Alabama?" the man asked without a smile.

"Arkansas. This is Arkansas, isn't it?" Alexis asked stupidly, completely flustered.

"Seemed to be the last time I paid taxes," he answered with a laugh that sounded a lot like a cackle. Reluctantly Alexis smiled.

"Look, you're in Stone County," the man said. "Whereabouts in Stone County are you headed exactly?"

"Mountain View."

"And why would you be going there?" He didn't seem eager to give her directions unless her answer satisfied him.

"I'm a writer. I'm going to do some magazine articles on—"

"A writer, eh? How about that? Just what we need around here—a professional windjammer 'n' scriber...."

"I beg your pardon?" Alexis said, beginning to feel annoyed. "Would you please bo so kind as to tell me the way to Mountain View?"

"I don't suppose Ellen Sue Carver's going to welcome you into town."

"And who might Ellen Sue Carver be?" Alexis's

impatience didn't go unnoticed by the old man, but he replied with the deliberation that apparently characterized his speech.

"She's a writer, too. Only one we need around here, I reckon. Don't get your dander up, missy. It don't do for a lady. Get back onto that road, and when you reach the fork, go in the other direction instead of the one you took. Should be in town inside of ten minutes."

"Thank you," Alexis said, but the man had turned back to his work, a gesture that indicated he had wasted enough time already.

Making her way back to the car, back onto the highway, Alexis felt considerably less free, less optimistic than she had. Not only had she ruined a pair of two-hundred-dollar boots, which now lay in a heap on the floor in the back of the car—she had also got the distinct impression she wasn't going to be met with open arms in the town she'd chosen.

As she drove into Mountain View and saw its pretty houses, its tidy lawns, its charming shops, her spirits lifted somewhat, but she still felt a long way from home. She hadn't seen any humor at all in the way the old mountain man had treated her. She had no way of knowing his easy manner with her was as much a sign of hospitality as otherwise. She had a lot to learn, and as she viewed the town and its environs in the fading light of early evening, she felt a strong uncomfortable attack of culture shock. This mountain town was clearly nothing like Chicago—nothing at all. For the first time she entertained second thoughts about what she was doing in the middle of not even nowhere.

But she felt a little better when the attendant at a service station pointed down the street toward a white clapboard house. A sign was posted on the front lawn: Tourists Taken. Alexis hadn't ever seen a tourist home, though she'd read about them. And she couldn't help thinking the sign's message had several possible meanings!

"I SPENT SOME TIME IN THE CITY, in Tulsa," the woman told Alexis as she showed her to her room. Lizzie Cabe was the proprietor of the tourist home, an attractive person of about forty-five, and quite talkative. Obviously she was enjoying the opportunity of speaking with the stranger from Chicago. "I've been taking in tourists for five years now, ever since my husband died. This house was my daddy's, but he's gone, too. My mother lives in Atlanta with my sister, now."

"It's a lovely home," Alexis commented with sincerity. Each room in the large house was decorated with old-fashioned country touches—white lace curtains, country-pine furniture, gleaming woodwork.

The room Lizzie showed her guest to, decorated in delicate shades of blue, suited Alexis perfectly, except for one detail. "The bath is down the hall," Lizzie said without apology.

"Down the hall?" Alexis repeated. "Do you mean it's shared?"

"Of course," Lizzie answered, a little deflated, maybe even insulted.

Alexis noticed the woman's reaction and hastened to smooth things. "That will be fine, thank you. I'll be pleased to take the room.'' She had never shared a bathroom with anyone in her life. First time for everything.

IT ONLY TOOK HER ABOUT AN HOUR to settle in. Though it was certainly different from any other room she'd stayed in, this room in Lizzie Cabe's house had such a comfortable atmosphere that Alexis soon felt relaxed, though not quite at home. She bathed and changed into a dark gray crisp cotton dress in a style that seemed closer to the more casual clothes people around there wore. The dress was also cooler than her traveling clothes. The average temperature in Arkansas in March, as Lizzie had told her, was fifty-four degrees. She felt quite "dressed down," but she had no idea how the fineness of her clothing and accessories set her off, would continue to set her off from the natives of the mountain town.

When she finished dressing, she headed down the stairs toward Lizzie's living room, which served as sort of a lobby. Though she was tired after her long journey, she didn't think she wanted to nap just yet. In fact, she was eager for company.

As she reached the hall leading to the living room, she realized Lizzie was not alone. From the depths of the room came the melodious baritone laugh of a man, a laugh so rich, so genuine that for one moment it filled Alexis with the ridiculous conviction that she had never really heard a man laugh before she heard that sound.

She hesitated at the doorway, but only briefly, for both Lizzie and the man saw her almost immediately, and Lizzie beckoned her in. As for the man, he stared at her for a moment, his expression blank except, perhaps, for the slightest hint of surprise. Then he smiled widely and said, ''Well, now, a stranger—and one that's as startlin' as a red bird in winter!''

Alexis smiled weakly, wanting to be polite but having no idea what the man's quaint simile might mean. Her first impression was that his manner was too familiar—too easy. But she wasn't used to the ways of these people, and she knew she had to make allowances for customs and behavior different from her own. She remained poised, almost aloof, as Lizzie introduced the man simply as a neighbor from down the way.

Sometime later, it would occur to Alexis that she had noticed a remarkable number of things about the man in a remarkably short period of time. It could only have been seconds between Lizzie's introduction and Alexis's nodded acknowledgement. Nevertheless, in those few seconds she noticed that though the man was dressed in faded jeans and a rough cotton shirt, there was a kind of elegant grace to his carriage that belied his casual clothing. He was obviously proud of the easy way his body moved. He straightened from where he'd been leaning against the top of one of Lizzie's cabinets; clearly, he was over six feet. In fact, he seemed large in every way. His shirt did nothing to hide his unusually broad shoulders and massive chest. The worn denim of his jeans emphasized his powerful thighs, and Alexis found herself imagining what that muscled hardness would feel like if she were to lay her hand on the soft fabric of his trousers. Large though he was, the man was well-proportioned. He looked healthy, robust, as though life flowed in him strongly, even, perhaps, joyfully. His vitality was so immediately evident that Alexis, looking at him, felt her own tiredness disappear, the way one is sometimes aroused from drowsiness by observing the vigorous activity of others.

He seemed to be between thirty and thirty-five years old—in the prime of life. He was a handsome man, no doubt about that, and yet there was a frankness and openness about him that made Alexis think his looks, good though they were, were superseded in attractiveness by his manner. Even in those few moments, observing him as one stranger scrutinizes another, she could see that he looked like the kind of man a person could fall back on—could trust.

His hair was a tawny light brown, golden where light fell on it, and quite short. It was also thick, shiny, a little unruly—like the man himself, it very likely had a mind of its own! She got a good look at his eyes, so bold was his glance, and she could see they were a clear bright blue, without a hint of mystery or a trace of sadness. Looking into those eyes was like looking straight up on a morning in May—nothing but clear blue and enough of it to make your heart sing.

"Welcome to Mountain View," he said, again surprising Alexis with the deep tone and smooth rhythm of his voice. It didn't occur to her then that despite the quaintness of the man's first comment about her appearance, a quaintness she would later come to respect as part of the poetry of mountain speech, the man had no accent. His tones were not softly slurred like Lizzie Cabe's. Had Alexis been thinking about such things, she might have realized that either the man was a stranger there himself, or else he had spent some time away from Mountain View, or else he had made an effort to rid himself of his accent.

But she wasn't thinking those thoughts or anything like them, for quite without warning the man extended his hand to her, and Alexis was unaccountably flummoxed to see that anticipation of her touch. She hadn't really felt social awkwardness in years—not since she'd been a young teen. In the instant that the man stood awaiting her response, Alexis had time to wonder how anyone as well brought up as she had always considered herself could feel so at a loss.

The man took her fingers into his own. His skin was slightly more heated than hers, hinting at the warmth of the sun or even the soil, considering that he might be a farmer, judging from his dress. She noticed, quite without intending to stare so hard, that there was a scar along his thumb. A knife, or the blade of some tool must have gouged him long ago. But his hands weren't as rough as she might have expected. His skin was smooth against her own, and she found a tingling excitement in the contact, as if their two hands stood for something more. Alexis began to wonder how it would feel to have the man's whole body close against her own, the way her hand was close against his at the moment.

The thought unnerved her, and she pulled away, not stopping to think her abrupt withdrawal might be taken as impolite. Indeed, the man seemed puzzled, and for a moment an expression of doubt clouded his face, as though he wondered whether he had somehow been impolite in assuming this elegant—almost exotic—stranger would be happy to shake hands with him.

But the smile soon returned to his face, throwing his features into fine relief, the wide lips, the well-shaped nose. "Nice to meet you," he said, nodding to Alexis. "Be a pleasure to run into you again."

Alexis nodded in return, not sure whether she would ever run into him again. Not sure she wanted to. She wondered who he was and whether he was indeed from somewhere else. Perhaps he, too, was just passing through.

"Be seeing you, soon, Liz," he said to the older woman as he turned and walked toward the door. Alexis's eyes followed his tall figure as he retreated. In the faded jeans, his legs were strongly muscled, his derriere temptingly outlined in a way that wasn't possible in any business suit!

"What's your neighbor's name?" she casually asked Lizzie, feigning polite interest. Actually, the skin of her hand still tingled a bit where he'd touched her. No, that was her imagination—she was sure.

"Him?" Lizzie said, affecting a casualness even Alexis, who had just met Lizzie, knew to be false. "That's one of the Webbers—Right John Webber, to be exact."

And then Lizzie let out a hopeless little sigh, the sigh of someone who yearns for something quite out of reach, but very, very desirable nonetheless.

CHAPTER FOUR

MARCH TURNED TO APRIL. In the woods surrounding Mountain View, tender green leaves turned a deeper shade; early mountain flowers were coaxed out from the rich earth. And like spring beginning to enrich the world with its wonders, Alexis began to enrich herself with knowledge of the place she had chosen as a temporary haven against—well, she didn't know what. But slowly Mountain View began to feel like a haven to her, and she gave in to the seductive charm of rural pleasures.

In her first attempts to explore the area, she took the simple expedient of driving the country roads in her rented car. It didn't matter to her that that was an expensive way to travel. Though she was by no means extravagant, Alexis had no very good idea of the principles of thrift, either. She needed the car, she could afford to pay for it, and that was that. It took her a while to get used to the country roads, especially the rough back roads, but it was those that led to some of the most interesting hollows, places where clusters of dogwood trees nodded their blossom-laden branches in the gentle breeze.

She passed countless cabins in her travels. At first, she paid little attention to them. Then she began to look more closely, occasionally driving up to a cabin that was obviously abandoned, getting out of the car and inspecting the usually small building. All her life, she had thought of log cabins as picturesque, perhaps connected with pioneers, with Abraham Lincoln, with history, dead and gone. Now that she looked more carefully, she could see buildings like these had been—were still—the homes of real people, people who had built them with their bare hands.

Alexis thought of the magnificence of her own home, the mansion in Kenwood, the only home she'd ever known. It seemed from a totally different planet than these simple wooden structures. She could see, by the state of the ruins of several cabins, that some men—and women, perhaps—were better builders than others. She began to understand how survival might depend on just how good a person was at wielding an ax, at cutting straight boards, at making good tight-fitting joints at the corners of the walls.

And then she took a closer look at other houses people inhabited in the Ozarks. Of course, there were many homes not that different from what Alexis might see in the suburbs of Chicago. It wasn't these that captured her attention. In the deeper recesses of the country, she found buildings made of log and covered with clapboard or siding. Many had the characteristic double-door construction she had read about in her extensive library research. It was hard to find a cabin without a veranda, and it was impossible to find a veranda without a rocking chair or two! Alexis thought about these homes, thought about the concept of home itself—and soon managed to work her ideas into a think piece that she sent off to an American architecture magazine. The article, to

Alexis's delight, would soon be accepted with few changes.

Her first weeks in the mountains were turning out to be a success from several points of view. The solitude of her country drives—and later, long country rides on horseback—gave Alexis plenty of time to ponder not only her work but also her life, just as she had hoped. The pace was so much slower there that it was already difficult for her to remember what it had been like to run from assignment to assignment, meeting Karl for lunch, or sometimes only for a quick drink between other appointments. She remembered the long evenings spent in concert halls, wondering why she didn't miss that as much as she'd expected. Sometimes she thought it was a shame that she'd never spent time in the country before. But when she thought about living in the country—well, that was a different matter entirely.

For one thing, she missed her stores. When she ran out of her regular shampoo, especially blended for her by a cosmetician in an exclusive boutique, she had to resort to an ordinary brand—from a supermarket. Alexis was disappointed, but not surprised, to note that the shampoo didn't contain the same sort of oil and conditioner as her own. And so her hair lost the sleek straightness of its former style as it grew. Left to its own devices, it waved a little in a way that made Alexis look less sophisticated, but more beautiful, though she couldn't see that herself.

And the country still seemed uncomfortably wild to her. Her reaction would have been silly to a native, to someone like J. Webber, for instance, but Alexis was always afraid of running into some wild animal.

So far, she had only seen the gentlest of sheep, cows, horses and pigs—yet she had been told the legend of the razorback, wild pigs living off the land. There might not have been a real razorback in Arkansas in a hundred years, if ever, but there was no convincing Alexis. As far as she was concerned, every hollow was a potential hiding place for that beast—or another just as awful!

And there was something else that made Alexis feel she'd probably not want to stay in the hills longer than her work demanded. The people. They were friendly—a little reserved at first but soon full of generous hospitality. Nonetheless, she couldn't get over how different they were from the people she'd grown up with. Their speech was like a foreign language to her; their manners remained a mystery. Despite the fact that she liked the area, liked the way her work was proceeding, she was a stranger still.

That persistent feeling didn't stop Alexis from accepting the many invitations extended to her. In the middle of April, she joined the crowd of people lining Main Street for the Annual Folk Festival Parade. The colorful costumes, the music, the silly, sometimes self-directed but always lively sense of humor of the parade's participants had Alexis laughing out loud. And she wasn't the only one. In the thick of the antics of one particularly funny "hillbilly" group, she heard a laugh she knew she'd heard before—that deep, rich, almost singing baritone. She glanced up sharply, scanning the crowd, hoping to catch a glimpse of tawny hair, of bright blue eyes. She couldn't see anyone she knew, so she turned her attention back to the noisy parade.

One afternoon she and Lizzie took what was locally known as a "Dogwood Drive," a ride into the country specifically to see the blossoms. Alexis had grown to enjoy Lizzie's company, had come to depend on the woman for news of what was happening in the community.

"Everyone's going to be there..." Lizzie commented, breaking off to stare out the rolled-down car window. "Well, now, will you just look at that!" she expostulated. "Pretty as a June bride. Those trees are just the best ever this year. 'Course, I suppose we say that every year. Maybe they're getting better and better!" She laughed at that, and Alexis noticed not for the first time that there was a sadness in Lizzie's laugh.

"Everyone is going to be where?" Alexis prompted.

"At the dance up at the church on Saturday. You know, time was they'd never allow dancing in that church—or any church. You ever hear of play parties?"

Alexis shook her head.

"Well, it used to be thought that dancing was against the Bible. I suppose that some folks still feel strongly that way, but we don't at our church anymore. When we did—back when I was a kid—we had what we called 'play parties' as opposed to dancing parties. There was plenty of socializing, and music, too, even without the dancing. There are those who say hell is full of fiddlers, but nobody'd take that to heart these days. Our best fiddler is Right John—and he's one of our best men to boot. Nobody's gonna find that particular fiddler in hell—for sure!" Again Lizzie let out a laugh tinged with sorrow.

"Lizzie," Alexis said carefully, not wanting to pry

but feeling she knew Lizzie well enough to ask. "Do you find Mr. Webber especially attractive?"

"Course I do. Who wouldn't?" Lizzie answered a little petulantly, as though the matter were none of Alexis's business. "Anyway," she said after a pause, "he's ten years younger than me. Don't do me any good to think he's handsome."

Alexis was sorry she'd broached the subject. She still hadn't learned much about the dance the next Saturday. "What sort of a dance will it be? Will there be an orchestra?"

"An orchestra?" Lizzie gasped in amused incredulity. "Good heavens, no. An orchestra! Oh, no, I should say not. Not around here!" Her laugh this time was full and rich, without intending unkindness, but fully at Alexis's expense. Alexis was so embarrassed that her face turned an unhealthy shade of red. She hadn't made a mistake like that in days—forgetting where she was, forgetting that the kind of music she was used to would be as out of place at a country dance as a banjo would be in a Beethoven symphony.

"Sorry, honey," Lizzie said, laying her hand on Alexis's shoulder as the younger woman guided the car through the narrow corridor of dogwood trees hugging the country road. It was Sunday afternoon, and neighbors sat on verandas taking in the April air and making friendly conversation. "No, what there'll be is a band, the usual: Dean Hamby on the guitar, and Grover Ledford on his guitar, if he's in the mood. We'll have Lester Hine playing his banjo. There may be a few others, as well. And Right John on the fiddle—when's he's not dancing, that is. The man loves his dancing. You'll come, won't you? Square and round. Something for everybody.''

"Square and round? What does that mean?" Alexis knew she was risking Lizzie's laughter again, but she had to ask when she didn't understand something. Otherwise she was defeating her whole purpose in coming to the Ozarks.

"Square dancing and round—ballroom—dancing. It's easy to do the square dancing, even if you've never done it before. As for the other, everyone'll ask you to dance, no worry about that."

Despite herself, Alexis wondered how she would handle dancing with the local farmers. There was only one local farmer with whom she could imagine doing any kind of dance. If he *was* a farmer.

"What does Wright—uh—John Webber do?" Alexis asked casually. After all, the more she knew about local life, the better.

"He helps run Old John Webber's place."

"That's his father?"

"Lord, no!" Lizzie answered with some emphasis, but she didn't elaborate for a minute. "Old John is his grandfather. Right John helps out now and then, to hear him tell it himself. But everybody knows the place would fall apart without him. There's some people think Old John has seen better days in the thinking department."

"What?" Alexis asked.

Lizzie smiled. "Old John's a bit eccentric—always has been—but Right John dotes on him. He's followed the old man around since he himself was knee-high to a garter snake. . . ." Lizzie's voice trailed off, but the smile stayed on her softly lined, still-pretty face.

"So he *is* a farmer?"

"By profession he's a musician. He— Oh, look out!"

And Alexis swerved to avoid a whole line of pigs who had decided they had the right of way across the country road. It wasn't really a near miss, but the incident made her quite nervous. For the remainder of the drive she concentrated on getting home, forgetting not only about the blossoming dogwoods but also about the man who was the object of her growing curiosity.

SHE WAS LATE for the dance. She told herself that was because she had to hem her new skirt herself. It was the first time in her life that she'd sewed anything. She'd been ashamed to ask Lizzie how to do it, but eventually had swallowed her pride. Predictably Lizzie was amazed, then amused, then patient and kind. Yes, it had taken a good long time to lengthen the full, swirly skirt of bright blue cotton decorated with ribbon and braid. But nothing else Alexis had was suitable to wear to a square dance, a fact that had prompted her to buy the skirt at a shop a few doors from Lizzie's house.

After the skirt was hemmed, she wasn't sorry, either for the purchase or the painstaking labor. It was just the right length for her tall frame. To complete her outfit, she wore a white eyelet blouse with a wide elasticized neck that was meant to be worn off the shoulders. The soft April night was warm enough for bare shoulders, especially under the shawl Alexis intended to take along, but when she tried the blouse that way, when she looked down and saw her shoulders were pale, vulnerable looking, she pulled up the neck of the blouse. Any gown she had worn in Chicago since the age of eighteen had been more daring than that white cotton blouse, yet she had never before felt so exposed, as though she was assuming a modesty that wasn't exactly welcome. The sight of those bare shoulders had filled her with the same nameless fear that was her real reason for being late for the dance. Fear that she would stand out, that she would seem more a stranger than she had seemed before. Because she would be associating with the people of Mountain View en masse, in a social setting.

"Everyone'll ask you to dance," Lizzie had said, and Alexis knew it was so. Because it was polite, because she was a stranger they were trying to make welcome. She admitted to herself that she was nervous about talking to many of these people, maybe because she was unused to their topics of conversation, maybe because she sometimes lost sight of the fact that her fine background made her no finer than anyone else. Maybe because one of those farmers was John Webber, and she knew that she wanted his words, his touch—not only the touch of a native inviting a visitor to dance but also the touch of a man inviting a woman to wherever desire might lead—beyond white eyelet, beyond any clothes at all.

She was afraid. She was ashamed. She was Karl Hulst's woman, wasn't she? His lover, wasn't she? But she was full of desire. Not just the desire that resulted from being without her lover for weeks. The desire for a particular man, a man, as yet, she had seen only once. There was no explaining the effect seeing him had had on her. And no explaining why she longed to see him again.

"Come on, Alexis, please!" Lizzie called up, and sighing, the younger woman turned to descend the carpeted stairs. Lizzie stood at the bottom, all dolled up for the dance, looking beautiful. Her fashion sense was totally different from Alexis's, but refreshing for that reason. Lizzie's reddish-blond hair was festooned in a cascade of curls that began at her crown and swooped down the back of her shapely head. Her dress was a frothy pink affair with a low neckline that was nearly hidden by the matching jacket, onto which was pinned a white flower.

What made Lizzie beautiful was not the dress she'd chosen, nor her hairdo. It was the look of hope on her face, a look that said maybe this time, maybe tonight, something would happen to erase the pain of the years of loneliness since her husband had left her a widow.

Something of Lizzie's spirit communicated itself to Alexis. She felt less afraid, less a stranger. Taking the white flower Lizzie had picked for her, she pinned it into her honey-colored hair. With a gesture of defiance, she pulled down the neckline of her blouse, nodded and followed Lizzie out the door.

He was the first thing her eye fell on as they entered the decorated hall of the church, because he was onstage. In fact, he was graciously bowing, accepting what seemed to be rapturous applause from the people who filled the large room.

"Damn," Lizzie said. "We missed him."

It took Alexis a moment to understand what this meant, but when she realized her slowness in getting ready had caused Lizzie and her to miss Right John

Webber's performance, she was more sorry for the other woman than for herself.

Quite simply, she hated country music, and the thought of hearing him scraping away was repellent to her. She had to admit, though, that he looked wonderful. His jeans looked new, and quite without intending to make the comparison, Alexis noted that the stiff material didn't mold his muscular legs quite as closely as the worn material of his other trousers, yet there was no mistaking the marvelous physique of the man. He wore a black shirt, and from where Alexis stood at the entrance to the hall, she could see that the open neck revealed a scattering of curls darker than the sleek strands of hair on his head, hair that was a little tousled from the exertion of his playing.

What she couldn't see was the dew of perspiration that made his face glow a bit, that lent a musky, heady scent to the clean warm smell of his skin. What she couldn't see was the strong musculature of his arms, arms grown powerful not only from the exercise of making music but also from working the earth of his family's farm. What she couldn't see was the strength of his back, the curve of sinew beneath the smoothness of his shoulders, the full richness of his mature masculinity.

But she imagined all those things. She imagined touching him, imagined him responding to her touch. And she was instantly embarrassed to be harboring such thoughts. She had thought about him in that way before—the first time she'd seen him—and since then, too. There was no justifying it. Perhaps it had something to do with the changes she was going through in her life. Perhaps she had never really met a man like John Webber before, a man who exuded something very simple, but totally irresistible: plain good health.

And when his eye caught hers, she felt she ought to drop her gaze. But she didn't. The intensity in her blue-green eyes could tell him nothing across such a wide space. Nor could she see whether the brazen blue of his glance was as full of dancing light as she remembered. But he was staring straight at her as though there weren't at least a hundred people between them in the already crowded hall. When he raised his bow in a salute to her, she was surprised, surprised that he should acknowledge her after not having seen her for weeks. She nodded back to him at about the same time as she heard a giggle from the woman standing beside her, and remembered then that she had come with Lizzie, that she had heard John Webber say, "Be seeing you soon, Liz. . . ."

She was so embarrassed. Of course he was greeting his friend. Of course he probably hadn't even noticed her; the gesture would have been too much to expect. Again, Alexis felt that jolt of awkwardness, that feeling of not knowing what to do in a given situation. If she'd been at a glittering cocktail party in the private lounge of Karl's concert hall, she would have been perfectly poised, perfectly at ease. Here, among the farmers and other folk, she felt she had five feet and every one of them was wearing the wrong shoe. It would be a fine idea if the rich earth of Arkansas opened up and took her into its dark depths!

Lizzie had noticed nothing. Nor, apparently, had the middle-aged couple, Lester and Serina Hine, who appeared at Alexis's side.

"Nice to see you here, Miss Smythe," Lester said. He was wearing his Sunday-go-to-meeting best, and he looked quite different from the Lester Hine who spent his days at the pump of the local service station, or in the garage. It was said of Lester that he could fix anything he could get to the innards of— "providin' it ain't the sort of thing that runs on legs instead of gas," he always hastened to add. He was also rumored to play a pretty mean banjo. Alexis felt the same about the banjo as she did about the fiddle, but she politely remarked, "I hear we can expect some excellent banjo music...."

"Don't know about excellent," Lester answered good-naturedly. "Don't get in as much practice as I ought—"

"Seems to me you get in about as much practice as I can stand," Serina piped up. "Can't tear him away from that thing," she joked, shaking her head. Despite her words, Alexis could see the woman was proud of her husband, was looking forward to having him be part of the center of attention.

"There's old Dean Hamby right now," Lester said, pointing to a lad who couldn't be older than eighteen, though he was clearly more than six feet tall. "Get on over here, son. Time to get going."

By the time Lizzie and Alexis found a table, the musicians were tuning up again. It occurred to Alexis they didn't sound that much different from a full orchestra getting ready to play. There was something in that sound that had filled her with warm expectation ever since she was a tiny child. She didn't regret not being a musician herself because she so loved being part of an audience, part of the group who would benefit from this careful tuning of instruments, the listeners.

To her surprise, she enjoyed the music. The men weaved and dipped as they played, full of the rhythm of their tunes. After a couple of lively numbers that Lester Hine announced were intended to "get the dust off yer bones," he handed a microphone to an elderly man, who, in a perfectly deadpan but very effective style, began to call the square dances.

Of course, she had never tried it before, but it took remarkably little coaxing to get Alexis on the floor. Lizzie was so eager to dance that her mood was infectious. The two beers Alexis had drunk helped a little, too. She wasn't used to beer, and it affected her more strongly than champagne.

She was totally unprepared when four squares, four groups of dancers, suddenly became one huge circle. The hand now holding hers on the left was not that of her former partner but the strong large hand of John Webber.

"Nice seeing you again," he said, his smile as warm as the April night.

She opened her lips to speak, to acknowledge his greeting, but before she could get out a single word, the caller yelled another set of instructions that sent Alexis spinning on the arm of an elderly gentleman, who whooped with pleasure at the dance and the company.

The next time she caught a glimpse of John, he was swinging his own partner, a slim dark-haired woman of no little beauty, though she didn't seem to be much of a smiler. Alexis laughed to herself. She was beginning to think in the lively dialect she heard all around her. *No sir, Right John's lady don't seem to be much of a smiler. You'd smile if he were dancing with you,* her inner voice added. She tried to ignore it.

But it was true. She did smile when he asked her to dance. Even though she was worn out from the twirling and circling and the stomping and the partner-changing of the square dances. His arms were every bit as strong as she had imagined them to be, and the fact took away her breath.

"I haven't seen you around," he said, as though he'd been looking for her. No, of course he hadn't. He, like everyone else, was being especially neighborly this evening.

"I have been around," she answered smoothly, "but not around town much. I've been going into the hills to have a good look at the area."

"Like what you see?" As he asked the question, he swung her to avoid another couple dancing close by. The motion surprised her, and she glanced up at him, momentarily staring straight into his clear blue eyes.

"I—I beg your pardon," she stuttered. "What did you say?"

"I asked whether you like what you see here in— and around—Mountain View."

The only thing she was seeing at the moment was his face. It was amazing how the dark golden lashes that curved down over his eyes could be so pretty and yet so totally masculine. It was amazing how that one lock of unruly hair could give him a look of boyish charm, even though he was so unmistakably a man.

"I like what I see," she said. "I like it a lot."

She felt the deep ripple of his laughter before she

heard it close by her ear. He had pulled her nearer. "I mean, I like the scenery, the people. The people are so friendly...."

He knew what she really meant. And she knew her unintentional frankness amused him. What was wrong with her, anyway? She'd always thought it inelegant to be flirtatious. Besides, she had never really felt the need to flirt with anyone. Men came to her, not the other way around. That was the way it was supposed to be.

"Liz tells me you're a writer," John Webber said, breaking into her wayward thoughts. "What could a writer from Chicago have to say about Mountain View? Life must be a lot more exciting where you come from."

"Depends on how you look at it. To me everything here is new and fresh. If I can make things look like that to my readers, I've got it made."

"You mean big-city folk would want to read about pigs and cows and—"

"Well, not that, maybe, but—speaking of big-city folk," she said, noticing something curious for the first time. "You don't seem to have much of an accent."

"Don't I?" He smiled at her, a friendly smile that was very attractive but told her nothing at all. She didn't mean to pry. She already had a pretty good idea why he might speak as he did. After all, she had heard all about him from two separate sources. He had probably given up his accent when he moved to New York. Still, that had been a long time ago. She knew her curiosity wasn't polite, but she *was* curious, either because she had a hard time not following her reporter's "nose for news," or because there was something about this man that intrigued her so completely she forgot herself.

"It's just that you don't always sound as though you were from around here."

"Oh, I'm from around here," John Webber said. "No mistake about that!" His tone was friendly, jovial. Yet there was a hint of something else there, a strange mixture of hidden embarrassment and stubborn pride.

Once more Alexis got the feeling she had overstepped her bounds. Would she ever get used to dealing with these people? Yes, certainly, she would. She wondered, though, whether she could get used to dealing with a man like this. She wished it was an issue, wished she had some reason to believe she might get to know him better. But she hadn't seen him for a long time, and it might be a while before she saw him again.

They danced together in silence, his smooth motions guiding her across the crowded floor. She allowed herself to revel in his closeness, in the fresh outdoors scent of his after-shave, like grass and the bark of pine trees. She allowed his sturdy hand to hold her own, his strong arm to surround her back in a gesture that was protective, even gentlemanly, if such an archaic term could be used.

"Pardon me, John. Sorry to interrupt but...." It was the dark-haired woman who spoke, the woman who had been John's partner earlier. Her hand on his arm stopped the motion of the dance, and in order to avoid being bumped by the other couples, John followed her off the dance floor, guiding Alexis before him by keeping his hand on her shoulder. It was a warm, not unwelcome weight on her bare skin. She felt a little frisson of excitement shoot down from where his fingers were touching her. But she knew the dance was over—and the excitement, too. "Your grandfather's not feeling well, so I thought maybe we should be getting back. I regret having to intrude on your dancing...." At this comment, the woman nodded toward Alexis perfunctorily, but her face was lined with what seemed like genuine concern; she was looking through Alexis rather than at her.

"All right," John said. He seemed a bit puzzled at the interruption, surprised to hear his grandfather was feeling unwell. "I'll walk Miss...Miss...?"

"Smythe."

It wasn't Alexis who supplied the name. "Miss Smythe," John repeated, flashing Alexis a warm smile—in the glow of which she forgot to wonder why the dark-haired woman should have been interested enough to find out and remember her name. "I'll walk Miss Smythe back to her table," he said, his blue eyes still alight, his white teeth sparkling against the gold-toned smoothness of his face.

Despite her protests, he accompanied her to where Lizzie sat chatting with a few neighbors. "Thanks for the dance, Miss Smythe...."

"Alexis...."

"Alexis. Be seeing you around."

It was his usual casual greeting, she supposed, but she let herself pretend he meant the words, meant them for her especially. But Lizzie, too, nodded in acknowledgement before he turned and walked rather swiftly toward the table where his grandfather sat, with a lovely teenage girl whom Alexis noticed for the first time.

THE LAMPS HAD BRASS BASES, milk-glass shades and soft bulbs that threw pools of gentle light onto the braided rug beneath Lizzie's homespun couch. In the shadowed recesses of the living room, a glass-fronted bookcase gleamed. White lace curtains with sheers underneath hung at the windows, where a few potted plants set on the sill, were outlined darkly against the white fabric.

Everything about the room was cozy, comfortable, homey. Alexis sipped the coffee Lizzie had prepared. Both women sat with their legs up, Lizzie on the couch and Alexis curled into a huge armchair she had heard one of Lizzie's young neighbors call a "swallowing chair." Their shoes were on the rug before them, and it was obvious both women would soon be heading for bed and sleep.

"Did you have a good time, Lizzie?" Alexis asked.

"It was okay," the woman answered, her voice revealing tiredness and disappointment. "I danced enough, that's for sure. That young Dean Hamby cuts a rug better than a man twice his age. I'd rather have been dancing with a man twice his age!"

Alexis laughed at that. "Did you dance with John Webber?" She wasn't sure why she asked; it just seemed a natural thing to say.

"Didn't get a chance," was all Lizzie offered. She retreated into silence, the way she often seemed to do whenever talk turned to the topic of the handsome musician-farmer.

"Lizzie..." Alexis began. In the last little while she'd started to feel that if there was some way she could help Lizzie, she would like to. The older woman was sad so much of the time, trapped by the circumstances of her life. It wasn't only talk of the elusive Mr. Webber that brought out that sadness. "Do you ever have the opportunity to get away—to travel?"

"Travel? Me? Lord, no. Where would I go?"

"Anywhere—Little Rock, Atlanta, up north."

"Who'd look after this place if I went trotting off?"

"I'm sure you could find someone. There are only the two of us right now, me and the other boarder. I could look after things for you...."

"No," Lizzie said. "It's really kind of you, but it wouldn't do." She was silent again for a moment. "You know," she commented, "I used to travel all over when I was married. Even went to New York. But then Dave died, and shortly after I had to come back to help mom nurse dad. When dad died, mom considered selling this place, but we couldn't stand the thought of having our family lose the house. So mom and I were here together for a couple years before my sister got divorced and mom decided to go over to Atlanta to help look after her three kids...."

Her voice trailed off briefly. "Guess I've had my good times already. Never thought I'd end up back in the hills, but you never can tell. If I'd had my way, I'd have stayed in Tulsa. It's a funny thing about these hills—they grab ahold of you and they don't let go. They're paradise for some folks and the opposite for others. I suppose I could leave again, but I'm the last one of my family to live in the state. The first one came here more than a hundred fifty years ago. I don't know...." She stifled a yawn that was as much a sign of her unwillingness to talk further as it was of tiredness. "Think I'll go up now. Good night, Alexis. See you tomorrow."

"Good night, Lizzie." Alexis didn't go up to bed immediately. She sat for a while in the warm comfort of Lizzie's living room. This was such a lovely house, and yet, for Lizzie, it was a trap. She thought about family roots. Could a house, a mere building, demand that kind of commitment? She thought of the mansion in Kenwood, and her mother. Would she be willing to keep her family home in the absence of any other relative? She thought probably she would. But she seemed to have much more freedom than Lizzie, a woman two decades older than her.

Before she knew it Alexis felt the need to jot down her ideas. The germ of an article was beginning to flower into questions, then an outline. She decided to begin to learn about—and write about—the plight of rural women. By the time she finally turned out her light, she'd completed the outline of the first really important piece she'd done since Marilyn Bank's story.

CHAPTER FIVE

"THE HAND THAT ROCKED THE CRADLE was sometimes the hand that built it, too...."

Alexis glanced over her typed manuscript for the last time before slipping it into the envelope and walking down to Fred Henson's Groceteria for stamps. The article had only taken a week to complete, and she was well pleased with it, though it was as much Lizzie's work as her own. For it had turned out to be an extensive interview with what seemed a typical rural woman. Lizzie told her story with a passion Alexis was able to carry over into her writing. It was the story of a young girl who had grown up wanting nothing more than to get away from the small town in which she'd been born, a girl who, like millions of others, had dreamed of life in the city, who had bided her time until she was old enough to leave her parents' house and strike out on her own. Elizabeth Cabe had made it, eventually finding a job and a husband in Tulsa, where she'd been happy. Until her husband died. That she could have got over, but at the same time her father had fallen ill, and Lizzie had seen no alternative but to return to Mountain View.

Now she was alone and had no responsibilities except to herself. Yet she felt it would be ridiculous for a woman of forty-five to start out again the way she had at eighteen, when she was full of hope. Her story, because of the straightforward, yet poignant way she told it, made excellent reading, at least in part because Alexis was able to keep her own comments out of the piece. She let Lizzie speak for herself because she realized Lizzie spoke for so many other women.

"So what will you write about next?" Lizzie asked when Alexis returned from the groceteria and strolled into the kitchen via the back door. Even so simple a thing as a back door was a revelation to Alexis, who was used to the security-guarded entrance of Karl's downtown penthouse condominium, or the front door of the Kenwood mansion.

"I don't know for sure," Alexis answered, pulling the tab on a can of pop and handing the can to Lizzie before reaching into the brown paper bag she had brought back to extract one for herself. Though it was late April, it was unseasonably hot, and both women were dressed in shorts. Alexis's shorts were from a designer cruise-wear collection. Lizzie's were from the local bargain store. But both women looked good in what they wore, Alexis in a trim elegant sort of way, Lizzie in a comfortable friendly manner.

They sipped their drinks thoughtfully. "Maybe it's time I tackled the Ozark Folk Center," Alexis finally said.

"Tackle it?" Lizzie laughingly responded. "What do you think it is, a Razorback?" She referred not to the legendary wild pigs, but to the famous football team named after them.

"No," Alexis said. "I don't know why I put it

quite that way...." And she didn't, except that thinking about the folk center made her think of Right John Webber, whom she hadn't "seen around" all week.

"You'll like it out there. Strangers just love the place. Not that you're that much of a stranger here anymore."

"Thanks," Alexis said a little absently. She was already thinking about what sort of things to look for to use in her writing about the center. "What would be the best time to go out there?"

"Oh, any time. They've got a pretty full schedule. We'll give them a call." Lizzie opened a drawer in the kitchen table and pulled out the phone book. The casual gesture served to remind Alexis that she was far from home. She'd never even seen an old-fashioned wooden kitchen table with a silverware drawer before Lizzie's. She'd also never seen a phone book quite so thin. You could use the Chicago phone book for a step ladder if you had to!

Lizzie opened the book, but before she found the number she closed it again. "I've got a better idea."

"What's that?"

"We'll ask John Webber to show you around. After all, he teaches there. He'd be just the person to introduce you to people and to show you what goes on on a typical day. What do you say?"

"Oh, I don't want to bother him," Alexis protested. "He's got his hands full if he teaches at the center and runs the farm."

"He's got mighty big hands...." Lizzie meant the comment as a joke, but it brought back to Alexis the thought of one of those hands against the bare skin of her shoulder. She was momentarily at a loss for words.

"Maybe you feel you don't want to be beholden to strangers, is that it?" Lizzie asked. "Well, don't worry. I'm sure John doesn't consider himself a stranger to anyone around here. He'd be glad to help you out."

"I don't know. I—" Her statement was interrupted by the sound of a truck pulling up in front of Lizzie's house. Both women stopped talking. Lizzie, who had been glancing toward the window at the side of the kitchen, smiled widely and said, "Speak of the devil...." Before Alexis could ask her what she meant, she heard the rich baritone.

"Anybody home?" John Webber called in through the kitchen screen door. From where she sat opposite, Alexis could see he was wearing a blue Western shirt with beige details, and when he swung open the door, filling the kitchen with his presence, she saw that the color combination set off his own coloring—the golden skin, the azure eyes.

"Hi, Liz," he said, handing Lizzie a huge bunch of rhubarb. "Thought you might be able to use this for a pie or two."

"Thank you, John," Lizzie said, taking the gift from his hand and blushing as though it were roses.

"Afternoon, Miss Smythe."

"Alexis."

"Alexis," he repeated simply, as though tasting the name, testing it out somehow. "That's nice. A bit fancy for Mountain View, but I suppose it sits well in Chicago. It is Chicago you're from, isn't it?"

"Yes, Chicago."

"I've got a relative up there myself, though I can't say I've ever been to call, so to speak." His voice had a joking quality to it. Alexis pretended she didn't realize the relative he must be talking about was Evelyn Kain, his ex-mother-in-law. She hadn't given Evelyn Kain a thought in some time—which was a mercy.

"We were just talking about you, John," Lizzie said. "Alexis here wants to go out to the center. I told her you'd be glad to take her some time."

"Sure I would," John said, turning toward Alexis with one of his neighborly smiles. She was one hundred percent certain he would have smiled in exactly the same way at anyone he was offering a favor to. She liked the smile, anyway.

"I don't want to put you out. I'm sure I can drive there...."

"I'm on my way, Alexis. Come on out and hop into the truck."

"Oh, I can't go like this," she declared, glancing down at her pricey sports ensemble as if she'd picked it up at a church rummage sale. "I'll only be a minute."

When she returned she walked toward the kitchen quickly, but hesitated before opening the door. She could hear the low voices of John and Lizzie on the other side. Judging from the way Lizzie acted, Alexis was fairly certain John didn't return her interest in more than his usual friendly way. Alexis knew Lizzie was "warped on" him, a mountain person's way of saying she was infatuated. Alexis could well understand how a woman could get warped on Right John Webber—not a woman like herself, though, of course. Of course.

"Well, now," John said when he saw Alexis. She had changed into a pair of chocolate-colored tailored trousers with a matching blouse of silk one tone lighter. A narrow belt of finely finished leather circled her slim waist. She wore gold earrings and a long gold chain wound twice around her slender neck. The brown tones combined with the gold of her accessories accentuated her own lovely coloring—the honey of her hair, the pale creaminess of her fine skin, and above all, the startling blue-green depths of her eyes. "Well, now, you look lovely," John finished. "But things are pretty casual around here. I've only got the truck. I could go back to the farm and get the car—or maybe you'd like to borrow a pair of Patience's jeans. She left some in the truck the other day."

Surprisingly, Lizzie laughed at that. Alexis didn't think it was funny. Patience must be his girlfriend, the dark-haired woman at the dance. She didn't need to borrow Patience's clothes—or anyone else's for that matter.

"No, thank you," she said coolly. "I'm sure I won't spoil these clothes by riding in a truck."

"Suit yourself, ma'am," John said dismissingly.

She was piqued. He and Lizzie were laughing at her expense. But when he reached out and put his hand on her shoulder, leading her to the back door, she found her anger seeped slowly away, to be replaced by something else, by an excitement equal to what she had felt dancing in his arms a week before. An excitement her body seemed to remember.

"This way," he said, leading her to where the truck was parked. Walking behind him, she couldn't help but notice the width of his shoulders, the slenderness where his back tapered to his waist. She could almost feel her fingers tingle with the temptation to touch him. How absurd! She didn't know this man at all, had spent perhaps a total of an hour in his presence, and yet she longed for contact. Something about him appealed to her strongest physical instinct. It worried her that she didn't know how to fight that appeal—and worse—that she didn't know why she *should* fight it.

When she saw the battered truck, Alexis, despite herself, stopped dead in her tracks. She had ridden in a Rolls Royce more times than she could remember, but this.... It was actually in quite good shape by country standards, though she didn't know that then.

Seeing her hesitate, John again offered to come back with the car, but with good grace she took a deep breath and accepted the hand up he offered. As he gave the door beside her a good slam to make sure it was shut, she could hear the rich tones of his laughter above the rattling.

During the trip out of town, they spoke sparingly in the fashion of two people who know each other only slightly. In order to break the silence that fed her imagination, she began what she hoped was an appropriate conversation. "Some people seem to call you Wright, and some call you John," she began. "Which is it?"

"It's Right John," he answered with a smile. "That's R-i-g-h-t."

"Oh, is that a nickname?"

"No, that's my real name. Right John Webber."

"I see," she said, obviously intrigued but too polite to query him further.

He hastened to satisfy her curiosity. "My grandfather was the first Right John Webber and I was merely named after him. He was the last baby out of the sixteen that his mother, my great-grandmother, had. By the time he was born, the eldest of his brothers and sisters were already married and had children of their own. They had also moved away from the hills to live in the city. When my grandfather was born, his mother declared—she always thought she had the gift of prophecy—she declared all her other children would desert the land where they were born, but that this babe would stay 'right handy'—and he did. My grandfather was the only one of all of them not to leave Mountain View."

"That's a lovely story," Alexis commented politely.

"It's not the whole story, though, at least as far as my name is concerned," John Webber said.

"Oh?"

"I am sometimes known as Wright. W-r-i-g-h-t. There was a time when I, too, thought of leaving the hills. As a matter of fact, I went all the way to the Big Apple."

"New York." Alexis said the words softly, wondering what he would say about that time in his life, which must have affected him so deeply. Her mother's story was still fresh in her mind, though she had heard it months before.

"Yes. New York. To make a long story short, it doesn't sit right to be called by a country name in the big city. So I became J. Wright Webber. Pretty fancy, don't you think?'' His smile was so genuine Alexis had to agree that yes, that was a pretty fancy name indeed.

"I never did figure out how much a person's name makes a difference to how he feels about himself. But I've gone by both, and though some people still call me by my city name and some by my country name, I prefer to be called just plain 'John.' That good enough for you?''

"I beg your pardon?'' she asked, not exactly sure of his meaning.

"You call me John. I'll call you Alexis.''

"Oh, yes,'' she said. "Yes, of course.'' With that settled, she looked up to see they were approaching their destination. The eighty-acre Ozark Folk Center, operated by the Arkansas Department of Parks and Tourism, was just a bit north of Mountain View, and it wasn't long before Alexis saw the distinctive octagon-shaped cabins dotting the beautifully land-scaped site.

"The travel brochures call this 'a living museum of mountain heritage,' '' John said, "and I guess that's about the fastest way to describe it. You have to see for yourself what goes on here. I reckon it'll take a few visits, but I'll be happy to give you a taste of the music part of things, if that'll help.''

"The music part of things?''

"Yes,'' John answered. "The center is devoted to all the mountain folk arts—so many it's hard to re-member them: quilting, basket making, chair caning, papyrotamia—''

"Papy— What?''

"Papyrotamia. The art of paper cutting. The craft

of cutting clever and beautiful shapes out of paper.''

"I never heard of it."

"There's probably a lot of stuff around here a city woman like you never heard of,'' John Webber emphatically declared, but before Alexis could take offense she caught a glimpse of his warm smile and couldn't help smiling back.

"Well," she said, good-naturedly mimicking the speech she heard around her, "suppose you fix it so I hear about some of them!''

SHE WAS ENTHRALLED by what she saw and heard that afternoon. John Webber explained to her that the folk center had an active program of musical activities—workshops, concerts. He himself, as she'd been told by Lizzie, taught fiddling, folk violin playing. There were specialists in several areas of Ozark music and instrument making, and John introduced her to men and women whose knowledge of their field came not merely from study, but from experience, from having grown up with the sweet sound of mountain music in their ears.

She learned a little about fiddling, though John seemed more eager to have her learn about the other instruments. He implied he would tell her more about his own music later. She wasn't sure exactly what that meant, but she liked the idea that there might be a later, a time they might share alone together. However, for the time being, she was more than happy to meet the other musicians, and it pleased her to see the respect and genuine good feeling that was accorded to John Webber by everyone they talked to, teachers, students and staff alike.

Of course, Alexis was already familiar with some of the mountain instruments. John asked her whether she'd ever heard of Merle Travis. She had heard of the famous guitarist and songwriter, listening with interest when she was told he would soon be conducting a Finger-Picking Guitar Workshop, even though her own taste in guitar music definitely ran more to Bach and Villa-Lobos.

She hadn't heard of Grandpa Jones, though she certainly did know what a banjo sounded like. The same couldn't be said of the quills or the pickin' bow. She watched in wonder as an old man showed her with consummate skill not only how the instruments were played but also how they were constructed out of common materials mountain people found at hand.

A young woman with flowing hair and a face that approached the angelic played the dulcimer for Alexis. This instrument, related to the ancient psaltery, was shaped almost like the torso of a woman. As the strings were strummed, a droning melody of haunting beauty was released. It was a sound like the wind in the mountain hickory trees, like the sighing of lovers, like the singing of babes. The dulcimer music was characteristic of the hills, simple, full of the uncomplicated but deep passions of human experience.

John also introduced her to a man who played the Autoharp, similar to the dulcimer, and, like it, of the zither family. But the Autoharp, when played, was held against the musician's chest, whereas the dulcimer rested on the lap.

When it came to the mouth instruments, Alexis was entertained by lively demonstrations on harmonicas and Jew's harps. The woman who taught these instruments had a collection that went back hundreds of years, but despite the age of some of them she encouraged Alexis to try them out. Alexis, whose own upbringing had never included the pleasure of going into the five-and-dime with a handful of change and coming out with a harmonica, was surprised at the pleasure she got from trying out the small mouth instruments. She discovered right away that it was hard to play when she was laughing!

The last person Alexis met was an elderly woman who taught the old art of shape-note singing. This method of teaching songs to the musically untrained fascinated Alexis. Deciding the subject was worthy of an article, she made an appointment to return to speak to the woman. That alone would have made her afternoon worthwhile, but she had seen and heard so much else besides. She was grateful to John Webber for the time he'd spent showing her around.

"I can make my way back to town on my own," she said as they walked across the attractive grounds of the center. "You've been so kind. I've taken a lot of your time."

"My pleasure," John said sincerely. "But don't go rushing off. I'll take you back."

"But you must be busy. After all, you work here."

"Yes. I teach here but I didn't have classes today, and both my private students for today are ill. That leaves me free to ask you to join me for some lunch. What do you say?"

"Yes," Alexis answered. "Yes, thank you." Something always made her eager to share time with

John Webber—the thought that each time might be the last.

He took her to the restaurant that was part of the folk-center complex. It had a full menu, offering such country favorites as ham steak and chicken and dumplings. There was even a large selection of fresh-baked goods made right on the premises, but as it was a little late for lunch and a little early for supper, Alexis simply chose from the salad bar. John, whose own plate was heaped with ham and beans and biscuits with gravy, asked, "Aren't you even going to put any dressing on that heap of greens?"

"No," Alexis laughed. "I never touch the stuff."

"You go for garden sass, eh?"

"Garden sass?"

"Folks around here use the term for salad without dressing—basically a handful of vegetables brought right from the garden to the table."

"Sometimes I think I'll never be able to remember all the expressions, all the words I'm learning here...."

"You talk as though you thought Ozark speech was a separate language from everyday American English," John commented.

"Isn't it?"

"I don't think so. Folks from down here can be understood in New York—and Chicago...."

Alexis smiled at his comment, but again she noticed an unnameable undercurrent to his friendly words. Something bothered him whenever he spoke about his own ways as opposed to the ways of people in more sophisticated places. Eager to change the subject, she asked, "So your teaching schedule isn't so heavy that it demands all your time?"

"No," he answered. "I teach fiddling here all year round, usually two days a week. And I perform. There are concerts here regularly. During the school year I also teach violin at a college in Batesville."

"Batesville?"

"Not far from here. And then there's my grandfather's farm. Old John is. . . ." He paused for a moment, a look of chagrin on his face before the look changed to one almost of tenderness. That tenderness seemed to transform him, to make him even more handsome than usual. It lent an uncharacteristic sadness to his expression, clouded the clear blue of his eyes, made him seem not laughing and affable as he usually was, but touching—a little vulnerable. The expression was fleeting, so fleeting Alexis thought perhaps she'd imagined the momentary sadness. "Old John's a geezer and a coot—no question about it—but he's my family and I'm stuck with him!" John was laughing now. "So I help him out whenever I've got a spare moment."

Alexis remembered what Lizzie had told her about John's actually doing far more work for his grandfather than he admitted. Evidently he had to work very hard for a living, but it didn't seem appropriate to say anything about that. There was an awkward pause in the conversation, and if John hadn't ended it, they might have sat in silence for some time. "How would you like one final demonstration this afternoon?" he asked.

"Okay," Alexis said, not questioning what he had in mind. Judging from what he'd already shown her, whatever he wanted to show her this time was sure to be of interest.

He led her out of the restaurant and into another building. His hand on her back, his warm, exceptionally large hand led her down a corridor into a modern studio with white walls and only a few chairs and a spindly music stand or two to mar the resonating emptiness of the room. He offered her one of the chairs, and she took it, sitting there waiting as he left the room, promising to return in just a few minutes.

When he came back he was carrying a violin, a lovely instrument finished not with the usual dark stain but with a lighter varnish that made the instrument look golden in the bright fluorescent light of the studio. He smiled at her as he stepped to the front of the room. "Ready?" he asked, then tucked the instrument beneath his strong chin, not waiting for her answer.

It was vulgar. His fiddling struck her as absolutely vulgar. He stomped his foot, the strong muscles of his legs straining against the denim of his jeans. A lock of his shiny, unruly hair fell across his brow. His frank blue eyes were hidden by lowered lids. He was miles away, lost in the harsh, grating sound he was producing. His powerful arms moved with the rhythm of the lively piece. He was full of mountain music, of the music of his own people. But at that moment, those people didn't seem to Alexis even to be fellow Americans. She was appalled, and when the words "hick" and "ridge runner" and "hillbilly" shot through her mind, she could do nothing to hide her shame at thinking they applied to the man in front of her. She wished she could beg him to stop. She wondered wildly what she, Alexis Juneau Smythe of the Chicago Smythes, was doing trapped in this small room in the middle of nowhere with a man who was fiddling like the devil himself. Never in her life had she felt more out of place. More like running away.

For a few agonizing moments he continued, not really aware of his audience of one. Then he happened to glance up, to catch the expression on Alexis's porcelain-pale face. Without missing a beat of the rhythm, and with the consummate skill of fine training and long practice, the musician before her slid effortlessly out of the romping mountain music into a passage from Beethoven's "Spring" sonata, a passage of exquisitely delicate, yet poignant passion.

His foot didn't stomp any longer, though he still moved with the music, swaying his large and perfect body to the melody that his hands spun from the violin. If she had been shocked before, she was stunned at the moment, and listening to him, Alexis remembered the story of his immense talent. It was true. It had to be true that once he had surprised the musical elite of New York. His skill, his sensitivity was suddenly so evident to her.

She listened in wordless admiration as the passage came to a close, the beautiful strains fading into a silence that sat between them like a boulder in the brightly lit room. What could she say? It must have been obvious to him that she'd hated his fiddling. To praise his classical playing would be clear admission of that fact.

But he solved the dilemma with his usual charming

friendliness. "I suppose you figure I've got hogs in
my tune patch," he commented with a small smile.
Seeing the puzzled look on her face, he added, "I
mean that it appears you don't care for fiddling?"

Silently she nodded her head. There was no point
in hiding her distaste. John Webber said nothing, nor
did he smile. It seemed when he was holding his
violin, it did the talking for him, for he lifted it again
to his chin and began to play a traditional American
folk song of such loveliness that tears sprang to Alexis's eyes. She had heard "Shenandoah" many times
before, but in John's hands the gentle sorrow of the
tune pierced her heart.

And he played another tune and another. No other
sounds intruded on their privacy. Around them, the
busy folk complex buzzed with the activities of artists
and students, tourists and staff. Beyond them, the surrounding mountains hummed with forest sounds—
the calls of birds, the stealthy footfall of rabbit and
deer. But in that room there was only music, the plain,
ordinary folk tunes of her country. Not a symphony
orchestra. Not a string quartet. Melodies that reached
out of the past of her land, out of her own past to
touch her heart, to let her know the man who played
for her was as sensitive as he was talented.

Finally, after many a tune, he took the violin from
his chin. His eyes were lowered, and he stood for a moment in the absolute silence he'd created. Touched by
what she'd heard and by the tall man's contemplative
stance, Alexis rose from her chair to move toward
him. She was about to speak, about to thank him for
the music. But before she had a chance, and without
relinquishing the violin and bow he held in one hand,

Right John clasped her tall slender body to his own broader one.

Without hesitation she welcomed the warm power of his arms. They surrounded her the way the sunlit waters of a rushing stream surround a hillock in its course. Beneath the silk of her fine blouse, she could feel her breasts strain to press up against his chest under the cotton of the blue shirt. Her whole body seemed to tingle with excitement, more intense, more complete somehow than what she had felt when they had first danced. The scent of him filled her nostrils—the scent of soap and cleanness. She shuddered to be so suddenly close to him, so close that she stared at his shirtfront rather than his face. Then his lips sought hers, and she knew she couldn't deny the invitation of his wide sensuous mouth.

His lips were not teasing, not gentle. They were hot and they were hungry. There was nothing of the poignant sadness his music had infused into the room, into the afternoon. There was only the demand of those lips, a vigorous questing warm that took her mouth without asking.

In return she felt the power of her own passion rise to meet his. Her tongue was a dart that sought the moist recesses of his mouth. Without quite realizing what she was doing, she ran her hands through the springy locks of his hair, then let them fall to the nape of his neck. She could feel the corded muscles, the tenseness of him as his mouth drove against hers with a fervor that she matched, kiss for devouring kiss. They were suddenly even more completely strangers then they had been—being lovers was new to them. All afternoon they had been so polite to each other. Now they melded with a desire that surprised them both, as if they had suddenly become other than who they really were.

Such abandon couldn't last long. With a tremor, she felt him pull away, felt the heated strength of his lips leave her parted mouth.

"Oh, my Lord," he said, his voice soft yet strangely wounded. "Oh, Alexis, I'm sorry."

She looked at him. His hair was tousled. His lips were soft from the effect of her kisses. He was leaning toward her slightly, and the light of the room caught in his blue eyes and made them blaze with an emotion he didn't try to hide, though she wasn't sure what it was.

"Sorry?" she said, smiling only a little. "What for?"

CHAPTER SIX

THE TIME WAS GOING SO QUICKLY it seemed to Alexis she'd been in the hills only weeks, when in fact it was going on three months. In May, the woods were alive as never before with a rich canopy of green leaves overhead and a thick carpet of forest flowers below. From her window she could look out over Lizzie Cabe's backyard and see the green-blue hills stretching into the misty distance as though the whole earth were made of mountains, as though beyond the beauty of this ridge there were no troubled cities, no countries at war, no suffering at all. The hills of heaven. The hills of home.

It amazed her, but it was true. Since she'd come to the Ozarks she'd felt more at home than she had in all her years in Chicago. A hard feeling to explain, for surely the room at Lizzie's, comfortable though it was, was nothing like her own wing of her mother's house up north. No, this sense of being at home wasn't really connected to a house or room. It was connected to the sense that in the Ozarks she could be herself, free from the expectations that other people had of her. Free from her past, too, though there was nothing in that past to be ashamed of. Unless her real parents.... Every once in a while she thought about the shadowy pair who had been her mother and father. At this distance, they came to mind more often than when Alexis had been surrounded by elegant things. Of course, she still didn't know who they were, nor what it meant to her that she had come from them and not the fine family she was used to calling her own.

Living at Lizzie's was working out exceptionally well, not only because the proprietress was such good company but also because the space was ideal for Alexis's work. The other boarder had moved out at the end of April, so she had taken his room as a study. On this bright morning she sat at the window, reflecting on what she had accomplished so far in her two months in Mountain View.

First, there was the truck. That she'd managed to do it was still a wonder to her, but John Webber was a marvelous teacher. He had to be to teach someone like her to drive a pickup! She had returned the rented car because John had left the truck at her disposal, insisting his new one was all he needed at the farm. During the past few weeks, she'd spent a lot of time taking the truck into the hills, stopping to meet and interview as many country women as possible. Glancing over at her desk, she was filled with satisfaction at the sight of the pile of cassette tapes there. Each one held an interview, and Alexis already had so much material, she was sure she could write article after article on the things she was seeing—and learning.

Many of the current interviews dealt with country crafts. She'd found out there was quite a market for that type of article. At first, she worried that she was unskilled in writing how-to pieces. But then she realized that since she was good at interviewing and enjoyed it so much, what she should do was to interview women who knew how to do the crafts—and let them tell her readers how. The technique was working well. Alexis had recently accepted an assignment on country quilting. She was almost finished with that one, but still the names of the quilt patterns danced in her head: Rocky Road to California, Wagon Tracks, Texas Tears, Arkansas Traveler, Drunkard's Path....

There was other material on the tapes, too. Wherever she went, the women talked about their lives, about their hopes and how those hopes had been met—and often—frustrated. This material was more serious, not what Alexis could work into the lively kind of article magazines liked to buy on a regular basis. She wasn't quite sure what she would do with some of the deeper interviews. But the lighter articles were doing very well. In her just over two months in the Ozarks, she had sold several major articles, and she had letters from editors clamoring for more.

Other letters had come her way. In fact, as she sat in the rocking chair by the summery window, she held two of them in her lap.

The letters Margaret Smythe sent her daughter were far different from the telephone conversations the two frequently had. On the phone, Margaret was breathless and nervous. It was funny, but despite her wealth, she still retained a sense of thrift inherited from some of the MacIntyres. About half her phone conversations consisted of the words, "This is going to cost a fortune, dear...."

But in writing she was leisurely; she expressed her thoughts in long elegant sentences. Reading her mother's letters always gave Alexis a warm, comfortable feeling, the same feeling she got when she sat beside the library fire at home and spoke with her mother.

This letter was saying that though Margaret would certainly love to see her daughter, she had the notion, both from Alexis's correspondence and from the articles she'd seen in print, that Alexis was happy in the hills. She advised her daughter to stay, even though she missed her, even though the large house was empty without her.

Margaret mentioned Evelyn Kain now and then. Alexis wasn't really interested in the activities of that distinguished lady. She had almost forgotten about Evelyn's part in making her decide to come to Mountain View.

Alexis put the stationery back in its blue envelope. Then she unfolded once again the letter Karl's secretary had typed for him. Like Margaret, Karl wasn't very useful on the phone, but for different reasons. He was always so busy, so rushed, that he gave the impression she was lucky to have the opportunity to hear him talk, never mind the opportunity to talk back! His letter showed none of the understanding evident in Margaret's. It was slick, sarcastic, contemptuous. He described the latest social happenings and more or less hinted he hadn't attended them alone. Nonetheless, he swore he missed her. He wanted to know when she intended to "dump the hillbilly routine and come back to civilization."

Somehow, reading Karl's words made Alexis think of John Webber—not that she needed much provocation to think about him. Since the afternoon he'd played for her in the studio, he hadn't overstepped the bounds of neighborliness to kiss her. This, as far as she was concerned, was only right, since he seemed to have an attachment of his own, as she had Karl. But she couldn't help feeling more than a twinge of regret that weeks had gone by since that afternoon.

She had had plenty of opportunity to see him, of course. Mountain View was a small place. Everyone was friendly. And practically everyone agreed Right John Webber was just about the most neighborly, helpful man in town. He invited Alexis to the farm twice; both times she was much obliged to accept. Absently clenching the letters from faraway Chicago, she thought about how John Webber looked as he worked on his grandfather's place the afternoon he'd asked her to "set" and keep him company while he chopped wood. He had a way of using the mountain phrases as though they were in quotes, implying he knew how people talked in the mountains and that he might choose to speak that way himself, but that he also knew a more urbane way of speaking. There was some mystery about this, his feeling about being a mountain man. Yet, Alexis couldn't pin down what told her that he was hiding something—some emotion perhaps—whenever he laughingly used a mountain phrase.

How he looked at his work! She'd sat and watched his strong body move with the rhythm of his labor. His hands were firm on the ax, his fingers gentle as he tested the blade for sharpness, his voice cajoling as he shooed away the tabby cat that seemed to follow him everywhere in unquestioning devotion. He wasn't anywhere near as old as Karl. She didn't know his exact age, but she figured he must be thirty-three or thirty-four. Still young enough to have the full power of his manly strength—that was obvious in the way he swung the ax effortlessly, stroke after stroke, for more than an hour without stopping, and without ceasing to talk to her, either.

He was old enough to understand life. It was a simple truth, yet it was clearly so. He was so good with people, so patient, for instance, when he had taught her to drive his truck, that he must have had plenty of experience in dealing with people, including his lost wife, including his present girlfriend—but Alexis didn't want to think about them.

She was even coming to like his fiddle music! Though she wasn't one to be convinced that "understanding" something would necessarily make a person enjoy it, she had to admit when John had explained a few things to her about fiddling, her interest had been piqued, and after that, her appreciation had increased. He'd told her the differences between fiddling and violin playing weren't easily explainable, but one difference was in the position of the hands as they fingered the strings. She had a hard time watching his hands on the violin without thinking about them on her skin, without wishing she could once again experience that sensation. Nevertheless, she listened and she learned.

He told her about different styles of fiddling, was even able to show her various ones, playing the way fiddlers did in Great Britain; in Cape Breton and Quebec, Canada; in New England and the southern states. He told her about the legendary Bill Monroe, a blue-grass fiddler who made concert appearances occasionally in Arkansas. And he told her about himself, how no one had ever taught him to fiddle, how one day, when he was seven or eight, he'd picked up an old violin he'd found lying around his grandfather's place and begun scraping away. He had kept at it until he'd discovered how to play.

She was enthralled by him. She loved the way he moved, the way he talked and made music. She loved how different he was from any other man she'd ever met. He was the real thing slick men like Karl were only the imitation of.

But she had no right to be so interested. She had no reason to judge Karl against this stranger. She was a stranger there herself, and she knew it would be to her advantage not to forget that fact.

And yet. The months had gone by like mere weeks. Alexis felt more alive, more hopeful than she ever had before. She knew it might be an illusion. Any night could be one of the nights the phone rang and she found herself speaking to Margaret or Karl—instantly back in their world, into their way of talking, of seeing things. When she spoke to them she felt she'd never left Chicago, that she might turn the corner and be again in Kenwood among the fine furnishings and leather-bound tomes. . . .

But then, too, she could hang up the phone. She could look around and realize she wasn't in Chicago. She was here, here at home in the Ozarks. For days an idea had been haunting her, starting at first like a funny little tickle at the back of her mind. At the moment it was nearly full blown. She let it come, the idea that had been teasing: she should leave Lizzie Cabe's, look around and buy a place of her own in the hills.

CHAPTER SEVEN

SHE HADN'T COUNTED on the speedy way gossip travels in a small town, though she was well aware of that phenomenon in the big city. *Some things are the same everywhere,* Alexis thought as she ran a brush through her now-wavy, a bit sun-streaked hair. Her jeans, not designer jeans this time, but ones she had bought in a local store for a fraction of what she usually paid, hugged her slim hips, her long legs. Her country cotton blouse was one Lizzy had found too small for herself.

It was the only hand-me-down Alexis had ever had. The fact that Lizzie had given it to her pleased her, as did the pale pink cotton of the blouse, which made her look fresh, even girlish. On her feet she wore not the strappy-heeled sandals she would have worn in the city, but sneakers!

Tell a goose, tell the flock. Well, she didn't consider Lizzie a goose, but she wondered whether it had been wise to let the older woman in on her sketchy plans to look around for a place of her own. Because everyone seemed to know what Alexis had in mind, including John Webber. At that very moment he was down in Lizzie's parlor, waiting for Alexis so he could take her into the country to show her what sort of place she might expect to find if she was seriously considering buying.

She hadn't asked. She'd been surprised—very pleased—but very surprised to answer Lizzie's front-door bell and see him standing on the veranda, straight as a high pine among hickories. In the morning sun, his tawny hair had glinted with the shiny good health it always showed. It was getting longer, she'd noticed. Maybe now that his teaching duties would soon be lightened because of summer vacation, he was letting it grow. She'd looked at his beige jeans, his white cotton shirt rolled up at the sleeves, and decided for about the hundredth time that he was probably the best-looking man she'd ever seen.

She was as ready as she'd ever be to hop in his car and take off with him, wherever it was he seemed so anxious to take her.

"Ready?" he asked when she stepped into the parlor.

"Yes, but I really wish I had more of an idea where we're going...."

"Well," he said, putting his large hand at her waist and leading her from the house to his car, "I heard you'd taken a notion to look around not at the scenery anymore, but at real estate. That's true?"

"Yes," Alexis answered. "I've been considering it, but...."

"I thought maybe you'd like a little guidance." She waited beside the car for John to open the door for her, remaining silent until he came around to his own side and slid in. She marveled at the way his long legs, powerful torso and shoulders filled the space beside her. A hint of his light, summery after-shave; the scent of grass and moss, met her nostrils, mingled with her own perfume, which had been blended especially for her in Paris, France.

"Guidance?" she asked.

He was silent for a moment longer as he started up the car and pulled away from beside the picket fence. When they reached the end of the street and turned in the direction of the highway out of town, John's eyes left the road, and he flashed her one of those smiles she was getting used to, but in no way took for granted.

"To tell the truth," he began, the melodious tones of his voice blending with the smooth sound of the car, "I'm quite concerned about you."

"About me?" she asked, genuinely surprised. Though she herself had thought about him often—too often—since the afternoon of their passionate kiss, somehow it hadn't occurred to her that he might be thinking of her. The idea gave her a little frisson of excitement, but she ignored it. "Why should you be concerned about me?"

"Well," he said thoughtfully. "Lizzie tells me you're seriously considering taking a place here—I mean buying one of your own. I don't know a lot about such things, but I guess that there are better ways to invest your money."

His voice was perfectly level. There was no hint of anything like contempt. But something about what he said struck Alexis the wrong way. Did he think her interest in this area was limited to its possible value as a real-estate investment?

"I assure you I don't need any assistance from locals with regard to my investment portfolio. I have very competent accountants and attorneys—"

As soon as the words were out, she regretted them. She hadn't meant to sound so arch, so superior. She glanced at the man beside her. His face was still, his eyes glued to the country road that dipped and circled, now passing through clumps of gum trees and dogwood, now cutting across the streams or fields plowed, sown, green with increase. There was no expression on his face that Alexis could read, but when he spoke his voice seemed to have lost its singing quality.

"No doubt only the finest will do for a lady like you, Miss Smythe. I do hope you don't have the impression that I would presume to offer you financial advice."

He was being sarcastic, and his sarcasm coiled into her like a snake, striking at her feelings and arousing anger. "I don't quite understand, then, Mr. Webber, why you're wasting my time this morning. Where are you taking me?"

"You'll see."

Several minutes of uncomfortable silence passed, minutes in which Alexis thought about the surprising anger that had sprung up between them. "Perhaps you consider me an intruder?" she asked.

"An intruder?" he repeated in a tone that let Alexis know he hadn't thought of that before. "No, no, Alexis, of course I don't. I must admit that first day I saw you up at Lizzie's, you looked as out of place as an orchid in a weed patch, but you've fit in really well here. We're all very glad to be neighborly with you."

"But not glad to have me as a neighbor?"

He didn't answer that one, and she found herself staring down at her slender hands folded in her lap. It took her a moment to realize what she was feeling must be exactly what people had felt when her own neighbors in Chicago had gently let them know their interest in buying property on their street was not appreciated. For the first time Alexis was the victim of that kind of prejudice, and its sting was a cold sharp shock. "I see," was all she could say. She wished she could answer in anger, but the hard feeling of rejection sapped her strength.

"No, I don't think you do see," Right John Webber said. His voice was soft but there was authority in it. He obviously felt qualified to decide what her place was in this scheme of things. She resented that. Who did he think he was, anyway—king of the state of Arkansas? "Let me explain," he went on.

"I don't see what there is to explain," she snapped. "Last I heard, Arkansas was still part of the Union, and America was still a free country."

"Oh, so they teach that up Chicago way, do they? Guess our coming up isn't so different, after all."

"Our coming up?" she asked, her curiosity momentarily getting the better of her anger.

"Our raisin'," John answered with one of his all-consuming smiles. "Our backgrounds."

"Oh," Alexis had to admit, "I think our backgrounds are pretty different—very different, indeed."

"That's exactly what I'm trying to tell you," John said. "There's not one person in Mountain View who's met you who wouldn't be pleased as punch to have you as a neighbor. But that's a whole different thing from buying a place in the hills out here. How could you run a place, a farm? Why, I bet you've never even spent a whole night on a farm."

"I have, too," Alexis retorted automatically. She wasn't sure an overnight ski trip in the Alps, which included staying in a Swiss chalet whose proprietors kept a herd of goats, counted as a night on a farm, but she wasn't about to quibble.

"Even so," John went on in a dismissive tone, "there doesn't seem to be much sense to your taking on a place you couldn't run."

"I could hire people to run it for me, couldn't I?" She was a little surprised at John's quick, obviously angry answer.

"That's typical," he sneered. "That's totally typical of people like you. There's just no problem in this whole world a little of your precious money can't solve. I'll hire. I'll pay. I'll buy.... Well, maybe it's about time you learned there are some things all the money in the world can't purchase."

Had she not been so angry at his words, she might have stopped to ask herself why this man who was normally so pleasant, so good-natured, should suddenly be moved to almost violent bitterness. But she was angry, and her first reaction was to think of her own defense. Just who did he think he was talking to, anyway? "Never," she said. "Never have I met a person not interested in money and what it can do. You must be quite interested in it yourself to work as you do—three jobs!"

"My 'jobs,' as you call them, are none of your business—"

"And my purchasing of real estate in this county is none of your business—"

"I never said it was. All I wanted to do was show you what you were talking about when you mentioned buying a place. Pardon me, but I still don't think you know."

"Well, then, Mr. Local Know It All, just suppose you show me."

"But that's what I *am* doing!" he answered. There was a pause, a silence in which both of them drew in their breath. And then there was laughter. A rich, throaty baritone laugh. The silvery laugh of a woman taught to be ladylike.

"We seem to have reached an impasse," he said, and she knew he wasn't talking about the country road that continued to wind out beneath the singing wheels of the car.

"I'm sorry," Alexis said simply.

"Me, too. Let's start over again."

"All right. Begin by telling me what you intend to show me."

"You've already missed half of it," he said with a teasing grin. "I wanted to show you the country here, south of Mountain View. But I don't think you've looked out the window once since we left Lizzie's."

"I don't have to look out a car window to know this region is one of the most beautiful I've ever seen. All you have to do is look up wherever you are, and that beauty is there."

John glanced at her. It was an appraising glance from a man who had perhaps underestimated a woman but was about to correct his mistaken notion of her sensitivity or her intelligence.

"What do you know about this region?" he asked.

"Not a lot, I must admit, though I read up on it before I came. I know, for instance, that these hills, these mountains are among the oldest in the world."

"That's right," John said, "and unlike other mountain ranges, this runs east and west instead of north and south. It was formed in an unusual manner, from a high, wide plateau cut by many streams that eventually became some of our famous 'float streams,' or canoeing waters.''

Alexis nodded. She knew these things. She also knew that though Arkansas itself was rich agricultural land, especially nearer to the Mississippi, the Ozarks were traditionally considered a less than prosperous, less than progressive part of the state.

Reading her mind, John Webber broke into her thoughts. ''Part of the problem with strangers buying land here is that they're not always aware how proud mountain people are of their land—of themselves. It's hard to be poor in a rich man's country. It's hard to be considered backward when all your fellow citizens pride themselves on being among the most advanced people on the face of the earth. Everybody's seen parodies of hillbillies,'' he said, frowning a little as his wide well-shaped lips formed the words. ''People around here can laugh at themselves—make no mistake about that. We're a fun-loving people, same as anybody, I guess. But it's hard. . . .'' His voice trailed away.

After a pause, he went on. ''When you've lived here all your life,'' he said carefully, ''I suppose it's hard to imagine what life is like beyond the hills. Of course, things aren't as isolated here as they once were. I imagine television alone would have been enough to change our view of things forever. But still, seeing things on television isn't the same as seeing them for yourself. There are people here still who have never been farther than fifty miles from the building they were born in, people who would be

scared stiff if they had to do the things you do all the
time without even thinking. Can you imagine what a
subway would look like to someone who's never seen
one? Or an escalator? Well, there are people around
here who would be terrified of an experience like that.

"But there are also people," he said, his voice growing softer. "There are also people for whom money is
not the only, not even the main thing. Believe it or not,
there are those who would much rather be free than
rich, loving and giving than sophisticated and wise.
Of course, there are lots of selfish people in these
hills; there are people everywhere who are less than
what they might be. Nonetheless, it sometimes seems
to me that my folk, the people from around here, are
held up to more ridicule than most, and I have to admit I find that hard...."

"But I would never—" Alexis began, then remembered the words that had come to her mind the first
time she'd heard Right John fiddle.

"Of course, I'm not accusing you of anything like
that," he said. "It's just that I wouldn't want someone like you...."

"A stranger?"

"Yes. I wouldn't want a stranger to get involved in
the life here without appreciating our ways, our
values. I'm sure you'd feel the same about someone
like me suddenly showing up at one of your fine parties in Chicago, for instance."

"Someone like you?" she asked, not understanding
what he was getting at.

"A hillbilly."

She blushed to the roots of her hair, but he was only
teasing, and the ensuing silence was a companionable

one. After a few minutes John turned off the road onto a narrower dirt path that led to a wide double gate made of sagging wire and weathered boards. He stopped the car, got out, opened the gate, got back in, drove through the gate, got out, closed the gate, got back in the car again—all without batting an eyelash. Obviously he was quite used to driving on country paths.

When they reached the end of the narrow drive, the car crested a low rise and came to a stop. About twenty yards in front of them, a wide stand of trees blocked the view for quite a distance on either side. Behind them were the unplowed fields they had passed through, and farther, the ever-present dark shapes of the hills.

"Is this the place you wanted to show me?" Alexis asked, pivoting on her heel to take in the landscape that was pretty much indistinguishable from, no less attractive than most of the area they had covered that morning. If John was trying to dissuade her from buying land, it made perfect sense for him to show her undesirable property. Somehow she had expected him to be above a petty trick like that.

"This is one of the places," John said. He reached out to put his hand on her shoulder. Through the cotton of her blouse, Alexis could feel the warm vibrancy of his skin. He was so alive; energy radiated from him, infusing itself into anything he touched. There was such power in the hand that led her toward the stand of trees—the power to wield tools, the power to make music, the power to make her body sing with the pleasure of love. She had thought about this last thing a lot, and knew it was so; what she didn't know was whether it would ever happen. Whether the tall, perfectly proportioned body of the man at her side would ever blend with her own body in a harmony that would be theirs alone.

Alexis shook that idle speculation from her mind as they neared the trees, and saw that a path ran through the stand of hickory and sassafras. John walked ahead of her, his arm extended backward in order to keep her hand in his, his wide shoulders blocking her view. So when they cleared the trees, she didn't immediately see what it was he'd brought her there for. She stopped when he stopped, tripping a little in a way that made her reach out her free hand and place it on his back for support. Feeling that hand, he turned and took her by the wrist, and for a moment he was holding both her hands in both his. She looked up at him, into the sunny depths of his eyes, and in them she saw his smile—as open and friendly—as inviting as the smile on his lips. Her own eyes were captured by his gaze, but not for long. He dropped his eyes, staring at her parted lips as though the temptation that had led him to kiss her once was still present, commanding.

Go ahead, she thought. *Kiss me.* Had they stood that way for a moment longer, she would have taken the initiative and kissed him. But he shifted so that he was no longer standing directly in front of her. As he moved, he held out his arm in a gesture of presentation that said, "Here is what I brought you to see."

Lifting her eyes, she beheld a sight so beautiful that her only response was a gasp followed by a deep sigh. For the stand of trees behind them was actually the top of a ridge overlooking a wide, deep valley of incredible loveliness. From their very feet a carpet of white flowers like large stars swept down the side of the hill. Here and there the white floral wave eddied around clumps of smaller flowers—pink and yellow and blue. And where the flowers didn't hide it, there was grass, the bright green grass of late spring.

This flowery panorama was a meadow that led down to a winding river visible far below. Its blue light danced in the full sun of late morning, shot through with other shades of luminescence—gold and silver and emerald, an emerald that caught and reflected back the deep green of the treed hills that climbed up from the river's sloping banks. If someone had asked Alexis to describe the landscape of paradise, she would have described just such a scene as the one before her wide eyes.

"It's—it's magnificent! Surely you're not showing me this because it's for sale?" That would be too good to be true.

"No," John answered, moving closer to her in the soft grass, white flowers nodding at her ankles. "I'm showing this to you not because it's for sale—it will never be as long as I'm alive. I'm showing it to you because it's mine."

"The whole valley?"

"Yes," he answered, smiling at the innocent amazement in her sophisticated voice.

"The whole valley—the meadow, the hills, the river itself—though I reckon no man owns a river. . . ."

"But why did you want me to see this? I thought that to discourage me, you'd probably want to show me . . . ."

"Some of the poorer farms this area is famous for?

Littered with the remains of old cars and appliances and rusted tractors and tools? No, Alexis, I didn't bring you out today to trick you. I wanted you to see what there is here to treasure—and to respect. Money can buy land, that's for sure, but it can't buy a home.''

She understood. How could she not understand the deep love he felt for this land? She remained beside him, silently surveying the beauty before her, and when he lowered his long body to the grass, when his strong hand reached up and took her wrist, inviting her to join him, she sank wordlessly to the earth, stretching out her long legs beside his.

At first, she felt only the slight touch of his fingers smoothing a lock of her hair, gently tossed by a scented breeze that swept up the meadow to where they sat.

''Your hair isn't the same as it was the first time I saw you,'' he commented.

It seemed a remarkably unsophisticated thing for him to say, as though he'd been thinking about her and wasn't able—or willing—to hide the fact. Somehow his comment pleased her, though she knew that if someone else had said it, if, for instance, a man had come up with a line like that at a cocktail party, she would have told him where to get off.

''It's different because it's been cut by Jenny White instead of Raoul,'' she answered frankly. John knew Jenny was one of the two hairdressers in Mountain View.

''Why cut it at all?'' he asked. And now five fingers twined themselves in her tresses, five fingers whose tips grazed her tender scalp, sending an unmistakable shiver of desire through her every limb.

She laughed, if to hide her growing nervous excitement, she didn't know. "I have to get my hair cut now and then," she said, her voice low. "Otherwise I'd look like a wild person."

He wasn't listening. His gaze was trained on her lips again, the bronze sweep of his lashes hiding the glowing blue glints of his eyes. Though Alexis, too, was tall, John towered over her. She quite purposely shifted a little closer to him, so that when his arm came up to encircle her shoulder, she was sitting very near, and when his handsome head descended toward the upturned planes of her creamy face, his lips had only a little distance to go before they reached her waiting mouth.

Warm as the sun of the upland meadow were his lips on hers. Softer than mountain breezes, the little sigh that escaped him when he relinquished her lips only long enough to say, "You are beautiful. You are more beautiful than any other woman I've ever seen."

And wilder than the rushing rivers of the hills was her own response to his kiss, to his words. She thrust her tongue into the hollows of his welcoming mouth, feeling his tongue meet and challenge hers. At the same time he lowered her so that they lay beneath the sky. His hand reached for the buttons of her cotton blouse, and she waited breathlessly for the slow release of each button, and the final button that allowed him to push aside the fabric, to cup her breast with his calused palm, its slight roughness an enticing contrast to the smoothness of her own skin.

Beneath his gently probing fingers, she felt desire stream from the place where he touched, into every pore of her. She arched toward him, closer and closer. And in his own eagerness, his lips, his hands gained an urgency that rent the country peace with primitive abandon. For endless moments passion carried them on its pulsing drift, until her hand reached down to where the zipper of his jeans was rigid, strained. She felt no shyness, only eagerness, only the desire to release the power she could feel underneath her hand, underneath the taut denim.

Then she heard it, and he did—hoofbeats. Before they could even think about what they were doing, both were sitting up, adjusting their clothes in a way that embarrassed Alexis deeply, though when she looked at John's face, she could see a twinkling laughter there. "Caught!" he said, smiling in such a teasing way that Alexis felt anger begin to bubble up in her. Maybe it was a fairly regular occurrence for him to be surprised by complete strangers in the middle of intimate pleasures. If he thought he could throw her down on the grass, paw her then laugh about it when they were caught like a couple of kids. . . . She forgot she'd been as willing a participant as he. . . .

It wasn't a stranger, after all. The sound of hoofbeats on the path grew louder as Alexis and John stood up and walked toward the trees to await the dark-haired woman—John's friend. As the woman cleared the trees and came up to them, her face revealed her surprised displeasure that John wasn't alone. She nodded at Alexis, yet her words were directed solely at the man. His expression revealed nothing of what he felt at seeing her.

"The fence is down along the east concession line," the woman said. "I thought maybe this afternoon would be a good time to. . . ."

At first Alexis showed polite interest in their talk, but as they went on and on, she gradually tuned out. It was slightly insulting to be standing there while these two went about their business. She wished she could get away. She was suddenly sorry she'd come along on this jaunt. Thinking about the beautiful land in front of her eyes, she wondered what he had hoped to accomplish by showing it to her. "I've got mine, but you won't get yours," his gesture seemed to say.

And as for his kiss, his exploration beyond the kiss, she wondered what that had been intended to prove. She looked at the two who stood a little removed from her. They were deep in discussion about something she couldn't care less about. Cows, fences—what were such things to her? She had to hand it to John. He was correct about one thing—she'd be a fool to buy a place out there. That was a pipe dream.

His caresses were part of a pipe dream, too. When she walked away from John and the woman, they didn't even notice. She went back to the place where the crushed grass showed the imprint of her own body and sat there, this time leaning, not toward the strong body of a man of the hills, but against the hill itself. Once more she surveyed the beauty of the valley, but suddenly it seemed a cold beauty. As though it weren't living, vibrant earth but a picture on some poster advertising a foreign, inaccessible land.

CHAPTER EIGHT

"ALEXIS. ALEXIS?" His voice was a ripple of sound that cut into her dream like the recurring melodic theme of a Beethoven sonata. "Alexis, you fell asleep."

She noticed the scent before she opened her eyes, the scent of flowers and warm skin not far from her face. His hand was on her cheek, his palm cupping its curve.

"I'm sorry," he said. "I'm sorry both for the interruption and for the fact that Mary and I took so long." He helped her to her feet, steadying her when he realized she was still a little dazed from her sleep.

"Mary?" she asked, not understanding whom he meant. "Who's Mary?"

"Who's Mary?" John repeated. "Haven't you met Mary Holmes?"

Alexis shook her head, then looked toward the spot where she had last seen the dark-haired woman. Horse and rider were gone.

"Mary's my neighbor and good friend."

I bet she's a good friend, Alexis thought, but what she said was, "I thought her name was Patience." She had so often heard John's name linked with that of Patience. She had just assumed the two were a couple. Did John have two women, then?

"You thought her name was Patience?" John asked, laughing a little. "No. Patience is a little younger than that...."

If the comment was meant as some sort of joke, Alexis didn't get the point. "Oh?"

"Patience is my fourteen-year-old daughter. You've probably heard her spoken of as 'Pat.' She insists her real name is too old-fashioned. No one uses it except immediate family."

"I wonder why I've never met her," Alexis commented. "Doesn't she live with you?"

"Of course she lives with me," John said abruptly and rather sternly. He was silent for a moment, until Alexis got the feeling perhaps all was not well between this man and his daughter. "You've seen her," he said. "She was with us the night of the square dance."

"Oh, yes," Alexis responded, remembering a slender teenager with long tawny hair sitting beside an elderly man whom Alexis knew by this time was Old John. The girl had looked about as bored as it is possible for a human being to look.

"Like most kids her age," John was saying, warming to the topic, "Patience is pretty elusive. She spends a lot of time at her cousins' place. And every spare moment that's left she spends practicing on her clarinet. Right now, that's the major love of her life."

"So," Alexis said, smiling. "She's going to be a musician like her father?"

"Why no," John Webber answered. "Not like her father—like her mother." He was silent, his eyes lowered. Across the wide valley a bank of clouds drifted, momentarily darkening the sky. Alexis said nothing. She felt rather guilty. Had she mentioned something she shouldn't have? But it wasn't long before he sighed lightly, then glanced up at her, his usual warm smile gracing his handsome face. "Come on," he said, again placing his hand on her shoulder. "You and I got some visiting to do."

"Visiting?" she asked, turning to follow his large strides through the stand of trees. "Who are we going to visit?"

"Family," was all he would answer as he ushered her back to the car, helped her in before he went around to the driver's seat. As they negotiated the bumpy country path, Alexis kept her peace. She wasn't at all reluctant to go wherever John planned to take her. She felt refreshed from her unexpected nap, lucky to be with him, to be sharing his day.

As the hours of that day progressed, she began to lose the other feeling he so often inspired in her, the uncomfortable sensation that any time she was with him might be the very last time. She couldn't remember feeling that way with a man before. Yet somehow, with John Webber, she could never quite forget his world was so different from her own, that her being in it at all could only be a temporary thing. Sometimes, despite the fact that she felt so at home in the Ozarks, she thought the months she'd spent there were merely a dream. She might awaken, and instead of finding herself beneath the handmade quilt on her bed at Lizzie's, she would be lying beneath the pale green silk coverlet in her mother's house, or beneath the furlike spread in Karl's Chicago penthouse.

She let her eyes stray across the front seat of the

car to the man beside her. In profile, his face was strong, the broad forehead sloping to the well-shaped nose; the cheekbone and jaw solid, giving the unmistakable impression that in this person physical strength was matched by strength of character. The curve of his lashes and the wider curve of his mouth made her think not of sterling character but of hot kisses, of temptation, the temptation to run her tongue, not her eyes, caressingly along the curves.

He turned as though her scrutiny had been obvious to him the whole time. And to her surprise, she wasn't the least embarrassed to be caught studying him. He smiled at her, more lazily, a bit more languorously than usual. She replied with a smile of her own.

They drove on in silence for a little while. They reached the highway after Alexis had taken a turn at hopping out to open and close the gates of a fence. The hills rolled out beneath the tires of the car, forest and field and rows of crops flashing by, the latter alternating with strips of earth. Alexis could see the deep rich dark brownness of soil that had been well tended, lovingly cultivated. She saw other farms that were less pleasing to the eye, too.

There were, here and there, houses that were little more than shacks, fields that were spiky with stubble or overgrown with weeds. And often, she saw yards littered with car seats and other automobile parts, old farm equipment, appliances.... Seeing her staring, John remarked, "A rather sad display."

"Yes," she answered. "It certainly is. Why would anybody want to keep all that junk around? It's really quite disgraceful."

John smiled at her use of that word. Perhaps he was

also smiling at the way her small, delicately shaped nose wrinkled.

"Well, now," he said, "I don't know that I'd quite call it disgraceful. After all, a man is entitled to his own property. Seems to me that's somewhere in the constitution...."

"Really," Alexis said, warming to the topic, and without realizing it, resuming a formal tone she didn't know she'd abandoned weeks ago. "I hardly think we're discussing the freedom to own private property. What we are discussing is the propensity of certain people to make a mockery of their own homes and an eyesore of the landscape. I find it abominable that some people have absolutely no respect for others. That—"

She stopped when she heard him laughing. After only a second's glance, she demanded, "What's so funny?"

"You. Do you often go on like that?"

"Like what? What are you talking about?"

"As though you were giving a speech about civic responsibility. Look, Alexis, out here a man's land is his own. His neighbors might be miles away. He might see them only a few times in a whole year. What does he care whether his front yard meets with their approval? Of course, many people out here care greatly about such things, but some don't—and it seems to me it's their right not to. If a man wants to surround himself with his collection of used car parts, I think it's only fair to let him."

"It's fair, all right, but it's damn ugly."

"You just never can say what's ugly and what isn't. One time, when I was a teenager, we convinced Old

John and Elly—that was his second wife—to come to Fayetteville to see a visiting company of ballet dancers. Well, Elly, she just thought Swan Lake was the most beautiful thing she'd ever seen. But Old John—Old John said he'd never seen anything in his life as ugly as a bunch of starved, plucked chickens strutting around like there was something wrong with their legs, besides."

"I get the point," Alexis said, more to be polite than to indicate she was convinced. But she soon forgot her displeasure, for the landscape changed again, and they were moving through acres of carefully plowed fields, grassy meadows sweeping away from the road in wide swaths of glowing shades of green. Here and there, stands of tall trees separated the fields. There were sheep and lambs in the fields, even the occasional young goat who seemed to gambol with joy at the freshness of life, at the bounty of the clean and abundant earth.

As the car ascended a hill, Alexis caught sight of a man on a tractor in a far field. The redness of the tractor almost sparkled against the sunlit, soil-brown field. When the man, evidently seeing them, raised his arm in greeting, Alexis felt the impulse to wave in return. She didn't do so because it seemed silly to wave to a stranger. But John waved.

"He'll be down to the house in a shake now that he's seen my car," he remarked.

"To the house?" Alexis asked. "Are we stopping here?"

"Yes. This is my cousin Roosevelt's place. One of the prettiest little farms in these parts. I thought you'd like to see how a real farmer manages things, although I should tell you Roosevelt's run into a little trouble recently...." John didn't continue, for they had turned off the highway and were bundling along a gravel road leading to a fine, large white house with red shutters, a barn with several outbuildings and a paddock, where Alexis was enthralled to see two tiny colts as well as several larger horses. She loved horses, had had several over the years. Red Star, her current favorite, was boarded in a stable just outside Chicago.

The car pulled up in front of the house. The screen door opened, and a generously proportioned middle-aged woman in a flowered cotton dress hurried down the steps toward the car. It came to a stop on the graveled drive.

"Right John!" the woman cried, going to the driver's side and leaning in the open window. "It's so good to see you! You ain't been around here in two weeks, though that kid of yours is a lot more neighborly than you are yourself!"

"Patience been wearing out her welcome?" John asked, getting out of the car and giving the woman a hug and a peck on the cheek. Alexis joined them.

"This is Alexis Smythe from Chicago," John said, putting his arm around Alexis's waist as he made the introduction. The gesture was not unusual for someone making a friendly introduction, yet the feel of his arm gave Alexis a little shock. She missed most of what the woman said in greeting, though she did manage to nod hello. "And this," John went on, "is my cousin Ethel Webber, Roosevelt's wife. Where's the kids, Ethel?"

"The teens—Harriet, Blanche and John's Pat—" she added for Alexis's benefit "—are up in the girls' room moonin' over some singer or actor. Lon is down at the Ledfords' helpin' Grover with the roof. That Grover's slow as sorghum at Christmas—Lon's been goin' over every day for a week. And little Taylor, he's up there hidin' behind the porch swing. He's a mite afraid of visitors, even if they are his own kin. Get on down here and say hello to your cousin.''

From behind the porch railing came a boy of about six. He was dressed in old overalls with no shirt, and his feet were bare. He looked like a child out of a depression-era photograph, but Alexis had to laugh at his getup. She could tell by the neat appearance of the farm, Ethel's simple but fresh and stylish dress, that the family wasn't lacking in essentials. This child, dirty and rather ragged as he was, was probably dressed in a way he'd chosen himself. He came shyly up to Right John, who got down on one knee and extended his large hand. A much smaller one reached out, but the instant the hands touched, John Webber grabbed the boy in an enormous hug and squeezed the child until, giggling, "little Taylor" begged to be set free. John, laughing his deep rich laugh, obliged.

"That kid looks like God's own orphan no matter how I dress him," Ethel remarked. "And as for shoes—well, might as well shoe a goose as that little fellow. Come on up to the house, Miss Smythe," she continued. Seeing that John and Taylor still had some roughhousing to attend to, Alexis followed Ethel through her parlor into the larger, sunny country kitchen.

THE AFTERNOON PASSED in a wave of color, some confusion and lots of noise. Alexis shared a country lunch with the whole family, including John's daughter. Patience was a tall child of willowy beauty. Unlike girls her age in Chicago, she wore no makeup, and her hair wasn't cut into the sometimes fantastic styles northern teenagers favored. It flowed down to her waist, a cascade of tawny tresses the exact shade and texture as her father's.

Alexis was treated royally, but in a friendly manner that made her feel right at home. She toured the garden, Ethel's pride and joy. She was shown around the house, where patchwork quilts on the beds, braided rugs on the wooden floors and framed photographs of family, old and new, added up to an atmosphere of cozy comfort.

She got a tour of the farm, as well. Roosevelt, John's first cousin, was a little older than John, and he was serious, almost solemn, a taciturn man. As he showed Alexis around he said little, merely agreeing with his cousin when John explained various aspects of running the farm. It became apparent to her that Roosevelt's dairy operation was at the center of his enterprise, and it was in this area that Roosevelt was experiencing the difficulties John had alluded to earlier. An important piece of equipment was on its last legs. It had been repaired a number of times, but the last time, the company that serviced the machine had warned Roosevelt it couldn't stand much more repair. To replace it would cost well over ten thousand dollars, a sum Roosevelt, who, like many farmers, was already in debt, could ill afford.

This problem had something to do with a middle-aged man with a clipboard. The three ran into him twice during their tour. "Who's that?" John had asked when he saw the man studying the farm, making notes.

"Man from Little Rock," Roosevelt said in his terse way.

"What's he doing around here?" John pressed.

"Government study of some sort, I guess. Lon knows all about it. Has something to do with that course Lon is taking by correspondence. Said the government was doin' some sort of study on small farmers. I don't know. He don't bother me, that man; seems like a nice sort."

As they made their way back to the house, the sun was beginning to descend toward the hazy tops of the distant hills. Approaching the back door, Alexis could hear happy sounds in the farm kitchen. The giggly, high-pitched teenage voices of the cousins were punctuated now and then by the lower, more assertive tones of Ethel, who was no doubt directing them in the preparation of supper. Those voices, the smell of the farm all around her, the still-bright but softening light of the spring sky filled Alexis with such a sense of well-being, following by such a sense that for her all this was only temporary. Then, in nearly the same instant, she felt John's hand again at her waist. All afternoon he seemed to have been touching her, on her shoulder, her back, even once, the outer curve of her thigh. His touch pushed away all sorrow for the moment. She, Roosevelt and John came up onto the wooden porch, Roosevelt opened the screen door and they all stepped into the kitchen.

"You're stayin' for supper, ain't you, John?" Ethel asked.

"No, thank you, Ethel. We've imposed on you all day. Time we were getting off. That means you, too, miss," John said to his daughter, who looked up from where she and her cousins were setting the table.

"I can't go now, daddy. We didn't eat yet...."

"You eat far too many meals over here, Patience," John answered. "Roosevelt and Ethel already got four mouths to feed—no need to lend them a fifth."

"Ah, come on, daddy. I'll go home right after."

"You've got chores, Patience—chores that won't wait. I don't want to come home and find your grandfather or Almeda has done your work."

"Daddy, I'll do my chores. Please...."

Eventually, John gave in to his daughter's desire to stay, yet Alexis couldn't help noticing a low-level but ever-present tension between them.

Ethel tried once more to persuade John to stay for dinner, but he evidently had other plans. As he led Alexis back to the car, he waved goodbye to Roosevelt and Ethel, who stood on the front porch with their arms around each other's waists. It occurred to Alexis that the two of them must have been through many a hard time together.

For no reason she could think of, the image of some of the couples she and Karl knew in Chicago flashed through her mind. Though many of them were couples in their late twenties and their thirties, few were actually married; most didn't seem to stay together long. There were times when it was hard to remember just who was with whom, and Alexis and Karl were a bit of an anomaly, having been together four years. These thoughts made Alexis uncomfortable for several reasons, not the least being the fact that, daily, she was thinking about Karl less and less.

It was a consolation to her that he, too, seemed to be cooling off. At this point he called only once a week. Still, she hadn't by any means dismissed their relationship. Four years wasn't something a person threw away lightly. She imagined the Webbers must have been together for about twenty years. . . .

"What do you think of my Patience?" John asked, breaking the silence that had filled the car since they'd been back on the road.

"Patience is a lovely child," Alexis answered sincerely. "She seems to look a lot like her father, a very good-looking girl."

"Thanks," John answered. "Thanks on behalf of us both," he added jokingly. "That kid can wrap me around her little finger easier than drinking water in a rainstorm, but I guess I don't mind. She's a good daughter, and I'd be lying if I didn't say I'm proud of her. Be good if she didn't plant herself over at Roosevelt's all the time, though."

"The farm is so well kept. Are they really having financial difficulties?"

"At the moment, yes. Things are always, well, delicate for small farmers. One thing goes, and the whole operation is thrown off. It's a shame in this case, because cousin Roosevelt is one of the hardest-working men I've ever known. He's no lazy good-for-nothing fiddler."

Alexis laughed at the joke he made about himself, but she knew how hard he, too, worked.

"Are you hungry?" he asked.

She hadn't been thinking about eating, but now that he mentioned it, it occurred to her that it had been some time since the generous lunch Ethel had served them. Alexis nodded, and John answered, "Good. Because just around the bend is one of my

favorite places to eat. It won't compare to what
you've got up in Chicago, but I guarantee you won't
be hungry when you leave.''

"Fine by me," Alexis said, anxious to see what
sort of place John Webber preferred. She wasn't
disappointed, though the restaurant he pulled up
beside looked not at all fancy. It was a largish cabin
of varnished cedar. Several cars were parked outside,
and when they entered the spacious dining room,
Alexis saw that several families were enjoying their
evening meals.

Much to her own surprise, she put away quite a
supper, though nowhere near the heap of food
necessary to sustain the man who sat opposite her.
She watched with amusement as John tackled a
mound of fried chicken, corn on the cob, potatoes
with country-fresh butter—and a good-sized basket-
ful of hot biscuits he ate with the thickest, richest,
smoothest gravy Alexis had ever seen the likes of.
Not even in the finest restaurants in Chicago, Paris
or New York had she been served gravy as good as
that!

Over coffee for Alexis and apple pie with vanilla
ice cream for John, they talked in a leisurely fashion.
The day had been so easy, so happy in a casual,
almost accidental way, that Alexis was beginning to
feel sad it was coming to an end. Already it was dark
beyond the windows of the restaurant. She stared for
a moment at the reflection of the other diners. "The
people around here sure are friendly," she commented, as much to herself as to John.

"Aren't they friendly in Chicago?"

"I suppose so. It's just that in the city, one spends

so much of one's time with strangers—surrounded by strangers. Here it's different. . . ."

"There are strangers here, too, Alexis," John said, and she looked up at him sharply, for his voice had changed from the conversational tone he always used with her to something deeper, softer, a tone she couldn't immediately understand. As her eyes sought his, she saw their usual brightness was dimmed. "You and I, for instance, are strangers," he continued, reaching his hand across the table to take her fingers.

His hand on top of hers was a warm weight, a heaviness she welcomed. She turned her own hand palm up so her fingers could clasp his. She felt unreasonably shy, like a girl who wasn't used to the touch of a man. It was ridiculous for a woman of her experience to feel that way, but there was something about Right John Webber that told Alexis she didn't know as much about men as she had always thought she did. "We don't have to be strangers," she said boldly, allowing a hint of something more than friendliness to seep into her voice.

"Is that so?" he laughed. His fingers left hers, but he lifted his hand from the table to draw a line along her curved cheek. "And how do you propose we go about becoming more than strangers?" he asked teasingly.

She was a little miffed at his flippancy. Perhaps she'd misread his earlier seriousness. Perhaps he was playing with her. "Forgive me," she said rather angrily. "I didn't intend to be forward."

"Forward?" John repeated, as though the term wasn't one that he used often. "Look, Alexis," he said, "don't get on your high horse, okay. If you don't want to be a stranger, why don't you tell me a little about yourself. I know you're a writer, but why come down here? Isn't there plenty to write about up in Chicago?"

"I wanted a change," she answered tersely, not sure whether he was merely being patronizing in listening to her.

"A change from something—or from someone?"

She wondered why he wanted to know. "Both," she answered succinctly, a little shocked by her admission about Karl.

John seemed satisfied on that score. He asked her a few questions about her work, her home and her family, and she had no difficulty carrying on an easy conversation about her life, what she was beginning to think of as her past life.

Then it was her turn to question him. He told her about his boyhood spent in the city, in Fayetteville where his father had been a businessman. About summers spent on his grandfather's farm. About his music, and even about his training at Juilliard. He didn't mention Caroline Kain, his first love, his wife. And she didn't ask, because she had no reason to and no right.

"It would be hard to find two people with more different raisings, wouldn't it?" John asked as the conversation wound down. "The way you've been brought up sounds pretty fancy to me—those schools, the clubs, the parties. Not to mention the glamor of life in a big town. I suppose a country man like myself must seem to lead a pretty dull life compared to what you've got up there in the Windy City!"

"No," she said sincerely. "Of course your life isn't

dull.'' The image of him at work came to her without bidding. There was certainly a kind of quietness, a kind of simplicity in the life of a farmer, just as there was in the life of a music teacher. But she would never have thought of John Webber's life—or of the man himself—as dull. There was no way she could tell him the real reason she didn't find him dull—that whenever he was near her an excitement that seemed to come out of nowhere filled her, growing stronger with every passing hour. She wished she weren't so different from him, from the women of his own state. Of course, the woman he had married had been every bit the socialite, but that had been a long time before. Alexis wished there was some connection between her and Right John Webber. She felt almost ashamed of her ritzy upbringing, almost sorry about the mansion she called home, though she would never be sorry for the generosity of the parents who had raised her with such love and devotion.

Then, for the first time in her life, she thought she might like to tell someone that Margaret and Wallace were not her real parents. Perhaps choosing to tell John Webber was the way she could say, ''Look, we're not so different as it seems. I, too, don't really come from a grand family.'' It might be a kind of comfort to tell this long-held secret to someone who would listen and not be shocked.

''You know,'' she said, ''I could have had a different what you call 'raising' altogether.''

''Oh?'' John said, showing genuine interest. ''How's that?''

''I was adopted. I never knew my real parents, but I believe they came from a very different part of Chicago than the one I was brought up in.''

He was thoughtful a moment before replying, "It's strange the unexpected twists fate has in store for a person, isn't it? I suppose it's very lucky things turned out as they did. Though, in a way, it doesn't matter, does it?"

"What?" Alexis asked.

"It doesn't matter where a person comes from—who a person comes from. What matters is what you are. Come," he said, taking her hand and leading her away from the table. "Let's go; there's one more thing I'd like to show you."

It was very dark beneath the trees just outside the restaurant; and it took a few minutes for Alexis's eyes to adjust. She followed John, her hand in his as he led her down a path descending from the rear of the building. She could hear the ripple of a stream as they walked. Now and then she caught the glimmer of silver between the tall trees that lined the path. They walked in silence, the sound of the water changing, becoming louder and deeper. Finally they reached a place where the trees separated to reveal that what had been a stream was now a wide river. In the blue light of the full moon, the glinting water rushed over rocks in the water's course, forming falls that gleamed silver, white, blue, black in the night.

"This is beautiful," Alexis said simply. The power of the waterfall stilled her voice. John, too, was without words. They stood, the tall man, the woman who was also tall, with their arms around each other's waist, not thinking about anything but the natural beauty before them. After a few moments, John drew her toward a flat rock at the water's edge, a safe place above the swirling current. He beckoned for her to sit, easing down beside her. Beneath her jeans she could feel the slight coldness of the rock. But along the side of her leg, she felt the heat of John Webber's body. His thigh touched her own, and neither pulled away to give the other more room. She looked at him. His eyes were trained on the rushing water. In the silvered darkness, the planes of his face were solemn, a look unlike his habitual cheerfulness. He appeared to be thinking about something so serious he couldn't speak about it. In the moonlight, his hair was a bright swath, its tawniness turned to white gold. Glancing down, Alexis saw that his strong hands were splayed against the rock, balancing his weight as he leaned back. She noticed once again the scar, shining white in the brightness of the moon.

And without even thinking, without considering the possible consequences of her bold act, Alexis bent and touched the scar with her closed lips—a kiss not of passion, but of compassion. To lean over that way exposed the nape of her neck, her golden hair falling away from the creamy skin. When she felt his lips on that spot, the heat of his wide mouth on her neck, a shiver shot through her whole body. John must have felt it, for he took her by her slender shoulders and turned her body so that he held her entirely in his arms, her head cradled near his shoulder, her arms around his neck, her breasts against the powerful plane of his chest.

The kisses, when he began to bathe her face with them, were soft, gentle, like the lapping of the silver waters against the base of the rock where they sat. His lips brushed the top of her head, his breath stirring in her hair. Held close to him, she was enveloped by the scent of the man—the mossy rich overtones of his lingering cologne, but also a deeper, more sensuous fragrance. Of his hair, his skin, his breath. She forced herself not to respond to the way his lips sought the curves of her face, her closed eyelids, her cheeks. Forced herself because she didn't want to rush the moment, didn't want to follow her strongest impulse, which was to grab him and force wide his mouth with the intrusion of her own eager tongue. No. She remained still beneath the rain of kisses. She let the feel of his lips along the line of her jaw tease her with a languorous pleasure that communicated itself to her every nerve.

It was he who gave in to impatience. With a sudden movement, his mouth sought hers. His tongue thrust into the recesses of her mouth. Again and again she felt the strong rather teasing stroke of it against her own tongue, her teeth, the sensitive planes of her gums. His kiss was like no other she had ever experienced—had ever even imagined.

All the strength of their bodies was concentrated in the kiss, for he held her lightly in his arms, and her own arms around his neck seemed to have little power to grasp. Yet, even so, when he lowered her so she was lying beneath him on the flat surface of the rock, her arms didn't relinquish their grip, and his arms continued to hold her. They lay close along the length of each other, the moonlight silvering his back, his hair; the moonlight filling her eyes with softness as she stared up at him.

"You are the most beautiful woman I've ever seen," he breathed, his low tones mingling with the sound of the rushing stream. She shook her head wordlessly. She didn't want compliments; she wanted his lips on her own lips again—and elsewhere. She wanted his mouth to touch all the secret places of her, though she couldn't seem to let him know.

Sensing exactly what she wanted, he slid a bit to one side, propping himself on an elbow. With his other hand he began a slow exploration of her body, at the place where her cotton blouse parted in a deep vee, revealing the tops of her breasts. His fingers were exploratory, touching the paleness of her skin almost as though he were asking permission. *Yes,* her inner voice cried as she felt his fingertips graze the dusky hollow between her curves. *Oh, yes, please.* She knew where this exploration would lead, and she remained still as his fingers moved closer to the buttons that would release the barrier between his hand and her hungry flesh. In the depths of her, that excitement she always felt when he was there began to build with a new, undeniable intensity.

He didn't open her blouse. His hand hovered over her for a moment. When it descended slowly, inexorably, it was to cup her breast in the heat of his palm, a heat she could feel through the fabric that still separated her skin from his. She could never have anticipated the thrill that shot through her then, a sensation combining the coolness of the cotton with the heat of him, the slight roughness of the fabric pressed against the smoothness of her skin. But above all, the straining of her curve toward the curve of his cupped hand as though that thin barrier of cloth could be burst by the power of her very desire.

His caresses were slow, unhurried, alternately heavy and light so that as his wide hands discovered her body, she felt desire ebb and flow until the high wave of her longing threatened to engulf her. Through her clothes, she could feel his fingers so near her most intimate centers of pleasure—and yet so far away. She wanted his bare skin on her bare skin—wanted it so much that ultimately, she pushed him away until there was space enough between them for her own fingers to pull loose the buttons of her blouse . . . she reached up toward the front of his shirt.

His lips, hot at each tip of her fingers, stayed her hand. But only for a moment. He leaned back a little, let her slide the buttons from their holes, let her part the shirt until she could put her palm against the wiry roughness of his chest. She felt him shudder, and in response, she removed her hand, let it drop to her own blouse, which she parted, exposing her breasts to him. She was full of feeling, but she had no way of knowing what John was thinking.

In the blue light of the high moon, her skin gleamed like the finest porcelain. He had never hoped even to see such beauty, let alone touch it. It seemed a long time since his fingers had traced the secrets of any woman, and he felt unaccountably shy, like a youngster who might have something for the asking but will never have it because it's far too good to ask for. He merely gazed at her for a while. Her hair, spread out against the grayness of the rock, shone like the riches of kings. Her eyes, eyes that usually invited him into their blue-green depths, seemed not to gather light, but to reflect it back, as through a dark silvered mirror. Did he see his own desire reflected there, or only imagine it? He had no time to wonder, for Alexis raised her hand, cradled his head, drew it down for his mouth to meet the peak of her lovely breast.

His lips there, the moist warmth of his mouth on her nipple, the springiness of his hair between her fingers, the smoothness of the skin of his back beneath her hand—all of it filled Alexis with a tempting pleasure that sang in her limbs the way the water sang below the moonlit rock. Surge after surge of excitement flowed through her. Each kiss, each touch of his lips or his hands, was a partial satisfaction and a teasing promise. She felt as though time had stopped; the round white moon might sail there above the trees all night and never shift position in the blue-black sky. She felt as though she wanted to offer to this man all her body could give in return for all his body might give hers.

But it was not to be. Not yet. It took both of them a while to realize where they were. Luckily—or perhaps not so luckily—one small fact broke through the dizzying haze of their passion: it wasn't likely, but it was possible that other patrons of the family restaurant were just as interested in seeing the waterfall in the moonlight, as John and Alexis had been before desire had made its sudden claim.

CHAPTER NINE

MAY TURNED TO JUNE, spring turned to the balmy days of early summer, and everybody in Mountain View and the surrounding countryside was busy as a fiddler's elbow. In some ways, busiest of all was Right John Webber, followed closely by Alexis Juneau Smythe. She made it part of her business to get to know even more deeply this simple-appearing but actually very complicated man.

As the weather grew pleasant, the demand for outdoor concerts of country music increased. The audiences at the folk center, and other places where John was called upon to play, included lots of tourists at this time of year. The "foot-stompin' fiddlin'" still seemed a little strange, a bit coarse to Alexis, but many were the evenings when she and Lizzie, after finishing the supper dishes, headed down to the center or to a park to listen to John and other neighbors playing up a storm. Sometimes they were joined by George Fox, a pleasant man of forty-five or so residing temporarily at Lizzie's. She had opened the seldom-used upper floor to provide another bedroom and office without displacing Alexis. George was working on a government survey of small farms in the area. The first time he came to Lizzie's, Alexis remembered him from Roosevelt Webber's place.

Even though she got a great deal of pleasure from the musical events she attended, Alexis wasn't merely passing idle time. In the weeks since she'd visited the folk center with John, she'd been drafting a series of articles on mountain music. She was still doing the craft pieces, as well, so she was busy full-time. There seemed no end of handicrafts to deal with—and a wealth of musical material, too. The editor of a widely read music magazine liked Alexis's proposal for a continuing series on country music, written on location. She had a contract tucked away in her desk at Lizzie's.

But the evenings she spent at the concerts were social, too. Often, when a concert was over, Lizzie and George and she and John would meet for coffee at a restaurant or back at the guesthouse. Almost always on such occasions, Alexis would have time for a few private moments with John. They spoke of how their work was going, and Alexis could tell that considering the summertime duties on the farm, the increased number of concerts and the fact that the summer teaching program at the center would soon be in full swing, John had little time for himself or her.

She knew, though, that it wasn't just a matter of being so busy that prevented them from being alone together more often. Each of them seemed to be exercising a kind of caution, as though their moonlight tryst had proved to both that their mutual attraction was dangerous; it had the power to blow apart their separate worlds if it wasn't approached with the greatest care. Or at least that's what Alexis told herself. It was hard for her to be patient, because she wanted to spend more time with John.

She could see from the way he acted whenever she was present that he hadn't forgotten their shared moment of passion. She could tell by the way his eyes so often met hers across spaces inhabited by other people, by the way his wide hand so often lingered on hers when they accidentally touched, by the way his voice seemed to grow softer when he spoke her name. He treated her as something more than a neighbor, something more than a friend.

As well as watching John perform, Alexis had the occasional opportunity to see him at work as a teacher, once or twice at the center, where his fiddling students took lessons, and once at the college in Batesville, where he taught not fiddling, but classical violin. Seeing him at work with young people who obviously looked up to him with a touching devotion, she learned he was a patient teacher, demanding, enthusiastic but serious. One student told her John was currently practicing classical pieces for an upcoming concert, but Alexis didn't ask when it might be.

She was beginning to feel a little uneasy about the future, because she was starting to get gentle pressure from her mother to come back to Chicago. Pressure from Karl Hulst was practically nonexistent. His infrequent rushed phone calls and the typed letters from his secretary seemed to say he was quite used to Alexis's absence. In fact, he almost seemed to prefer it. Alexis felt she might be reading something more into his apparent indifference because of her own growing lack of feeling for him, which was hard to explain, even to herself. She wrote him long letters about what she was working on, yet she never went beyond that. She knew she should go back to Chicago, at least to be with Margaret for a while, but she just couldn't force herself to pick up the phone and make a plane reservation. She told herself she would go just as soon as she finished this article or that. But when the time came, there was always some other excuse handy, every excuse except the real one, which was that she didn't want to leave the hills—not even for a holiday—because to do so would break the enchantment of her present happiness. Her contentment included having John Webber always at the edge of her consciousness, across the room looking at her with those frank blue eyes, across the valley thinking about her. She knew he was thinking about her.

As she couldn't help thinking about him. John was full of a physical energy that drew a physical response from Alexis. She sometimes drove out to see him at Old John's farm—not just to see him, but to watch him as she had done that first time. When he had jobs to do, lifting and loading, for instance, he worked without a shirt, the bronzed expanse of his torso rising above the tight denims molding his powerful thighs, his slim but temptingly curved derriere. In the heat of the Arkansas sun, his body shone with a thin film of perspiration that set off the tan hours of working outdoors had given him. His tawny hair was tossed by the wind and tousled by the work, so he looked a little wild, a little more "natural" than any man she'd ever been with in Chicago. The sun that had darkened his skin had lightened his hair; the dark gold strands were interspersed with threads of paler gold that caught the summer light and sent it dancing into the eyes of the watching woman.

He kissed her sometimes. More than a friendly peck. Less than the kisses of passion they had already known. When his lips met hers like that, she wished she could grab him and kiss him the way she wanted him to kiss her. But she didn't. Of course, she didn't. Right John Webber was biding his time, either because he was being a gentleman, or because he wasn't sure of himself, or because he wasn't sure of her.

There were two other reasons why the man whose body aroused in her such hunger might be stifling his own hunger: the memory of Caroline Kain; the presence of Mary Holmes. Alexis didn't like to think of either woman, especially the latter, who had the ability to show up like a bad penny when she was least expected. Alexis didn't want to think at all when it came to John. She just wanted things to unfold, the way the endless vistas of the misted hills unfolded—hilltop to hollow, valley to ridge, sunny rise to shaded, secret wood.

She didn't honestly know whether there could ever be a future for her there, with this man. Yet the sight, the nearness of him filled her with desire. She did know that if the opportunity arose, she was going to make love with him. And that decision made her see something else clearly for the first time—the hunger she felt was not only the hunger of her body for his. . . .

With his students, with his daughter, with his neighbors, he was provident, kind. She had seen him patiently listen as Old John Webber told him one of his famous "stories," a story that Alexis, in three months, had already heard twice. She knew John must have heard it countless times. It was he who held Old John's life together—without his work on the farm and his presence in the household, much of the joy of the older man's life would have been dimmed, even if he did have a wife to help him out, too.

Of John's intelligence and sensitivity, Alexis had ample proof in his music, while his work as a farmer made her aware of the seasons and cycles of the earth, of its openness and its gifts. Whenever she was with him, even whenever she let her mind turn fully to thoughts of him, she felt completely alive, completely in tune with the whole planet.

But there was another feeling, too. It hovered at the back of her consciousness, mingling fear and the promise of disappointment to come. No matter how much she might like to ignore that aspect of things, Alexis had to admit John was, above all, a man of the mountains. There would be no transplanting him, the way there is no transplanting the mountain hickory—not a tree for the indoor gardens of the northern rich. Alexis's growing involvement with him was tinged with the painful certainty that her world was not and never could be his.

She remembered how once he had said she looked like a red bird in winter. That could only mean she'd been conspicuous, out of place. It never occurred to her that the red bird is all the more beautiful because it seems exotic and foreign—a splash of lush richness against the starkness of the winter landscape. She never thought that Right John Webber, son of the gentle hills, might grow to love her, might even be starting to love her right then, partly because she had come from a world so different from his own.

"NOW TAKE ALMEDA, HERE," Old John was saying.
"Please." Everyone groaned at the elderly man's
trite teasing of his pretty wife. He was, by his own
admission, "an old coot who's earned the right to be
cantankerous." His long beard and battered hat, his
patched ragged denim overalls with their brass
buckles and buttons made him look exactly like
everyone's idea of a hillbilly. He delighted in this
fact, often relating how a man had come down to the
hills "fer National Geography," meaning, Alexis
understood, on assignment for *National Geographic*
magazine, to do an article on the people of the
Ozarks. While all his neighbors had dressed in suits,
as they thought proper attire for meeting the visitor,
Old John had insisted on his usual outfit. "Only
wear a suit for a weddin' or a funeral," he was fond
of saying. "And at my age, I ain't always sure which
is which...."

The *National Geographic* photographer had, of
course, been intrigued by Old John, as any reporter
worth his salt would have been. Outlined by a rather
crooked frame from the five-and-dime, a portrait of
Old John hung near the stove in the kitchen, where
the visitors sat. It was a page torn out of "National
Geography."

"Take my Almeda, here," Old John repeated.
"Now's she a Laplander."

"She's from Scandinavia?" Alexis asked with interest.

"Scandanavy? Lord, no," Old John answered.
"She's from over yonder, up by the border where the
hills of Arkansas lap over into Missouri. Now what
they say about Laplanders is...."

Alexis had spent all day at Old John's farm. It was a Sunday, a real country Sunday, a bright June day that had begun with church. Some people in the neighborhood still referred to the service as "meetin'," apparently harking back to the religious services called camp meetings that would sometimes last for days, filling the mountain hollows with the echoed strains of the old hymns.

After church there had been a pancake social under the trees of the church grounds. Alexis hadn't ever seen—let alone eaten—so many pancakes in her life. She shuddered to think of the calories in the mounds of farm-fresh butter, the gallons of maple syrup that had been consumed in two short hours. When she had come to Mountain View, she had been ten pounds lighter, yet she wasn't exactly sorry to have gained weight.

Karl had always liked her to be a little thinner than she thought right for her tall frame. Nonetheless, when lunch was served outside at the farm, Alexis declined to eat anything. She preferred to sit on one of the porch rockers, watching the crowd that included Old John and his wife, Right John and Patience, all the Roosevelt Webbers, and surprisingly, Lizzie Cabe in the company of George Fox. Mary Holmes had dropped by, too, but she had stayed only long enough for a hasty conversation with John. It could have been business—or something else. Alexis refused to allow herself to wonder.

Perhaps because she was from far away, Alexis took such pleasure in watching the doings on this typical country Sunday. Perhaps she watched because she was a writer to whom the art of observation

was at the center of all her work. Or perhaps because—though she barely dared to hope—someday
she might be totally at home in this setting.

She noticed that Patience, for all her youth and in-
genuous charm, was more sophisticated than her
cousins. They spoke with the characteristic Ozark accent that was noticeably absent in Right John and
softened to the merest drawl in Patience. The two
teenaged girl cousins, who might actually have been a
little older than Patience, seemed to hang on her
every word, as though she knew things—or perhaps
planned things—that were, as yet, beyond them.
There was a maturity to Patience that puzzled Alexis
because it seemed to have a negative element, though
Alexis couldn't put her finger on what it might mean.

As for Right John, a person would have to walk a
country mile on a windy day to find anything negative about him. His voice, his smile revealed his
sense of fun, of family. There was only one moment
out of the whole Sunday when Alexis saw that rare
trace of sorrow cross his face. It happened when
Taylor, the littlest, raggediest Webber, had been
horsing around with John. The boy had been screaming bloody murder, as though the teasing and tickling
John was gently inflicting were about to finish the
kid off.

But suddenly Taylor stopped screaming and
squirming, turned in John's arms as the man knelt on
one knee to be level with the boy. The boy threw his
scrawny arms around Right John's brawny neck and
planted a kiss on the man's rough cheek before high-
tailing it around the corner of the house, out of sight.
John stared off in the direction the boy had disap-

peared, and Alexis read in the solid planes of his handsome face such a look of longing, of loneliness that her breath caught in her throat in a deep wrenching sigh. He recovered his equanimity without realizing she'd seen him.

An hour or so later he entered the kitchen and extracted her from what he called "a whole gaggle of womenfolk," who were crowded around the sink doing the lunch dishes. "How about escaping from here for a while?" he asked her, coming up behind her and tugging at the ties of the apron she had borrowed from Almeda. His touch on the flowered fabric seemed to communicate itself to her in some mysterious fashion. She had known it was him before she even turned around.

"Escape?" she said, not hiding the smile in her eyes. "Okay. Where?"

"How about a drive in the country and some dinner? I know a sort of fancy place just outside of Batesville. . . ."

"It's a little early for dinner, isn't it?" she asked, motioning toward the other women. "We've just finishing up the lunch things, though I myself haven't fully recovered from breakfast."

"Guess you city spindly-shanks aren't used to country eating," he laughed. "Well, then, tell me what you think of this idea: I'll drop you back at Lizzie's for a while so you can have a nap or such. Then I'll come and get you in a couple hours. We can make it a late dinner."

She wasn't sure why he thought she might need a nap. Perhaps it was an excuse. Perhaps he wanted to get her away from the family crowd to tell her something, something about himself and her. She let the little thrill of hope—hope she very well knew could be false—circle inside her, lending excitement to his offer. "Okay. Sure," she said, taking off the apron and following him out of the kitchen.

But when they got into town and pulled up at Lizzie's, he didn't even get out of the truck to escort her to the door. "Off you go," he said, giving her yet another of his infuriating pecks. "See you later."

"See you later," she repeated as she hopped out of the truck, going quickly up the walk so she didn't have to turn to wave goodbye. She couldn't risk letting him see the disappointment on her face, a disappointment that almost amounted to anger, though she didn't see how she could accuse him of any misconduct—except the misconduct of obviously not wanting her as much as she wanted him.

Two hours passed slowly, measured by the grandfather clock that ticked away in Lizzie Cabe's house and reverberated throughout, like the sound of a heart that has only a limited number of beats left. As Alexis went from her own room to the bathroom at the end of the hall, she heard that sound and cursed it, not knowing why she should. She drew a tepid bath in the claw-footed tub and sank into the warm water. She would have liked to doze off for a bit, but she found her thoughts were too fresh and sharp to be put aside.

Karl.... It was so easy to decide she must tell him their affair was over. Their relationship simply hadn't weathered the separation, it simply couldn't weather the fact that she was in love with someone else. Though that thought crept up on her, she accepted it the first time.

Yes, she was in love with Right John Webber. And Right John Webber was not in love with her. A man in love makes his feelings known. A man in love is not satisfied with stolen kisses, with passion momentarily shared and then forgotten. She hadn't forgotten his mouth against the yearning hunger of her skin, but he must have. How else to explain why they hadn't been intimate again. She had been going with the same man for four years, but that didn't mean she didn't recall what a man acted like when he was becoming interested, what Right John Webber would have acted like if he was as interested in her as she was in him.

Shyness wouldn't have posed a problem. She would have just told him how she felt and let him take it from there. But John wasn't shy—not at all. He was one of the most open, confident men she'd ever run across. He was indifferent. Friendly but indifferent. Definitely indifferent. She made herself repeat the word over and over until she convinced herself finally and utterly that it was the right word, notwithstanding the fact that as she did so, the hot tears running down her face fell into the bathwater with no sound.

It was even harder to decide what to do than to decide she must do something. She could no longer pursue him. That's what she'd been doing—always around when he was, always accepting any invitation from anybody, providing the social affair would put them in the same room or the same house, or even the same damn county—for Pete's sake. Of course, he'd done a lot of inviting, too. But now she realized she'd misread his invitations. Sure, he had invited her to his concerts and to watch him teach. He knew she was working on articles about country music and he was a professional musician. Why should he refuse to help her in her work, when it was easy for him to do so? And as for inviting her so often to his grandfather's farm, hell—who wasn't invited out there?

There was really only one thing she could do—stay away from him. After all, a woman who pursues a man who plainly isn't interested stands a good chance of making a fool of herself. *Doesn't she,* Alexis asked herself, *dammit, doesn't she?*

Sure, she was attracted to Right John Webber. Who wouldn't be, with a body like that? She tried vainly to minimize the feelings for him that had been growing all those months. In the end, she decided on two things: to admit to herself that it was the man himself and not any single aspect of him that had won her love and her deep admiration; and to tell him, however much he might think her silly, that she didn't want to be alone with him again. To love him, to be with him in the open friendly way anyone might be with him would hurt too much.

Alexis chided herself for her lack of sophistication. Surely a well-bred woman should have the ability to at least appear comfortable in any social situation. Yet, she just couldn't. She just couldn't bear to sit with him in his car, his broad shoulders only inches from her own, his wide hand as likely as not to accidentally brush her own. She wouldn't sit across from him at candlelit restaurant tables, his blue eyes strangely soft in the glow of the dim romantic light.

Just a trick, she told herself. *Just a damn optical illusion.* Those eyes had never been alive with anything but kindness, no matter how much she wanted to read in them some other, some entirely different emotion.

After toweling herself dry, Alexis put on a white two-piece batiste dress, its deep ruffle setting off the perfection of her long neck. Her honey-blond hair was swept up, a few tendrils falling about her creamy forehead and the fine chiseled lines of her jaw. She outlined her delicate mouth with lipstick, but the bright shade seemed to jar against the more subtle tones of her skin and hair. She wiped if off, leaving her deep blue-green eyes the brightest of all her colors.

As she put the finishing touch to her ensemble, she made up her mind to tell John that she felt they had spent too much time alone together. She would point out that, of course, she had enjoyed being with him, but that coming from two different worlds as they did, they would soon run out of things to say. She would rather they ended things before each of them became so bored they would have to feign interest to be polite.

It didn't make perfect sense, but Alexis felt the argument would work. It was the best she could do.

I'm ready for him, as ready as I'll ever be. She stood by her bedroom window gazing out at the mountains glowing deep blue and purple in the twilight. She noticed them without granting the ridges her full attention. Nor did she hear the nightfall songs of a dozen different birds. For a while she heard nothing at all, and then, as though her ear were attuned to a single sound coming from the greatest of distances, she heard his car.

It seemed an eternity before she saw it pull up in

front of Lizzie Cabe's house, a second eternity before Right John opened the door and stepped onto the street. It had grown dark enough for the town's street-lights to come on, and by that light, she noticed he wore a summer suit, the first suit she'd seen on him. The color was light, emphasizing his lean but powerful physique in a way different from his other clothes. Dressed as he was, he would have looked at home in Chicago, in New York—in Paris, itself, Alexis thought. No man that perfect, that lithe and hand-some and strong, could be at home in her heart, no matter how much she wanted him. He looked so—so beautiful—so totally desirable and therefore so inac-cessible that unbidden longing caused tears to spring to her eyes.

Had she not been so nervous herself, she might have realized he, too, was nervous. She did see that he closed the car door, came around to the front walk, then turned and went back to the car. Alexis watched silently as he leaned in and took something from the front seat, a large bouquet of mountain flowers. Even from the second-story window, she could see their delicate beauty contrasted sharply with the powerful masculinity of the hand holding them.

Her eyes stinging with tears of wanting and regret, she watched him take the veranda steps two at a time before disappearing beneath the roof of the porch.

And then she heard the front bell. She imagined feeling the finger that pressed the button, imagined that finger pressing her laden heart and stopping it in its beat.

CHAPTER TEN

THE THIRD ETERNITY was the time it seemed to take her to get downstairs to the door. In fact, she ran all the way and had to stop for a moment to catch her breath before walking up to the screen. He was outlined beyond it, filling the dark square.

As soon as she opened the door, he was close to her, closer than he'd been in days. Before she had time to say hello, she felt a little rush of scented air brush her cheek. And then his lips were on her, not in the kiss of friendship, but with a deep hunger evident in the moist demand of his tongue as he probed the depths of her mouth. He held her to him with one arm across her back, pressing her up against the strong planes of his body, imprisoning one of her slender hands between them so she could feel the warmth of him through the fine fabric of his suit. From his hand dangled the almost forgotten bouquet. It brushed her thigh, and as if his fingers had touched her there, she shivered, causing an instant response in the man who held her, an instant tightening of his hold.

For a moment she was motionless in the circle of his arms, her lips relinquishing his. She wanted simply to stand by him, quiet and close, while she gathered her thoughts. She needed to decide whether all her other decisions were meaningless in the face of this kiss.

"I almost forgot this," he said, pulling away from her and handing her the bouquet of flowers. They were beautiful, but they were wild—not the hothouse roses, not the waxy-white gardenias, not the air-fed orchids she had had in abundance for as long as she could remember. No, this was a spray of daisies and black-eyed Susans, tiger lilies and a host of smaller flowers she couldn't name. She lifted the bouquet, not to her nose as one would expect, but to her lips.

The man before her saw only that she had bent in order to breathe in the scent of his humble gift, saw only the sweep of her lashes against the pale pink porcelainlike cheek. He hoped she would never discover how her loveliness filled him with a shyness he hadn't felt in all the many years since he'd left New York City to come home. "Picked 'em myself," he said, his laughing tones low and melodious, making her believe his greatest music was the music of his own fine voice.

Alexis looked up in surprise. She didn't quite know whether to be charmed or embarrassed. But at the sight of his confident stance, his large yet graceful body filling the summer suit, she knew the man before her was not some country boy. He was a rural man, all right, a man as strong as the hills that had bred him, who seemed as confident of himself as he was that the sown seed would grow into crops.

"Thank you," she said softly. A small silence stretched between them, an empty minute into which rushed the grandfather clock's slow, inexorable ticking.

"John, there's—" she began, but even as the words left her lips, she realized he was speaking at the same time.

"Alexis, there's something I have to tell you." He looked up at her, catching her own stunned expression.

Despite her previous resolve, Alexis was flooded with apprehension. It was ridiculous, but suddenly she feared he'd come to the same realization she had, that they were from such different backgrounds that nothing was really possible between them. Though she had intended to tell him so, she longed to deny that very conclusion. She was wordless with a kind of panic she didn't understand.

John, however, seemed as collected as ever. When he shot her one of his famous sparkling smiles, her panic evaporated as quickly as snow in the sun. "Let's sit down," she said smoothly, motioning toward the couch in Lizzie's parlor. On the coffee table she had set a bottle of white wine, not the French brand she was used to, but a California white she quite liked—and four glasses.

"Are you expecting someone else?" he asked in surprise as they sat down.

"I thought maybe Lizzie and George. . . ."

"Oh, I was supposed to tell you," John said. "Lizzie and Georoge have gone off to Harrison."

"They have?" Alexis asked, her tone clearly suggesting that she hoped the friendship she had seen between those two was growing into something deeper. Lizzie Cabe had been lonely for a long time, and George Fox was a fine man—and a widower.

"Don't get your hopes up," Right John laughed.

"They're fixing to spend a couple of days at Lizzie's sister-in-law farm. George wants to take a look at it for that government study he's doing."

"Funny, she didn't say anything to me about it."

"Does she tell you everything?" John asked teasingly.

"Well, anything important...."

"You two have become fast friends, haven't you?" Alexis nodded. "In fact," John continued, "I'd say you're quickly loosing your status as stranger." She smiled at the comment, but she could see from his unusually serious expression that he was no longer joking. "Which brings me to what I want to tell you, Alexis...."

She felt her heart skip a beat, but she kept cool, her hands folded in her lap. Maintaining her composure was difficult, for as he spoke, John's long fingers began to trace a path from the roundness of her slender forearm to the smoothless of those still, perfectly manicured hands.

"What I want to tell you, if I may," he began, "is about myself."

"But I already know—"

"No," he interrupted her. "Listen. Please, Alexis, listen to me."

She leaned forward, away from the intensity of his voice, from his fingers that were causing her skin to tingle. She poured wine for them both, settling back to sip from her frosty glass. "Okay," she said, still not understanding what this was all about. "I'm listening."

"As I may have told you once," he began, "I wasn't born in Stone County. My folks—who are retired and live in Houston, by the way—were prosperous business people in Fayetteville. Now," he said, the teasing quality returning, "Fayetteville most certainly ain't Chicago—and it ain't New York, neither...."

She laughed at his imitation of the accent she so often heard from nearly everybody but him. Soon, however, he was serious again. "No, most definitely not New York. But it is a city, and my parents were—are—city folk. My father ran an insurance brokerage, the biggest in western Arkansas. Like every father, he had high hopes that I would follow in his footsteps. And like many children, I could not have cared less about what was so fascinating to him."

He was silent for a moment, lost in thought, and for no particular reason Alexis wondered whether Patience was a disappointment to him. "No," he went on, smiling and shaking his head in a way that sent the low light of the room dancing through his sun-streaked hair. "I didn't have much use for insurance in those days."

"What *did* you want to do?" Alexis asked, curious not only about his past, but about why he wanted to reveal it.

"I wanted to be a musician. Then a farmer. Then a musician.... There was some confusion." He laughed gently, reminiscently. "The thing was that when I was in town, in Fayetteville, I filled nearly every waking hour with my music. Everything else was boring to me. As I think I may have mentioned, when I was quite small I found a fiddle at my grandfather's farm. It set me to playing music, and before long the violin was to me what the baseball bat is to some kids. I lived by it, for it and because of it. All winter long I took lessons from a teacher on our street. She was a terrible teacher, and the only reason I continued with her was because it gave me an excuse to practice—as well as a good source of sheet music. I started as anyone starts to learn music formally, scraping away at the scales, etc. And then, after a few years, Mozart, Haydn, Bach.''

Alexis guessed the casual way he spoke hid the fact that, even then, it must have been obvious he had an exceptional talent. She waited patiently for the point in the story where this fact would be discovered. She knew it was coming because of what she had heard of his history from her mother.

"But," he went on, "that was in winter and in town. In summer, it was different. In summer it wasn't Bach and Mozart. It wasn't the lovely little Stradivarius reproduction my maternal grandfather had brought me from Atlanta. It was my paternal grandfather—and that same old fiddle, which I myself reconditioned—who shaped my life.''

"Old John?''

"Eccentric Old John Webber, the original ridge runner,'' John said, unable to keep the affection out of his voice despite his words.

"I'd spend all summer with him, every summer. My parents would come for a weekend in June to drop me off and a weekend in September to pick me up. My father left the farm the minute he could get away. He was as citified as a man could be, and I understood, even then, that he was ashamed of Old John. He always pressed money on my grandfather when he saw him, money Old John said was for the express purpose of purchasing store-bought whiskey. That was a joke—Old John never drank any other kind—but I think he liked to scare my father into thinking there was a still somewhere in the woods. I guess dad never really worried much about Old John, because my Uncle Charlie, Roosevelt's father, looked out for him, helping him on the farm. Old John has always been a better dreamer than farmer.

"As soon as I was old enough—which is to say, as far back as I can remember—I helped out on the farm, learning from Charlie how to do things. But I learned from Old John how to love the land. He had a visionary's regard for his property. 'Someday all this'll be your'n, boy,' he used to say, gesturing with his scrawny hand across the expanse of his scrawny fields—"

"Scrawny fields?" Alexis interrupted, thinking of the rich green acres she had visited that very day. "Old John's farm certainly can't be called scrawny these days."

"I've been working that land for more than a decade," John said, his voice edged with determination. "I'm going to get it back to where it should be if it takes three more decades."

"Is it true it'll be yours someday?" she asked, hoping the benefit of his labor would fall to him, who so clearly deserved it.

"Oh, I don't know," he said, as if the question of ownership wasn't of much importance. "I don't need to own it in order to work it. My father and Roosevelt are the legitimate heirs now that Uncle Charlie's gone. Dad was the oldest son, so I suppose I'm in line for it, according to tradition. But Old John's so damn quirky. He may have a will somewhere leaving it to what he calls "the meeting," in lieu of never once having graced the inside of a church. Or he may be leaving it to one of the cats or the cows— Anyway, I'm interrupting my story." He leaned forward to refill his glass after offering some to Alexis.

John stretched out his long legs, crossing them at the ankles. The muscled strength of his thighs was clearly visible beneath the taut fabric of his slacks. When he asked whether he might take off his jacket, she saw that beneath his shirt, too, the rippling power of his body wasn't hidden. She noted these things, storing them in her mind, unaccountably sure she would have time and cause to pay closer attention to that body later. She took his jacket and hung it in the closet, and when she returned to the couch she noticed he had stretched his arm across the back, across the space where she'd been sitting. He beckoned to her to sit beside him; he pulled her close, his arms around her shoulders now. She felt tense at this closeness, his side pressed against her, his thigh along her own thigh. But he wasn't at all tense. As he resumed his story he absently, gently stroked her arm, reaching up beneath the ruffle of her dress to where her shoulder curved softly.

"I'm going to rush along here," John said, "because there's not a whole lot to tell. For the first seventeen years or so of my life, things were pretty much the same. Except that when I was fifteen, I got a really first-rate teacher. It was she who turned me into a real violinist, and it was also she who taught me about ambition. In some ways, I've lived to regret that lesson, but an artist who doesn't know ambition is not a real artist." He was silent for a moment. In that quiet, Alexis thought about her own work. She didn't consider her writing art, or herself an artist. But she understood about ambition. She remembered the day she had decided there was something more—much more—for her than the lovely little press releases she was writing for her mother's foundation.

"By the time I was seventeen," John Webber went on, "I was no more sure whether I wanted to be a farmer or a musician than I had been ten years earlier, when the two possibilities had first occurred to me."

"At the age of seven?" Alexis asked. "That's pretty precocious."

"Runs in the family," John said simply. "I finally decided, at the prompting of my teacher, and with the full and enthusiastic support of both my parents, to go to New York. I'd been accepted at Juilliard. That, they assured me, was a chance that would never again come my way. They were right." Alexis was struck by the desolation in his voice as he made that assertion, but he didn't explain his feelings.

"When I told Old John I was going—something it took me weeks to prepare to do—I could hardly keep the tears out of my voice. I felt so torn, so much as though my going was an act of the greatest disloyalty. When I finally got up the courage to tell him I was headed up north, probably for good, he said, 'New York, eh? I once met a man who lived in New York. Said it was so crowded there a drunk could stand up straight as a preacher!' And then he looked me in the face and said, 'It don't do for a man to cry, son. Anyways, you'll be back.'"

"And?"

"And so I went to the Big Apple. Musically, it was, of course, like nothing I'd ever experienced. But there was something wrong about it, even about the music. It all seemed extraneous somehow. It hadn't ever really mattered to me whether I had an audience or not. I always felt the music was something that happened between me and the composer and my instrument.

"In the two years I spent at Juilliard, I learned that was wrong. Music isn't a private art—or at least it isn't only a private art. It's social, too; it's a way of making a statement about life, about the world, about music itself. I had wise teachers to point that out to me, and I spend a lot of time pointing it out to my students. What I'm talking about, of course, is performance. In New York I learned not to be a musician—which I already was—but a performer."

"And you were a good one?"

"I still am!" he joked, drawing her a little more closely into the circle of his arm. She caught the fresh fragrance of his after-shave and the deeper scent of his skin.

"The most important thing that happened to me in New York wasn't professional, it was personal," he said, and Alexis knew he was about to tell her about Caroline, his wife. "I learned for the first time a lesson everyone needs to know. I learned where my home was—and it wasn't in New York. I thought I would die of homesickness, that I would wake up one morning and just start walking until I saw the Ozarks looming up ahead. I missed home so much I thought my body would take off in that direction without my mind having any say. And I learned about loneliness. Here in the country, a man can get away when he wants to be alone, but he can also find company when he needs it. Now, of course, company alone doesn't cure loneliness, but it helps. What helped me in New York—what saved me—was Caroline.''

Again there was a pause. Again a look of sorrow crossed his face, as though, even after all this time, the person he spoke of was so dear to his heart that her name on his lips caused him unbidden anguish. He drew in a deep breath, and as he did so he took his arm from Alexis's shoulder. Leaning forward, he rested his forearms on his knees, his hands folded in front of him. She could no longer see his face, realized he needed that little space, that privacy, in order to tell her what he wanted her to hear. She still had no idea why he wanted to reveal these painful things, but she respected the subtle distance he'd just put between them. She could see the tension in his strong neck beneath the silky strands of hair that curled a deep brown gold.

"Caroline was my wife, Patience's mother," he said. His voice was deliberately flat. "She was from your territory. In fact, I wouldn't be surprised if you knew her. She came from a wealthy family—the Chicago Kains.'' Alexis nodded at the name, but John didn't turn around. He continued his narration, and despite himself his voice became more lively as the pleasure of his memories began to outweigh the pain.

"Caroline," he said, smiling. "Caroline was a thoroughbred, all right. She wasn't beautiful; she was handsome. She was a damn handsome woman—spirited as a filly that's got the whole valley to herself. First time I ever saw her, she came right over to me in the Juilliard cafeteria and said, "I need you for a paper I'm doing on economically disadvantaged areas." I thought she was some mouthy obnoxious brat. But that opinion changed in about the first ten minutes I knew her. The thing about Caroline was this: once she decided she wanted something, there was no one on the green face of this earth, no one in God's starry heaven, either, who could stand in the way of her getting it. She decided right off the bat she wanted me. I'd been in New York for a few months by then, but I'd kept pretty much to myself. Caroline changed that. She said I was so quaint she just had to show me off. It was her way of saying she didn't think it was healthy for me to spend so much time alone.

"I was completely bowled over by her. She used to call me her 'wild boy,' but it was she who was wild. Her mother was always writing her what Caroline referred to as 'a final-warning letter.' When I met her, she was only seventeen, but already she was engaged to a prominent Chicago lawyer. She ended that with admirable finesse, a skill I had yet to learn. There are a million ways I owe what I am to her. She even taught me how to talk. She said my accent sounded like somebody jumping up and down on a tin roof in their stockinged feet. She had a good ear, Caroline. She was a fine musician, though she didn't love her clarinet one iota more than her car or her horse or her good clothes."

"But she loved you...?" Alexis's voice was a soft interruption. She could tell by the fondness in John's voice that her question wouldn't be thought of as too personal or otherwise out of place.

"She sure did. She loved me harder than anybody I ever ran across. Even though I was an only child, I wasn't made that much of—I mean I just had your normal upbringing. But to Caroline I was a marvel. Now I've got to say that a young man finds that intense admiration a lot more charming than a man who's more mature. But I, too, was seventeen when I met her...." He was lost in his private thoughts for a while, before he smiled softly and said, "I'll make a long story short, Alexis." He leaned back and, looking into the depths of her watching eyes, revealed, "I married Caroline despite the protests of her family. I brought her here, and soon we had Patience. For three years we were as happy as God ever meant for a family to be. Then Caroline was killed speeding her car down a mountain road in the middle of the night in a rainstorm. She always drove like a fool, but there was no telling her...."

"I'm sorry," Alexis whispered. It seemed an inane thing to say, but she didn't know how else to respond to his revelations.

He nodded his head in acknowledgement, then raised his hand and softly stroked the plane of her cheek.

"That was more than ten years ago now," he said. "In ten years, a man forgets most of the hurt. I loved that woman from the first moment I ever saw her to the last. I thought I wanted to die when she did, but now, of course, I thank the Lord I didn't. And not just because of Patience. Life is good. My life is good. But...."

"But?"

"Alexis," he said, his hand still but not leaving her

face. "I'm not a man who speaks about these things easily. Caroline was the only woman I ever loved. For a number of years, Mary Holmes and I have had an—an arrangement...."

Why was he telling her these things? At the mention of Mary, Alexis moved away from the touch of his hand on her cheek. She poured a bit more wine into her glass, and when she settled back, it was at a small distance from the man beside her. "Why do you think I should know—" she began.

"Alexis," he said, his hand against her slender neck as though to draw her more closely to him. "This afternoon after I dropped you off, I went up to Mary's place."

Alexis shrugged almost imperceptibly, as though to say, "So what? What's that to me?" Feeling that motion, John again began to stroke her skin, gentling the soft curve of her shoulder.

"I was with Mary for more than an hour, and in that time I told her, as kindly and fairly as I could, that I felt the time had come when she and I must realize our friendship is just that. I don't mean to imply we haven't been intimate—we have, off and on for some years. But whatever there has been between us has never grown, never become anything greater than it was at the very first—doesn't promise to become anything greater."

"I don't see why—"

"Listen to me for a minute, okay?" The hand that had stroked her shoulder now clasped it, and he took her other shoulder so that he held her facing him with no possibility of escape that wouldn't seem rude. Alexis sat patiently, not at all sure what he was about to say. Hope and hopelessness seemed to be singing a duet in her heart. Was he going to tell her goodbye— or something else?

"I told Mary I had met someone who, after a number of months, seemed to me to be more suited—"

She did pull away then. What did he think she was— some sort of applicant for the exalted position of his woman? She stood, but before she'd taken a single step away from the couch, she found herself spun around, pulled tight against his powerful chest.

"Damn!" he said, his breath fanning her face. "I never learned the kind of fancy talk—" And he stopped trying to talk, instead using his mouth to capture her parted lips. She felt the thrust of his tongue, the sweep of it against her own tongue, her teeth, her gums. All of her was sensitized to his touch. Where his arms crushed the fabric of her dress, frissons of excitement sped along her back, communicated themselves to the inner recesses of her body. She didn't resist him. Why should she when his embrace was what she had hoped for for so many weeks? It wasn't because she had been months without sharing the passion of a lover that she was so hungry. For months she had been watching this man, his body a constant temptation, a forbidden delight that had hovered at the back of her consciousness almost from the first day she had come to the hills. There had been nights, too, when she had dreamed of the coolness of his bare skin against the hot desire of her own. With him this close, this obviously hungry, she knew she had a chance to get from him what she longed to have—the sweet stolen hour, the languorous pleasure of a summer night, the fulfillment of his body joined to hers.

But she reined in her eagerness. Because her feeling for him was more than physical hunger. Because she loved him, and to make love with him just to stop the swelling waves of her longing would be not fulfillment, but a further cruel teasing of herself—and him. So she pulled away.

But only for as long as it took him to realize she had increased the small distance between them. His arms tightened; his lips relinquished hers to rain kisses over her forehead, her closed eyelids, her cheeks, before lowering to brush for an instant her lips. They swept down to her neck, and beyond, to where the white ruffle of her dress revealed the sensitive tops of her breasts.

His kiss sent a shiver through her, making her feel the late-June night had suddenly turned frigid as winter.

"Listen to me, Alexis," John said, raising his eyes to stare at her. Even when he was dead serious, the light danced in those blue eyes, the light of life, a life he had said was so good. "Listen to me...."

"All right," she said. "All right." She stayed exactly where she was, so close to him she could feel his heart beat beneath her trembling hand, where it rested on the front of his shirt.

"I told Mary Holmes I was about to ask you whether there was a chance—"

"Yes."

"What?" he breathed, surprised she had answered before he had even asked the question. Maybe she'd been too quick, but she didn't give a damn.

"Yes." Her voice was so definite, so without the shadow of a doubt that Right John Webber stared at her for a moment almost in consternation. Then he realized that, of course, she understood. He was asking her whether she felt, as he did, that they already had might blossom into something more, much more. He looked into her blue-green eyes. They reminded him of the jewels he'd seen at Cartier's and Tiffany's when he'd lived in New York. He made up his mind that someday he would buy her two gems to match her eyes. Someday. The thought of the future intruded on the perfection of the present. "You know what I'm asking?" he said. "You know what might happen if we follow this—this attraction between us to its ultimate end?"

"How could I know that?" Alexis asked. "I can't tell the future any better than you can. I only know that I want it, that I want you."

"I told you about my past, Alexis, because I wanted you to understand I can't leave here, not again, not ever."

"I know...."

"And I could never ask you to stay. I did that with Caroline, and...."

"I know."

"This could be foolish—this could cause us both a lot of hurt. The day might come when you wake up and ask yourself what you're doing in this godforsaken neck of the woods rather than up home where you belong—"

"Damn it, John, I know!" There was only one way to still him. She pressed the whole length of her body against the length of his, leaving only a small space in which to reach up and teasingly place her finger across his lips in a gesture that said, "Be still and come hither." He kissed the tip of that finger. He reached up and took her hand in his, guiding her palm to his lips. His tongue drew a suggestive, teasing circle there, and she giggled, but the giggle caught in her throat, turned to a huskiness he read correctly as invitation. He stared into her eyes, seeing there exactly what she was asking. Wordlessly he led her toward the stairs, up to the second floor of Lizzie's house, where he knew the bedrooms must be.

Later she would try to remember whether they had spoken at all in those first few minutes. She couldn't recall any words—or much shyness either—though at first, when he took off his shoes and socks and began to undress, he turned from her. Without the least hesitation, she took him by the shoulders and made him face her so that as he unbuttoned his shirt, she could watch the bronze skin of his chest become exposed to her sight. She had seen that before, of course, and he had seen what she revealed when she raised her arms and pulled her dress over her head, then her camisole. He had seen her breasts before; nonetheless, he drew in his breath sharply, stepped toward her.

"Alexis," he said, "Alexis, you are the most beautiful creature...." She knew that when he said "creature," he was speaking as farmers speak of the wonders of the rare perfect creation, and she was deeply flattered. His hands, a little rough from his work, were still the sensitive hands of an artist, and his touch on her breast, then on her nipple set her to quivering the way the strings of his violin quivered into exquisite music beneath those same fingers. So light was his touch, so teasing and tempting, that she wanted to thrust herself up against him, wanted to feel her own skin against his, immediately and intensely.

But he pulled away. Like her, he was an experienced lover who knew the value of restraint, that waiting could hone the pleasures of the moment to keenness. Slowly, he removed his trousers, the briefs he wore beneath. It was Alexis's turn then to draw a deep breath of surprise and appreciation. He, too, was beautiful. He was not evenly tanned because he so often worked in jeans and no shirt, yet there was no part of his body that was pale. His skin seemed to glow, whether because of his obvious good health, or because desire was clouding Alexis's eyes and making her see things in an unreal light, she couldn't tell. His body was so large, so well proportioned. Colossal—was that the term she had learned in school—the technical term for a statue of a man that was larger than the man himself? She stared at the width of his shoulders, at the trimness of his waist, at the musculature of his thighs. And then, only then, did she allow her eyes to fall on the full glory of his masculinity. Almost involuntarily her hand reached to touch, to grasp. . . .

But he stayed her, his wide hand encircling her slender wrist. A laugh like a song rippled through the still air of the bedroom. "Just a darn minute," he said teasingly. "Fair's fair. I'm not going to be the only one naked as a gosling just out of the egg. Come here. . . ." Something in his tone was so playful that she responded not by rushing into his arms, but by rushing away.

The only place to go was around the other side of

the bed, and he was on her before she got halfway there, both of them laughing like children. But then that laughter changed to silence—to the silence of a passion whose impending fulfillment hung in the air—a rich promise. Soon, oh, yes, soon.

He had grabbed her from behind, his hands on her shoulders. Slowly those hands descended, brushing her tender skin but not grasping, until both hands came around her breasts and in a single strong but totally pleasurable clasp, he held her fullness in his palms. For a moment she stood powerless, spellbound by his touch, before turning her head ever so slightly. With him standing behind her, she could just reach the skin of his encircling arm with her tongue. She gave it a flick, tasting the saltiness of him. He remained still. Again she flicked his skin with her tongue. She felt him loosen his hold on her breasts a tiny bit; she pressed her derriere gently but firmly against him. Even through the fabric of her skirt, she could feel the effect this had on him, and she didn't stop. Slowly she circled her hips, so that her body's unmistakable desire for his could be spoken in its own language. And he answered. He answered by reaching down and in one swoop removing her skirt and underthings.

They were both as naked as new things, naked as nature intended them to be. There seemed no place too private for either to touch. The hands of the woman explored the body of the man. The arms of the man lifted her to the bed, where he, too, let his hands roam in discovery, in a joy that was new to them both, not because they had never before experienced these pleasures, but because they had never before experienced each other.

It might have been hours. It might have been minutes. It might have been all the days of their lives that
they touched like that, until the touch of lips, of
fingers, of legs and shoulders and arms was not
enough. Until kissing was not enough. Until simple
caressing, however passionate, was not enough. Until
only complete union could fulfill their mutual longing. Strong limbs entwined, they each allowed the
other the ultimate intimacy, rocking with the motion
of shared ecstasy until on a wave of sweet oblivion,
they were swept away from all consciousness except
the consciousness of their pleasure.

Without their being aware of it, the benign evening
breeze, scented with the rich perfume of mountain
flowers, fanned the white curtains before gently
wafting over the bodies of Alexis and John as they
explored their newfound love.

CHAPTER ELEVEN

ALL THE MONTH OF JULY was like a dream to her. *Liebestraum*, a dream of love. The mountains were bathed in a deep blue haze from dawn until dusk. In the valleys and meadows, waist-high sweet grasses stood still in the breezeless afternoons of brilliant sun. The forest floor was dappled with the shadow of thick foliage, sprinkled yet with flowers in shades of purple, pink and white. The scent of the hickory trees, the gums and the sassafras mingled with the cool earth smell of moss. The birds sang their most ambitious songs—long trilling runs of notes through the wood. And all this Alexis interpreted with love, her love for John Webber, accepted by him and returned to her, enriched by the ardor of his own heart.

They were discreet. They wanted to keep their feelings secret for a while, to savor the wonder without anyone else knowing this marvelous thing had happened to two people who hadn't been expecting it, hadn't even known it was possible. When they met accidentally in town, they strove to act the way any two Mountain View neighbors would. It was exciting for Alexis to calmly ask Right John how things were going at his farm, without revealing that she already knew how things were going in his heart.

He wanted her to get to know his daughter. At

first, Alexis felt slightly intimidated by the idea. Her experience with teenagers was limited, but when she put herself in Patience's place, she could see that her own presence in John's life might very well seem an intrusion to the girl. Once or twice, Alexis had tried to speak to Patience, but neither of them could think of much to say. School was over. Alexis knew nothing about the music Patience and the cousins listened to all day and most of the night. Talking about the endless stream of scrawny boys that tromped through the girls' lives was clearly taboo—and that about covered Patience's interests. Or so it seemed at first.

One afternoon, around the time when Alexis had given up with the girl, she was visiting Old John Webber and his wife Almeda. Right John was working at the folk center, so Alexis thought she and the two adults were the only ones in the farmhouse. They sat in the kitchen eating Almeda's famous giant oatmeal cookies, sipping tall glasses of lemonade made with honey from a neighbor's bees. Old John was in the middle of one of his incredible tales, when Alexis heard the distant strain of what she recognized as a Mozart piece. "What's that?" she asked.

"I said 'the damn thing was quicker 'an double-geared lightnin'—jest took off, 'n afore ya knowed it—"

"Yes," Alexis said, "I heard you. What I mean is, what's that sound?"

"What sound?" Both Almeda and Old John pricked up their ears and screwed up their faces, but they didn't seem to be hearing what Alexis heard.

"The music. . . ."

"Oh, that," Old John said with a dismissing smile.

"That's nought but the sprig tootin' her horn."

"It's Pat practicing on her clarinet," Almeda explained. She often acted as a sort of walking footnote to Old John's utterances, explaining what he meant, adding things he'd forgotten. She knew every one of his stories better than he did himself. Alexis was constrained to listen to two more of those stories before she managed to excuse herself, ostensibly to use the washroom, but really to follow the sound of the music until she could get close enough to better judge Patience's playing. She couldn't get much of an impression from the snatches floating down to her from above.

Leaving the kitchen, she made her way through the dining room and parlor of the farmhouse, which Right John had helped renovate when he moved in. Once on the second floor, Alexis momentarily lost the thread of the music. She was familiar with the house and knew Patience's bedroom was on the third floor, but there was a music room on the second. Lately, John seemed to be spending quite a lot of time there. Often when she came over, she could hear his violin, though he always stopped practicing when he realized she had arrived. She approached the door to the room, which was open. Glancing in, she saw Patience Webber, and the sight touched her heart.

Several music stands were set up beside the piano. John sometimes had musicians from the center or from Batesville over to the house to play, but at that moment there was only Patience, seated at one of the stands, the sheets of music in disarray in front of her. Her long golden hair fell forward, hiding her face, but Alexis could tell by the shaking of the girl's shoulders, and by the low sound of something other than music, that the girl was weeping. She held the instrument between her hands. Perhaps she was crying because she was frustrated in her efforts to coax from the clarinet what was in her mind—the sound that had been in Mozart's mind. Alexis's years with Karl, her acquaintance with many of the members of his orchestra had made her aware of the frustrations of musicians. Her own work made her familiar with the pain of having an exquisite idea but inadequate means to get it across to anyone else.

Not wanting to intrude on the girl's privacy, Alexis turned from the door, intending to slip away. But Patience had heard her and called out, "Who's there?"

"It's me, Alexis. Sorry to disturb you. I was just on my way back downstairs."

"You're not disturbing me," Patience said, coming to the door. Despite the fact that her eyes were red from recent tears, she was smiling. A smile very similar to another person's heartwarming grin. "Come on in," she said. Whether Patience was just being polite or whether she was genuinely interested in making friends, Alexis wasn't sure, but she didn't want to pass up this rare opportunity to at least begin to get to know John's daughter.

"How's the practicing going?" Alexis asked, realizing the moment the words were out that that was exactly the wrong question. She couldn't help it; she was nervous. She had been nervous and awkward more times in the past five months in Mountain View than she had during her previous twenty-six years in Chicago. That was all right. She was coming to understand being ill at ease was a sign of growth.

Perhaps that was part of Patience's problem, too.

"The practice? Oh, it's okay. Sit down." She motioned to one of the folding chairs, and Alexis moved a music stand out of the way to sit down. "Pardon the mess," Patience said. "Daddy had some students over last night. You sure got pretty clothes."

"Why, thank you," Alexis murmured, a little taken aback by the swift change in topic. Her dress was linen in three shades of gold, simply designed—three rows of gathered fabric held up by wide straps at the shoulders. The dress set off her light tan and the golden wildness of her curls. Her hair had grown a lot in the last little while, and the humidity of the summer air had caused it to bush out in natural waves quite unlike the sleek style she had once worn.

"That dress come from Chicago?" Patience asked.

"Yes."

"Must be some place."

"Because of the dress?" Alexis asked, smiling.

"No, of course not—not really," the teenager answered, returning the smile.

"Haven't you been there?"

"Only once when I was small. I went to visit my grandmother, and I remember nothing about it at all. But I think it must be a wonderful place to live. I can just imagine the stores and the concerts—not to mention the mansions. My grandmother lives in a mansion." Patience uttered the last word with a tiny shrug as, though the concept of a mansion was a bit unreal to her, something out of a now-discarded fairy tale.

"I know."

"What? What do you mean you know?"

"I know your grandmother—Mrs. Kain."

"Wow," Patience cried. "Is that ever freaky. How could you know my grandmother?"

"It's easy," Alexis said jokingly. Suddenly she felt much more at ease. "She's from Chicago. I'm from Chicago. She lives in a mansion. I live in a mansion."

"You're kidding—aren't you?"

"No," Alexis answered simply, momentarily surprised by the strange sensation of realizing she wished she was kidding. "No, I live in Kenwood, same as Mrs. Kain, who just happens to be my mother's best friend."

Patience was quiet for a moment, which seemed to be all the time it took for her to accept what she'd just heard—and apparently to begin to formulate a plan.

"Will you be going back to Chicago soon?" she asked.

"I don't know." Alexis knew she should go back soon. There were several editors she wanted to see, not to mention Margaret. As for Karl, she wouldn't be seeing him. When she'd sent him a carefully worded letter of goodbye, he'd answered with a telegram— "Fine with me. It's been fun." "Yes," she said, "I'll probably go back for a visit soon."

"Maybe I can go with you?"

Alexis was surprised by this. It seemed odd that Patience should go, in one fell sweep, from hardly knowing her to offering herself as a traveling companion. But when Alexis thought about the girl's weeping, she recognized there was an element of desperation in this whole scene. Perhaps Patience was grasping at straws. "And why would you want to go to Chicago?" Alexis asked, keeping her tone casual.

"To see my grandmother, of course," Patience replied evenly. But there was a pause, and when she continued her voice was loaded with emotion, growing more and more excited as she spoke. "I want to see my grandmother. I want to visit my mother's house. My mother was a musician—a clarinetist, just like I'm going to be. She got to go to New York to study. She didn't have to hang around a place like this...."

"Like this?" Alexis asked. She was unnerved by the girl's sudden passion, but some instinct gave her the confidence to listen patiently so that she might be able to somehow help.

"This place is nowhere. I hate it. I don't want to be a farmer's daughter."

"But your father is an artist."

"My father is a hick—"

"Patience!"

"I don't want to be like him. I don't want to go around in stupid jeans all my life like a farmer."

Alexis fought to hide a smile. "Patience," she said. "When you do get to Chicago, you're going to see more pairs of jeans there than you see even here."

"That's not what I mean. I— Oh, what's the use...." And again she began to cry. Alexis knew the girl would be embarrassed later to have lost control in front of a stranger. Suddenly, it was as though a door opened in Alexis's heart. Quite apart from the fact that Patience was the daughter of the man she was growing to love more day by day, she wanted to help Patience, to befriend her. She knew she would have to do it slowly, but she was willing to bide her time.

Reaching out, she put her hand on the girl's shoulder. "Patience," she said softly, "you're upset now, and I think you need to be alone. You know I'm at Lizzie's in town. Call me if you want to talk about all this when you're feeling calmer, okay?"

In response to her overture, Alexis received a nod, which was confirmation enough that she and John's daughter might be able to establish a rapport.

OVER THE WEEKS, Patience did call. She began to come to Lizzie's often, and she and Alexis soon found plenty to talk about. Everything about Alexis—her clothes, her accent, her experiences— fascinated the girl, who seemed to regard the woman somewhat the way her father did—as a mysterious stranger from afar whose ways were exotic, whose person and manner were beautiful and rare.

In her dealings with Patience, Alexis was torn in several directions: loyalty to John, fairness to the girl, recognition that Patience was strongly attracted to her as a role model. And at the back of Alexis's mind was always the niggling memory of that conversation with Evelyn Kain so many months before, when the pesky matron had insisted Alexis should keep an eye on her grandchild. Alexis was convinced Mrs. Kain's demand was meaningless, though it had occurred to her briefly that she shouldn't encourage Patience's obvious desire to visit Chicago.

She dealt with Patience and her problems well, though sometimes she had to figure out what to do from one minute to the next. Eventually she felt it was right to promise Patience she would talk to Right John about letting the girl go up north for a visit in the near future. She didn't agree to ask John about high school in Chicago. It was too soon for such a request—too soon in every way. But daily Patience mentioned how wonderful her life would be if only this one wish could come true. . . .

CHAPTER TWELVE

"WELL, I'M THE ONE who should know whether I've ever done it, aren't I?" Alexis's voice was impatient, though not angry. She and John were sitting in Lizzie's kitchen. It was past dark. Through the screen door Alexis could see moths buzzing around the back-porch light.

"I just find it so hard to believe. Never in your whole life?" John asked again.

"Never in my whole life."

It was August, the time of "laying by," when the farmer's work, planting and cultivating his crops, is over and his work harvesting them hasn't yet begun. In the deep still heat of midsummer, Right John Webber had finally found time to take a break from all his activities except the one he loved most—being with Alexis.

"I've simply always had a roof over my head," Alexis went on. "I don't see what's so unusual about that. After all, this is a civilized country, isn't it?"

"Yes."

"This is the twentieth century, isn't it?"

"Of course, Alexis. But every kid has slept outside in the summer. You never put up a pup tent in the backyard?"

"In Kenwood? Of course not."

"You never went to camp?"

"I went to camp. Sure. Yes, I went to camp."

"Okay, so didn't the camp have tents?"

"No."

"Well, then, where'd you sleep?"

"In the lodge," she answered in a barely audible voice.

"What?"

"I said we slept in the lodge."

"Oh, is that so?" John laughed, getting up from the table and coming around to where Alexis sat. He stood behind her, putting his arms around her shoulders and leaning down so that they were cheek to cheek. "And did the nice day maid roll up your little Gucci sleeping bag for you every morning?"

Swiftly she pushed both of her elbows back, catching him in the chest. She knew she hadn't hurt him, but he backed up, remaining stooped, grabbing his sides as if she'd mortally injured him, groaning as if any moment might be his last. "Cruel," he mocked. "There is no cruelty so great as that of the rich directed toward the poor."

"I'm not cruel, you're not poor and you're not funny, either. Okay, so I never slept outside under the stars—or under canvas, either. So what? I bet there are plenty of people—"

"It's time you left their ranks, miss," John said teasingly.

"I'd be a dead loss in the wilds. You'd throw me overboard ten minutes after we got on the river—if you could put up with me for that long."

"I'm as patient as Job in despair—anybody'll tell you that...."

'And modest.''

"Ah, come on Alexis," John said more seriously. "You'll love it. It'll be like nothing you ever did before."

"That's for sure," she answered. She couldn't even imagine what it would be like to canoe down a "float stream." She did know the rushing mountain streams, and the many state rivers, like the Little Red, the Spring, the Strawberry, were famous among canoeists. Not to mention the wonderous White that rose in the northern part of Arkansas, then meandered southeast toward the waiting Mississippi.

"It'll be easy," he insisted. He had come back to the table, but instead of sitting opposite her, he took the chair next to her. His leg touched hers beneath the table. They both wore shorts; her skin tingled at the contact with his. "I'll look after you, honey. You can count on it." His fingers stroked her cheek, and she raised her eyes to look into his. They showed such concern for her, such love. The way he looked when he was looking at her was so strong, so open an expression of his caring, she had to drop her eyes in the face of his intensity.

"I've never done anything like it before. . . ."

"I know, Alexis. There must be thousands upon thousands of things you've never done before. That doesn't mean you're never going to do them."

"No, but—"

"And there are lots of things I've never done before, either."

"Like what?"

"Oh, I don't know," he said. He stared off into the distance for a moment, whether to think of an example or to take the time to carefully phrase what he wanted to say, Alexis wasn't sure. He was always funny, sometimes flippant, when he joked with her about what he called her "raising," but at those times she thought she sensed an undercurrent to his teasing. There was something always at the back of his mind, some problem—not with her or with them, but with himself—some question that bothered him but that he couldn't bring himself to put into words.

When he did speak, she was certain his words didn't reflect the seriousness of his thoughts. "Fer instance," he said teasingly, "I ain't never played that there game they call squash. Ain't much call fer a fancy-pants game like that down here 'n the hills, but I hear tell all the folk up yonder in Chicago are stuck on that game like flies on a jam lid."

"Cut it out," she laughed, not bothering to respond to his silliness, though she had to admit his Li'l Abner routine was funny precisely because it was so different from his usual manner. He seemed as polished, as sophisticated as any man she knew up north, though she wasn't sure whether that was because of the time he'd spent in New York, or because of his own sense of self-confidence, his friendly yet somehow commanding presence.

In the end, Alexis gave in. She believed his assertions that he was an expert canoeist and camper. He promised that if she came along on the trip to the White River, he would look out for her, teach her some of what he knew about wilderness survival. He swore the area they would be traveling through wasn't really wild at all. When she protested that she had no equipment, he told her there were plenty of outfitters along the route to supply her with anything he couldn't give her. He apologized for the fact that there wasn't time for her to order a wilderness ensemble from the sportswear department of some posh boutique—and for his trouble received a playful punch that somehow developed into a passionate embrace.

It was then that she definitely decided to go. For his lips against the curve of her listening ear promised they would finally have some time alone together, time to explore this new thing that had grown up between them...the sweet flower of love with its rich, mysterious, elusive perfume.

"IT'S NOT MY FAULT. The damn thing keeps falling off."

"It doesn't matter whose fault it is, Alexis. Just go back and pick it up."

"You do it. I'm exhausted. When are we going to stop? I didn't realize we'd be walking the whole time. How much farther is it, anyway? These boots are killing me."

"All right," John answered, his voice strained with the effort to remain patient. They had come to a clearing in the forest. "You sit here and wait. Don't wander around. Just sit here until I find the bundle of tent pegs and bring it back. Can you do that?"

"Yes, I can do that," she snapped, turning from him and sitting on a flat rock. She heard him stride away, back toward the wood. She wondered whether the vegetation at the rock's base included poison ivy. She wouldn't be surprised to see it—not that she knew what it looked like. She wouldn't have been surprised to see a rattlesnake or a tarantula, either. The woods they had been tramping through all day long could hold anything, for all she knew. Though they surely didn't hold the creatures Old John had told her to expect. He had described three snakes: the hoop snake, which had the ability to turn itself into a wheel by putting its tail in its mouth and rolling along the ground; the joint snake, which fell into a dozen pieces when hit with a stick, then managed to reassemble itself; and the whip snake, which wrapped itself around a person and "whupped 'em" with its tail. Wide-eyed, Alexis had believed every word, until she'd glanced up at Almeda, Right John and Patience. They were trying so hard not to laugh, their mouths were contorted. Finally it was Old John himself who took pity on her, revealing that these were only "so-tales"—myths that had little—or no— basis in fact.

As she sat in the afternoon stillness of the sunlit clearing, Alexis reflected that if Old John had wanted to tell her something scary, he should have told her what to *really* expect. For instance, how hot it would be to walk mile after mile with a pack on her back. How thirsty and tired she'd get. He should have warned her about the insects, about the fallen trees they'd have to climb over, about the fact that the whole damn trip had seemed uphill so far. She'd never felt more tired in her whole life. And they had just begun. They hadn't even been in the woods for a whole day.

Early that morning, Roosevelt and Ethel had dropped them off at Bull Shoals, less than an hour's drive from Mountain View. Bull Shoals was where

the White River began, and it was also on the way
west to the resort town of Eureka Springs, where the
Roosevelt Webbers were headed for a rare vacation.
Alexis knew they'd saved for the trip for months. It
almost made her cry to think she could have gone to
the bank and withdrawn the same amount of money,
given it to them without even missing it. But she was
sure that had the money come as easily to them as it
did to her, they wouldn't have been in such a state of
happy excitement. That morning they had chatted
about their plans to visit a place not one hundred
miles away with more enthusiasm than Alexis could
remember displaying over trips across the Atlantic.
She herself said almost nothing on the way to Bull
Shoals. Quite simply, she was afraid.

The plan was uncomplicated, though it involved
three stages. The first had been the short drive to Bull
Shoals. The second was a twenty-mile hike southeast
from there, along the river to the outskirts of the
Ozark National Forest. The third stage was to be a
canoe trip on the White as it meandered past the
northeastern boundary of the forest. They planned to
go only as far as Sylamore, a point a bit north of the
Ozark Folk Center. As the crow flew, the journey
was forty miles. But the river twisted and meandered,
so the actual distance traveled would be longer.

Even the inexperienced Alexis understood the four
days they were taking for the trip was exceptionally
slow time; however, that didn't necessarily mean exceptionally easy. By the afternoon of the first day,
she felt as though she'd already been hiking for
weeks. When she asked John how far they'd come,
he said they still had two miles to go before they

reached the place he planned to stop. That probably meant another hour's hiking at the rate they were going.

Depending, of course, on how long it took John to find the small bag of tent pegs. The bag had been suspended from the frame of Alexis's backpack—she thought she'd secured it, but it had fallen off three times in as many hours. She didn't care. What did she know about knots—or whatever it was you were supposed to know in order to tie things to other things?

She wished she felt better about the whole trip. It wasn't that hiking in the woods had really been so difficult. After all, she was in good physical shape, and she certainly couldn't complain about the company. John was being as patient as anyone could be with such an inexperienced companion.

Not only that, but it was a pleasure to watch him as he hiked ahead of her. He moved through the woods like one born to them, which, of course, he was. His movements were sure, his limbs powerful with manliness and health. He carried his body with a rhythm that somehow echoed the swaying leaves of the woods, the beating wings of the overhead birds, the flowing streams they crossed, streams that fed the wandering river they were following. John was silent for the most part, not wanting to disrupt the delicate forest sounds with the sound of his voice. Yet even without speaking to him, she felt close to him.

And that made it worse. For Alexis understood that what made her feel so negative about the day was her own ineptness. As he moved smoothly and silently through the woods, she tripped and stumbled and bumbled along behind. Even if he didn't mind her awkwardness, it was a source of, well, the only proper word was "shame"—she was ashamed of herself. Mostly, she was ashamed to be so afraid. She just never knew what was ahead—or behind or under her very feet, for that matter. She had moved with confidence all her life. Everything in her upbringing had been designed to give her the feeling she was somehow special—she had been blessed with advantages others would, unfortunately, not be able to share.

So where were those advantages now? She didn't know. Her fine manners, her breeding, weren't much use to her there in the woods, especially since they weren't helping her to hide her clumsiness. As she sat, she slipped her backpack off and reached down to lean it against the rock before unzipping one of the pockets and taking out her compact.

It was a family heirloom that had belonged, not to a natural grandparent—from whom, of course, she had nothing—but to the grandmother of Wallace Smythe. Alexis had known the woman only through Wallace's stories, but she had always considered great-grandmother Smythe her favorite relative. She had been not only a beautiful lady but an intellectual, as well. From her, Wallace Smythe had always insisted, he got his brains. "And it was from her that you got your beauty," Wallace would joke. Her connection to great-grandmother Smythe made the young Alexis feel part of the family, as if that fact could maybe be or come true.

So she treasured this beaten-gold compact with its delicate floral pattern, colored here and there in the palest shades of rose and green. She opened it to peer into the mirror, but as she did so the reflection of the sun behind her glinted in her eye, and she squinted, jerking. The compact flew from her hand, rolled down a slight incline, landing with a plop in the swiftly moving stream not far from where she sat. So surprised was Alexis that she merely stared for a moment, before she sprang up and headed for the precious object. She got there just in time to see the current carry the shiny compact to the edge of a pile of stones, which were partly submerged. Beneath them the compact slithered, then disappeared.

Throwing off her hiking boots, Alexis stepped into the stream, but the rocks at the bottom were slippery, and before she had taken two steps she lost her balance, landing with a splash on the stream's hard bottom, her legs and arms flailing in a futile attempt to regain her balance. She was soon drenched from head to toe, her lovely hair hanging in dripping strands around her face. And before she had even caught her breath, she heard a sound that filled her with an anger so total, the intensity of it wiped out all physical pain.

He was standing not three yards from her, his head thrust back. The sun in the clearing glinted off the shiny, tousled, tawny hair. His parted feet were planted firmly on the warm earth. His jeans were stretched taut against his legs, and his ivory-colored cotton shirt was open at the neck, revealing the sun-bronzed column of his throat, from which issued the rich, rolling tones of his baritone laugh.

"What's so damn funny?" Alexis demanded, enraged.

John fought to control himself—almost, but not quite, succeeding. "I'm sorry," he choked, moving closer to the stream and extending his hand. "I know it's impolite to laugh, but the way—" Again the rippling sound of uncontrolled merriment.

She slapped his hand away, not even noticing the surprise and hurt in his expression. His laughter stopped. He put out his hand again, but she managed to scramble to her feet without his assistance, heading not toward the stream's edge, but farther out to where she had last seen her compact.

"Where are you going?" Right John asked. There was a note of anger in his voice.

Alexis caught that note, and it infuriated her further. "What do you care?" she retorted.

"Get on out of there, Alexis. What the hell do you think you're doing?"

"I'm retrieving my compact, if you must know."

"Compact?"

"It's a little round thing that holds powder—in case you've never seen one." It was ridiculous, of course, but her barb didn't miss its mark. He slipped out of his shoes and socks. In a moment he was headed toward the center of the stream, where she was stooped, searching under the rock pile. When she felt his warm dry hand on her chilled, wet shoulder, she flinched but didn't turn around. His voice, when it came to her from above, was more gentle than she'd expected.

"Leave it and come on out, Alexis."

"I can't leave it," she said, a little less angry than she had been. "It's real gold."

"So what?"

"What do you mean so what?" She was standing facing him. "I said it's real gold. It's not just some piece of plastic junk...."

"Like anybody else would have?"

"What do you mean? What are you getting at?"

"Look, Alexis, I just don't happen to be impressed by things made of gold. It's what a person is, not what they have that impresses me."

"Oh?" she asked through clenched teeth, thoroughly infuriated once more. "Oh, is that so? Well, then, Mr. Democracy, suppose you get out of my way and let me take care of this myself."

"Don't, miss. I don't need any fancy pants ordering me around...."

"And I don't need to be wasting my time in the middle of the goddamn woods—tramping all over the place like a savage—sweating, dirty. Maybe this is what people do for fun around here. But I've got better things to do with my time."

"Like searching for a damn piece of metal?" John was close enough to touch her, but his hands were tight fists at his sides, his face strained with anger. And had she cared to look carefully enough—hurt.

"It's a family heirloom. But, then, maybe you wouldn't understand that. Maybe your family wouldn't have had anything to pass along."

The moment the words left her lips, she was as shocked as she realized he would be. It was a rotten thing to have said—she'd clearly gone too far. She stood still, her eyes downcast, waiting for his retort. He had every right to point out to her that it was she, not he, who actually had no family—she, not he, who had no knowledge of her real parents.

The angry words didn't come. "No," John said quietly, with quiet self-respect. "No, that's not true. My family has been in this state since just before the Civil War. We have lots of things." He said no more. She glanced up at him, but he was looking past her. He took a step, accidentally brushing her. Her body was jolted into response at the slightest contact with him, the way it always was. Something told her that response was wasted this time. She wouldn't be surprised if he never touched her again.

She watched as he stooped down, picking up the lost compact. It glinted in the sun, but she didn't see that at first because she was looking at the way his hair glinted in the bright afternoon light. She was suddenly so sorry she had picked a fight with him. Because she wanted to touch the gold of his hair much more than she wanted the golden object he held out to her.

"Thank you," she said softly, taking it from fingers that did not touch hers. She looked up, but still he wasn't looking at her. His eyes were lowered, and remained so as he turned and walked toward the stream's edge, scooping up his shoes and socks with one graceful motion and striding away toward the edge of the clearing, where he had left his pack.

Alexis's sense of loss was complete. She struggled toward the water's edge and climbed back onto the rock near her own pack. For a moment she merely sat in total stillness until she could catch her breath.

And then the tears came. At first, as they slowly welled up in her eyes, she thought she must be crying because she was tired and hot and still afraid of being in the wilderness. Then the tears began to course down her soft cheeks, and she realized she was crying because she was a long way from home. She missed her mother. She *was* a stranger here, no matter how she tried to deny it. She should go back to Chicago, where she so clearly belonged.

And when the real sobbing began, when her hands held up to her face grew wet with her weeping, her shoulders heaving with the ebb and flow of her sorrow, she knew she was crying because she loved him, because Right John Webber wasn't like any man she'd ever known or was likely ever to know again. Because they would never be able to make a go of it. This was their first argument, and it would be their last. It was so obvious their backgrounds would always stand in the way of their happiness. *Forewarned is forearmed,* Alexis thought, keeping her face buried in her hands as the tears flowed heavier still. She was so immersed in her misery that when she felt strong hands on her wrists, she jumped.

John was kneeling before her, staring at her, his own eyes clouded. "You've got to stop," he said, his voice a low gentle song in her ear. His hands relinquished her wrists, took instead her wet cheeks and slowly stroked them as if to gather her tears in his palm and take them away from her. "Your crying has stopped the birds from singing—listen...." Alexis did listen, and the birds had stopped singing, though she didn't believe it was because of her. When she was little, Wallace had tricked her like that lots of times, once telling her he could make the leaves move on distant trees, when really the wind had been the cause.

The thought of that made her smile. "There,"

Right John said. ''That's better.'' And looking up, Alexis saw his eyes were alight with his usual sunny smile. ''You know what, Alexis?''

''What?''

''I love you.''

It was the first time he'd ever said it, and she was stunned. Wordlessly she stared at him, then lifted her hand to stroke the curve of his jaw. Beneath her trembling fingers, his skin was warm from the heat of the day, from the heat of his emotions. His lips were warm, too, as he turned his face into the caress of her fingers, planting a moist kiss in the cup of her palm.

His lips sent a shiver through her. Seeing her quiver, he reached up and drew her down until they were both kneeling on the soft grass of the forest clearing. The birds had resumed their song. High above, clouds scudded through the blueness of the mountain sky. All the world seemed scented with the sweet fragrance of full summer.

He touched her reverentially, as if her creamy skin were fine china, as if her hair were filaments of finely spun gold, as if the parted lips awaiting his fingertips were made from silk.

But she wasn't china or metal or silk. She was flesh, and her flesh yearned for him. Her hands were not reverential; they were eager, hungry. She tried to stroke his face with gentleness, but her hands found their way to the nape of his neck, rose to entwine themselves in the thickness of his hair, then pulled him close, so that her desire for the pressure of his lips on hers was unmistakable. And he obliged.

Would she ever grow used to the power of his kiss? His mouth tentatively explored, but even that light, initial touch sent its message to her nerves, which tingled with anticipation. His kiss grew stronger, his lips more wanton in their exploration, his tongue thrusting into the willing openness of her answering mouth.

Her arms around his neck, Alexis pulled herself up against his chest. Like him, she wore jeans and a cotton shirt, through which she could feel his heat. And surely John could feel the hot hunger of her, for the large hands that had rested on her waist as they kissed then descended toward the curves of her derriere. He cupped her firm buttocks in his fingers, shooting a dart of pleasure deep into Alexis's body. In response, she arched closer until she could feel the whole length of him pinned to her. His desire was evident, obvious against her belly. Gently she pushed, toppling him to the soft grass. She clung to him as he fell so that she landed on top of him.

For moments they simply lay that way, he on the woodland grass, she on top of him, communicating to every inch of his supine body the longing that infused her own body. Her head against his shoulder, her hand on his chest, she felt his heart beat beneath her palm. The thought of that, of the source of his very life under her fingers, filled her with a surge of caring that made her sigh. Feeling the motion of her soft expulsion of breath, John tightened his arm around her waist, but he said nothing. His own breath mingled with the forest breeze, stirring in the soft tresses of her hair, which was quickly drying in the August sun. The sun was beginning to lower, and the leaves of the trees cast dappled shadows around the couple.

Lazily Alexis reached up a finger to caress his rough cheek, to trace the curve of his jaw, to tease the lobe of his ear. Laughing a little, John clasped her hand, his fingers meshing with hers and drawing her arm down alongside both their bodies. Looking up, she saw that his blue eyes were closed, his bronze lashes a fan against his cheek. She wouldn't let him sleep, if that was what he had in mind.

"You know what, John?" she said.

"Hmm?"

"I love you, too."

He opened his eyes, then. His wide smile crinkled the corners of his eyes and his lips. "That so?"

"Yes."

"Know what that means?" he asked teasingly.

"No, what?"

"This...."

And swiftly he rolled over, so that she was under him. His body covered hers far more effectively—he was so much larger. She felt the warm strength of him along her entire length—his thighs against the planes of her thighs, his taut stomach against the rounded curve of her stomach, her breasts beneath the muscled masculinity of his chest.

And his greater masculinity hard against the place where desire was beginning to swell in her—a wave rising with every second they lay together. Then his mouth on hers was a demand—she met his eagerness, kiss for passionate kiss. Thirsty for the heady wine of each other's essence, they clung to those kisses, even while they shifted to remove the barriers of cotton and denim and whatever else was beneath.

Until, like the other creatures at home in the

beauty of the forest, they were naked, without barrier to the full pleasure of touching. John again lay supine. She was propped up beside him, in her hand a sprig of meadow grass. The top of it was tasseled with seed. Playfully she reached down and drew the grass along the well-shaped arch of his foot, toward his ankle. He laughed, shaking his foot a little, and she bent to kiss the places the grass had been. He was still once more as she drew her gentle weapon up toward his thigh. Again a soft laugh escaped him. Again she put her lips to the spot she'd tickled. Then she drew the grass up along the surface of the center of his manliness. He did not giggle then. A deep, desiring moan escaped his lips, and he began to rise as though to hold her. Firmly she reached up to push his shoulder back. She touched him again with the grass of August, there and there, and oh, yes, there, her lips sometimes following the motion of the slender wand and sometimes not, so he didn't know when she would next touch him with her moist tongue. He began to groan with the pleasure of her ministrations, and in her own body, desire started to make a claim so strong, her hands grew too weak to wield the blade of grass. Sensing that, he reached up to clasp her. She could no longer resist.

"Alexis," John breathed. "Alexis, oh, how I want you."

"Yes," she answered. "Oh, yes."

The thrust of his body was like the shaft of late sun penetrating the forest. And the arching answer of her body was like the stream pushing up against rock and singing as it broke into a thousand diamond droplets. The sounds they made—the sweet murmur of flesh

meeting flesh in the act of love, the moans of
pleasure, the sighs—were too soft to be echoed back
from the mountains that held them in an embrace.
The love of nature for its own. But those sounds
danced into the clean air of the forest and mixed with
the rustle of leaves, the chirping of birds, the
swishing of tall river reeds. And when the sounds intensified and burst in a cry of consummate joy, not a
creature was startled or moved out of the enchanted
circle surrounded by trees.

THAT NIGHT, the first of their journey, they slept in
their small tent pitched in the clearing. For supper
John had caught smallmouth bass, which he cleaned
and cooked over a little camp burner. When Alexis
awakened to the morning song of birds, to the rising
sun that filled the nylon tent with its light, she
wondered why it had taken her so long to discover
the pleasures so many others enjoyed.

The second day was much easier than the first. For
one thing, Alexis found she was losing her fear. The
insects were less of an aggravation. It helped, too,
that John had decided to give her lessons in the appreciation of nature. At places, the river was flanked
by hillsides sloping down to the sparkling waters.
Here redbud and dogwood trees abounded, and
though it was past time for them to be in bloom,
John pointed them out to her, showing her the shapes
of the leaves. He showed her other trees, as well, his
eyes alight with enthusiasm as he described how these
woods would look in a couple of months, when autumn blazed across the hills. It made her a little sad
to think about that, because she didn't know where

she'd be in autumn, whether she'd be hundreds of miles away, facing the prospect of winter descending on the city....

He knew the names of the forest flowers, the flowers of the meadows and hills. When they came to a species he wanted to show her, he leaned over the delicate blooms, taking them between his strong fingers, but not picking them. Against his bronzed hands, the small white or pink or yellow flowers glowed like jewels on velvet. He told her that he never took anything away when he was travelling in the forest. His objective was to pass through without a trace, to leave things exactly as he'd found them.

At one point, she asked him whether it would go against his philosophy for her to take a drink from the clear, singing stream they were passing by. For answer, he led her to the bank, stooped to the water and scooped up a brimming handful, which he held to her lips. She drank from his hands, a little embarrassed by such a gift—but touched, too. It occurred to her that though she had often been served champagne in glasses of crystal, no host had ever offered so gracious or so refreshing a drink as this taste of the mountain stream.

AT THE END OF THE SECOND DAY'S HIKE, Alexis and John came to a large clearing, where an outfitter was set up. Here they rented a canoe and bought a few other things they would need for their journey on the river itself. Alexis, surprisingly, was less afraid of canoeing than of hiking. There would be no snakes on the water—even Old John's legendary tales didn't run to water snakes. She had no canoeing experience, but she had plenty of experience boating and swimming.

She wasn't crazy about the idea of portage, carrying the canoe over places they couldn't navigate, but John told her those places would be few, that the canoe was lightweight, and that he himself could shoulder most of the burden. She found she was actually looking forward to the activity. The White River, she learned from a brochure she found in the outfitter's store, was considered to be one of the best float streams in the state.

And indeed, as they moved along on the river, she thought she'd never seen such loveliness. The terrain changed as they went. Sometimes the grassy hills of the Ozarks swept down in wide green curves toward river reeds marking the bank. Beyond those hills the mountains rose, not ruggedly, but gently, their treed heights a deep blue green in the distance.

At other times, the canoe moved through the forest, serenely floating almost at a level with the woods on the shore. It was along these stretches of river that Alexis began to see small animals—rabbits, racoons, and once, three graceful, spindly legged deer who had come down to the water to drink.

That first afternoon on the river, Alexis felt a peace she had never known, partly because glancing at the strong man behind her guiding the canoe made her feel secure. He removed his shirt, and in the sun his wide chest glowed, rippling with muscle, sheened with the dew of perspiration from the exertion of his paddling. Yet he wasn't straining; his motions were confident and easy. No doubt he had canoed these streams ever since he was a boy. Seeing him, as fully alive as the forest, the river, the summer day itself, Alexis felt a surge of his energy enter her own body. And for a moment, she allowed another image to intrude, a picture of how he must have looked during his years in New York.

Of course, he had only been a teenager then, without his fully developed masculine beauty. Alexis knew that wasn't the only difference. She imagined him walking the streets of the megalopolis, breathing not this invigoratingly fragrant air, but the fumes from thousands of cars. He wouldn't be strolling leisurely through bowing hardwood trees, but rushing along corridors of concrete and glass. She saw him not as a farmer who every day renews his acquaintance with his land, but as an alien who, in the depths of the city, couldn't remember that there, too, land was beneath his feet, though it hadn't seen the sun in hundreds of years.

Seeing John as he was, imagining him as he must have been then, Alexis understood more clearly than ever before what he meant when he said he would never again leave the hills. He probably felt he had made a mistake once, had been lucky to escape the consequences—at least some of them.

Alexis thought about herself, too, about the way she was in Chicago. Hers was not a bad life in the city. Her home, of course, was lovely. Her writing could just as easily flourish in Chicago as here in the Ozarks. Yet she had to admit the success she was having writing about Ozark life had been a most welcome surprise. She didn't mind life in the city—that is, she hadn't minded it. True, life in the hills suited her wonderfully. She felt healthy, calm, excited about her work.

Still, she couldn't deny there was really only one thing that made living in Mountain View better than living in Chicago had ever been: Right John Webber. She honestly didn't know whether her love for him was strong enough to make her give up everything she had up north. She did know the day would come when she would have to find out.

Like the landscape, the river, too, changed as they went. Sometimes it was a smooth, mirrorlike expanse reflecting the cloud-dotted blue of the sky. In places the banks were high bluffs, and there the reflections were spectacular, convincing Alexis she didn't quite know which way was up, because the tall columns of rock seemed to stretch to infinity, both above her in reality and beneath her in reflection.

But the river wasn't always calm; she knew that it, like all rivers, had its dangers. She would never have considered such a trip had she not been sure John knew exactly what the river was like, and had she not been such an excellent swimmer herself. Before setting out at Bull Shoals, they had stopped off to check with the U.S. Army Corps of Engineers at the Bull Shoals Dam, and to get a power-generation schedule. John explained the river could become very much swifter when water was released from the dam.

Even without taking that into consideration, the river seemed quite wild in spots. There were many bends, and riffles, places where the high riverbed extended across the bottom, causing broken water. At these places the canoe bounced along. The passage didn't seem dangerous, though, since the water was obviously shallow. Should they be dunked, it wasn't likely they would be pulled under.

Other spots scared Alexis more—where rapids resulted from swift water coursing over large rocks. She held her breath until they were well past, John navigating at the bow in tense concentrated silence.

After a while they began to see gravel bars here and there, flat areas extending out across the water. They all looked like perfect spots to pitch a tent in the lowering light of the sun. "Will we stop soon?" Alexis shouted to John. She was growing somewhat tired of paddling, even though she realized he'd been doing most of the work. Besides, she was hungry. She was still surprised that the outdoors could pique one's appetite so strongly, and that the simplest of foods seemed so remarkably delicious eaten in the open air.

When they did stop, it was at a lovely site. Across the river the trees came right down to the water, while on their side a gravel bar extended from a sloping grassy meadow for many yards out into the river. John suggested they set up on the meadow, but Alexis liked the idea of being out over the water. So after checking the schedules he carried in his pack, John picked a good place for the tent, and they set up.

After supper, after they had cleaned up, after they had talked quietly of nothing in particular for a while beneath the brightness of the wilderness stars, they crawled into the tent. Within minutes they were asleep, entwined in each other's arms, both tired from the long hours those arms had spent paddling. The second last thing Alexis heard before she dozed off was the gentle lap of water against the side of the gravel bar. The last thing she heard was the soft breathing of the man beside her. That sound meant safety, and she closed her eyes and slept.

IT HAPPENED SO QUICKLY, so completely without warning, that afterward she could never tell the tale adequately. She must have been half-asleep during most of it. One moment she was dozing off, the next she was nearly submerged in water, her sleeping bag soaked, her hands, her hair.... She'd opened her eyes, opened her mouth to ask John why suddenly everything was so very wet. Of course, she thought she was dreaming—until she realized John was gone, and felt herself being pulled out of the tent by the ankles, sleeping bag and all.

It was raining, hard. She could tell it was no longer night, for despite the rain, the sky had about it the look of early morning, of dawn. In that dim light, she struggled out of the sleeping bag and stood glancing around her, not yet awake enough to panic at what she saw. But soon the grim reality of their situation impressed itself upon her. The gravel bar they'd been camping on was almost totally underwater. Only the few yards closest to the riverbank were not yet covered. The water was a swirling dark mass everywhere, and against its power, John was struggling to secure the canoe, which had worked loose from its mooring near the bank. Alexis began to run toward him, but he saw her start and shouted, "I can handle this—get the packs!" She turned back toward the tent. Beneath her feet the submerged gravel bar was slippery, and at her first step she went flying, landing with a splash. When she struggled up she realized she had cut her hand on the sharp gravel, but it didn't hurt much, so she ignored the sting, pushed ahead through the sloshing water back to the sodden tent. She managed to retrieve both packs. They were thoroughly soaked, and so heavy she could only move them by dragging them along behind her in the water. She felt stupid. Surely there was a better way to save their gear, but she didn't know what else to do. She wanted to get to where John was, because she was more afraid for him than herself.

Alexis found she had cause to be worried. John had finally secured the canoe, at the moment bobbing wildly in the rising water. Seeing Alexis coming, he took a step toward her. And then, in an instant, an instant that was to haunt her memory for months to come, he simply disappeared from her sight. Without even thinking, she let go of the packs and went after him. Instinct alone guided her. If she'd had time to think, she might have lost valuable seconds deciding he was a strong swimmer and probably wasn't in danger. Yet, something told her his skill couldn't save him this time, and she followed that something blindly. When she got to the spot where she had last seen him, she sat at the edge of the gravel bar and slid into the flowing water. She couldn't take a chance on diving; she didn't know how deep the water was.

It was deep, and she didn't find him right away. There was no panic in her, only complete determination to get him and get him out of the water. She succeeded. It was only when she'd managed to drag him to the bank that she realized he'd struck his head. His face and her hands were stained with his blood, which mingled with the now-lightly-falling rain. But he was breathing. He was alive. He moaned, opening his eyes, reached for her hand and held it to his heart. Panic filled her then. A deep, shaking horror that she had come so close to losing him. . . .

THEY LOST THE TENT and all their food and cooking equipment. Luckily the one pack Alexis finally managed to retrieve contained their clothes. John was weak, too weak to paddle himself, but strong enough to guide Alexis for some of the twelve hours it took to reach campers who could help get him to a hospital. And he was strong enough to joke—he didn't mind being hungry when he had to ask strangers for help, but he would have hated to do so in the all together. "I've noticed," he said, his blue eyes glazed with pain but twinkling faintly, "that there's only one situation in which a naked man has any clout!"

He was in the hospital in Batesville overnight. After some hours of observation, the doctor decided there was nothing to fear from the injury to John's head. Exposure to the rain and the subsequent hours on the river had made him quite ill, but his condition improved rapidly, since he was in such good general health.

Alexis tried not to think about the fact that she had saved his life because she didn't want to think about the fact that he had almost lost it. They returned to Mountain View, physically a little battered but closer than ever before. They still hadn't talked about the future—about whether Alexis could stay—about whether she and John would become husband and wife.

CHAPTER THIRTEEN

SHE FINALLY DECIDED September would be the best time to leave. She had put off visiting Chicago for so long, she was almost embarrassed to let Margaret know she'd be coming home in a short while. Her whole life had changed during her months in Arkansas, but her loyalty to her mother was finally making its claim. What would happen after that, she wasn't sure.

Surprisingly for one so healthy, Right John seemed to be suffering lingering effects from his head injury and his twelve hours spent in the bottom of the canoe. Alexis was worried about him. His doctor told him he had to take it easy, but John didn't pay him much mind. Though Roosevelt was helping Old John, Almeda and Patience with the farm chores, more than once Alexis came over to find Right John listless and white as a sheet after having insisted on practicing his violin for hours, or having refused to cancel his students' lessons.

Alexis would have gone north earlier, but she hated to leave him like that. There were other reasons for the delay, too, the main one being her work. She'd got a little behind in her writing lately. She certainly hadn't missed any deadlines, but two assignments would soon be due, for which she hadn't yet completed the preliminary research. Both involved interviewing elderly local people dedicated to preserving folk arts in danger of being lost forever.

So one typically bright and lovely afternoon, Alexis set out for the Ozark Folk Center to interview Miss Bessie Kilgore, the shape-note singing teacher. Miss Kilgore, a charming lady in her sixties, explained she'd learned the old art from her grandfather. "Seems strange to me," Bessie said, "to be teachin' the old kind of singin' in a fancy new place like this center, but it's a good idea, 'cause if we don't teach these things the young uns'll forget there ever was such a thing as the shapes—or Fifth Sunday, either."

"Fifth Sunday?" Alexis repeated. "Could you speak a little on that. . .?" She had her notebook and pencil in hand, ready to take down the important parts. Like every good writer, Alexis knew the heart of her article would be the quotes. Without them, her writing would seem lifeless. She had to be careful both to bring out the best in her interview subject and to capture what the woman said as accurately as possible. She didn't use a tape recorder, though. Unlike some other writers, she found her subjects froze a little when faced with a machine.

"Well," Bessie said, settling back against the bench. They were sitting in a grove of trees outside the folk center, a soft breeze stirring in Bessie's silver hair. "Fifth Sunday is your regular prayer meeting, only with supper after, and singing. In the old days, and now, too, sometimes, the folks'd learn new songs just for that day. It all goes back a long way— to the time of Queen Elizabeth the first—the shape notes go back, that is."

"And how did this type of thing get all the way down here?"

"Well, first you gotta understand that the shape notes are a way of *teaching* singin'. Once you've learned the song, it'll sound the same as any other way of singin'. The shapes are for people who can't learn by reading music; they learn these shapes instead of notes. The way it got down here was that in the 1700s, the people in New England set up all sorts of singin' schools. After a while some of those Yankee singin' masters came to the frontier, like all the other kind of folk who were pioneers. These masters traveled from town to town, teaching the people, then moving on. In most every town there was someone who learned from the master, then set up for himself and kept up the teaching. All's you need is a blackboard and a knowledge of the shapes."

"What do the shapes stand for?"

"Well, now," Bessie went on, "each shape stands for one note of the scale. Here, let me show you. . . ." And taking Alexis's notebook and pencil, she began to draw neat, small diagrams. "This here triangle right side up—that's 'do.' Whenever a singer sees that, he or she knows they gotta sing 'do.' This next one here, the cup without a handle—" she drew a semicircular figure "—this here's 're.' The diamond is 'mi'; the triangle pointin' down is 'fa.' 'Sol' 's an oval; 'La' 's a rectangle, and 'te' would be another triangle, 'cept it's round at the top." Bessie made a diagram that looked like the outline of an ice-cream cone before handing the notebook back to Alexis.

"And people find this method of learning to sing easy?" Alexis asked. She let the woman talk.

"The reason it's easy is that people don't have to read music from a staff. Around here now, at this center, there's people who are famous musicians right around the world, but country music—I mean the music of country folk—it's not always written down. Music, some folks say, isn't a matter of writing; it's a matter of hearing. Still, you've got to start somewhere. And with the shape notes, what you do is sound out the song while the students have the shapes in front of them. Before long, they've got the melody. Then you add the words and you're all set."

"Is this way of teaching found only here in Stone County?"

"I don't think so," Bessie replied thoughtfully. "Since I came to work at the center, I've run into people who've at least heard of it in other places in the south. Also, there are other primitive ways of teaching people to sing, though primitive don't seem exactly the right word."

"No," Alexis agreed, "it doesn't. Is the shape-note type of teaching used only for hymns?"

"It started that way," Bessie answered, "and part of my work here is to collect the old hymns. Many of them are similar to ones sung in England and Scotland a long time ago. There are versions that belong to the Ozarks alone, though. I, of course, am not the first one to collect hymns here, but we're trying to get as many as we can on tape. As for the shape notes, I use 'em to teach all kinds of folk songs, like the old lovers' songs."

"Could you give me an example of one of those?"

"Sure," Bessie replied. "Here's one called 'My Sweetheart Went Down With the Maine'...." Her soft, pleasant, plaintive voice sang out, "Once I had a sweetheart, noble brave and true, fearless as the sunrise, gentle as the dew. . . ."

THE OTHER ARTICLE was on papyrotamia. When she'd first encountered that word in her conversation with John, Alexis had tried to find a book about it, to no avail. She looked in three dictionaries to confirm that papyrotamia was the art of paper cutting. Her expert on this craft was a gentleman of eighty-five who lived by himself in a cabin deep in the woods. Alexis had no trouble finding the place. If her months in the hills had taught her anything, they'd taught her how to follow directions given in Ozark dialect. She no longer shuddered when someone told her a place was "over yonder up beyond that there rise behind. . . ." She even knew just about how great a distance would be considered "two whoops and a holler"!

Though his hands were now and then bothered by arthritis, Orvil Buchanan still possessed the dexterity with scissors necessary to his strange and wonderful art. Before Alexis's enthralled eyes, he created shapes that seemed downright miraculous. He kept up a steady banter as he folded and cut strips of newspaper into long rows of dolls—"ladies and laddies," he called them.

"Most old geezers like myself take to whittlin'," he told Alexis. "Some say this here papytamy's fer women. I don't know that it makes a mite o' difference whether I whittle wood or cut paper. Seems to me one waste o' time's as good as another." Deftly he pleated another strip of paper, then began to cut away a sliver here, a slice there. Alexis watched in fascination, not taking notes at the moment, but letting all she saw sink in so that she could recall it later, recreate it for her readers.

"Run up the house an' git me some o' that white tissue paper from the drawer o' the parlor chifferobe," Orvil directed to his barefoot grandson, who stood at the side of his chair. He was a boy of about eight, whose wide eyes watched now the old man, now Alexis. "Light a shuck, boy," the old man said, giving the child an affectionate pat on the behind. "This fine lady ain't got all day."

From the tissue, Orvil cut snowflakes of such intricacy that Alexis knew she could never describe them adequately in writing. She asked whether she might have one or two of the snowflakes to send to the magazine. She knew the editor would have them photographed and would give credit for the cutouts to Orvil.

"You mean my name's gonna be there in that magazine?" he asked.

"Of course," Alexis answered with a smile. "Without you, I wouldn't be able to write this article. After all, it's your work the article's about."

"Ain't what you'd call work...."

"Well, your craft then...."

"My waste o' time," the old man laughed.

THERE WAS ONE OTHER THING Alexis knew would have to be settled before she set off for Chicago. She spoke to Lizzie about it one evening. It was a little harder to get Lizzie to sit down at the kitchen table for a chat than it had been, because these days she seemed to be spending a lot of time with George Fox. He often stayed in Mountain View, even though his work, and his permanent home, were elsewhere.

"I don't know what to do about Patience," Alexis said.

"I thought you two were getting along just fine. Is there something wrong?"

"No," Alexis answered. "Not exactly. We *are* getting along fine—so fine, in fact, that she asks me every time I see her whether she can come up to Chicago with me."

"And you don't want to take her?"

"I'd love to take her. That's not the problem."

"But John Webber is?"

"You've got it."

"She's been up to Chicago before, hasn't she?" Lizzie asked.

"Only when she was very small. According to her, it was only once and so long ago that she can't even remember. It seems odd that she's never been to visit since her mother died."

"Oil and water," Lizzie said cryptically. "John's never been there—ever. He's as afraid of his mother-in-law as a dog's afraid of a whip snake."

"I don't think he's afraid of anything," Alexis said with a small smile.

"Don't count on it," was Lizzie's soft remark.

"What do you mean?"

"Nothing. Listen, why shouldn't she go up there? It's not natural for her never to visit her grandmother. I've wondered about that before, too. I know she gets letters and presents from Chicago. I happened to be over to Old John's farm one time, and it was Pat's birthday. You should have seen the beautiful dress that came for her.... Maybe that's why John doesn't want her to go up there—because he can't afford to give his own kid stuff like that."

"I doubt it," Alexis said thoughtfully. "I don't think John would care about that. I think it goes deeper. Maybe he realizes Patience isn't happy here in the hills."

"She's only fourteen," Lizzie argued. "What does she know about being happier in Chicago than she is here?"

"What did you want to do when you were fourteen?" Alexis answered gently. "Seems to me you told me you wanted to leave here even before then...."

Lizzie had no answer to that one; she remained silent for a bit. After a while she said, "I think it *would* be fine for that kid to go up north—be fine for her to see what there is to look forward to. From what I hear, she's already pretty good on that clarinet of hers. I don't know a lot about music, but I'm willing to bet there's no clarinet teacher around here that's as good as John is on the violin. I mean, maybe she has to go somewhere else if she wants to be a musician like her father—and her mother."

"Did you know Caroline?" Alexis asked. It was off topic, but her curiosity wouldn't be contained.

"No, not really," Lizzie responded. "When they were together I lived in Tulsa with my husband. I met her once, though, at a Christmas party at the farm. She scared the daylights out of me."

"She scared you?" Alexis asked in amazement. "How could that be?"

"She wasn't what you'd call a quiet woman," Lizzie said. "Myself, I'm shy—especially at a party. But Caroline—well, nobody was a stranger to her. She'd just come on up and treat you like you'd known her for years. I don't like that, but it makes some people feel right at home. John doted on her, I know that much. When I first met him, he couldn't bring himself to talk about anything else a lot of the time...." Lizzie sighed as though she'd be willing to talk to John Webber about anything at any time, just to have his company. Lately, most of the local people had come to consider John and Alexis a couple. And Lizzie *was* seeing a lot of Mr. Fox. But still, Alexis knew Lizzie would always have a soft spot in her heart for John, though, to her credit, she never showed the least hint of any envy she might feel. He was one man she couldn't get past, couldn't forget. It didn't make Alexis any less sympathetic to know Right John Webber was one man she herself couldn't get past, either.

SHE GOT BOTH ARTICLES FINISHED. She made flight arrangements. She phoned Margaret, and Margaret phoned her back—often. Alexis's mother was overjoyed that she'd soon have her daughter with her again, though both were careful not to mention whether or when Alexis would be returning to the hills.

There was no question of Alexis moving out of Lizzie's. She left her room, and her study, full of her belongings. She'd accumulated quite a number of things since she'd come to Mountain View—handicrafts, clothes, handmade jewelry. Not one of those things was like anything she had at home in Chicago. But she wasn't leaving them behind because they'd be out of place in her mother's house. She did so to give her the feeling she had something to come back to—to Mountain View, to Lizzie Cabe's, to John. The items she'd collected were her hostages against the day of her return.

She had no luck convincing John that Patience should come with her. At first she didn't want to add to the stress of his slowly improving physical condition. Later, when he was obviously feeling much better, she did broach the topic—and met with evasion, until he refused to speak to Alexis about Patience at all. After a little more persistence, he finally agreed to consider discussing the matter in the near future.

And that was as far as Alexis had got by the time she was ready to leave.

CHAPTER FOURTEEN

WHAT COULDN'T BE ACCOMPLISHED by tact, persuasion, logic, cajoling or bribery was finally accomplished by tears. Patience broke down, and Right John Webber was rendered powerless in the face of her misery.

Alexis had been present at the beginning of the argument, wishing she could have stopped father and daughter from hurting each other the way they were so clearly able to do. John's health was not back to normal, though perhaps only Alexis, who looked at him through the keen eyes of love, could see that. The verbal battles with his daughter left him drained. After an hour or so of talking, John's voice would begin to waver in a way barely perceptible to others. Alexis could hear the difference and knew he was weighed down by hurt, by his own stubbornness and by a fatigue uncharacteristic of his usual robust constitution. Once he had stormed out of the room in the middle of an argument, and not five minutes later Alexis found him in the next room, stretched out on the couch as sound asleep as if he'd been lying there for hours. She had smoothed the tousled hair on his brow, and at her touch she could see the tense lines of his face soften. But he didn't wake up.

There was only so much Alexis could take of these

family arguments, mostly because she felt discretion dictated her absence. So one afternoon, the day before her departure, she left the two of them shouting at each other and headed back to Lizzie's to finish up the last-minute details of her packing. At about eleven that evening, Alexis heard the phone ring in Lizzie's downstairs hall. Lizzie called up to her, "It's for you!"

A triumphant young voice met her ear. "Daddy says I can come!" Patience announced.

"That's fine," Alexis answered. "I'll be glad to have you along. But we have to make sure we can get you a ticket—"

"It's all set. Daddy phoned the airport at Harrison and got me a ticket on the same flight as—"

"With an open return, like my ticket?"

"No." Patience lost just a little of her exuberance. "He said I can only stay one week. I have to go to school right on time, he says. I don't know why I can't miss a few days...."

"I'll get you back on time."

"I know. I promised daddy you would. But listen, I don't know what to pack. Come over and help."

"Now? It's late for you, Patience."

"I know, but if you don't help, I can't be ready on time." Before Alexis could reply, she heard a happy giggle, followed by the click of the receiver. She picked up her keys, and with a smile and a shake of her golden hair, headed for the door.

As it turned out, neither of them was ready on time the next day. Patience was throwing things into her suitcase, then taking them out, then throwing other things in, right up until the moment they got into the truck—which had run just fine earlier that morning. But the truck balked when John tried to start it for the trip to the airport. And when they finally arrived, there was a delay in processing Patience's ticket.

At last, though, they were ready to board. John bid his daughter farewell with a few more warnings and admonitions, which the girl agreed to with the ease youngsters exhibit when they've already got their own way. "Wait for Alexis on the other side, over there," John said, pointing to a place beyond where an airline employee was issuing boarding passes.

Alexis had been dreading this for weeks; the full impact of what was happening that morning hit her, and she knew she was near tears. "Every parting gives a foretaste of death." Was there something like that written somewhere in Schopenhauer? She couldn't remember, but the words were true.

"Come here," John said, enfolding her in the broad, warm circle of his embrace. In that moment she wished there were no airplanes, no journeys, no other place than this haven, this one small spot on earth dearer than any other—the spot where he stood. She felt tears spring to her eyes, and she didn't do anything to stop them. When he lifted her face with the slight pressure of one finger under her chin, when his wide lips came down on her softly curved mouth, he tasted salt in her kiss and responded by holding her more closely. Her head was against his shoulder as he stroked her hair with gentle power.

"Come on, now, Alexis," he said, and she could hear the smile in his voice without looking up into his handsome face. "You're just going visiting for a spell. You'll be back home before you know it."

"Yes," she said with a sigh. "Back in Chicago."

"No. I meant you'll be back home, down here, before you even have a thought of settling in anywhere else."

Alexis glanced up at him. His eyes were full of their usual sunniness. She remembered clearly the first time she'd ever looked into those eyes, the day he had said she looked like a red bird. Well, she was flying, however reluctantly. Her own eyes were clouded. Noticing that, he kissed her again, a warm promising kiss full of love and temptation. In response, she parted her mouth, ran her tongue teasingly against the fine whiteness of his teeth. She felt a shudder go through him then. His embrace tightened yet again, his thigh shifting so that the plane of her own thigh tingled beneath her skirt.

"When you come back," he said, his voice a throaty whisper, "we've got some talking to do...."

"About what?" she asked breathlessly, her very tone revealing her hunger for him, a hunger that was useless, considering it would have to remain unsatisfied for who knew how long. Not long....

"You all just make damn sure you get back here."

"Yes," she whispered. "Yes I will." And with one more passionate kiss, she tore away from him, turned, walked briskly to the place where Patience was shifting from foot to foot in eagerness to board.

"Ah, THERE SHE IS! Oh, my precious, how tall you are—so like Caroline...." Alexis watched quietly from a distance as Evelyn Kain, all her pink chiffon sails flying, swept into the Smythe drawing room to-

ward the at-first astonished, then amused Patience
Webber.

"This is your grandmother, dear," Margaret said
in her easy, well-modulated voice. "Since it's been
several years, she might seem a stranger to you."
Though they'd only been at Margaret's for an hour,
Alexis and Patience had already been made to feel relaxed after their journey. Alexis had eyes mostly for
Margaret, studying her mother carefully and coming
to the conclusion that she looked well, very well, indeed.

Patience was a model of politeness, quite shy now
that she was out of her own element. Acting as discreetly as she knew how, she obviously couldn't help
sneaking glances at the things around her—the like of
which she'd clearly never seen before. There was no
homespun here—nor was there much warmth. *This
place looks like a museum,* Alexis thought, and was
so stunned by the disloyalty the thought implied that
she blanched.

"Is something wrong, dear?" her mother asked.

"No, mother." Alexis paused before commenting,
"It's good to be back with you."

"It's good to have you back, dear. You look wonderful. Though I do think Raoul is going to scold."

"Raoul?" Alexis was momentarily puzzled.
"Raoul— Oh, the hairdresser!"

"Yes, the hairdresser. It looks as though he has
quite a challenge ahead of him."

Alexis smiled a little stiffly at her mother, sup-
pressing a pang of what felt remarkably like homesickness. For, unaccountably, she remembered the

last time Right John had run his fingers through her hair. "Just like wild wheat in August," he'd said. "Thick and gold and full of sun." Of course, the style—actually, it was no style—she'd let her hair grow into wouldn't be suitable for the sort of affairs she knew her mother would have planned for her. But she had thought the chignon would hide the fact that her hair hadn't been cut, streaked or conditioned by anything other than rainwater in months. She was wrong, apparently.

"I'll see Raoul tomorrow, if he'll have me," Alexis said, and Margaret nodded before turning her attention back to her guests. Evelyn stayed only as long as it took for Patience to finish the lemonade Ms Buckner, the housekeeper, served her. The silver tray and crystal glass seemed to fascinate Patience in the same way Almeda Webber's plastic tumblers had been a bit of a revelation to Alexis.

At first the girl appeared quite intimidated by the overbearing matron Kain, but it didn't take Evelyn long to figure out how to gain her granddaughter's complete approval. The mention of a shopping spree, for instance, was a good start. With promises to call Alexis the next day, Patience left, following happily in the wake of the grandmother she had insisted on visiting.

ALEXIS WAS IMMEDIATELY THROWN BACK into her old life. The phone rang a dozen times that first evening—several of her friends from the club calling for lunch and cocktails. Because she hadn't thought about it much, it surprised her that a number of people seemed to want to hear all the gory details of her breakup with Karl. To her, it hadn't been so much a breakup as a fading away. She tried to tell her callers that, but they insisted there was more to the story.

Perhaps that "more" was John Webber, but she found she couldn't even mention his name to these people. She wasn't ashamed of him—quite the opposite. She liked carrying her love for him the way a poor man carries his own piece of gold—a wonderful secret in his shabby pocket, a talisman, a ticket—the touch of which carries him away from all else around him. When Alexis thought of John, she wasn't there in Chicago among the glittering people who had once been her only friends. When she thought of him, she was back among the mist-shrouded Ozarks. And what filled her was a poignant mixture of love, and that other emotion she'd noticed before. She looked forward to seeing her old friends again, of course, but she was homesick. She was already homesick for the hills.

One of the people who called her was Karl himself. Surprisingly, Alexis had no difficulty talking to him. He was full of news about the Scandinavian tour he and the orchestra were about to embark on. He asked her whether she'd like to have lunch with him, and she couldn't think of any reason to refuse, even when he said he'd have his secretary call her back to let her know when he would be free.

The opportunity to be with Margaret again outweighed many of the more negative aspects of returning to Chicago. The weather was cool for September, cool enough that they could have a fire in the library late in the evenings. Over crystal glasses full of the finest imported sherry, mother and daughter caught up on the news of the months they'd been apart. Though there had been frequent letters and phone calls, nothing was quite the same as chatting, and there seemed to be no end of topics to discuss.

"The garden up at the lake was magnificent this year," Margaret said. "It's a shame you had to miss seeing it."

"Of course I'm sorry to have missed it, mother," Alexis replied, "but I haven't exactly been away from horticulture during the summer...."

"There's a difference between horticulture and agriculture, my dear," Margaret said with a ripple of her lovely laughter.

"Not always," Alexis replied, her smile wistful as she recalled Almeda's farmyard flower beds.

"What's kept you there, Alexis—what's keeping you there?"

This sudden change of topic—and of tone, for Margaret's voice was now intense—took Alexis aback.

"Why, my writing, mother. My job."

"You were a writer here, too, dear."

"Mother, you've seen my articles; you know what I mean."

"Yes," Margaret conceded. "I can certainly understand how you'd want to keep up the work you've been doing lately. But I still don't understand why it's taken you so long to come back home. And I know, believe me, that you're just here for a visit."

"Well, I. . . ."

"*Who's* keeping you there? Is it Wright Webber?"

She hadn't heard that version of his name in a long time. In fact, she hadn't heard his name spoken aloud in days. Silly as it was, the sound seemed to fill the room, and in response Alexis trembled ever so slightly, too slightly for the movement to be seen, had she not been holding the glass of sherry. A single dark drop of the liquid skidded out of the glass and slid down the side. Margaret watched that drop as though it were an omen. "I can only assume the fact that you've been entrusted to bring his daughter to Chicago means you've made his acquaintance."

"Yes, mother."

"And more?"

"Yes, mother."

"I see."

They sat in silence for a little while. Alexis thanked God for her mother's discretion. Margaret MacIntyre Smythe might be the descendant of a crusty old prospector, but she was every inch a lady, not only because she was finely bred but also because she was a fine person. She wasn't about to ask Alexis any more questions. Perhaps the day would come when Alexis would tell her mother all about John Webber. And, Alexis found herself hoping, perhaps on that day there would be at least a little more to say than there was at the moment. She didn't feel she could speak about any future just yet.

To fill the silence between them, Alexis turned to other topics, eventually deciding to tell her mother about Roosevelt Webber and his dedicated family. Alexis, writer that she was, was an excellent storyteller, and her description of the Webbers' valiant struggle to hold on to their farm appeared to touch Margaret deeply. At the conclusion of Alexis's narration about the difficulty of raising money for the equipment to continue Roosevelt's dairy operations,

Margaret sighed and said, "What's to be done to help people like the Webbers? Farmers are the backbone of our country, and yet we treat them so poorly. What's to be done for such people?"

Alexis suspected her mother's view of agricultural life in America was based more on what she read in novels than on hard fact, but she also knew her mother was sincere. "I don't know what's to be done, mother," she said. "I wish I did."

HER LUNCHEON WITH KARL was a strange mixture of mild embarrassment and pleasant nostalgia. On seeing her, he'd registered what could only be termed shocked displeasure. She'd been to Raoul, and surprisingly, the hairdresser had loved her new wildness. He had cut her hair only a little and in a way that made it seem not less unruly, but more so. Karl found the style inappropriate for one of Alexis's age and bearing. He also thought it a little distasteful that she was so tanned—in all their summers on the Riviera, he commented, she had never allowed herself to become quite that brown. Of course, he conceded, it was Victorian of him to object. Still, she had such fine skin; it was a shame.... And when she referred to the salad as "garden sass," he didn't find the term amusing. And when she remarked that the waiter was "yonder" beside the steam table, he looked up at her almost in disgust. On the other hand, they did have memories to share. They talked about old times in the gentle, bittersweet way of lovers whose mutual interest has faded.

When they parted he kissed her hand. At that gesture, a little dart of pain shot through Alexis, for she knew without a doubt that there had only been one other time he'd done that—the first time they met. As his lips touched her skin, it was as though her whole relationship with Karl passed before her eyes.

They'd had their good times and their bad, mostly good, she had to admit. But somehow they hadn't really changed each other, hadn't been able to teach each other. The Karl she said goodbye to was the same Karl she'd met years before, at a time when it seemed he could teach her so much. If love had no power to change one for the better, what power did it have at all? She knew her feelings for John were different. She wasn't thinking about passion, though it was true her physical longing for Right John was always intense. No, she was thinking that she could say goodbye to Karl and have the waters of her life join seamlessly over the spot where he had disappeared.

With John it was so different. She couldn't say whether her time with him would stretch into all the years she wished she might have with him. But even so—even if, heaven forbid, she should never see him again, she knew he had changed her, changed her life. She wasn't quite sure yet what those changes meant, but she could already see that the Alexis Smythe who had left Chicago in March was not the Alexis who had returned in September.

SHE TURNED OVER THE PAPERS in the file folder slowly, trying not only to take in what was written on them but also to understand why those pages were there at all. The woman sitting opposite her, trim in a well-tailored suit, waited patiently for a response.

"I'm thoroughly amazed that you've taken such an interest," Alexis finally said. Her voice, however, revealed not amazement, but cool self-confidence. "You don't seem to be missing a single item." She thumbed through the pages again—photocopies of the sixteen feature-length articles she'd written and had published between January and September of that year.

"It's pretty impressive, Alexis," remarked Janice Hart, features editor of the Chicago daily that had published Alexis several times. "I'd say the eight or nine months' work represented there outshines the three or four years' worth preceding it. The variety, the depth—not to mention your style. But none of those things impresses me as much as your ability to get people to talk. When you were doing those profiles of executives, I used to wonder how you managed to make each of them sound so individual—because, quite frankly, interview subjects like those can come off sounding like carbon copies of each other. It takes real skill to get past people's defences, but now that I've studied these backwoods pieces, I see you've got something else, something no mediocre reporter has and no great reporter lacks."

"What?" Alexis asked with a small smile. She couldn't guess what Janice was about to say, didn't know how impressed the editor was.

"Guts."

"I beg your pardon?"

"Courage. Look, I'm going to be perfectly candid with you. The first time I published something of yours, I did it because I needed a piece on the man you'd written about. The work was perfunctory—acceptable, but no earth shaker, if you know what I mean.''

"If you'll pardon my saying so," Alexis commented, "that was some time ago. Every professional has to start somewhere."

"Of course," Janice answered, turning a gold pen between her perfectly manicured fingers as she spoke. "The point is, you've come a long way. I felt I was going out on a limb when I assigned you to that welfare-mother story—"

"The Marilyn Bank piece?"

"Right. Our response on that was good. I thought about it for a while, and I decided I'd been wrong to be less than enthusiastic about your doing some follow-up pieces. I tried to get in touch with you, but you'd gone south."

"You could have contacted me there."

"Sure, I could have. But the idea I have in mind couldn't be handled from down there. Then I found out you were headed back to Chicago. Listen, I've kept track of you. I've kept this file all year because I think you would be a natural. Your work down south—all these interviews with the farmers and the mountain people—has strengthened my conviction that you're the right person for what I've got in mind."

"And what have you got in mind?" Alexis asked, closing the file and placing it on top of the editor's wide chrome-and-ebony desk.

A discreet smile lit Janice Hart's face, a smile that hinted at triumph, as though she was quite sure she could convince this writer to do the sort of work she was eager to publish. "Well, first of all, I'm not talking about a single article."

"A daily column?" Alexis asked, not pleased. She respected columnists, but she couldn't handle the idea herself; she felt that having to churn something out to deadline every day would rob her work of the freshness she constantly strove to achieve.

"No, not a column," Janice answered. "A series. What I have in mind is a series of twelve full-page features in the weekend edition—one a month for a year."

"On what?"

"On our readers' absolutely favorite topic. . . ."

"Chicago?"

"You are sharp, aren't you? Yes. I want you to do for this town what you've done down there in the hills. I want you out on the streets talking to the people. I want you to get them to tell my readers what this city is really like from every point of view you can come up with. I want you in those ritzy penthouses I know you're familiar with, and I want you in the tenements."

"What makes you think I could handle something like that? When I came to you after you'd published the Marilyn Bank article, you pretty much said, 'Don't call me, I'll call you.' "

"Yes, well, I *did* call you."

"Why? Why did you change your mind? What makes you think I'm more capable of doing this now than I was six or eight months ago?"

It didn't surprise Alexis that Janice didn't answer right away. A woman in her position wasn't about to be pressured, even by the questions of an experienced interviewer. Alexis knew the editor's silence was a means of dissipating some of the tension that had come into the conversation. After a few moments Janice put down her gold pen, folded her hands on her desk and looked Alexis straight in the eye.

"When you first came in here, I thought you were a bored rich gal looking for a little diversion. Pardon my candor, but I just didn't think you had it in you. I thought maybe you were toying with the idea of a career and had decided writing was as good a one as any."

"You're a pretty tough lady," Alexis said coolly, insulted but not intimidated by the editor. "But I'd say you're a bit confused. You're the one who assigned me the Bank article."

"By that time I suspected I'd been wrong about you, but it wasn't until I saw what you'd done in the country that I realized just how wrong. Forgive me, Alexis—I didn't mean to insult you. I spoke as I did now to let you know how much respect I've come to have for your work. My original estimate of you was just plain prejudice, reverse snobbery, you could call it. Now I don't care where or who you come from. All I care about is having you on my team, on my payroll, too.

"Look, I'm offering a contract for the series—no writing on spec. I'm talking about a year's worth of exposure. And not just local, either. There's a national edition and an overseas one on the weekends. Besides that—and more important I'm sure you'll agree—is the chance to do something really big, to get in there and get stories like you haven't got before. I'll give you free rein. What I want is a portrait of Chicago that comes right from its own people—and I'm one hundred percent convinced nobody can do it the way you can. What do you say?"

Now it was Alexis who paused to gain control of her thoughts, and the situation. If she'd had an offer like that months ago, she'd have jumped at the chance. It didn't take much imagination to figure out what would happen if she took on the assignment. First of all, she knew she could succeed at it. The work would push her skills to the limit, but she knew she'd be able to grow into whatever the challenge demanded; her months in the unfamiliar reaches of the hills had shown her that much. And then there was the exposure. Any future editor seeing the scope of the present project would realize Alexis could handle a major job with thorough competence. She had long ago learned what every freelancer soon finds out if she wants to survive: work leads to more work. No, she felt confident she could handle the project—and that it would be well worth handling. Even as Janice was outlining the concept, ideas had started to flow, ideas that would serve as a good start on the work.

But at the center of the story's concept was the necessity for Alexis to remain in Chicago. Obviously, the man-in-the-street angle was what made the idea unique and appealing. That angle demanded complete honesty, not only on the part of the people Alexis would be interviewing, but on her part, too. There was no way this could be a halfway measure. She'd have to immerse herself in the city in order to write the in-depth articles Janice Hart was seeking.

"How long do I have to decide?"

"I'd be lying if I didn't say I'd like you to decide before you leave this office, Alexis. I also think you know if you don't do this, someone else will. When I get an idea, I usually see it in print sooner or later—

preferably sooner. But the idea can hold for a bit. A month is the absolute maximum, I'd say. Think it over, give me a call. I'll send you a letter on it just so everything will be clear. I'm not frantic, but I am in a hurry. You know what I mean?''

Alexis nodded, stood up and shook the woman's hand. ''I'll give it careful consideration. I'll call you soon.''

But she knew even before the next morning that she couldn't take on the assignment. She kept hearing John say, ''You all just make damn sure you get back here.'' If she really had courage, she'd have to go for the thing she truly wanted. And if she was really so good a writer, refusing one assignment, even a major one, wasn't going to spoil her career. Whereas, to turn against what her heart told her to do, what her heart told her to wait for, might spoil her life. She didn't call Janice Hart and eagerly accept the offer.

But neither did she refuse it—and even she couldn't say why she was being so careful to leave that option open.

ALEXIS STARED AT THE GIRL in consternation. It was gone. The beautiful, flowing, tawny hair that had blown around her young shoulders in the mountain air, hair so like her father's, was gone. Except for the short cap that swept up behind her ear on one side and swooped down to her jaw on the other, giving Patience a look that was no doubt considered fashionable among some young people, but that just skirted ugliness in Alexis's opinion.

''Oh, Patience, what have you done to your hair?''

she gasped as Mrs. Kain's maid ushered her into the front room of Evelyn's home. "And the makeup! Oh, Patience!"

"I've been to Raoul," the girl answered, unable to contain the happy pride in her voice. "Grandmother says it's not right to travel without dressing up."

Alexis surveyed the dress Patience had chosen for her home-going. Like everything else about the girl's appearance, it reflected the damage a week with Evelyn Kain had wreaked on the country child. She now looked like an imitation of a city kid: her hair; the makeup that made her still-childish face look like a beautifully constructed mask; the dress, garish and short, as was the style among her newfound peers; her shoes that were nothing like the sneakers she'd been satisfied with before.

Yet Patience's manner hadn't changed in the week. She retained the almost-shy reserve she usually exhibited when in the company of adults. The contrast between the way she looked and the way she acted touched Alexis's heart with pity and mitigated her anger somewhat. This whole outfit was undoubtedly part of Evelyn Kain's larger ploy, one that Alexis saw through immediately. What better way to buy the affection of a fourteen-year-old than to let her dress like someone three or four years older? What better way to capture her devotion—at least momentarily— than to let her act out any fantasy that entered her head—clotheswise, anyway!

"Did you have a good week?" Alexis forced herself to ask. She didn't feel it was her place to criticize Patience, whatever her own views.

"It was wonderful! Oh, Alexis, wait until I tell you

where we went and what we did. It was the most wonderful week of my whole life. I'm never gonna forget this. I wish I didn't have to go back.''

"Your father will have missed you. . . .''

"I know, but—''

Their few moments alone in the elegant room, with its red velvet curtains and needlepoint-covered Victorian chairs, were soon over, for the double doors opened to reveal a rather flustered Evelyn Kain. "Oh, dear, I'm so sorry to have been delayed. The charity committee is meeting this afternoon, and I've spent the whole morning in the kitchen giving instructions to the cook for the luncheon. You'd think he'd know by now how I want things done. I'm so glad I didn't miss you, Alexis. Have you brought your chauffeur, or would you like mine to take you to the airport?''

"The baggage is already loaded in my car. There was rather a lot of it, Evelyn.''

The disapproval in Alexis's tone went right over Evelyn's head. "Oh,'' she said gushingly, "my girl and I did a little shopping, didn't we, dear?'' And she actually pinched Patience's cheek, giving the girl the opportunity to live up to her name. She stood absolutely still, not even flinching the way she did when Old John Webber tried similar tricks.

Fortunately, there wasn't any time to waste. Patience's plane was due to take off before long, and Alexis had promised to escort her to the airport. She was glad their tight schedule prevented a long visit with Evelyn.

As the matron escorted them to the front hall, she whispered to Alexis, "I owe you so much, my dear.

to go all the way down there just to rescue my poor granddaughter.... I don't even mind how long it took. I know these things take time. That's why I can be patient now, knowing it won't be long before the child is back here to stay. You and I both know this is where she belongs, here in her own mother's home. Thank you, my dear. Without you, I'd never have gotten my daughter's girl back.''

Alexis was used to dismissing Evelyn's flamboyance—verbal or otherwise—as absurd. It never occurred to her that the woman's sentiments might come back to haunt her—might seem less extreme to others involved in the future of Patience Webber.

CHAPTER FIFTEEN

No THREE WEEKS ever seemed as long to Alexis as the three weeks of her visit to Chicago. True, she enjoyed seeing her friends; she loved being with her mother; she valued the opportunity of renewing important business contacts. But in the end she realized the old friends she had in the city weren't more important to her than the new friends she had in the country. She realized, too, that the time had come when she must finally move out of her parents' house, though she didn't like the idea of leaving Margaret virtually alone. As for business, she managed to put off giving Janice Hart a definite answer without losing too much face. Even so, the editor was clearly disappointed and hinted that her patience was not unlimited.

When she'd completed all she'd hoped to do, after staying on an extra few days to please her mother, Alexis felt it was finally time to leave Chicago. She headed for the airport feeling more lighthearted than she could remember having felt in years. She was genuinely going home—home to the hills. And home to Right John Webber.

Alexis had talked to him on the phone several times during her absence, though to hear his melodious voice without seeing him was like hearing the sound track of an opera. Good, but not good enough. Not nearly. Her heart skipped beats every time she thought of being with him again. She was so excited she forgot that each time she had spoken to him, he had sounded a little unlike himself...tired. As she was driven out to O'Hare, as she boarded and made small talk with the stewardess in the sparsely populated first-class section of the plane, she let her mind drift now and then to him, imagining how it would feel to see him again, the warmth of his blue eyes revealing his pleasure at her return.

She imagined how it would feel to once more have the sweet pressure of his lips on hers, the tender strength of his arms surrounding her, the smoothness of his cool skin against her own.... Thinking of his touch, of the way each had of communicating with their bodies, the deep feeling between them, she forgot where she was. She was daydreaming so completely that when the stewardess asked her whether she would like champagne and got no answer, she moved away, assuming Alexis was asleep.

John didn't meet her at the airport. She was puzzled by that. In fact, she tried to hide her disappointment in confusion. Perhaps he hadn't understood that her connecting flight would bring her to Harrison. She hoped he wasn't waiting for her in Little Rock. She was sure she'd been clear in her explanation of her plans. Maybe he'd had trouble with one of the trucks, or with the car. But it seemed impossible that all his vehicles would be out of commission. Perhaps he just didn't care that she was coming home—coming back. That seemed impossible, too, yet the thought of it stung her, actually bringing tears to her eyes.

In the end she made a deal with a local cab driver to take her the sixty miles to Mountain View. As she neared Lizzie's house, she felt the excitement begin to rise in her again. In a little while, she would be showered and changed. In a little while, she'd be able to call him. It hadn't seemed right to call from the airport, but there was nothing to stop her from ringing the Webber place as soon as she got in.

"I think it's a little late to be calling, don't you?" Lizzie had an anxious look on her face, rare for her.

"I think they'll want to know I'm back...."

"Look," Lizzie said, leading Alexis to the living-room sofa. "You've had a long trip. Why don't you just sit here for a spell, and I'll make us some coffee. You've got a lot of unpacking to do, I know, but it can wait until tomorrow. For now, why don't you just relax."

"Why don't you want me to call the Webbers?" Alexis demanded, not impressed by Lizzie's strained attempts at hospitality.

"Call in the morning, Alexis."

"What's going on over at their place that you don't want me to know about?"

"I guess being up in the city has really brought out the reporter in you," Lizzie said with a weak smile. "You sure sound like one, the way you're grilling me."

"Please, Lizzie, don't be ridiculous," Alexis said with more than a hint of exasperation. "I'm not grilling you. I just want to know why all of a sudden you seem to want to prevent me from contacting John." A thought flew into her mind, a thought she'd avoided all during her taxi ride from the airport. "There's nothing wrong with him, is there?"

Lizzie Cabe averted her eyes, and the gesture was all the answer Alexis needed. "I'm going out there. Right now. Is the truck here?"

Lizzie nodded. "Look, Alexis," she insisted. "You're tired. It's been a long trip. Why not wait until tomorrow?"

But Alexis was already halfway up the stairs; it didn't take her long to change into jeans and a sweat shirt. She found her sneakers at the bottom of the closet where she'd left them and hurriedly laced them.

She hadn't driven in three weeks, so it took her a little time to feel at ease in the pickup. Turning off the town road, she headed out into the country. The lights of the truck bounced off the roadside fences and trees. Despite her apprehension, despite the fact that it was very dark, she felt a little thrill of happiness to be back in the country. She rolled down the window and took a deep breath of the fragrant night air. It wasn't at all cold, yet the scent of the air reminded her autumn would soon lay its fiery finger on the hardwood forests of the Ozarks. It would be beautiful then. Perhaps she and John could go away again.... John. She accelerated a little, concentrated on the road.

It didn't take long to get to Old John Webber's farm, though it seemed to. Alexis was surprised to see the house in darkness—no one should be in bed yet. She got out of the truck and stepped onto the wooden porch with her usual light tread. The door was open; only the screen door was closed, and trying it, she found it wasn't locked. "Is anybody home?" she called softly, but got no answer. She turned, and would have gone back to Lizzie's had she not noticed a dim light flick on somewhere in the recesses of the house. Thinking that meant her greeting had been heard, Alexis opened the screen door, stepping into the dark parlor. "Hello?" she called, but still no one answered. Slowly she made her way toward the light, which she realized was coming from a small room the Webbers called their back kitchen—in the daytime a sunny room overlooking the kitchen garden, from which Almeda picked fresh vegetables and herbs nine months out of twelve.

Alexis carefully threaded through the maze of the living-room furniture, through the dining room, where even in the faint light, the sun-dried white cotton of the tablecloth glowed. She entered the kitchen. The gleam of Almeda's polished pots and pans, her spotless china displayed on the shelves, caught Alexis's eye, though it didn't distract her from her goal— that low lamp shining from the adjoining room. Something was leading her toward the back kitchen. The house was silent except for the distant ticktock of the grandfather clock. And then that regular sound joined with another rhythm: the sound of breathing, a sleeping person, a man. John Webber.

Alexis was amazed to see that a bed had been set up in the back kitchen near the window. She was even more amazed to see him lying there. Against the whiteness of the pillow, his bronzed skin seemed to retain its usual robust quality, but it took her only a moment to realize his face, his beloved face still in sleep, didn't look healthy at all. In fact, his suntanned skin was flushed with fever.

His bright blue eyes were closed, hiding their usual

vitality. Taking in the curve of his lashes on his too-rosy cheeks, Alexis was filled with such tenderness, such caring, that her breath caught in her throat, and she fought back tears. His hair was damp on his brow, the slightly matted locks tousled, as though the sleep he enjoyed for the time being had been long in coming and had cost him much tossing and turning. The sheet and blanket covering him were rumpled, though on top of those covers, his strong arms, his hands that were a farmer's hands, but those of an artist, too, rested in perfect stillness. He seemed to fill the small bed, and yet his size and strength couldn't make up for the fact that he was obviously ill and in need of her care.

She wanted to touch him. She wanted to lay her hand on the fevered plane of his brow. She wanted to smooth the covers for him. She felt such a surge of love that she wanted to smooth out everything that would ever come his way—all paths, all problems made easy. Silently she moved toward where he lay. Slowly she bent nearer to him, until she was close enough to feel the heat rising from his face, where a little stubble covered his jaw. In sleep, the fragrance of his skin was as enticing to her as heady wine, and she lowered her gentle lips to kiss him without rousing him.

But her lips never met his skin. At the last instant, Alexis felt a cold hard hand on her shoulder. The shock of it was so great that she jumped; the hand fell away. Turning, she was astounded to find the small commanding figure of Mary Holmes behind her. But Alexis wasn't too startled to detect a strange combination of concern for John, contempt for

Alexis and smugness in Mary's expression. Alexis opened her mouth to speak, but the other woman frowned, put her finger to her lips and shifted her eyes to John. It was an insulting gesture, as if Alexis had intended to shout into the heavy silence of the room. She felt her ire rise. This was no time to argue, however, so that when Mary motioned her out of the room, Alexis followed, noticing that Mary glanced back at John, then pulled the door closed with a distinctly proprietary air.

"Come this way," Mary said. Alexis was disgusted by her imperious tone. Nonetheless, she went into the kitchen with her.

"What's going on?" Alexis asked, not making any extra effort to be polite. Mary's manner bothered her, and she was too concerned about John to worry about her own manner. "What's wrong with him? How long has he been like this? He needs a doctor."

"Ms Smythe," Mary said, her voice so cold that Alexis again thought of the edge of autumn on the night air. "Perhaps it hasn't occurred to you that it *is* possible for rural communities to have adequate health care. Undoubtedly you have your own private physician. Well, things are a bit different here, but we do manage."

"Is that so? Then suppose you just tell me who's seen John and what he's said."

"It's not a he. The doctor is a she," Mary said archly.

"Very progressive—very progressive, indeed," Alexis answered with sarcasm. "I congratulate the community. Now what did the doctor say about John?"

"He's quite weak. He..." Mary began. The

smugness left her voice, replaced by genuine caring, and despite her previous feelings, Alexis saw and shared Mary's deep concern. "He's been less than well since the canoe trip, the doctor thinks, and he's got a lot worse in the past week."

"Why isn't he in the hospital?" Alexis asked. Suddenly she felt afraid; nothing mattered except that he be out of danger. "Shouldn't he be in the hospital where they can watch over him?"

"Look, Ms Smythe, down here we can look after our own. I don't know what it's like up in Chicago, but here, when a person's sick, he's got family and neighbors to help. Sure, we have hospitals for when they're really needed, but as I say, we can look after our own." She sounded as though she would much rather have said, "my own." Alexis wasn't surprised when Mary went on, "You know, the doctor said this is a direct result of that canoe trip John took you on. At the time I told him it wasn't going to be easy taking someone from the city into the wilderness."

Mary made it sound as if John had consulted with her before asking Alexis along—that thought didn't sit well with Alexis. "Are you an expert on wilderness trips?" she asked snappishly.

"Oh, I myself am a schoolteacher. We often take the children out on wilderness trips, so I know how difficult it is to be in the woods with someone who's afraid."

"I don't know what you think my being afraid has to do with John's being sick."

"An inexperienced person is always a handicap to an experienced one," Mary answered succinctly. Yet Alexis understood that the woman was implying more. Her manner was intended to remind Alexis that she was an outsider, a stranger. She didn't want to argue with the woman, though; she was too tired and too worried.

"What does the doctor say? Is he getting better? He seems so flushed."

"You needn't worry yourself," Mary replied. "Everything's under control. His fever is much lower than it was a day or so ago, and the doctor will be here to check on him in the morning. . . . ''

"Where did everyone go?" Alexis asked. She wouldn't have been so concerned about John if she could have talked to Almeda, who, along with all her other skills, was an excellent nurse.

"Pat is over at Roosevelt's. As for Almeda and Old John—they're down in Houston."

"Houston?"

"They're with Right John's parents."

"Well, did you call them to tell them how sick John is? Perhaps Almeda—"

"If you knew the family as well as I do," Mary began in her smug way, "you'd realize the trip down to Houston is a once-a-year occasion for Old John. Getting him to the big city is akin to carrying a mountain into a meadow. It's not likely to be canceled on short notice. Besides, it wasn't until they'd been there for a day or two that Right John took a turn for the worse. It isn't as though they left knowing he was sick. When I heard how bad off he was, I came right over. That was the day before yesterday. . . . ''

It didn't take much imagination to complete *that* sentence: *and I've been here ever since.* "How did you find out he was so sick?" Alexis asked.

"He phoned me."

"Right John himself phoned you, you mean?" Alexis asked. She had heard the answer, but it took a moment to sink in. Immediately, she felt left out of John's life. But perhaps that was ridiculous. After all, she had been hundreds of miles away.

"Of course that's what I mean," Mary retorted with such contempt in her tone and her expression that she might just as well have come out and said Alexis was a dolt.

"Naturally, as soon as I heard his voice and realized how different he sounded from usual when he phones me," Mary continued, "I threw a few things in my bag and rushed over. Luckily I was able to get a friend to look after my class for a day or so."

"That certainly was lucky for you, wasn't it?" Alexis commented. "And now it's lucky you can go back to work tomorrow."

"Oh, I don't think John's quite ready to be left alone just yet," Mary argued.

"I quite agree," Alexis responded. "And that is precisely why I'm going to take over here. So that you won't have to put yourself out any further. After all, it's real nice of you to be so neighborly and all, but there's no need for you to miss any more school."

"Listen here, Ms Smythe," Mary said. "We don't need any fancy Yankees coming down here to tell us what to do. If you think you can just walk into this county and start pushing people around, you've got another think coming. What does a person like you know about being what you so sarcastically call 'real nice and neighborly'? The way I hear it, nobody would treat you like a neighbor unless you hired them to do it and gave them a uniform to boot. You don't have neighbors—you have servants. And as long as you don't know the difference, you don't belong around here.''

"Ms Holmes," Alexis answered, pride making her struggle to keep her voice icy cold. "It's obvious you feel you have some sort of ax to grind with me. Under ordinary circumstances, I would be happy to point out that you seem to be the only person in Mountain View who holds the opinion that people from elsewhere are not welcome in this county. I could point out several examples of—well, let's just leave it, shall we? In the presence of a man who is quite ill, it seems inadvisable to carry on a discussion that might lead to voices being raised. It might wake him."

"I think you and I—" Whatever Mary was about to say fell into dead silence—both women stood stock still at the sound of the voice coming from the back kitchen. Their argument had already awakened him, or something else had. "Mary?" John called softly. "Mary, where are you? Come, please. I need you."

Without another word, but without missing the opportunity to throw one last supremely smug look at Alexis, Mary turned and made her way toward the man who was calling her for help.

Alexis didn't stop to think that had John known she was there, he might have called her name. She just turned and headed for the door. Tears blinded her, and as the screen door swished closed behind her, she stood for a moment on the wooden porch, letting the tears flow. Some homecoming this had been. She had waited for this night since the moment she'd left her love at the airport. *Her love.* The thought crossed her mind that perhaps he was no longer hers at all. Perhaps he never had been. They had never spoken about the future, had they?

She made her way to the pickup and climbed in, waiting a few moments for her tears to subside so she could concentrate on getting back to Lizzie's. Not on getting *home*, for quite suddenly Lizzie's seemed as much of a boarding house as it had the first time she'd ever set foot in it. The result of Mary's treatment of Alexis was twofold. Once more she felt like a stranger. Worse than a stranger. She felt like a foreigner.

Even worse than that was the overwhelming feeling that she missed Right John Webber. She had spent three weeks missing him, had looked forward to this night as eagerly as a child to her birthday. She'd dreamed of how he would look at her. Instead, she'd seen only the sweet curve of his lashes against his cheek. She'd imagined the strength of his arms around her. Instead, she hadn't even been able to touch him. She'd thought about the way it would feel to lie beside him again, the softness of her skin meeting the softness of his along the length of the two of them. Now she didn't know whether she'd ever lie beside him again. Perhaps it was a foolish fear. And perhaps not. "Mary," he'd said. "I need you, Mary."

After a while Alexis started the truck, turning out of the Webber's gravel driveway onto the road into town. She opened the window and let the swift

stream of night air blow away the hairstyle Raoul of
the other world had created for her. Absurdly, she
thought he might be the only man ever to touch her
hair again. She blinked away fresh tears, and with
that gesture, began to feel laughter bubbling up.

How could she be so silly? How could she be so
weak as to let someone like Mary Holmes get the best
of her? What did Mary know about John's feelings?
What did Mary know of Alexis's own strength?
True, the woman had been John's friend, and by his
own admission more than a friend, for a long time.
But that didn't mean John's feelings for Alexis were
trivial—or temporary. That didn't mean that when
he'd said, "Alexis, I love you," those words hadn't
been true. If she had any fight in her, she would be
able to take on the superior Mary Holmes and beat
her on her own turf. Not that she could conceive of a
physical fight, of course; the thought was disgusting
to her. Still, she wouldn't find it difficult to tell Mary
Holmes a thing or two about being neighborly. Alexis was so determined that she almost turned back in
the middle of the country road.

But of course she didn't. It was late, and since she
was tired from her journey and from what had tran-
spired since her arrival, she'd just head home to Lizzie's, have a good night's sleep and tackle things in
the morning.

And when she let go of thoughts of Mary Holmes,
thoughts of John rushed in to flood her mind. Later,
tired as she was, she lay awake for a good while. She
worried about the fact that he was ill, and a tenderness filled her, a desire to help him—the same desire
she'd felt as she stood over his bed. But he was

strong, a healthy man in his prime. And Mary had been wrong about Alexis's lack of confidence in rural health care. She was sure John would soon recover.

Her worry was seeping away. And it was then that the other desire filled her, the desire to speak to him with her body, her whole hungry, love-filled body. She wanted to feel the muscled contours of his chest pressed against her eager breasts, wanted the hot rain of kisses that had once descended upon her, opening to delight all the secret places of her longing. She longed to be one with him, to sway with the motion of his desire in a rhythm as natural as that of the golden grass swaying in his fields. She wanted to burst the floodgates of his most exquisite need, to hear him moan with pleasure as the broad river moans in its ecstatic rush toward the deep and distant sea.

"IF YOU THINK Right John Webber's going to go back on his raising again to get involved with another northerner who cares only about herself, you're dead wrong. He wouldn't be that stupid."

"Get away from the door, Mary...."

"You get away, Alexis Smythe. Get out of here. We don't need interference. Go back where you belong."

"Mary, get out of that doorway!" The woman was standing in the narrow passage leading from the dining room to the kitchen. Alexis was amazed that she would resort to such childish tactics to detain her. She didn't want to argue, and she certainly didn't want to push her out of the way.

"Please, Mary, be reasonable. You can't keep me

from seeing him; you know you can't. Now come on, get out of my way.''

"What's going on out there?'' As they had the previous evening, both women froze at the sound of Right John Webber's voice, much stronger this morning. Alexis raised her brows in a silent question, which Mary answered by sighing and moving aside. Alexis rushed toward the sickroom without noticing—or caring—whether Mary followed.

It seemed he hadn't expected an answer to his question. He was sitting up in bed, clearly feeling better. But he was staring out the wide window, past Almeda's garden, past the harvested fields that had richly repaid him for the season's labors, toward the gentle, distant hills. His strong hands were resting on the blanket, and Alexis looked again at the scar near his left thumb, the scar she had touched with her lips. To her, a scar on the hand of a musician could only mean some terrible tragedy had been narrowly averted. Yet when she had asked John whether he should be more careful with his hands, he had laughed and commented that the difference between a violinist and a fiddler was that a fiddler knew how to get his hands dirty!

Alexis had jokingly asked if he'd been fiddling the day he hurt his hand. He had flinched, though he'd answered evenly that he guessed you could say something like that. Alexis had dropped the topic, thinking her careless question had made him feel bad about being a fiddler part-time instead of having the full-time concert career he'd once planned on. Later Lizzie told Alexis where John Webber's scar had really come from. When he'd heard about his wife's fatal accident, that her body was still pinned beneath the wreckage of her car, he'd become hysterical and tried to pry her out with his bare hands.

As she stood at the threshold of the sickroom, Alexis could see that John's strength had only partially returned. His hair was just a bit tousled, curling a little at the neckline of his pajamas. Seeing those soft tendrils of tawny hair, Alexis was immediately and unaccountably struck by the man's vulnerability.

For all his physical strength, he had his weaknesses, his need for help. And for all his vital cheerfulness, he had also lost a promising career and a beloved wife. Alexis knew intuitively that John still grieved in some ways. There were areas in which he might welcome help in shouldering the burden of his many heavy responsibilities. He had worked so hard at his music; he had pulled the farm out of poverty and confusion; he had raised a child—all without having someone beside him who cared as much about him as he cared about his duties, year after year.

She wished she could have been with him during all those years. She prayed she might be with him for at least a little time to come. In her heart, she wished it could be forever. Just plain forever by his side. He was a strong man; he hid his needs. But he could no longer hide them from her. She saw him, at this moment, through the unblinkered eyes of deep love. He was not perfect, and that was good. Love had nothing to do with perfect beings; it had to do with imperfect beings urging each other to become better.

Alexis sighed, and hearing the small soft sound, John turned his head. His sky-blue eyes smiled before his lips had a chance to. Without a word, he raised his arms, and she flew into his welcoming embrace. For endless moments they merely clung to each other. For all his size, he felt small in her arms, and she cradled him closer to her, as close as she could. And he held on.

She should have asked him whether he was well enough for her to stay with him for a while, but she forgot about that the minute his lips met hers. His tongue found the eager hollow of her mouth, his hands cupping her face.

"It seems to me I've thought about you every moment you've been away," he said, his breath a warm moistness on her cheek. "Yet even so, I find I'd forgotten how exquisitely beautiful you are...."

She responded by again seeking the heat of his kiss. She slid his hand away from her face, toward the swelling curve of her breast. Obligingly, he moved his fingers where hers guided, and when she felt the pressure of his thumb against her nipple, she let out a sigh of pleasure that John answered by lying back down on the bed and pulling her over him.

They were the only witnesses to each other's ecstasy. In the joy of their reunion, they had forgotten there was another person in the house, who had followed Alexis to the door of the back kitchen, but who had very soon fled from the threshold in tears.

CHAPTER SIXTEEN

HE REMAINED AN INVALID for another week. Alexis made an uneasy peace with Mary, who continued to come over every day. It took a little while for Alexis to accept that Mary had a right to the friendship she and John had shared for so many years. When she thought about how proprietary she herself had been on that second day of her homecoming, she felt a little ashamed. She had been raised to be more self-controlled. It was crass to be that obvious about what one wanted, especially if what one wanted was a man.

But Alexis was finding she thought less and less about what she'd been raised to think and feel and do, and more and more about what she thought it right to do. By those standards, her behavior was still inexcusable, and when she apologized, the two women had managed a strained but revealing talk, during which Mary admitted she had loved John for years without ever expecting her feelings to be returned. Her confession brought Lizzie to mind, who had said something similar. In her happiness over her homecoming, it didn't occur to Alexis that she, too, faced the risk of becoming one of those women whose unfulfilled love for Right John would add a poignant sorrow to her years.

Her happiness over her homecoming.... Her homecoming. As John slowly recovered, she spent hours with him. He was impatient to be doing the dozens of things he usually did, and Alexis tried hard to take his mind off the fact that his students were missing their lessons—not only his students at the center but in Batesville, too, where the college's fall session was in full swing.

As for the farm, that was less of a problem. It was early autumn, not the busiest of times. Roosevelt Webber and his older son, Lon, came over two or three times to see how things were going, but they seemed to spend more time in the house than in the fields or the barn.

If anyone had told Alexis a year before that she'd feel strongly about a man like Roosevelt Webber, she would have denied the possibility. Yet her respect for the farmer was growing by the week. Roosevelt's face was lined by care, his skin leathery from years in the sun and wind; he looked considerably older than he was. But he was one of the kindest men Alexis had ever known. His hands were gnarled from a lifetime of manual labor, but she'd seen him lift a baby chick with such gentleness that the small creature didn't even seem to know it was being picked up. Roosevelt, unlike Right John, had no use for schooling, had never been formally educated. But his children regarded him as the source of all knowledge, and he never seemed unable to answer their questions. To his wife, he was a good provider, yet he never let her feel the things she provided were any less important to the family.

Sometimes Alexis played a game with herself. She

imagined the most elegant reception possible. She pictured the room where such an event might be held, all marble and brocade, with music provided by a small orchestra. The food would be caviar, oysters, filet mignon. The champagne would flow like a mountain torrent. And everyone, including the men, would be dressed in designer clothes.

Once she had this scenario in mind, Alexis would push her imagination a little further. Old John Webber would suddenly wander in on the scene, saying something like, "People wanna eat fish eggs it's their business, but where I come from we throw things like that on the compost heap."

Then she tried to imagine what it would be like if Roosevelt Webber entered such a scene. Being a man of quiet yet complete dignity, he would no doubt feel each person had his own way of enjoying himself, and that way must be respected. No doubt Roosevelt would simply turn and walk away.

Finally, she imagined how Right John would seem among the crowd filling her fantasy room. She knew he wouldn't be as out of place as his relatives. He would be more handsome than any other man there, and no more awkward. What that meant to her was that there were levels to this man she wasn't yet able to fathom, even though she'd known him for months. He was complex. She wondered how many years it had taken Caroline Kain to understand the man she'd married. She wondered if she herself would have time to learn to know him as a wife learns to know her husband. But he had said nothing; neither could she. That was one part of her "raisin'" she wasn't going back on. No decent woman ever asked a man to marry her. That would be going too far. Wouldn't it?

To be with him again, even after so short an absence as three weeks, filled Alexis with happiness, but the happiness of the homecoming began to wear a bit thin, because another homecoming was putting a great strain on Old John Webber's household. He and Almeda came back from Houston with stories of the good time they'd had, with gifts for Right John, Alexis and Patience.

It was Patience's return that caused the problem. In the two weeks immediately following her arrival home from Chicago, she had spent a lot of time at her cousin's place, Alexis learned. She thought it strange that the girl should do so when her father was sick and could have used her help, but perhaps the girl didn't want to be in the house while Mary Holmes was ruling the roost. Alexis didn't know. What she did know was that Patience was putting everyone on edge. For one thing, she seemed to be lording it over her cousins, Harriet and Blanche Webber, making Alexis want to reprimand her, though she decided she didn't have the right.

One day Alexis was sitting on the porch of the farmhouse waiting for Ethel to come back out, when she heard the voices of the three girls from around the side of the house.

"You two will never be able to do it," Patience said with finality.

"Why not?" the youngest of the three cousins asked.

"Because you ain't smart, enough, squirt," her sister replied jokingly. But there was no joking in Patience's voice as she took up the conversation.

"If you want to get a good job up in New York City, you've got to go to college."

"So?" the older girl asked. "Lots of people from around here go to college. A person could go to Fayetteville."

"That's not what I'm talking about," Patience declared. "I'm talking about going to a really fine school—the best."

"College?"

"No. You got to go to this school before you go to college—like high school."

"High school..." the younger girl sighed, as though she just couldn't wait to get to that mythical place of joy.

"The school I'm talking about is a lot better than any stupid school around here. For one thing, you get to wear uniforms."

"Like in the army?" the younger girl queried.

"No, dummy," Patience replied. "You get to wear a tunic."

"What's that?"

"It's a special sort of outfit that only students at certain schools wear. This whole school is special."

"Wow," said the youngest.

"If it's so special, how are *you* going to get in?" the other girl asked.

"My grandmother...."

"The one that lives in the *mansion*..." the older of Patience's cousins said with more than a hint of sarcasm. Clearly, she wasn't as impressed with the traveler's tales as her sister. "You better forget your old grandma. Your daddy ain't gonna let you go to school up north."

"He is *too*," Patience nearly shouted, and Alexis was shocked by the quick anger that filled the teenager's voice. She was even more shocked by what followed. "I *am* going to Chicago," Patience insisted. "I'm going to Chicago again, just like I did last month. Only this time I'm going to stay. I'm not hanging around here. I'm not going to be a lousy hick."

"What's a hick?" the younger girl asked.

"You, squirt," her sister answered good-naturedly, and Alexis heard the high squeal and rippling giggles that always resulted when the two sisters began to tease and tickle each other. Apparently, Patience was keeping silent during the fracas, for Alexis didn't hear her voice again.

Several days after that, Patience tried another tactic. When she first met the girl, Patience had shown Alexis the sort of shy deference one might expect a girl of her age to show toward an adult stranger. As Alexis had come to spend more time at Old John's, Patience had become a little easier in her presence, until the day Alexis found her in tears over her frustrating attempts to perfect her clarinet playing. From then on they'd been friends.

The trip to Chicago had made them closer than ever, and the day Alexis had taken Patience to the airport, she'd managed to convince the girl to change out of her outlandish outfit and wash her face clean of makeup before boarding the plane. That evening, when Right John had called Alexis to say he was ready to "pitch a fit" over what had been done to Patience's hair, Alexis had managed to smooth things over, all the while hoping John didn't pitch a fit over her own new hairdo!

She and John's daughter had indeed established a rapport, but what Patience was up to now was a different thing altogether. She had some trick up her sleeve, which involved idolizing Alexis to the point where she didn't know what to do with the girl. Every time she turned around, Patience was there telling her how beautiful she was, begging to be allowed to borrow this or that item of clothing, this or that piece of jewelry. Patience had decided there was something to be gained by imitating Alexis, but it was hard for the woman to understand what the girl was trying to accomplish. It wasn't that she begrudged the child anything, of course; it was just that Alexis was sure it would be healthier if Patience spent more time with her own young friends. In fact, Patience seemed to be losing the friends she'd had all summer. John commented that they never came around, that Patience never bothered to call them back when they phoned the house for her.

Alexis would have been content to let this idolization of her person and her possessions continue until it ran its natural course, had there not been another, more serious, component to the problem. Patience was becoming more sassy by the day. When Alexis first met her, she was struck by the girl's quiet manner. It wasn't much in evidence these days. The teen wasn't particularly mouthy with her father, perhaps because she respected him too much, perhaps because she was afraid of being disciplined. But she was a holy terror to Old John. At first, he thought it was funny that she should all of a sudden become what he called "spunkier 'n a puppy in a hen house." But he thought it a whole lot less funny when she called him a "know-nothing old geezer," and he wasn't amused at her cavalier treatment of Almeda, either. When Alexis decided to speak to Patience, the girl snapped that her behavior was none of Alexis's business. Immediately afterward, she was so apologetic and obsequious that Alexis was more angered by her apology.

There was one good side to Patience's changed behavior: she began to dedicate herself to her music more ardently than ever. Often when Alexis was at the house, Patience would be up in the music room practicing; her technique was definitely improving. Right John seemed pleased as punch about this, and for the first time he suggested Patience and he could learn some pieces together, he with his violin, to be performed at the house. That was unusual, because though he often fiddled, John never seemed to play classical violin except when he was teaching, or the odd time when he played only for Alexis. She asked him why he practiced so much for so little playing, but he had only winked, telling her he was preparing a surprise. That was all he'd say. So the offer to play a recital with his daughter was clearly a special thing to Right John. And when Patience agreed to the plan, John acted as though he'd reached his child in a way he never had before. Alexis wasn't so sure. She was beginning to distrust Patience's acquiescence, fearing it might be more insidious than her negative behavior.

She watched as, daily, Patience began to exhibit, once again, small but unmistakable signs of rebellion. There was nothing Alexis could do except hope whatever was bothering the girl would work itself out, causing minimal damage to Patience herself, and to her father.

"He's looking to settle around here on a permanent basis...." Lizzie Cabe refilled her coffee cup from the enamel pot on the stove, then came back to the table and sat, tipping two legs of her chair up off the vinyl floor.

"Oh?" Alexis responded. "When did he decide that?"

"Well...." Lizzie's manner was a little more hesitant, a little shyer than usual. "Well, it sort of came up about a week ago—sort of in the course of another conversation."

"What do you mean 'another conversation'?" Alexis asked with a smile, beginning to suspect what Lizzie was really trying to tell her.

"Oh, you know, a—a conversation." The woman rose from the table again and walked to the window over the sink. She peered out as though looking at the distant hills, but it was pitch-dark. From where she sat, Alexis could see Lizzie's reflection in the dark square of glass.

"It's starting to get dark a lot sooner, don't you think?" Lizzie asked. "Be winter before you know it. Another winter."

"Don't wish winter on me already," Alexis said, laughing. "I haven't even seen one of your famous Ozark autumns yet."

"Any day now..." Lizzie answered, but in such a wistful tone that Alexis wasn't sure the woman was still talking to her.

"Come on back and sit down, Lizzie; you're making me nervous."

"I am restless, tonight, aren't I?" The older

woman returned to her chair and took up her coffee cup. "I feel skitterish. Jumpy as a fly."

"Why? What's wrong?"

Lizzie was silent for a moment. Then she took a deep breath. "Alexis," she began. "If I tell you something, you promise you won't tell anybody else?"

"Of course, Lizzie." In the months she'd lived in Lizzie's house, Alexis had become close enough to her landlady for them to share secrets. To Lizzie Alexis had confided her fear that Right John might never get around to thinking about marriage. Lizzie had admitted that John took his time about most things, so she could imagine how long it would take him to make up his mind about marrying again. It had embarrassed Alexis even to admit she wanted John to propose to her, but Lizzy didn't seem to think there was anything unusual in that. "What is it?" Alexis questioned Lizzie.

"He—George Fox—he's almost certainly got that new job with the university."

"Oh, that's wonderful! He's been waiting a long time to hear. So he'll get to set up the experimental farm."

"Yes," Lizzie answered. As she spoke, her eyes lit up with excitement and pride. "When he first came here from Little Rock, he had no idea this area was best for the study he had in mind. The state government was in on the research, you know, and he'd gone all over Arkansas checking the soil, the crops— lots of things. But it wasn't until he did his report on Old John's farm that he really got the attention of the federal Department of Agriculture, and the university.''

''Why Old John's farm?''

''Well, I know you know that Right John brought that farm back from nearly nothing. Took him years to do it, but it's in prime shape right now.''

''Yes,'' Alexis said with a warm smile she didn't try to hide. She was proud of John, even if she didn't understand, still, the first thing about farming. ''But what's that got to do with George?''

''George's studies are on something called 'agricultural reclamation.' You see, what he's interested in is using new techniques to rescue old farms. Now that both governments and the university are interested, they're willing to fund George so that he can buy a place to run all on his own, incorporating the techniques he's developed. Those techniques are only on paper now, but with a place to run. . . . Well, who knows?''

''It sounds great. What's the problem? There *is* a problem.''

''Yes, you're right. There's a problem. Two problems. The first is that there's no place for sale right now in the immediate area. Apparently, the land around here—in a big circle around Mountain View—has something special about it that's important to George's theories. I don't know about those things. Anyway, there's only one farm for sale in the area, and that whole piece of land is on a slope facing west. I don't know what difference that makes, but some of what George wants to do involves solar energy, and the direction and angle of the main fields on that farm are wrong. So. . . .''

"If he can't find a farm here, does it mean he loses the contract with the university?"

"No, I don't think so," Lizzie answered. "But it could mean he'd have to make adjustments, would have to start pretty much all over again somewhere else."

The two women were silent for a moment. They heard an old car or truck draw to a noisy halt outside the house. Both women looked up, waiting, but they didn't even hear the car door slam, let alone a knock on the door. Of course, there were other houses on Lizzie's street. Dismissing the sound, they resumed their conversation.

"What's the other problem, Lizzie?"

"He's asked me to marry him, Alexis." Lizzie's voice was low, her eyes cast down onto the cotton tablecloth with its print of bright flowers.

Alexis laid her hand on top of Lizzie's. She spoke softly in the quiet kitchen. "And why is that a problem?"

Lizzie looked up, but not at Alexis. Her eyes seemed to take in the sparkling kitchen. Though the rest of the house was old-fashioned, this room was modern, equipped with the latest appliances. Yet Lizzie wasn't really seeing what was before her, Alexis could tell. "From the time I was little," Lizzie said, "I promised myself I would never be a farmer's wife."

"But what's wrong with being a farmer's wife?" Alexis asked. She wanted to know the answer for more than one reason.

"Nothing—for some people. But for me—" Her fingers beat a mindless little rhythm on the table. "I never wanted to be tied down that way. I never wanted to be married to the land."

"Lizzie, pardon me for saying so, but I don't understand how it would be any different from being married to this house, the way you are now."

"I *am* married to this house, aren't I?" her landlady asked in the manner of one who has been thinking about a thing for a long time. "I keep telling myself I'll sell out, that I'll move on. But I've never had the courage to do it. I left here once. I know now I never should have come back, because a person almost never gets a second chance...."

"That's not true, Lizzie. You're looking at things in far too negative a light. Maybe George is your second chance. He's not an ordinary farmer. If you marry him, you have the opportunity to learn all sorts of new things, to see—" She stopped in her tracks. "Unless, of course, you don't love him."

"I do, Alexis," Lizzie said, looking at Alexis squarely for the first time that evening, revealing the painful questioning in her eyes. "I do love him, but everything is so uncertain. I just don't—"

They were interrupted by a knock on the front door. The sound surprised the two women, because Lizzie had quite a nice set of door chimes. Whoever was at the door either hadn't seen the button or didn't want to bother with it. Before they got into the living room, the knock sounded again.

"I'll get it," Lizzie said, moving toward the door. Alexis stayed close behind her. There was something ominous in the air, though there was no reason for the women to suspect anything was wrong.

And indeed, when Lizzie opened the door to reveal

Roosevelt Webber, both women let out a sigh of relief. Alexis hadn't ever seen Roosevelt in Lizzie's house before. In fact, she couldn't recall ever having seen him in town, but he must come in now and again. It occurred to Alexis that his visit might mean there was something wrong at his farm—or at Old John's.

"Good evening, Roosevelt," she said. "Is everything okay at your place?"

He didn't answer immediately. He was normally a taciturn man, not given to idle talk. Yet the silence that met Alexis's question was too prolonged, even for Roosevelt. Alexis looked at him more closely.

Unlike Right John, who was large in just about every respect, Roosevelt was small and wiry like his grandfather, Old John. He'd dressed for the visit in what Alexis recognized as his Sunday best, an ill-fitting suit that made him look even skinnier than he was. His thinning hair was slicked back, revealing his broad forehead. There was a look on his weathered face that Alexis couldn't read accurately...a combination of anger and shame. Then she realized he held something, an envelope that looked as if it had been much handled.

"Come on in and set for a bit, Roosevelt," Lizzie said. She was more capable of eliciting a response from the man than Alexis. He thanked her and moved toward a chair, but he didn't sit. After a moment's pause he spoke.

"Lizzie," he said, "I'm real sorry to be bustin' in on you at this hour, but I gotta talk to Miss Smythe here. And it's gotta be private...." His voice was strained with some emotion Alexis couldn't name.

She felt a little twinge of fear shoot through her, but when Lizzie glanced questioningly in her direction, Alexis nodded.

"I'll be upstairs if you need me," Lizzie said, then walked toward the steps. Once she glanced back doubtfully, but Alexis caught her eye, throwing her a warning look. Lizzie went on up the stairs.

"Won't you sit down, Roosevelt?" Alexis asked, taking a seat herself on the couch. He hesitated for a moment, then lowered himself onto the chair opposite her.

"Would you like some coffee?"

"I ain't come for a tea party, Miss Smythe."

Ignoring his sarcasm, Alexis asked, "Why don't you call me by my first name? You always have before." The man's behavior was puzzling, but Alexis was more annoyed than afraid.

"It don't much matter what I call you, ma'am. What matters is why did I get this here letter?" And Roosevelt thrust the crumpled envelope toward her. She had to lean forward to take it. As she did so, she saw his fingers were trembling.

Slowly she extracted a folded letter from the envelope. As she opened it, another piece of paper fluttered out, landing in her lap. She ignored it because she was shocked—the letter bore the unmistakable signature of Margaret MacIntyre Smythe, her mother.

"Why would my mother be writing to you?" she asked. She began to read to answer her own question. And when she finished, she glanced down at the slip of cream-colored paper still resting in her lap. It was a check. Made out to Roosevelt Webber. For five thousand dollars. "I'm not sure I quite understand..." was all she could think of to say.

"It's pretty clear from that letter, ain't it?" Roosevelt said, anger evident in his voice. "I been thinking about this all day. I even set outside Lizzie's here for a while before I come in to talk to you. I figure it this way. When you went up north a while back, you told yer ma about a nice little charity case, didn't you? A nice little charity case for her foundation." He said the last word with such disgust that Alexis cringed. "So she gets together with her fine lady friends, and they empty their fancy piggy banks and come up with a contribution. Well, Miss Smythe, I think you should know the Webbers don't accept no charity and never have. Even in the Great Depression we didn't go on the dole—and I ain't on the dole now. You just take this here check and you send it back to your ma and you tell her where she can put it, okay?"

Before she could utter a single word in response, he'd brushed past her. He stomped to the door and was through it before she could even stand up. She simply sat there, her mother's letter in her hand. At first, she felt numb, then defensive. She read the letter again. It was on the letterhead of the foundation Margaret and Evelyn had established years before. They called it a "heritage" foundation, because the women's cause was to preserve something of America's traditions.

They must have decided the operation of Roosevelt's farm was an American tradition worth preserving. Of course it was, but how Margaret could be so blind as to think Roosevelt would blithely accept five thousand dollars out of the blue, she didn't know. Still, she felt she should have defended her mother. Margaret's heart was in the right place, even if her usually accurate understanding of the pride and dignity of people had misfired.

If Roosevelt had stuck around, Alexis would have pointed out that her mother was trying to be kind. *And perhaps he would have pointed out that mother, whatever her intentions, had actually been very unkind, indeed.* It suddenly occurred quite forcibly to Alexis that Margaret had unwittingly treated Roosevelt Webber as though his own struggles were meaningless—as though one piece of paper was worth more than all the worry and work he himself put into his farm. The check *was* an insult, a way of saying, "Here, let our money do what all your work hasn't been able to do—save your farm."

Alexis understood. She was ashamed, for Margaret, but more for herself. She should have understood sooner. She should have made Roosevelt stay long enough to accept her apology. She should—her thoughts were interrupted by another knock on the door. So he'd come back. He must have realized it wasn't fair to run off like that. She went to the door, grateful to have the opportunity to set things straight.

CHAPTER SEVENTEEN

"JOHN!"

"Hi, there, lady." Before she could utter his name a second time, the door swung closed behind him, and she found herself enveloped in the warmth of his familiar embrace. His arms held her lightly, but it wasn't the power of his muscles that kept her close to him; it was his sheer presence. His lips met hers in a kiss that began in tenderness but moved swiftly toward the passion that had grown ever stronger with the passing months. His slightest touch made her want him. In the circle of his protecting, enticing arms, every season seemed the spring, every hour of the day seemed morning. Everything was at the beginning, full of promise and hope and joy.

"Just a minute...let go of me, will you?" she teased, pulling away from him, but not resisting when he drew her back. The fabric of his shirt was warm, soft beneath her hand. Her fingers were imprisoned against him, and she could feel the solidity of his strong body. She lifted her face to seek another kiss. He had pretty much recovered from his recent illness, but she needed the reassurance that his vitality, so appealing a part of his nature, was back to normal.

He obliged. He kissed her again. And again. He

doubted he'd ever be able to let her know just how much pleasure it gave him to taste the sweetness of her lips on his. To have Alexis Smythe in his arms made him the prime, number one, ace candidate for the position of happiest man in the world. He didn't have any way of telling her that. Words wouldn't do. He could never get past feeling that any words he uttered would sound less than elegant to a fine woman like her. It would have to be his kisses that spoke for him. He kissed her again. And again.

"What are you doing here?" she managed to ask, making her getaway when he finally had to relinquish her lips to take a breath.

"I've been teaching in Batesville all day. I had six students pretty much one after the other. After that I did some practicing in the studio there."

"Why didn't you go home to practice?"

"I had a pianist at the college. He—"

"You were practicing with a pianist?"

"Yes," John answered a little sheepishly.

"How come?"

"Oh, he just happened to be there, and...."

"You've got something up your sleeve."

"What?" John laughed, backing away from Alexis, who was coming after him with a devilish grin on her face. "You all get away!"

She kept after him, even though he began to back around the couch and the end table in a halfhearted attempt to escape her clutches. "Let me see what's up your sleeve," she teased. She reached for the long sleeves of his shirt, missing him the first two times, but grabbing with a strong hold the third time. And when she had him, she began to tickle. It never ceased to amaze her that a man of Right John Webber's size would absolutely crumble at the touch of a few well-placed, gently jabbing fingers. He tried to pull away, gasping and giggling, his shiny hair falling over his forehead, his blue eyes as bright with laughter as any two eyes could be. "Stop it!" he begged. "Get yer paws off me!"

But she didn't stop until she'd got him where she wanted him—on the couch. She pushed him down, nearly sitting on top of him. She was laughing almost as much as he, but she managed to get out, "Tell me what you've got up your sleeve. . . ."

"An arm, sugar. In fact, two of them—see?" And with that, he exerted more strength, enough to grab ahold of her and halt her teasing hands. He halted her breath itself with a deep kiss that matched the ardor of his embrace. She stopped laughing, too, thinking of nothing except the kiss and the wave of desire swelling in the depths of her. The hands that had tickled him caressed the soft, smooth strands of his hair.

Molten gold it was. To hold him was to hold the most precious treasure. Sometimes Alexis thought about another kind of gold, the kind stored in a Chicago bank. That was her gold—not jewelry, but bullion—bars of it. She knew in her heart that the gold of his hair between her eager fingers was worth more than all the bars in her family's vault. With that thought, she drew even closer to him.

He shifted so that he was lying full length on the couch and she was on top of him, her head on his chest. For a moment, he cradled her head in his palm, then drew his fingers along the pale skin of her cheek. With his other hand, he caressed her back, moving slowly toward her derriere. When she felt his fingers gently but strongly press into her flesh there, she shivered, for his touch sent such a jolt of excitement through her that she felt momentarily dizzy. Sensing her reaction, he moved his other hand down, so that both muscled palms massaged her rounded buttocks. She arched up, eager to feel as completely as possible his strokes through the silk lounging pajamas she'd put on earlier for her evening at home.

"Where's Lizzie?"

"Hmm?" she asked, unable to focus on the question, lost in the waves of pleasure and promise that were slowly gaining momentum in her hungry body.

"Alexis, honey, you'd better rein in your horses— unless you want a witness...."

"What, John?"

"I can hear Lizzie moving around upstairs. She hasn't gone to bed yet, and I don't think she'd appreciate having to stay out of her own living room because...."

"Okay, okay," Alexis said, laughing, stifling disappointment. She slid away from him. As he eased his large frame into a sitting position, supporting himself momentarily with one hand, Alexis heard the sound of a piece of paper being crunched. They both looked down at the same time. She realized immediately what the paper was, but John grabbed it before she had a chance. He stared at it for a moment, a look of surprised displeasure passing across his face.

"What's this?" he asked, examining the check closely. "What the hell is this?"

"It's a check."

"No kidding?"

She was totally unused to sarcasm from him. "Give it to me," she said, speaking more sharply than she ever had to him. She put out her hand. He ignored it.

"Just a minute." Again he examined the check. "What is a check addressed to Roosevelt Webber doing here? More to the point, who owes my cousin five thousand dollars? What's going on around here?"

"Nothing. It's just a mistake...."

"A five-thousand-dollar mistake?"

"Look, John, I can explain if you'll just—"

"I think you better explain—I don't like the looks of this at all. Did you buy something from Roosevelt?"

"What's Roosevelt got to sell me?"

The question was an honest one, not intended to suggest Roosevelt's belongings were in any way beneath Alexis. John took it the wrong way.

"Roosevelt Webber's got plenty of things you could use. Like the quality of being open and honest, for one thing."

"What do you mean open and honest?"

"Did you buy land from Roosevelt? Is that what this is all about? I thought you decided against that a long time ago."

"I did decide that. What are you accusing me of? Of course I didn't buy land from your cousin. I didn't even know he was selling. Is he?"

"So you *are* interested?"

"What if I am? What's the matter with you? No—no, I'm not interested in buying land from Roosevelt. I...."

"Then what have you bought?"

"Why are you always so damn sure about that?" Her anger was growing. He was being ridiculous, and she felt obliged to point that fact out to him. "I get a little tired of being accused of buying my way out of trouble—or into happiness. Just what do you take me for, anyway? Do you think I'm out to buy you? Because if you do, John Webber, I think you ought to know that five thousand dollars is too high a price. Five cents is too high...."

"Look, Alexis," he said, putting his hands on her shoulders in a gesture of conciliation. "I'm sorry. Don't fly off the handle like that. I didn't mean to accuse you of doing something behind my back. I'm just a little confused, that's all. Cousin Roosevelt doesn't often see five thousand dollars in one place at one time, so whatever this is about, it's obviously something big. Why don't you just sit back and relax and explain it to me. Let me see that check again." He studied it for a moment, then asked, "What is the Amtrad Foundation?"

"Well, it's not me," Alexis said a little poutingly. Her anger was slow to dissipate.

"All right," John said patiently, "it's not you. Now tell me who or what it is."

"It's a charitable foundation."

"A charitable foundation is giving Roosevelt five thousand dollars? I don't get it."

"The foundation is under the directorship of my mother and your mother-in-law."

"Evelyn Kain? Oh, my God...." He blanched at the name. Alexis could actually see his complexion pale a shade. "Oh, Alexis, how could Evelyn have got her hooks into Roosevelt? This is terrible. He's sold his soul to the very devil. . . ."

Alexis was appalled at the strength of John's loathing—or was it fear—of Evelyn Kain. She wished she could ask him why there was such enmity between the two of them. The right time had never seemed to come. This wasn't the right time, either. "John," she began, "Roosevelt is not in Evelyn's clutches, nor is he in any way under my mother's power. He's refused the gift of the foundation."

"The gift of the foundation? Gift? What are you talking about now?"

"Amtrad was set up to raise and distribute money for the preservation of certain aspects of American tradition and life-style that, in the opinion of the directors, are in danger of extinction. Evelyn and mother must have convinced the other members the Roosevelt's farm was a worthy project."

"Project?"

In that single word, Alexis could detect his virulent anger. His large body was ramrod stiff against the upholstery of Lizzie's homey-looking couch.

"Well, not a project exactly. . . . A. . . a. . . ."

"Look, here, Alexis, my cousin's farm is not some little toy charity case for a couple of dotty old ladies with nothing better to do with their dirty money than spread it around like bad manure—"

"My mother is not a dotty old lady—"

"Well, she hasn't got a whole lot of sense, Alexis. You people should know better. You just never stop and think, do you? You think you can buy whatever you want—clothes, jewelry, cars, farms, farmers. . . ."

"How dare you!"

"How dare I what, ma'am? How dare I talk this way to a fine lady like yourself? Pardon me, ma'am. I guess I just forgot my place there for a minute. I guess I just forgot exactly who I was talking to." John sprang up from the couch and headed for the door. Not wanting him to leave in such terrible anger, Alexis lunged after him, once again catching him by the sleeve. This time there was none of the playfulness of only moments earlier. Reaching down, he touched her hand where it rested lightly on his arm.

At the contact of his skin on hers, she felt the familiar tingle that always signaled her body's ardent response to his. They stood like that, and she had time to think his hand would tighten in a gesture of love and reassurance, stopping the silly argument.

That wasn't what happened. Gingerly he took one of her fingers between his thumb and forefinger and lifted her hand from his arm the way one lifts something one is very reluctant to touch. The gesture was entirely contemptuous. "You all mustn't soil your fingers, ma'am," he said, gently dropping her hand.

She wanted to hit him. He was mocking her cruelly. It wasn't she who was acting superior—it was he—and he wasn't being clever at all. She searched her mind for something to say, something to get him to leave her sight. He was rejecting her just because of something her mother had done. She wished she could strike back at him as hurtfully, but it just wasn't in her. What she finally said in her own defense had little bearing on what had just happened. "You hate me being born rich, I know, but I told you once before I wasn't—"

"Alexis," he said, turning toward her, his voice softer than it had been. "I'm sorry, but I don't buy that story of your being a woods colt."

"A woods colt?"

"A person of uncertain parentage."

"You don't believe me?"

"I think there's probably more to the story than you've been told. Anyway, it doesn't matter. I don't care who or where you came from. I care about you. I *do* care about you. But there's just so much you don't understand, and quite honestly, I don't know if you ever will understand."

He was being cool. Suddenly Alexis wanted his anger, because the coldness seemed to cut him from her entirely. His voice was even, almost emotionless. "I understand what's happened here," he said. "You offered Roosevelt the check, and he refused, right?"

"I had nothing to do with it personally, John. I keep trying to tell you."

"How did your mother and my mother-in-law find out Roosevelt's farm was in trouble?"

There was no answer to that. The scene with her mother passed before her eyes—her mother completely enthralled by the story Alexis was telling her.

"Alexis. . . ." He said her name with the tenderness she was used to, yet he didn't touch her. "Alexis, it's going to take Roosevelt a long time to get over the shame of this. That may be hard for you to see, because you just can't think the way we do. I know you try. I try to think your way, too. But it just doesn't make a whole lot of sense to me. I. . . . I just don't know. . . ."

And with that, he turned and put his hand on the doorknob. Before he turned it, he swung around. She thought he was going to kiss her. He didn't. He shrugged, turned back to the door and, without another word, let himself out.

EIGHT DAYS. Eight whole days. Alexis had been over his words so many times that she was good and sick of thinking about that conversation. Besides, thinking about what Right John Webber had said to her didn't help her understand why he hadn't called in all that time. At first she'd been afraid something had happened to him, but after a day or so Patience had called. The girl had been over to Lizzie's to visit Alexis, too. In fact, she was being even more of a clinging vine than before, which Alexis didn't mind at the moment. Being with John's daughter was a substitute for being with him. That seemed unfair to the girl. But at least Alexis could ask Patience what and how John was doing, though the girl was far more interested in other matters, such as whether and when Alexis would be going back to Chicago. The longer she went without hearing from John, the more likely it seemed that Alexis would soon be heading back north.

She would have called him, except that she was too proud at first. The afternoon she'd swallowed her pride and dialed, Mary Holmes had answered the phone.

Every day the situation grew more hopeless. Alexis didn't understand how John could have dropped her so quickly, so completely, after all they'd shared. No matter how often she turned the matter over and over in her mind, it always came out looking the same. He should at least have had the decency to tell her to her face that he'd changed his mind about her. She couldn't believe she'd so misjudged him. But evidently she had.

She looked up from the forest floor. For the past hour she had been sitting so still, so deep in thought, that the birds had resumed their song. They seemed to sense that this quiet woman, her honey-gold hair waving about her face, her deep blue-green eyes staring into the distance was no threat to them or their woodland home. She sat on top of a smooth rock at the edge of an opening in the wood, overlooking, from a great height, a wide valley.

When she'd come to Arkansas in the late winter, people had told her there was no sight more beautiful in the world than the Ozarks in the fall. At that time, she hadn't the least idea she would still be in the hills in October. Now she realized the locals hadn't exaggerated. As she looked out at what seemed to be miles of hardwood forest, Alexis had to concede this spot just might be the most beautiful place in the world, after all.

From where she sat, a hillside meadow, the grasses dried to gold and shimmering in the sun, swept down to where the trees began again, closer to the river. Every leaf seemed individually visible in the sun of this October afternoon, each a different dazzling shade of red or gold or bronze. Close to her, the colors were so bright they nearly hurt her eyes, but as the stands of trees stretched into the distance, their colors melded, blended with the ever-present mountain mist until they faded into shades of the softest blue brown and burnished orange. Nearby, a single tree blazed redder than all the rest, and watching it, Alexis realized that what she had taken for the motion of the wind in the leaves was actually two red birds. Their plumage blended in so perfectly that she didn't see them until they flew away from the tree, twittering at each other, crossing each other's path, then winging in a wide arc over the valley before disappearing into the distance.

All her life, Alexis had thought about the birds flying south at this time of year. Now she was in the south, though she didn't know enough about such things to know whether those red birds might be headed farther south to where the winter sun turned to the sun of summer. It had made her sad, even as a girl, to think of creatures relinquishing their homes year after year. At that moment she felt akin to birds on the wing, to other creatures that had left behind something familiar and sure to venture beyond.

Things had gone so wrong since she'd come back from Chicago. For one thing, she hadn't had one decent idea for a story for weeks. She knew every writer had dry spells, but she hadn't experienced one in a long time, and the feeling of discomfort—of downright loss—that came over her at such times was creeping up on her.

There was also the whole Roosevelt Webber fiasco. Quite apart from the rift that had developed between her and John as a result, Alexis had had to deal with her mother. It had taken all the diplomacy she could muster to call her mother and explain why the generosity of the foundation was being refused. When Alexis had finally got through the whole explanation she had so carefully prepared, when she'd answered all her mother's questions, when she'd reassured Margaret that she understood the intentions of the foundation had been good, if somewhat misguided—when Alexis had been through all that, Margaret in all innocence had asked whether there might be another farmer in the area who could use the money.

As for Roosevelt, Alexis had driven out to apologize, but had only spoken to Ethel. Roosevelt was, reportedly, far too busy to see her. Ethel said her husband was in town doing business with George Fox, but as Alexis couldn't imagine any business those two might have, she was fairly certain the story was an excuse. She had been rejected by a family she had come close to loving.

Patience, too, had gone from bad to worse. The girl was so skittery lately, so nervous, that Alexis was beginning to fear she might be ill. Every once in a while, she prefaced a statement with "When I go to school in Chicago," as though that were a fait accompli. If Alexis tried to pin her down, Patience sometimes even denied having said anything of the sort. Alexis had no idea whether the girl was still being sassy to Old John and Almeda, since she herself hadn't been out to the farm, but she suspected as much. Her suspicion was strengthened when, one afternoon, Patience snapped at Lizzie and received for her trouble an invitation to leave Lizzie's house and not to come back until she could keep a civil tongue.

Everything seemed to be falling apart. Sometimes Alexis actually wondered if she'd dreamed the per-

fect months before her return to Chicago. Had she
dreamed the summer evenings on the lawn of the
town park, listening to John playing some softly sen-
timental American folk song? Had she dreamed the
frequent suppers in the warm embrace of the Webber
family—Old John's and Roosevelt's combined? Had
she dreamed the beautiful, gentle girl, the sweet
country child Patience had been?

She couldn't have fantasized her love for Right
John. The stroke of his fingers against her naked
skin. The cool draft of his kiss, like chilled wine
against the heat of her thirst. What she felt for him
had colored all her days with the joy of knowing
simply that he existed, colored all her nights with a
longing to be one with his body, to sleep in the circle
of his arms, to wake beside him, as his lover.

What a fool she'd been on every single count! If he
loved her—if he'd ever loved her—where was he?
Looking out over the hills ablaze with the red and
golden leaves of autumn, Alexis felt she might as well
be looking at the red desert landscape of the planet of
Mars. She was still a stranger, a foreigner, an alien.
"You just can't think the way we do," he had said.
And he was right. She'd given it a try, but it hadn't
worked. If it had, she wouldn't be completely dried
up for writing ideas. The Roosevelt Webbers would
be able to stand to talk to her. Patience wouldn't be
such a trial. And John would be here beside her instead of God knew where.

Never in her life had Alexis felt quite so alone. She
realized she was separated in one way or another
from almost everyone she cared about. She felt like
an orphan. Once again, as was happening more and

more often of late, she thought about her real parents. She remembered John saying he didn't buy the story of her being a "woods colt," but she knew she'd been adopted by Margaret and Wallace—she'd even seen the papers.

It was also true that she didn't know anything at all about her real parents. She had just assumed they were from a different class than the Smythes. How could they not have been? Why would a couple adopt a child unless they could take her out of unfavorable circumstances and provide her with a better life? Alexis admitted to herself that she'd bult up quite a myth about her real parents. Because they weren't fancy or rich or in any other way different from millions of their fellow Americans. It was a myth she retreated into when her life became a little more unhappy than she could bear. It was the myth of poor but happy. She then retreated into it.

This time it took the form of a determination to write about people like her natural parents. Whoever they were, she convinced herself she owed it to them to make the best use of her talent, writing about people who must struggle to get the necessities of life, people not born with silver spoons. And the best way to do that would be to accept the Chicago editor's offer—if it wasn't too late.

Alexis had plenty of time to think about all this, eight days of contemplating her life. It hurt to realize what a mistake she'd made, imagining she could stay in the Ozarks forever. Yet she couldn't say she'd wasted her time. She had written good articles there. She had learned how other people lived. She had seen a new part of the country, got a fresh perspective.

She had made a damn fool of herself and let her heart get broken besides.

For the first time in a while, she let the tears come, until the whole fiery landscape swam before her eyes. She should have known better. She should have realized from the beginning that she'd be out of place here in the hills. Blinking back her wayward tears, she stared again at the panoply of color spread out across the valley, displayed against the sharp blue sky. She took a deep breath and felt the beauty of the hills enter her the way the fresh mountain air entered her lungs. She felt a little better then. Eventually she might be able to accept that all this beauty had been hers to borrow for a time.

It had been the same with John. How could she ever have expected their love to flourish? For a while they had ignored the differences between them. Their relationship had been foolish from the start. Suddenly she understood why he hadn't called. He had undoubtedly come to that same realization, that their love was and always would be impossible. "I don't know if you will ever understand...." She would understand until the day she died that he was the one man she would want to build a life with. But he was right. His ways were not hers. His people were not her people. This beautiful blazing land was not her territory. She rose; she turned away from the valley and its views. Her eyes were once again cast down. She was thinking of what she would say when she called him, for this time she had the courage. She was thinking of how best to phrase the sentiments that— any way she said them—would spell goodbye. And because she was so deep in thought, because her eyes were cast down, she ran smack into the immovable obstacle.

His hands grasped her shoulders. His lips stifled the surprised little scream that skittered out of her mouth. His arms came around her, and the crisp air of the October forest was suddenly as warm as the summer of his embrace.

"How do you manage to hide yourself?" he asked. She shook her head wordlessly, shocked that he should walk out of her imagining and into the sunlit forest. "I've been trying to get in touch with you for three days. . . ."

At this bit of news, she pulled herself together. She was eager to ask him what he meant, whether he'd really been seeking her out, but she kept her cool. Just because he'd apparently come back and taken her breath away with his kiss didn't mean she would forget her resolution. "I tried to reach you once, also," she said calmly, pulling away from him and returning to sit on the rock. He followed her. Tentatively he reached out a strong hand to cup her face. She longed to cover that hand with her own, perhaps turn her face a little so she could plant a kiss against the callused skin of his palm. But she didn't move. Slowly he began to stroke her rosy cheek with his thumb.

"I called a million times, sugar, but every time I got through, Lizzie said you were out."

"I've been spending a lot of time in the woods. . . just thinking," she answered softly. She hadn't seen him in so long that he felt like a stranger again, and she felt unaccountably shy in his presence, timid even to look at him, especially to look into his eyes.

"Alexis," he said, his melodious voice a whisper. "Honey, look at me." He put a finger beneath her chin, raising her face until she was confronted by the warm blue light of his gaze. "I'm sorry, honey. I'm so sorry...."

"For what?" she asked, a little too sharply. She turned her head away, her eyes meeting the blue sky. It was exactly the same shade as his eyes, and it made her turn back to him. She wanted to maintain her composure. Eight days without him had taught her there was at least a possibility she could live without him. She had to make that possibility a certainty— for both their sakes. She must not give in, even though her body was already beginning to send signals of impatient desire. Her heart felt near to breaking in two. "There's nothing to be sorry for at all, John. I've thought over what you said the last time we were together, and I now think you were one hundred percent correct."

"Correct about what? Listen, sugar, forget what I said then. Just pay attention to what I'm saying now. I was wrong. I want.... Oh, Alexis I want you to...." He reached for her, but gently she pushed him away. As she did, her hand brushed the warm skin of his arm. She ignored that enticing contact. She had to.

"You were right, John. You were right when you said I may never come to understand what life down here is all about. I'm still a stranger here after all these months. I realize I'll always be a stranger. That's why I'm going—"

This time he was too quick for her. His strong arms came around her, pinning her own arms to his chest. She should have struggled, resisted the temptation of his lips as once more they sought the soft curves of her mouth; should have rejected the hot thrust of his seeking tongue. So long had she gone without him that when his hand slipped beneath the collar of her shirt, when his fingers began to make a languorous circle around her breast, narrowing and narrowing until the peak was teased by his thumb and forefinger, her body arced toward him, one admission of desire, one plea for more.

But he withdrew his hand, and instead of seeking to satisfy the growing hunger in them both, he moved away. He was still, appearing to gather his thoughts. Finally he sighed and spoke. "Alexis, I've spent the past week thinking about things—about us. . . ."

"Oh?" she answered coolly, making a strong effort to mask all feeling.

John seemed not to have heard her. "And you know what? I still haven't come to any conclusions." His voice was even, so lacking in passion that he sounded like a scientist disclosing the results of his latest experiment.

"What conclusions had you hoped to come to?" Alexis asked stiffly. She couldn't believe this man, with whom she'd spent hours of such intimacy, could now discuss their love, their future, so dispassionately.

There was a moment's tense silence, invaded by the rustling of deep mountain grasses, the sighing of the wind in the wood, the occasional cooing and twittering of forest birds. In that small space of time filled only with the song of the hills, he looked at her. He felt he could hear her breathe with a soft rhythm at one with the rhythm of nature around them, and suddenly he was overwhelmed by such a rush of tenderness that he forgot the self-doubt gnawing at him. He forgot everything but her, this woman who had come out of nowhere to fill all the longing hollows of his heart. He reached for her. He wanted to hold her, never to let her go.

HIs embrace was a total surprise to Alexis, his rough gesture reminding her of the few times he'd embarrassed her slightly by the unsophisticated openness of his actions. But she wasn't embarrassed this time. She let him clasp her against his warmth. His embrace was like a haven, like a home, and despite herself, she wanted nothing more than to stay there as long as she could. Forever wasn't too much to ask in that shared moment.

For a long time neither spoke, and he bent his head so that his cheek rested on her crown. He filled her heart with his vitality, the way the autumn sun filled the gold and red forest. "Alexis," he finally whispered, "I've thought and thought about the future, but I always come back to the same question, the one I don't want answered: how long would it take before you tired of me, before you began to see me as nothing more than a plain dirt farmer—a clod?"

His words stung her. In her anger and pity, she wanted to deny them. He suffered so badly because he misjudged his own worth—he was so blind. But she said nothing. She wanted to swear that never, never would she see him as less than simply the most wonderful man she'd ever known. How could she utter so simplistic a thought? She had to be realistic. Their worlds were as different as two alien planets. There was no guarantee love could breach the huge gap between them—however much she wanted it to.

She couldn't speak. What was there to say? She wished the love she felt for him could be a talisman to ward off all future sorrow, but it couldn't. She began to cry silently, the tears coursing down her cheeks, soaking into John's shirt. He held her, motionless himself, until he felt those tears touch his skin.

"Stop it, Alexis," he demanded softly. "Stop it, honey."

"I can't help it," she choked, the words catching in her throat. "This is hopeless—this is just hopeless." She hadn't expected him to contradict her. He didn't. His arms tightened, his wide hand coming up to cradle her head. After what seemed an eternity of comforting silence, he spoke. "I've got a surprise for you, sugar. . . ."

"A surprise? What surprise?"

He pulled away a little, grasped her slender shoulders and stared into her eyes. She waited without breathing, unable to imagine what he was about to say.

"Alexis, I've thought about our future all week, and I'm no closer to knowing what it will be. But I do have a surprise and I've got to tell you about it."

"Okay. . . ."

"Do you remember the first time I ever played the fiddle for you?"

"Yes," she said quietly, careful not to reveal any emotion.

"And you hated it. . . ."

"I—"

"It's all right. I know you don't feel that way anymore. But when I saw your face that afternoon, I made up my mind to do something I've been, well, afraid to do for a very long time."

"What?"

"I've accepted an offer that's been extended to me over the years. I've always turned it down until now." He paused, and his face showed not its usual sunny smile, but the clouded expression of a man who feels a momentary twinge of nearly forgotten pain. "When I was at Juilliard," he said, his melodious voice a low song against the soft rustle of the autumn leaves, "I had one friend other than Caroline. His name was—is—Bill Williams, and Bill is a fine violinist. He's also a very persistent man. For years Bill's been trying to convince me to make a concert appearance. He knows I've never played classical music outside my own home or classroom since Caroline died...." Again the clouds passed over the handsome planes of his face. Alexis said nothing, waited for him to resume. He spoke in the slow way of someone who wants to make clear the importance of his message.

"When Caroline was alive, both of us used to do guest performances all over the state. Caroline was more often asked than I, but that worked out fine because she had more time to practice, not having to do farm chores." An unexpected smile skittered across his face. "No, sir," he said with a warm little laugh, "Caroline wasn't one to do chores, that's for sure." Again he paused, and the smile disappeared.

"Anyway, after Caroline died, I couldn't bring myself to take on any concert engagements, and no one asked, either. But after a while the invitations started to come again. To make a long story short, I refused so often that orchestra directors and others who set up recitals and concerts gave up on me—

except for Bill. Every year he writes to tell me that if I want to play with the Arkansas Symphony, all I have to do is give him a call. He wrote to me in the spring, about a week after I first played my fiddle for you. And this time, I called him.''

''You mean you're going to do a concert performance?'' she asked. ''Is that what you've been practicing for?''

''You knew I was practicing? It was supposed to be a secret. I've been at it all summer, Alexis—longer, in fact. I've been at it since the day I saw you wrinkle that fine nose of yours in disgust at my music.''

''No—not disgust. I—I—''

''Look, honey, this performance is a gift to you. It's a way of saying thank you. . . .''

''Thank you?'' She wondered for one agonizing moment whether thank you was the same as good-bye.

''Alexis,'' he said, one long finger stroking her cheek, ''all this week all I've been able to come up with is that I'm not ready to think about our future. I don't mean I don't. . . .'' For an instant his blue eyes burned into hers with such intensity that she knew he was looking his love, though he didn't speak it. ''But I do know you've opened my eyes—my heart. You've made me feel again, Alexis. There were times—there were whole years—in which I thought I'd never be able to feel deeply again. It's been a long time since Caroline. For a long time I've carried the burden of losing her. It wasn't until you came that I was able to lay that burden down. Because you showed me *I'm* not dead, that my feelings are still alive.''

''But how could I—''

"By being yourself, Alexis—bright and beautiful and brave."

"Brave?"

"Yes. And now, I, too, am brave," he said with his usual joking sunny smile. "Brave enough to face the Arkansas Symphony Orchestra, the students and faculty of the University of Arkansas, and the adoring—I hope—public."

"The University of Arkansas...?"

"Yes. That friend of mine, Bill, teaches music there. Very shortly, next week, in fact, the orchestra—which is actually based in Little Rock—is doing a guest appearance at the university in Fayetteville. And the featured soloist is me. And the guest of honor is the person to whom I'm dedicating my performance—you."

OF COURSE SHE WENT with him. Like John, Alexis put aside thoughts of their future. In her own heart there wasn't the slightest doubt that she loved him, more deeply than she could imagine ever loving another man. But she hadn't forgotten the insights that had come to her that afternoon in the blazing autumn forest. Her first months in the mountains had been like a dream, but if she was to live there, it could not be as a dreamer. The world was real. She was real. Her love for Right John Webber was real, too, but that didn't mean it could conquer all her problems, could wipe out the fact that she had come from a far different world, which she couldn't continue to ignore.

On the way to Fayetteville, they stopped to spend a day in Eureka Springs, a remarkably picturesque town built into the hills, claiming the distinction of having no two streets crossing at right angles. And indeed, as John and Alexis wandered the curving, tree-lined avenues, Alexis had to admit she'd never walked in such an unpredictable but lovely place. It seemed to her that each time they turned a corner, yet another storybook house met her eyes. The town was an enclave of Victorian elegance. She delighted in gables and verandas, mansard roofs and cupolas, gazebos and porticoes. Besides being a veritable museum of turn-of-the-century American architecture, Eureka Springs was an artist's colony, and Alexis found great pleasure strolling in and out of studios and shops, speaking to potters and weavers, painters and doll makers.

To her mind, the best thing in the whole town was the magnificent Crescent Hotel. Constructed before 1900, but still in operation, the hotel rose like a castle from among the golden trees of the hills. Looking out the windows of the suite John had booked for them, Alexis could see the whole town spread below. The little shops, the stately homes, churches, stores— all were nestled under trees whose boughs, laden with the richness of autumn, seemed to cradle them in an enduring peace. If only she, too, could find some peace from the doubts about where she should be, who she should be.

She was so deep in thought that she didn't hear John come through the double doors separating their rooms. The suite was old-fashioned in the Victorian style but painted in light colors—shades of beige and pale mauve, with white furniture and sheer white curtains beneath off-white drapes. When he came up behind her, his bare feet silent on the cream-colored rug, she didn't turn—not until he bent his head to kiss the shoulder revealed by the large towel she'd wrapped around herself. "Oh," she said with a little shiver of delight. "You surprised me." She turned then, and caught her breath at the pure masculine beauty of him.

He was dressed only in a white terry-cloth robe. He had one of the hotel towels around his neck because he'd just come from the shower. The thick, tawny mass of his hair was tousled, but the disarray did nothing to hide the shiny vitality of his locks. His skin smelled freshly washed, and he hadn't lost any of the summer tan that set off the indefatigable sparkling blue of his eyes.

The front of his robe was open to the waist in a deep wide vee, revealing his muscled chest and light sprinkling of curly golden hairs. Looking at him, his hands lightly holding on to the edges of the towel around his neck, she felt that even if she didn't know what a good character he had—what a provident father he was, what a dutiful grandson, what a good teacher and farmer—she would still have loved him. Just for the gorgeous way he looked.

Then it occurred to her that what he was determined how he looked, at least to some extent. She doubted, for instance, that his body could ever have been so fine if he didn't work so hard. Thinking of that, but also hungry for him, the way seeing something delicious looking makes one hungry for food, she stepped toward him and placed her hand on his chest, teasingly twining her fingers in the short little curls. He covered her hand with his own, pressing her fingers against his flesh.

"You've finished your shower, I see," he said. "Are you ready to dress for dinner?"

"Not just yet," she answered. The place where his hand touched hers seemed to pulsate—or was it where her hand touched him that tingled? Both, she decided, reaching up to pull the towel from around his neck, replacing it with her own slender arms. As she drew herself up to him, she felt his whole body stiffen, then instantly relax in response. She knew he was as hungry for her as she was for him. Teasingly she began to kiss him. Though she was tall, he was taller, and she had to stand on tiptoe to pepper his wide brow with kisses, to touch his closed eyelids with her soft lips, to continue down along his cheek, his strong jaw.

When she reached his lips and captured them with her own, her tongue thrusting into the willing recesses of his mouth, she took her hands away from his neck, in one swift motion tore open the terry robe, revealing the wonder of his powerful body. Eagerly welcoming her advances, he shook the robe from his shoulders; it landed in a soft pile at his feet. He reached for her, but teasingly she stepped away. He looked at her with a sly grin, as though he enjoyed the game she was playing, would willingly play along. He stood stock-still, waiting.

And she eliminated the little distance between them by extending both hands and closing them around the firm curves of his derriere. He gasped at her touch, but the sound he made was no more impassioned than her own soft moan. To feel his flesh beneath her palms was an enticement, a promise exciting in itself, more exciting in the fulfillment. She kneaded the pliant curves of him, drawing him even closer, feeling his response to her touch in the hard pressure against the towel she still wore. Her hands roamed up to his waist, the sinewy planes of his back. She kept her lips locked to his, her tongue flicking his mobile, working tongue.

She felt her own towel give way. One of his large hands captured her breast, while the other captured her buttocks, kneading, pressing, shooting such spasms of pleasure through her that she thought she'd melt beneath the unrelenting pressure.

His mouth was a devouring heat against her own. His hands teased, touched, pressed, released. Her breath, when it came at all, came in a ragged pattern of deep gasps and sighs. But so did his. So did his. Her hands on his fine, strong body evoked an equal response. Time and again, she felt him shiver as she teased him, skirting over his chest, stopping to caress his nipples, then smoothing down along the flanks of him, reaching for his inner thighs. And then touching where she most wanted to touch—the full power of his manhood.

It was a long time before either of them dressed for dinner. It was a long time before they thought about dinner at all.

CHAPTER EIGHTEEN

ALEXIS TURNED OVER THE PROGRAM in her hand. It
wasn't printed on the thick, creamy, deckled stock
the Chicago Festival Orchestra used. It had been
typewritten and photocopied, and it didn't sport a
photograph of the concert hall, though the modern
Fine Arts Center Alexis was sitting in was well worth
photographing, in her opinion. So charmed had she
been by the university and its friendly personnel that
she had spent the afternoon interviewing professors
and students; she knew she could turn the information into saleable articles. She'd managed to interview a few of the artisans in Eureka Springs, too. It
felt good to be back on track in her work. There was
her first decent article ideas since she'd come back
from Chicago. John had joked that if he'd known
she was taking a working vacation, he would have
had her interview *him*. She took him seriously, telling
him she would do so immediately following his concert.

They had spent the day apart, because John had
had to rehearse with the orchestra. Alexis had no
trouble filling her free time on the university's downtown campus, which had been established more than
one hundred years before and now had fourteen
thousand students. The older parts of the campus in-

terested her especially, and the fact that it was autumn made her tour of the school all the more heartwarming, since it reminded her of Wallace Smythe. As a tiny child, she had gone with him "to work" at the University of Chicago once or twice a month. He told her much later that he'd done it so she wouldn't think he disappeared into nowhere every day.

As the afternoon had progressed, Alexis had grown more and more nervous. She remembered the first few times she'd been in the audience at performances conducted by Karl Hulst. She was as nervous as it was possible to be. But one day it occurred to her that Karl himself didn't know the meaning of the word. He was cool and calm, like a plumber approaching a familiar tangle of pipes. "The score is simply a tangle of notes," he had joked when she had spoken to him about his lack of stage fright. "I don't like to be distracted before a concert because I don't want my concentration disturbed. But nervous? Never, my dear."

It was different from Right John. He hadn't eaten a thing at dinner, even though Dora Williams, Bill's wife, had gone to great lengths to make the dinner special. So concerned was John about hurting Dora's feelings, that at one point when both host and hostess left the dining room, John asked Alexis if she wouldn't mind eating some of his dinner. She obliged, but she herself was nervous—and full. She ate John's food in silence, determining that someday a long time from now, she would jokingly tell him just what a sacrifice she'd made for the sake of his honor. She didn't even notice that her usual doubt about there even being a "someday" was absent.

The Williams family—Dora, Bill and three children older than Patience—had welcomed John and Alexis as if the visiting couple were royalty. Not only had they provided dinner, but they also offered a place to stay overnight after the concert. The members of the university's music faculty were exceptionally hospitable, as well; they seemed to recognize John by dint of his reputation. She noted with pride that John carried himself with a sophistication totally appropriate to a guest artist. Once again it occurred to her that there were layers to this exceptional man's personality, layers it would take years to uncover and appreciate.

Dora, Bill and the children sat beside her in the second row of the concert hall. Once in a while Dora made some polite comment to Alexis as they waited for the rest of the audience to file in until the hall was full. Then members of the orchestra began to come on stage. Alexis smiled a bit. *Orchestras all over the world must be the same,* she thought as she watched the musicians, all formally dressed. One or two of them chatted and laughed nonchalantly, as if the prospect of performing wasn't frightening at all. Others practiced some passage or other over and over again in a last-ditch effort to make sure they had it as near perfect as possible. Most plucked, struck, blew or hammered their instruments in a final tuning that filled the concert hall with the anticipation only that sound can bring.

Alexis wasn't sure that what she felt should be called anticipation. *Maybe terror would be a better word for it,* she thought. Her heart was in her mouth. John hadn't played like this for more than a decade.

Even though music was his livelihood, there was a difference between fiddling with a country band and soloing with a symphony orchestra. Alexis didn't even know what he was going to play. She hadn't asked him, not wanting to be overly curious about the "surprise."

When she opened the program she'd been idly toying with, she got two shocks. The first was that John was going to play the immensely challenging Beethoven violin concerto. Secondly, beneath the announcement of this fact on the program, there was another statement, set off in italic type. It said, "Our guest artist gratefully dedicates this evening's performance to Alexis Juneau Smythe."

The warm smile on her lips was visible to no one as the houselights dimmed and the conductor stepped onto the stage to welcoming applause. For a moment Alexis felt totally disoriented, because this was the first time she had sat in the audience of a symphony orchestra since she and Karl had parted company. It was the first time in a long time she'd seen anyone but him conduct. When she had adjusted to that fact, she realized John would be stepping onto the stage as soon as the overture was over. This particular selection was not one of Alexis's favorite pieces. In fact, she usually found it interminable. But tonight it seemed to fly by. The audience applauded, the conductor bowed and left the stage. The orchestra squeaked and grunted with more tuning. And then there was silence, a silence in which Alexis imagined the sound of her own heartbeat was filling the hall, pounding in nervous love and expectation.

The people at the far right of the hall saw him first

and began to applaud before Alexis caught sight of him. He entered from the wings, preceding the conductor to the podium. At first, she wasn't thoroughly convinced the performer was John. He was dressed in black tails. Even the most formal of clothing couldn't hide the fact that he was a very large man. His shoulders beneath the perfectly tailored jacket with its black satin lapels were obviously wide. The jacket was nipped in at the waist, flaring slightly at his narrow hips. Beneath the jacket he wore the traditional white silk cummerbund and multipleated shirt. A white silk bow tie completed his formal wear.

He looked like a magnificent stranger. His tawny hair was perfectly groomed, sweeping across his wide brow. Alexis wasn't one hundred percent sure this man, easily the most handsome she'd ever seen, was also the man she loved, until he lifted his eyes to the applauding audience. Ah, yes, it was like looking into the May sky—clear blue—and enough of it to make your heart sing. For one instant his eyes sought and found hers, seeming to pierce the darkness of the hall. There was no doubt in her mind anymore. No doubts about anything at all.

He stood poised as the orchestra began, the opening drumbeats of the piece echoing her own heartbeat. The exquisite theme winged its way out into the theatre. Then it was time for the solo entry. John lifted his instrument to his chin. His powerful hands were not then the hands of the farmer, hands Alexis had seen sift the rich soil of his grandfather's land. Nor were they the hands of the lover, their touch making her body one song for his singing. They were the hands of the artist, not only sensitive, but sure.

As his bow came down upon the waiting strings of his violin, the sound that Beethoven had intended for the piece filled the hall. It was the tone not only of beauty but of authority, also, and hearing the opening notes, like a drawn breath magnificent in the restraint of its passion, Alexis already knew John's playing would be masterful.

He had told her she had taught him to feel again. If she needed any proof of the truth of that statement, it was in the music he played that night. When the music was impassioned, he played with a power that held the audience spellbound. When it was tender, the musician was unspeakably touching. And when the soul of the gruff composer took flight and soared away from the mundane world to the clean, unfettered heights, Right John Webber flew, too, his bow as light as wind, his touch as swift as a wingbeat, as compelling as the flight of a single bird. Alexis felt her love for him swell with the strains he was playing.

When the final notes echoed, then faded to the farthest recesses of the hall, there was a moment's respectful silence, before rapturous applause. He was called back for three bows, after which he did an encore, a Paganini showpiece that left the audience gasping before they again demanded his presence on stage so they could accord him the ultimate tribute: a standing ovation.

He was thrilled. His reaction was nothing like Karl's, the times he had received such a tribute. Karl would remain cool, offering a slight smile, a courtly bow in response to the audience's enthusiasm. Not so John. He was positively beaming. When he opened his strong arms as though to embrace the whole audience, their clapping became even louder, even more approving.

But a little while later, seeing her walk backstage, he grabbed her tightly. She could tell he was trembling, even though he was happier than she'd ever known him to be. "I did it, sugar," he whispered for her ears alone. "I *did* it!"

"You certainly did, love—you were wonderful," she said in the moment they had together before he was swamped by admirers. He hid the lingering effects of his nervousness so well that only Alexis knew he wasn't at all as calm as he seemed, greeting the dozens upon dozens of well-wishers.

There was a reception afterward, not oysters and caviar and a little too much champagne, as there always had been at Karl's reception. Here there were homemade sandwiches and cakes and a little champagne, which Bill Williams used to toast what he called "the reawakening of a major talent." A reporter from Little Rock monopolized quite a bit of John's time, and when the reporter left, John turned and winked at Alexis, saying she'd just have to interview him later when he had plenty of time to reveal his private side. She laughed at his teasing, as did Dora and Bill, the only other people close enough to hear. The joke served as the cue for Bill to spirit John and Alexis away from the reception, explaining that the guest artist had had a long and tiring day.

THE NEXT MORNING at breakfast, Bill was full of plans for future concerts. John told him he could make no promises, but all Bill would say was, "We'll see. We'll see." He begged John to stay longer, at least for the day, but John explained that they'd been away for a couple of days, and that he felt a little uneasy leaving his daughter. She seemed a bit under the weather lately. Bill nodded at this. As the father of teenagers himself, he appeared to understand John perfectly.

With heartfelt gratitude and many promises of future visits back and forth, Alexis and John pulled away from the Williamses' suburban house. But instead of heading for the highway and home, John took a turn toward the center of Fayetteville.

"Where are we going?" Alexis asked when she realized the direction they were headed.

"I have to show you something," John answered, and it wasn't long before he pulled into a pleasant street, not as new nor as prosperous as the street the Williamses lived on. Alexis watched in silence as they passed dozens of ordinary homes. She hadn't spent much time in neighborhoods like this, though she realized millions of average Americans had grown up on just such a street.

"Where are you taking me?" she asked. There was no concern in her voice, just interest.

John didn't answer immediately. In fact, he didn't answer at all until they'd pulled up opposite a small frame house exactly like every other house on the street. "I can't take you in because I don't know who lives there now, but I lived there once. Until the day I moved to Old John's farm, I called that house home. It's been a long time since it was good enough for my mom and dad, who, as you know, have moved to Houston."

"It's a lovely house," Alexis said, partly to be

polite and partly because she didn't know what else to say.

"No, it's not, Alexis. It's an ordinary house, as ordinary as can be. I wanted you to see it for a reason."

"What reason?" she asked apprehensively. She was getting the feeling something important was going on—she couldn't put her finger on what exactly.

"I want you to see where I come from, Alexis, because I wanted to make sure you understand what I am—what I'll always be. Eventually my father found me, as well as the house, not good enough for him, which is why I never much see him anymore. The same is true of your mother's friend, Mrs. Evelyn Kain. She did everything in her power to convince Caroline I was worthless. Caroline, God love her and rest her soul, never listened to a word her mother said. I, however, almost came to believe Evelyn's opinion of me must be correct."

"I wasn't aware you'd even met her."

"I met her only once—at Caroline's funeral—on which occasion she did me the honor of slapping me in the face in the presence of the assembled bereaved, for the sole reason that I was, in her words, 'a dirty uneducated hillbilly.' "

"Oh, my Lord!"

"Over the years, she's made a number of efforts to get Patience up there—most of them directed at proving me unfit as a parent. If she'd been more reasonable about things, I would have been happy to let Patience spend time in Chicago. But she hasn't been reasonable. At times she waged what amounted to a smear campaign against me—letters, phone calls, visits from her lawyer. When Patience was ten or so, she seemed to give up. All she accomplished was to destroy any desire I might have had to encourage my daughter to maintain contact with her mother's family. As for myself, my dealings with Evelyn Kain have renewed my determination to stay where I belong.''

He was silent for a moment. Then he leaned over, and taking her hand in his, gazed into her blue-green eyes. ''Alexis,'' he said softly, ''when I'm away from the hills I don't know what I'm worth. I've done the best I could for Old John and for Patience, and for my music. But I'm not any sort of a fancy man. I'm not rich, and I'm not sure that a woman who's known the kind of men you have would find me handsome. But I do know one thing. I love you. I know, too, that the world you come from is not like the world I offer. No matter how much I think about it, I can't figure any way out of our situation, except one. I want you to come and live with me, Alexis. And around here—at least among the Webbers—that means one thing: I want you to marry me. I want to know whether you will.''

She could have told him she had already decided it would be better for them both if she just went home and resumed her career. She could have told him that yes, their worlds were as different as diamonds and dust, that when she thought about their future, she couldn't visualize it. She could have told him she had never dreamed she would someday be considering marriage with a farmer who didn't even own his own farm—or a musician who lived by such a seemingly chancy thing as talent. She could have told him anything.

She told him yes.

CHAPTER NINETEEN

IT WAS ONLY A HUNDRED OR SO MILES from Fayetteville to Mountain View, but they took their time, stopping now and then to view the remaining autumn leaves that were pale gold and brown instead of the blazing reds and oranges of a week before. They stopped at a country restaurant for a leisurely lunch. As the strain of John's concert appearance had dissipated, he'd regained his appetite, and Alexis watched in amazement as he put away a truly man-sized lunch.

At one point she excused herself to use the ladies' room. When she stepped back out she was surprised to see the proprietor and his wife and the two waitresses gathered around John. Approaching the table, Alexis saw that the proprietor held an open newspaper. The women were obviously offering words of admiration, and John was graciously accepting their praise. "What's going on?" she asked as she came up behind the proprietor, glancing over his shoulder. There, in all the splendor of his formal attire, stood J. Wright Webber beneath the headline, "The Reawakening Of A Major Talent."

"We recognized you soon as you came in," one of the women said.

"This here's the *Arkansas Gazette*," the proprietor explained, apparently for Alexis's benefit. "Most famous newspaper in the state."

"Yes, yes, of course. I've heard of it," Alexis answered. She didn't add that she herself had had an article published there not long ago, nor that she knew the paper was a metropolitan daily with a substantial circulation. As she read the rave review of John's performance, she couldn't help but be pleased as punch that he was getting that kind of exposure.

When the admirers left the table, insisting John take the paper free of charge, Alexis said, "Oh, John, how wonderful! Did you read what they said about you?"

"No, I—"

"Listen—just listen to this—"

"Don't read it to me, Alexis. I've never read a review of my work yet, and I don't intend to start."

"Why not?"

"Things like that give you a swelled head. I don't need it."

"But that's unprofessional."

"Alexis, if I read about how wonderful that reporter thought I was, I may get scared that I'll never be able to play that well again, or give another concert."

"You mean there's a possibility you might do more concerts?" She couldn't keep the hopefulness out of her voice.

"We'll see," was all he'd say.

ALEXIS WAS RATHER QUIET for the rest of the ride home. She was preoccupied with the thought that she'd accepted John's proposal. Her manners prevented her from asking him to stop on the highest peak of the Ozarks so she could shout her joy to all the world. But nothing prevented her from feeling that joy—not even the fact that there were a million things to think about, to take care of, that hadn't been there that morning. She would have to break the news to Margaret. It wasn't going to be easy, telling her mother she was about to marry a man Margaret had never met. Yet Margaret knew about John Webber and had seemed very sympathetic about his past. Alexis hoped she would be as sympathetic about his future!

There was her career to consider, as well. Alexis was still stalling on the question of the inner-city newspaper series. Marrying John would mean the project would definitely be off. Alexis would have expected to feel more disappointed about that. Over the weeks, she'd been deliberating on every angle of the project, and she had to admit her enthusiasm for the series had increased only as the possibility of a future with John decreased, a defense mechanism. She felt remarkably easy about the career aspect of things. She *was* a real writer, and she would find stories. In fact, she was living a story she might some-day have the objectivity to tell—''Chicago Socialite Opts for Hillbilly Home!''

She smiled at the imaginary headline, but the facts behind it were no joke. When she had accepted John's proposal, she had said yes to farm life, to southern life. The implications of that decision might just take her the rest of her life to work out. She glanced over at the strong profile of the man she loved, and saw that he didn't turn to acknowledge her look, keeping his eyes on the twisting mountain road because he knew their safety was in his hands. And she was filled with a faith that canceled any fears. It wouldn't be easy adopting a whole new way of life. Yet it was easy to love John Webber, and that love would carry her through the rough spots. She was going to work from that moment on to preserve the feeling between them.

By midafternoon they were on the outskirts of Mountain View, and John asked Alexis whether she wanted to go directly to Lizzie's. She said no, she'd rather go with him to the farm. He understood without asking that she wanted to announce their news to his grandfather. Reaching over, he tenderly caressed her hand before turning onto the farm road.

At the sound of the car, Almeda and Old John ran out to the wooden porch to greet the returned travelers. So full of good news—about the concert and themselves—were John and Alexis that they didn't notice how tense the older couple were. "Welcome back, son," Old John said when his grandson stepped up and put his large hand on the old farmer's skinny shoulder. Right John leaned over and kissed Almeda. Alexis, standing a few steps behind, noticed that kiss didn't elicit the broad smile Almeda usually offered in exchange, but she didn't make anything of the fact.

"Come on in, boy," Almeda said, putting a hand on John's arm.

"How'd the concert go?" Old John asked as they all headed back toward the kitchen.

"Here," John said. "You can read all about it." And with a broad grin, he handed his grandfather the newspaper. It was folded at the page where John's photograph appeared, and when his eye fell on the picture, Old John's face absolutely glowed with pride.

"Well, now," he said. "Will you look at that...."

Almeda took the paper, and in a moment, her face, too, broke into a pleased smile.

"I want to show Patience," Right John said. "Where is she?"

Both Old John and Almeda raised their faces to him. Alexis noticed at once that their smiles had faded, their eyes expressing fear and sorrow.

"She ain't here, son," Old John said.

"Is she over at Roosevelt's?" John questioned. "I'll just phone and—"

"I think you better sit down, John," Almeda said.

"What?" John asked, not yet understanding that something was wrong—very wrong, indeed. Alexis, with her reporter's instinct, had already figured out the older couple's nervousness was uncharacteristic enough to indicate some major problem.

"Why should I sit down? What's going on around here? Where is my daughter?" Right John was white as a sheet. He did sit down—in fact, he sank into the nearest chair. Alexis rushed over and put her hand on his broad shoulder, but he seemed not to notice. "My God." His voice filled with an emotion Alexis didn't want to name. "My God, something's happened to Patience...."

"Son," Old John said, standing, too, beside the younger man and putting a frail hand on his strong back. "She's gone. She's just up and took off. She ain't been here since the night you left. We've had the police. Last night they asked us questions near to all night long. 'Meda and I, we ain't—''

"What do you mean she's gone?" John cried, turning so sharply that both Old John's and Alexis's hands fell away. "You were supposed to be keeping an eye on her."

"We couldn't watch her every second, John," Almeda answered. "She's not a babe."

"She's only fourteen years old, for God's sake," John said. His voice was husky, with none of its usual melodiousness. "What the hell is a fourteen-year-old girl doing away from her own home for two nights? Did she go with someone?"

"Nobody else's gone missin'," Old John said sadly.

The word "missing" hung like an ominous presence in the air.

"My God!" Right John shouted. "She'll be at the mercy of anybody that runs across her. My God!"

"Stop cussin', son," Old John said. "Time to be prayin' rather than cussin'."

John paid the old man no heed. He went for the telephone in two giant strides and grabbed at the receiver. Alexis could see his fingers were shaking as he dialed. Whoever he was calling answered almost immediately, and John didn't waste any time on pleasantries. "Barton," he demanded into the phone, "you light a shuck and you get on down here. I want to talk to you, understand?" There was a pause. As he listened to the other man speak, the lines of tension in John Webber's face seemed to deepen. Alexis wanted to go to him, to smooth those lines with the delicate touch of loving fingers. But she didn't move.

She waited breathlessly for him to say something more, hoping whoever this Barton was would have some answers.

"Not in two days?" John asked. "You've had your cruisers all over the county and you haven't had a single clue in two days?" Alexis understood then that he was talking to the police. He listened, bowing his head and covering his eyes with his hand. Alexis started for him, then, fearing he'd heard bad news, but Almeda stayed her, putting her hand on the younger woman's arm. There was another pause, and when John dropped his hand and revealed his eyes they were full of tears. Nonetheless, he kept his voice steady as he said, "I realize what the dangers are, Barton. You don't need to point them out. Could you come out here, please? I'd like to talk to you and your boys."

In the next twelve hours, Alexis watched as his mood swung from hope to despair and back again a number of times. He made a valiant effort to control his emotions, but there were times when the possible consequences of a fourteen-year-old girl being lost in the hills were just too much for him to think about. Alexis tried to comfort him, realizing with dismay that she didn't know him well enough to know what to do.

She remembered how differently she and Margaret had reacted to the tragedy of Wallace's death. Her father had seemed in perfect health one morning as he left for his office at the university. Later that same afternoon, he'd been found slumped over his desk, dead of a heart attack. Alexis had spoken to as many of his friends as she could contact in the weeks that followed. Somehow, being among those who had known him eased her pain. Margaret, on the other hand, had locked herself away, insisting she couldn't bear to see anyone. Alexis had learned there are different styles of grief, different means to console and comfort.

It seemed to her that what John wanted right now was no comfort at all, because he didn't want to acknowledge there might be a need for any. He grilled poor Almeda and Old John, going over and over the details of the last time they'd seen Patience. He questioned Roosevelt's family. He questioned the neighbors. He harangued the police for not intercepting him in his journey to Fayetteville. They insisted he couldn't have done anything, anyway. After hours of talk leading nowhere, John was showing unmistakable signs of exhaustion. He sent everyone home. There was nothing anyone could add to the information he had, or subtract from his sadness and worry. Even Almeda and Old John slipped away.

Only Alexis was left in the untidy kitchen, where the man she loved sat down at the kitchen table and laid his weary head on his folded arms. She came up to him and gently put her hand on his shoulder. He didn't lift his head, but he did lift a hand to caress her fingers. At this sign that he wanted her near, she sat in the chair beside his and stroked his tawny hair with her free hand. She could see his shoulders relax, and moments later his deep even breathing. She sat motionless for a while, then made to rise, intending to leave him to his hard-bought sleep.

Her motion awakened him, and as though he hadn't been sleeping, but thinking, he said, "I know people disappear every day. But I just can't believe it could happen to Patience. Not just because she's mine— though there's that to it, too—but because she's never been one to do much wandering on her own. In all the time she's been around, that kid has never even so much as strolled into a meadow by herself. I used to joke with her that she wasn't really a country kid at all...." Suddenly his expression changed entirely. Alexis saw there the first sign of real hope.

"What is it?" she asked, her emotions ping-ponging between optimism and fear.

"Evelyn Kain!"

"What?"

"How in the hell did it take me this long to figure it out?"

"What are you talking about?"

He didn't answer. Once again he went for the phone. She heard only a single sentence. "I want the number of the residence of Mrs. Evelyn Kain in Chicago."

It wasn't long before he slammed down the receiver in frustration. "Unlisted," John spat through clenched teeth. "Of course it's unlisted." Another idea came to him, and he went over to one of the kitchen-counter drawers, rifling through its contents; coupons, paper bags, little rolls of string went flying as John dug. Realizing all four members of the household kept things in that drawer, things they seldom used but wanted to save, Alexis knew John was searching for the slip of paper one of them had written Evelyn's number on. Reaching for her purse, she extracted a small leather-bound, gilt-edged book and handed it to John. "The number's in here."

He took the book without comment, headed across the room and again grabbed the phone. After a few moments he hung up. "It's a recording," he said. "It's a recording made by one of Evelyn Kain's lackeys, announcing that madam's personal secretary will receive calls after ten in the morning." The disgust in his voice was undisguised, but it quickly changed to determination. "I'm going to call the Chicago police," he said, picking up the receiver.

"No!" Alexis cried, rushing over to cover the phone dial with her hand.

"What are you doing?" John asked in consternation. "Don't you want to know whether my daughter is safe?"

"Of course, I do, John. But you can't send the police banging on Evelyn's door in the middle of the night."

"Why not?"

"She'd die of shame, for one thing."

"So what?"

"John, it's not necessary to— Look, if Patience is with Evelyn, she's safe. If she's not with Evelyn, what good will it do to scare the wits out of an old woman?"

"Alexis," he said, his low voice strained with the effort to control his fatigue—and anger. "I've long ago given up any shred of consideration I might have had for my ex-mother-in-law. Before you came here, I hadn't spoken to her in nearly five years. As far as I was concerned, that wasn't long enough. When Patience discovered she was a friend of your mother's—" Again he stopped in the middle of his sentence, as though the words themselves had made him realize something. Watching the changing expression on his face, Alexis felt her heart sink. He looked up at her, and in the blue depths of his eyes a new light shone, the light of ice. "Alexis, you don't want me to send the police because you know she *is* there. You *know* my daughter is safe in her grandmother's damn mansion."

"I...w-well, as soon as you said..." she stuttered. Somehow she was sure.

"And not only are you sure of where she is—you helped her to get there."

"What? What are you saying?"

"How could I have been so stupid? How could I possibly have accepted the story that you had come down here to the Ozarks to write? Mountain View is a dot on the map, not that different from a million other dots all over the country. Why should you come here? Let me rephrase that. Why should the daughter of Madam Kain's very best friend just suddenly show up here in the middle of nowhere to write pretty stories about us hillbillies, unless she had some other little task in mind at the same time...?"

"I don't know what you're talking about."

"Yes. Yes, you do, Ms Alexis Juneau Smythe." His low voice was as melodious as ever, only at the moment it was full of such contempt, such distrust, that Alexis cringed to hear it. "You came here with a plan, and tonight that plan finally came to fruition, didn't it? You and Evelyn Kain have got what she wanted all along—revenge for what happened to Caroline. In the form of getting my daughter away from me. If you were going for the one thing that would hurt me the most, you've succeeded."

"John, how can you accuse me?" She was near tears, but she had no defense. If he asked the question she feared he was about to ask, everything would be finished between them—for good this time. There was a moment's tense silence. A moment in which she gathered her thoughts. But it was too late, too late to tell him she had come not to do as Evelyn Kain had bid, but to meet *him*. That would have sounded just plain ridiculous, even though it was true.

"Alexis," he said coolly, "I want to be fair. Until tonight, until these past few moments, I never questioned your being among us. I believed you'd come down here because of the folk center. It never occurred to me to even ask whether you'd ever written about folk art before. And when you told me, quite accidentally, that you hadn't, I let it pass. Now I'm going to ask you point blank. Did Evelyn Kain request that you come down here because of Patience?"

She waited as long as she could to answer. It seemed she could hear all the minutes of her happiness, the few remaining minutes, tick away into the silence. There was nothing she could tell him but the truth. "Yes," she said. "Yes, Evelyn did ask me. And I didn't refuse." She heard him sigh then, a mixture of disappointment and despair. She had no intention of begging him for forgiveness. She knew she'd done nothing wrong, but she could feel the hard ache of coming tragedy already beginning in her heart. Calmly she attempted to explain, "Evelyn Kain has asked me for many favors over the years. Generally, I pay lip service to her demands, because she's such an old friend of the family. I merley listened to her plans. By the time I'd been down here for a few weeks, I forgot all about her request..."

"But it was you who convinced Patience to go with you to Chicago the last time."

His insinuation was patently unfair, but she maintained her poise, as she'd been so well trained to do. "No," Alexis said with dignity. "I'm afraid you're wrong. It was Patience herself who was dead set on getting to Chicago. The girl had dreamed about it for months. My coming here was just a lucky accident as far as she was concerned. You shouldn't underestimate that girl. She has her own ambitions, her own dreams."

"I don't think I need you to tell me about my own child," John said sharply. He was still very angry, but Alexis could sense the focus of his anger was shifting—perhaps he was beginning to see she would never have betrayed him.

"I'm going up there, right now, to Little Rock. There's got to be a plane first thing in the morning."

"John, don't do it. If you yank Patience out of her grandmother's house, you're going to cause a rift that'll never be healed."

"Good. That's just what I'd like between me and Evelyn Kain. That woman has wanted my skin from the first moment she ever heard my name."

"I'm not talking about a rift between you and Evelyn. I'm talking about between you and your child."

"So what do you suggest? That I leave her up there and let Evelyn turn her into the sort of useless nothing she tried to turn Caroline into?"

"Let me go get her."

"You? Why should you. . . ?"

"Because I can talk to Evelyn—and to Patience. Because I know the territory, John." Tenderly Alexis placed her hand on his shoulder. He brushed it away. He'd had many hours of fear, worry, and now anger. His gesture caused anger to rise in her, too, but she stifled it. She remembered her vow that morning, to preserve her love for this man. If she let negative feelings conquer her, she would be untrue to herself and him. "Let me go and get her and bring her home."

"All right," he said. "All right. But if anything happens to her—if she suffers any damage from this whatsoever—I'm holding you personally responsible. As far as I'm concerned, you're a spy for Evelyn Kain. You can give me any fancy excuse you want to about why you've stuck around down here, but the way I see it, there was only one reason for your coming in the first place. I'm going to bed. Call me in three hours, and I'll take you to Little Rock. Good night." And he strode out of the room, leaving Alexis standing alone amid the ruins of all her dreams.

Soon she would feel hurt, so hurt that she would wonder how someone so unfairly treated as she knew herself to be could continue to draw breath without sobbing. Soon she would ask herself over and over how he could ever have loved her if he could mistrust her so. Soon. At the moment the only emotion she felt was anger—total rage, which sparked its own crude energy. She would go and get Patience, all right— she'd go and get the willful girl. She'd bring her home to her equally willful and thoroughly detestable father. She'd give each of them what they deserved—each other. And then she'd bid good riddance to them both!

CHAPTER TWENTY

ALEXIS DIDN'T WAKE HIM. She didn't go to Little Rock with him. She didn't even leave him a message. She slept on the Webbers' couch until dawn. Then she called Lizzie and got her to come out and take her to the airport at Harrison, where Alexis managed to get a flight before noon.

She knew her mother was shocked to see her with no advance notice, but she put up as good a front as Margaret did. "What brings you here, dear?" the older woman calmly asked, as if Alexis had dropped in for tea. She answered that she had some urgent business to conduct. When Margaret asked whether that business had anything to do with Evelyn Kain's young visitor, Alexis breathed a sigh of relief. She left the house the minute she had showered and changed, knowing her mother would understand the reason for her abrupt departure.

It was late afternoon when the Smythe chauffeur pulled up the circular drive of the Kain mansion. He left his car for a moment to see Alexis to the door. This, of course, wasn't standard procedure, but she was arriving unannounced, so there would be no one to greet her when she arrived. Without hesitation she gave the huge brass knocker a sharp rap. The door was answered by an employee familiar to Alexis. She nodded in dismissal to her chauffeur, even though Mrs. Kain's employee hadn't asked her in. In fact, the employee was very cold, insisting Mrs. Kain was occupied serving tea to a guest. Alexis replied that that was quite all right; she was there to see the woman's granddaughter.

"I believe you are mistaken," the employee said in clipped tones. "Madam's granddaughter lives in the south." As the woman spoke, Alexis glanced past her. In the well-lit recess of the wide entrance hall stood Patience. The girl was poised on the bottom step of the marble staircase, as though she'd been about to step into the hall but had frozen at the sound of Alexis's voice. Without thinking of the consequences, Alexis pushed the woman at the door aside and ran across the hall, heading for the stairs. She ignored the woman's discreetly voiced protest. It was the first time Alexis had ever entered anyone's home without invitation—but she couldn't care less. All she cared about was catching up with Patience, who had darted back up the stairs.

Patience was faster than she was. As Alexis mounted the last of the stairs, facing a long corridor stretching in either direction, she heard a door slam a short distance away. She was familiar enough with Evelyn's home to know that door lead to the library; Patience must be taking refuge in the huge room. Alexis made her way to the heavy oak door, knocked hard. There was no response, so she tried again. This time she heard a muffled, "Go away."

"Patience," she called through the door, as loudly as she dared. "I've just crashed in here. Any minute now a security employee is going to throw me out—

unless you let me in that room. I want to talk to you. It's just me—nobody else is here. Let me in, honey.''

At first there was no answer, and Alexis panicked for a moment when she heard voices from the bottom of the stairs. The woman who had answered the door was giving instructions to a guard. Alexis almost turned and headed back down the stairs, but just then the large wooden door opened a crack; a slender young hand beckoned Alexis in.

Patience looked not at all as Alexis had imagined she would. For one thing, she wasn't dressed as she had been the last time Alexis had come to pick her up at her grandmother's. Today the girl wore faded denims and a soiled T-shirt. Though her tawny hair was shiningly clean, she hadn't bothered to style it. It stuck out wildly from her head, emphasizing the look of fear that sat on her young face like a ghost on a tombstone. Alexis's first impulse was to hug the girl, to tell her she didn't have to be afraid. But she didn't approach her. She stood before the door Patience had hastily locked and waited for John's daughter to speak.

"Did daddy send you to rescue me?'' Patience asked, her voice hovering between defiance and begging. She must have spent a lot of the past three days crying. Her young face was puffy, and she wore none of the expensive makeup her grandmother had bought her.

"No, not exactly,'' Alexis said carefully. "Your father knows I'm here, but he didn't send me. I offered to come.''

"Why?'' The word shot out at her, a challenge. Alexis remained calm.

"Because I care about you. And because I care about your dad. Do you realize how you've frightened him?"

"Frightened? Him? He's not afraid of anything." This wasn't said as a boast. It was a way of indicating Patience didn't believe John cared about her. Alexis understood this intuitively, tried to find a way to convey to the girl that her father cared more deeply than she could imagine.

"Patience," she said gently, "your father thought you were in grave danger. He thought you might be dead. Do you understand what that means? You are his own flesh and blood. You are dearer to him than anything else in this whole world. And not only that, you're all he has left of your mother...." She couldn't go on, because Patience was weeping. She stood, her slender hands over her face, her young body racked with sobs. Quickly Alexis took her in her arms, held her until her sobs subsided a bit and she was able to talk.

"He's going to kill me," Patience said brokenly.

"Of course not," Alexis soothed. "He's never laid a hand on you in all your life."

"No—no. I mean he's going to hate me. He's going to think I hate him.... I never should have done this. I never should have run away. But if I go back now, I'll never be able to come to Chicago again. I'm going to be stuck in one place or the other for the rest of my life...."

Despite her concern, Alexis couldn't help smiling at the girl's simplistic way of stating what was obviously a very complicated problem. If she could get Patience to talk about things a little more sensibly, they might come to some understanding that would satisfy the needs of both father and child. Gently Alexis led Patience over to one of the library's many overstuffed, red velvet sofas. As they sat down, Alexis heard a knock on the door, and a man's voice, evidently that of the security guard, called out, "Are you all right, Miss Patience?"

"Get lost, Henson," Patience yelled back at the top of her lungs.

"Very well, miss," the man answered, not revealing in his tone how he felt about being insulted by a fourteen-year-old. If Patience was to stay at her grandmother's any longer, she needed a good lesson in how to treat household employees.

"Do you think you'd like to talk about things a bit?" Alexis began, not sure what to say.

"What's there to talk about? I ran away. I'm sorry I hurt daddy, but...Alexis, he deserves it."

"I don't really understand how anybody could deserve to be hurt, Patience, though surely people do deserve to have their mistakes pointed out to them." She thought about a few mistakes she herself would like to point out to Right John Webber, but she'd have to deal with that later. "What is it your father did that was so bad it drove you from home?"

"He doesn't understand anything," Patience declared. "And he doesn't care about anything but that stupid farm. He doesn't even care about music."

"Patience! How can you say a thing like that? He's one of the finest teachers at the center. Everybody says that!"

"If he cared about music, really cared, he'd play real music—not hillbilly stuff. You know that recital he promised we'd have, the both of us together? Well, we never did it. We—"

"He was busy, Patience; he was practicing for his concert. Didn't he tell you about that? About playing Beethoven with the orchestra?"

"Yeah, he told me. He invited me to come, but—" The girl stopped. Her face took on a strange expression, a look balanced somewhere between defiance and shame.

"But you didn't want to come? Why?" Alexis was silent, awaiting the girl's reply, but when Patience didn't answer, she suddenly suspected the reason for the girl's hesitation. "Had you been planning this for some time?"

"What do you mean?"

"The escape—running away. Had you planned all along to do this to your father as soon as you got a chance?" There was anger in her voice now. Quite without wanting to, she found herself defending John, taking his side, even though she'd lost nothing of her feeling that she was an outsider as far as his family was concerned. Her own anger communicated itself to John's daughter, who responded heatedly.

"No! No, I didn't plan anything. I didn't go with daddy because I knew he wanted to be alone with you. I only ran away when I couldn't stand things one minute longer. Everybody thinks Old John is so funny. I think he's a pain. I just made up my mind I didn't want to stay with him anymore. We had an argument, and I went running out of the house. I was headed toward Lizzie's. I forgot you weren't there. I got halfway down the road when I remembered. I was so mad I couldn't think straight, so I sat down in the woods for a bit and I just went over everything in my mind, and I decided I wanted to strike out on my own.''

"But Patience, you're only—"

"Daddy wasn't very old when he went to New York. And that was a long time ago. People are smarter earlier now. Everybody says so. Besides, I knew there was somebody I could go to in Chicago...."

"But how did you get here?"

"I went back to the house. I pretended to make up with great-grandpa. I went to bed, and so did he and Almeda. The two of them sleep sounder than a rock in a rainstorm. I waited. And then I...." She hesitated for a moment, shrugged her shoulders. "Then I just ran away."

"What do you mean you just ran away?" Alexis had no intention of succumbing to the girl's evasions. She could see Patience was hiding something important. "Where did you get the money?"

"I didn't steal anything, if that's what you think!" Patience jumped up from the couch, but she didn't go far. She stood with her back to Alexis, her shoulders thin and vulnerable beneath her T-shirt. Her head was bent. She seemed to be thinking hard, trying to decide what to say, what to do.

"Patience," Alexis said, nearly whispering, "what's going on? How did you get here?" She rose and put her hand on the girl's shoulder. Patience didn't push her away. There was a moment of perfect stillness, the lovely woman and the rumpled teenager poised like two beautifully executed statues. Then Alexis felt the slender shoulder beneath her hand begin to tremble with renewed weeping. Without turning, Patience began to talk brokenly, to tell Alexis the full story.

"When I was here the last time, grandmother told me all about Caroline—about my mother. She said my mother was so talented it was certain she'd be a soloist with any orchestra she wanted to appear with. Grandmother said that when my mother went to Juilliard all the teachers raved about her. She was going to be one of the best clarinetists ever.

"And then she ran into daddy. I know from what Old John told me, and from granddaddy who lives in Houston, that daddy could have been a star, too. Grandmother Kain said it was daddy's fault neither of them amounted to anything. She said he was just a farmer and that's all he'd ever be and he shouldn't have wasted his time going to New York in the first place." Here a sob caught in her throat, but she shook away the urge to cry, clearing her throat and going on. "Grandmother Kain said daddy ruined two brilliant careers—that it was all right with her that he ruined his own, but she didn't see why he thought he could ruin my mother's and get away with it. She said daddy would ruin me, too, if he knew I might someday be as good as my mother. But grandmother said that wasn't necessary—I could come here. And... and...." Patience took a deep breath.

"That was when I was here before. Well, she—grandmother—she gave me an airline ticket. She arranged it especially so the ticket would be good whenever I wanted to use it. She told me just to hop on a plane and come whenever I had the notion to. I didn't mean to use it—I didn't mean to run away, Alexis, really, I didn't...."

The girl swung around to face the woman. Her eyes were red, full of tears. "I didn't want to leave daddy. I don't believe he would ruin anyone's career on purpose. I know he's a good father, but when I had that argument with Old John, I just couldn't stand it anymore. I just wanted to get out, so I hitched a ride to Harrison and stayed outside the airport all night long, until the sun came up and I could get on the plane and it wouldn't seem suspicious. I know I shouldn't have, but I couldn't help it. Now daddy's going to hate me forever. I can't go back there.... What am I going to do?" And she flung herself into Alexis's arms, a hot misery infusing her young body.

Alexis led her back to the couch. From her purse she took a white linen handkerchief edged in lace and offered it to Patience, who dried her tears. "What am I going to do?" she repeated.

"First, you're going to calm down," Alexis said softly. "And then we're going to talk for a bit. Would you like something to drink? We can ring for someone."

"No—I don't want any of grandmother's servants to come."

"Honey, we don't call them servants."

"I just want to talk to you, Alexis. But...I don't know what to say, where to begin."

"Why don't you begin by telling me what it is you want? Do you want to stay here with Evelyn?"

Patience shrugged her shoulders. She thought for a moment and slowly shook her head.

"Well, then, do you want to go home?"

The teenager lifted her eyes from her hands, folded in her lap. She looked nor at Alexis, not at the elegant room, but into the distance. Her eyes clouded again, soon filling with tears.

"I miss home," she said evenly, not giving in to the emotion that threatened to rack her. "I already miss the way it looks, even the way it smells. The city smells bad to me—too much pollution. But I don't want to stay there, Alexis—I don't want to stay in the hills. You don't understand what it's like to be in a place where nothing ever happens. I don't want to live in the country, in a little nowhere town, all my life. I have talent; I know I have, and I want to use it. I don't want to be like daddy—I just don't. I know he's a good man. But he's just a hillbilly fiddler. I don't think it's going to make one bit of difference that he played with that orchestra. He's happiest in the hills. He always will be. Not me. Music is everything to me. That's the difference between daddy and me...."

Alexis was amazed at the maturity of Patience's explanation. She could see in the girl the same forces that must have pulled at Right John when he was only a little older than his daughter. She could also see something of herself. Someday she must write about the effect the places where they grew up had on the dreams of people—young people especially. It seemed almost silly that so simple a thing could determine one's destiny. Alexis thought about people in Mountain View for whom the choice of where to live, where to stay, had never been a problem. She could think of only two—Old John and his grandson, Roosevelt. Everyone else—Lizzie, Right John, George Fox, Patience, Caroline Kain and she herself had been transplanted, or wanted to be. She understood the girl's anxiety, though she had no answer to Patience's dilemma, which was also her own. She wanted, however, to offer what help she could.

"You know," she began, "I think it's wrong for a person to think where they are necessarily determines what they are. Maybe a person isn't really defined by her circumstances. Maybe she can keep an open mind, make the best of more than one world. After all, there are plenty of people who move easily from the country to the city and back again many times in the course of their lives."

"Daddy couldn't do that," Patience argued.

"No." Alexis's voice was full of a wistful sadness, her blue-green eyes glazing with a secret pain. "Your father is as much a part of the Ozarks as the mountain mist. He's a mountain man if ever there was one. You'd sooner get a briar out of a boar's ear as get *him* out of the country...."

"You really love him, don't you?" Patience asked quietly, and Alexis, who'd been thinking not about her doomed love for John, but about the man himself, was startled. It took her a moment to compose herself, to hide the tears she was suddenly on the verge of shedding. Patience compounded the problem by asking, "Are you going to marry him?"

"No," Alexis answered carefully, straining to control any evidence of her sorrow. She wanted to be fair to Patience. She didn't want John's betrayal of her to mar a reconciliation between the girl and her father. Alexis would have time to vent her own pain later—all the time in the world. She drew a deep steadying breath. "I think you have a right to know your father asked me to marry him, honey. But no, I'm not going to. I've been thinking about this all the way up here, and I can see now that for me—and for your father—it's too late to change, too late to compromise. I've got family and work here in Chicago, while your dad's whole life is down there in the hills. We—John and I—we are already what we are. I don't think we can ever be different, right for each other. When he realized you were up here, he blamed me...." The truth of that hurt so much that Alexis bit her lip, turning her head to hide her face from Patience. But the girl sensed the woman's distress.

"I didn't mean to—"

"I know you didn't mean to cause me any trouble, Patience. The point is that where there's no trust, there can be no...." She had intended to say "no love," but the words froze in her throat. "Listen, dear, all that is beside the point. What I wanted to say is that it's not too late for *you*, Patience. You can be anything you want. Not just one thing, not just one kind of person, but many—all at once. Go back to the hills for a while. Learn the good things the country has to offer. Be open, be patient. Then, when you really understand where you came from, you can set off on a strong footing. You can go elsewhere—Chicago, New York—anywhere and everywhere. But don't start off as a runaway, as someone without a home. And don't start off without a family. Your father loves you. That love is too good just to throw away."

Patience was deep in thought for a while before she answered, "But I want to go to school here. I want to study music here."

"I think you'll be able to do those things, only just

not right now. Maybe your father has been less patient, less wise, than he should have been, but he's
had you to himself almost all your life. He's not used
to sharing you. Maybe in this next year you can help
him to see that you're becoming your own person. If
you act worthy of his respect, you'll earn it. But not
just that, Patience. You have to help him to understand that you appreciate all he's done for you. He
doesn't always realize people *do* appreciate him.

"You see, when he gave up his chance to be a concert soloist, he also gave up the opportunity to be instantly recognized. Anybody can applaud the efforts
of a star violinist. But who applauds a simple music
teacher, a plain fiddler, a farmer, or father? Your
dad has spent the past ten years of his life without
much recognition—without the people he cares about
most telling him how much they care back. He's
never told me this, but I know because. . . ."

"Because you love him. . . ?"

Alexis looked at this girl, so like her father. She
was suddenly stabbed by a new and even deeper pain,
realizing she hadn't only lost John—she was about to
lose Patience, Old John, Almeda. She couldn't answer Patience, but with a little nod of her head, she
indicated yes, oh yes, she did love Right John Webber.

"Then why can't you marry him?"

"Patience, we're talking about you, not me. Will
you go back?"

"Will you come back with me?"

"I can't."

"Do you mean you're going to stay here forever?"

"I don't know about forever," Alexis said, fighting hard for control. "I've been offered a writing assignment here that I've decided to accept. I'm going to stay."

"Then so am I."

"Oh, come on, Patience. Don't be childish and stubborn. You can't blackmail me."

"I can't go back alone. I can't face daddy. You've got to come with me...."

Alexis didn't want to see John Webber again. That was what she'd told herself over and over on the trip to the airport, on the plane, in the limousine on the way to Margaret's, and again en route to Evelyn Kain's. If he couldn't trust her now, he'd never learn. And not just that. His life had been fine before she'd come along. He'd had his farm and his teaching. He'd had a satisfactory relationship with Mary Holmes and a good relationship with his daughter. His emotional wounds had healed, and if his life wasn't exactly passionate, it was at least pleasant.

What did he have now? For her, he'd played in concert again, resurrecting all his old doubts about his career. Because of Alexis, he'd given up Mary Holmes. No doubt that good lady was more than willing to step into the breach left by Alexis's departure, but still.... And because of Alexis, as he saw it, his daughter had run away. Not to mention the fact that his cousin Roosevelt had received a stunning blow to his pride. Of course, it was true that she'd told John she loved him, even that she'd marry him. She realized his unfair accusation had been spoken in a moment of terrible stress. He had probably been deeply hurt by what he must have seen as Alexis's desertion of him without goodbye.

But she wasn't going back. Not because she didn't love him. Because she loved him so much. She saw clearly just what a major disruption she'd been in his life. The incident with Patience, even though it had come to a head over the course of only a few hours, had so drained Alexis that she felt afraid, afraid it *was* her fault this had happened. She couldn't bear the thought of having caused John such trouble and grief. She wanted to spare him. She wanted him to go back to his former uncomplicated life, before she'd so foolishly burst in. It hurt her to come to this conclusion, but she decided she'd rather bear the pain of losing him than cause him more anguish. The way he'd been during the hours when he didn't know his daughter's whereabouts had shown her how much John Webber was capable of suffering. She never wanted him to suffer like that again.

"I can't go with you, Patience. I can't."

IN THE END, she did agree to go. She agreed to take Patience as far as the airport in Harrison and to help the girl find a way to spend more time in Chicago. She couldn't speak to John about Patience's future, though. And she couldn't resist treating Evelyn Kain to a few well-chosen expressions from the Ozark dialect!

CHAPTER TWENTY-ONE

A DAY LATER Alexis and Patience headed for Arkansas. It was very early in November, and the weather was uncertain over much of the central United States. In Chicago there were such high winds that Alexis was apprehensive about whether the plane would be able to take off. But after some delay it did.

There had been a tearful call the night before to Mountain View. Only Patience had spoken to John. When Patience held out the receiver to Alexis, she shook her head, and Patience said to her father, "Guess she'll talk to you tomorrow...." Alexis probably would have to talk to him, though what words she'd use for goodbye, she didn't know. She was trying so hard not to waver in her determination. She could only think of one thing at a time. John hadn't insisted on speaking to her. Maybe he, too, had finally seen the impossibility of their ever being able to build a future together. It would make things easier if he understood that, she told herself.

As the flight progressed, the weather got worse. This was evident from looking outside the window of the first-class section, but also from observing the steward and stewardess, who were becoming more falsely reassuring by the hour. Patience seemed more daunted by the prospect of seeing her father than

worried about the possibility of plane trouble. Perhaps she wasn't sophisticated enough, Alexis
reflected, to understand that the almost frantic friendliness of the airline personnel masked a fear unusual
among employees noted for their unflappable poise.

Was it Alexis's imagination, or was it getting colder
in the plane the farther south they went? She did know
the sky was unnaturally dark for the middle of the
day, and at one point, when the dark mass of clouds
beneath them parted momentarily, she glanced out the
window, expecting to get a peek at the landscape.
What she saw was a raging blizzard obscuring her view
of the earth.

When the honeyed tones of the captain came over
the intercom, informing the anxious passengers the
flight was about to be diverted to Little Rock, Alexis's first reaction was irritation rather than fear. They
had planned to arrive in Harrison and would now
have to make alternative plans to get to Mountain
View, since no one would be on hand to meet them.
Patience was by then fully aware of the danger they·
were in. However, she seemed to think it was all very
exciting. Arkansas was a fairly warm place on the
whole, and the sight of snow, especially snow on the
second day of November, was new to her. Teenagers
in general and Patience Webber in particular were
certainly full of surprises. The girl who had accurately put her finger on the differences between her
father's ambitions and her own was bouncing up and
down in her seat, exclaiming, "A blizzard—great!"

She was far less enthusiastic about the storm, when
it came time to land in the midst of it. Neither Patience nor Alexis made any attempt to hide their ap-

prehension as the plane began to circle for what seemed hours above the snow-clogged airport. Even the airline employees abandoned their pretense that everything was normal. "I've never seen anything like this down here," the steward said, shaking his head. "Saw it in Winnipeg in October, once when I worked for a different company. But I've never seen this kind of snow south of the Mason-Dixon line, that's for sure!"

Finally the plane did land with no apparent difficulty, accompanied by a collective sigh of relief. Disembarking proved to be another matter. As the stewardess carefully explained, the airport maintenance crew was coping with the unusual conditions as best as it could, but the runways couldn't be properly cleared. What had seemed so smooth a landing to the passengers had actually been a near-emergency procedure. The plane had been brought down at a considerable distance from the terminal. No vehicles could reach the plane where it now sat, so airport officials had decided to have the passengers disembark and hike to the terminal.

It was twilight already. Steward and stewardess began to assist the first-class passengers to an emergency exit. There was a quick efficiency to their movements that did more to instill confidence than their earlier words had done. Still, as Alexis was helped down a shaky emergency ladder into a howling snow-filled wind, she felt a jolt of real fear. Patience must have been anxious, too, for she followed closely behind. When she reached the ground and stood beside Alexis, she grabbed the woman's hand and held fast as they set out on their trek to the terminal.

In the unnatural gloom of that strange afternoon, the straggly line of passengers stretched out ahead and behind Alexis were barely visible to her, not only because of the fading light, but also because every time she looked up, the swirling snow hit her in the face and forced her to lower her eyes. She and Patience were shivering. Luckily, they'd both worn boots that day, though not snow boots. Alexis was grateful she'd convinced Patience to change out of the running shoes in which she'd made her escape. In fact, she was dressed entirely in Alexis's clothes. She'd left several things at her grandmother's— almost as hostages toward her return, as Alexis had done when she left Mountain View the first time.

Though the temperature wasn't far below freezing, the wind was bitter. Alexis couldn't tell how much progress they were making as they slogged along. It seemed to be taking them hours, when in fact, she realized, they had only been walking for ten minutes or so. Every once in a while she glanced up, but all she could see were her fellow passengers bent down against the wind, some walking two or three abreast, but most in single file, a pale slow-moving line against the paler but infinitely more rapid snow.

The third or fourth time Alexis looked up, her eyes caught a dark figure moving toward the passengers. At first she thought she must be imagining the figure. She could, after all, only open her eyes for a few seconds at a time. Forcing her eyes up despite the wind and snow, she stared hard into the distance. This time, she got a good look at the figure. Despite the weather, he was moving quickly—she could see that it was a man, that he was striding forcefully past all the other passengers, glancing now and then at the peoples' faces. He was approaching her and Patience. He was Right John Webber.

And in the moment that Alexis realized it was he, he must have recognized her, for he began to run, his feet not slipping, sure even in the slush. She was amazed to see him, astounded that he had come to Little Rock, let alone found them in the midst of a blizzard! It took her only a moment to estimate how many miles he must have driven through the mountains in that snow. The thought made her nearly sick with the sort of anxiety one feels when a danger is past but the fear lingers.

When he came within a few feet of them and she could clearly see his beloved face, she began to cry. Large white snowflakes lodged in his windblown hair. His usually golden complexion was pale with strain and with the gloom of the twilit snow. His eyes, usually as bright a blue as the noonday sky, were lowered against the elements, and perhaps, too, against the strong feeling he felt it unmanly to show—relief after hours of fear. He was dressed in a dark jacket, dark jeans encasing his strong legs, and Alexis couldn't help but think the closer he came, the more solid he seemed, the less frightening the swirling snow.

In a moment he was upon them. He opened his wide arms. Alexis felt Patience's hand rip from her own as the girl flew into her father's embrace. Before Alexis even knew what was happening, she felt his powerful arms encircle her, his large hand shielding her face from the snow, holding her head against his shoulder so that she could make no reply when he whispered beneath the furious sounds of the snow-storm, "My two runaways. Old John says he's gonna peel ya both—but all *I* can do is thank God you're okay!"

He took off his jacket and made both of them huddle beneath it, not listening to their protests that he needed it as much as they. He insisted his thick black turtleneck was plenty warm enough. Despite her objections, Alexis was grateful for the extra warmth of his jacket. For it was quite a while later before they finally made it to the terminal, and a while after that before John coaxed his truck into action, out of the snow-packed parking lot. He traveled only far enough to find a motel where they could hole up until the roads were cleared.

Home. Was that where she'd just been? Or was it where she was headed? Maybe it was where she was at that moment, when she awakened from her nap and found herself cradled in a pair of strong arms she just knew hadn't released her all the time she'd slept.

John had booked a separate room for his daughter and seen her safely in. Then he'd taken Alexis to their room. He insisted on drawing a bath for her, on helping her remove her wet clothing. His gentle hands so near her skin had made her lose all desire to sleep. They brushed her neck, her upper arms, the tops of her breasts as he removed the silk blouse she wore. But when she had raised her arms to embrace him, he had gently disengaged her with a little unpassionate kiss. She'd felt a stab of fear then, was sure he didn't want her.

Yet she could read the desire in his eyes as he urged her to slip out of her lace-and-satin panties. He knelt to pull them down over her thighs. Tenderly he kissed the slightly rounded curve of her stomach, his lips as soft on her skin as the petals of a flower. She breathed in sharply, reached down and grasped his head; she just stood there with him kneeling before her. For a moment it was enough to have him close and safe and touching her.

But she grew impatient, for she was standing there wearing nothing, and he still had on his jeans and shirt. "Undress..." she said teasingly. "Undress...." Behind her, beyond the door leading to the washroom, the water began to cool in the tub. She didn't care. Nor did she care that she'd told herself only that morning that she was coming back to Arkansas just to say goodbye. "Undress...."

But he pulled away from her with a little shudder and stood up. She was lifted off her feet and gently placed in the tub. When he made to move away, she grabbed his wrist. "Don't you want me, John?" she asked, her voice more teasing than worried. She could tell, just by the way he touched her, that he wanted her very much indeed. He laughed and knelt beside the tub so that his eyes were even with her own. She felt then that she might drown—not in the tepid water, but in the bottomless blue wonder of those eyes.

"I want you, all right," he'd said, lifting a finger to tweak her chin. "But I want you to sleep first. You've come a long way, and it's been an awful day. I want you to nap. Then we'll have a late dinner. Then we'll see...."

So she had napped. And dreamed of Evelyn Kain and Roosevelt Webber and the plane—dreamed it had gone down in a swirl of flame and snow. But before she hit the ground, she felt a hand smooth her hair and cradle her head, and without waking she had realized she was safe.

Then she'd dreamed the plane had landed, in a mountain meadow full of pink and white and yellow flowers. There was a log cabin in the meadow. In front of it was a clothesline, and on the clothesline hung a quilt of an intricate and beautiful pattern. The quilt swayed gently in the breeze, now obscuring, now revealing the cabin porch, where Alexis saw two rocking chairs. One was empty. The other was occupied by a man. The man held some object. As she came closer, she knew what he held was a fiddle. He put it down when he saw her come running. He put it down and opened his arms.

Her eyes shot open. "Welcome home, love," John said. His embrace was warm, his arms encircling her shoulders and waist, his face so close that his sweet breath fanned her cheek and the curve of her chin. It took her a moment to realize the man who held her was not part of a dream, but part of her life.

Home.

He lay beside her beneath the warm covers of the motel bed. It wasn't an elegant room. But it was infused with a warmth that belied the early-winter cold outside. She was content just to feel him so near for a minute. She stretched her body a bit and let it touch his where it might—thigh to thigh, her arm across his chest. But when he planted a kiss in the open crook of her elbow, his lips hot on the tender, exposed skin, a shudder began in her chest and quickly moved down into the nether reaches of her body. She turned swiftly then, cleverly pinning him before he had a chance to protest. When he did protest with a laughingly uttered, "Hey, what do you think you're doing?" she silenced him with a deep thrust of her tongue into his open mouth.

For endless moments, their only motion was the motion of that long, languorous, exploratory kiss. Her body was feather light on his, her lips demanding as they came down on his, again and again. His mouth met hers with equal strength, his tongue teasing, pushing, sweeping along her pearly teeth before plunging deeper into the eager recesses of her mouth.

John's hands began a new exploration, at first tracing idly along her shoulder blades and the slender planes of her back. He drew his fingers down past her waist, ran his open palms along the curve of her hips before sweeping up to grab hold of her buttocks with the kneading motion that always drove her to distraction. She pressed closer to him, her breasts against the rough curls on his chest, her fingers entwined in his golden hair, her face against his shoulder.

She opened her mouth and tasted the saltiness of his skin with her tongue, flicking with a rapid motion that stilled his hands for a moment as passion began to assert its power in him. She slithered up a bit; both of them were dewed with the slightest sheen of perspiration. She slid up and traced the outline of his ear with her skillful tongue, running it first along the outside curve, and then more boldly teasing the inner curve with swift and tempting flicks. He drew in his breath, and she felt the breeze of it in her hair as he exhaled. Again her lips found his, and as they did so she moved one of her hands so that it grazed his side and the tops of his thighs—which was all she could reach.

Hungry for more of her, John turned, his strength making it easy for him to flip his body over on top of hers. Briefly, he merely lay still, his golden limbs covering her paler skin. Large as he was, he seemed weightless over her. She clung to him, as though to reassure them both that they were there, safe and together.

Her slender arms around his neck filled him with such tenderness that it was hard for him to fight back the tears. He didn't want her to see him cry, though he wished there were some adequate way he could tell her how much he wanted her. He didn't mean only sexually—though God knew he wanted that, too. More importantly, he needed her in his life. She was so beautiful—so fine that it still took his breath away to lay eyes on her. But there was more to it than that—much more.

All his life he'd lived according to his own dreams, no matter what other people had said. And he'd felt a stranger everywhere he'd gone. He had been a stranger in his own father's house because he wanted to be a farmer, and when he got to his grandfather's farm, he was a stranger because of the music that wouldn't let go of him. So he had followed the music, and look where that had led. He had been a foreigner in New York. Then he'd come home to find that being in New York made him a foreigner in the Ozarks. His life had been bearable as long as Caroline was there—she had been such a rebel that she'd almost made him forget he just couldn't seem to fit in anywhere.

But Caroline, Lord rest her soul, hadn't been there very long. All those years of being alone. How could he ever live like that again? How could he have lived at all before Alexis came to him? Unlike him, she wasn't a stranger anywhere. She'd come as though from a different planet, and within a short time had made Mountain View her home. He had wanted to be neighborly, to help her get used to the hills, yet she'd taken to the Ozarks so well that he felt she had something to teach him. In his heart he believed she might teach him to be truly at home at last. If she could forgive him for his rash cruelty.... If he could find the courage to ask for that forgiveness....

"Hey!" she teased. "Where have you gone?" Reaching up a slim finger, she traced the strong planes of his face, stroking his brow, his cheek, his chin, then drawing a teasing line around the sensuous curves of his mouth. He captured her finger in his teeth, hardly touching her but stopping her hand in its path. He kissed each fingertip that she laughingly offered to his lips.

"Alexis," he said, pulling back so that he could look into her eyes, but not shifting his body. "Alexis, I'm so sorry."

She didn't want contention to mar the closeness of the moment. "Sorry for what?" she asked. She had to turn her face away because she knew there would still be anger in her eyes.

"Look at me, sugar," he said, gently taking her face in his hands. "I'm sorry. I'm sorry I ever accused you of being a spy for that old bag of suet."

"John," she said, smiling despite herself, "I hardly think it fitting to refer to one of Kenwood's most distinguished matrons as an 'old bag of suet.' Besides, though I was never her spy—and never will be, I might add—you weren't wrong to ask me whether I'd come down here at her bidding. I didn't, though.''

''Why did you come?''

''A number of reasons,'' she replied, stalling for time to organize her thoughts. ''Certainly, I needed a change. Everyone does once in a while, I guess, but for writers a change of scene can mean the difference between work and no work. I was lucky that way, because as soon as I got here the ideas started to flow. But there was something else, two things really....''

''Karl Hulst?'' She had told him about Karl a long time before, but she herself hadn't thought about Karl in so many weeks that it actually took her a minute to recognize the name.

''He was part of it,'' she answered honestly. ''Chicago was another part. I'd lived there all my life—had lived a particular way all my life. It was beginning to look as though my life-style was all there was of me. I don't know if I'm making myself clear. It's hard to explain. It's just that sometimes it's necessary to separate what you are from what you do. In Chicago, I did a lot of different things—some pretty exciting things, by most people's standards. But every once in a while, I got the strong feeling that I didn't know what kind of person I really was. A very busy stranger seemed to be living inside my skin. I...I guess I was tired of that. So I came down here to find out who I was.''

''And who are you?''

Again she was forced to turn away from the intensity of his gaze. ''I'm Alexis Juneau Smythe of the Chicago Smythes....''

"Not for long," he declared, and laughter rippled through his deep tones, the same laugh that had preceded their first meeting, so many months before. Suddenly she thought of that other reason for her coming to Mountain View. She had fled to the hills not only to find herself but also to find him.

"What are you talking about?" she asked, looking up and trying to hide a smile, because she knew very well what he was talking about.

"Seems to me I asked you to marry me a while back."

She wrinkled her face in mockery of deep thought. "Did you?"

"I sure did. Seems to me you answered me, too."

"What did I say?" she queried in the same teasing tone.

"You said yes." He wanted to tease, too, but emotion, the pure joy, the relief, of having her back ripped through him and renewed the threat of tears so that he had to kiss her passionately to hide the depth of his feeling, to hide his telltale eyes.

And his lips on hers were like a seal marking the destiny she was finally ready to accept. She *was* Alexis Juneau Smythe, but that didn't mean she had to be one thing only. She could easily be her own person and the wife of Right John Webber. And the lover of Right John Webber. And the friend of Right John Webber. She wanted him more than she had ever wanted anything in her life. But that didn't cancel out her life. It enriched all the other things she had and did and was.

"I love you, John."

"I love you, too."

Outside, the too-early snow began to melt, running in rivulets down the sides of the hills, joining with mountain streams, coursing along until it met the mighty rivers of the state, perhaps to find its way to the mightiest of them, the Mississippi.

Inside the warm room, the tenderness of the lovers melted all their former anger and fear. Her hands were like little waves lapping at the willing surfaces of his strong body. When she touched his shoulders, kneading the strongly muscled flesh, he kissed her, drawing her to him by cradling the back of her head with his two strong hands.

She let her hands slip down along his side, his thighs, his powerful legs. The feel of him, the texture of him beneath her fingers was the most glorious thing she had ever experienced. Better than velvet or satin or silk.

His lips took hers again and again. His hands knew every curve of her. His limbs became entwined with hers. And the tenderness turned to passion and the passion to a desire that engulfed them both until they soared on the high wide wave of ecstasy, remaining at its crest for endless moments. Until, clinging to each other, they spiraled down, a long descent to where the peaceful eddies of spent passion washed them. And they slept.

CHAPTER TWENTY-TWO

EVERYWHERE CHRISTMAS IS THE SAME, and everywhere it's unique. In the Ozarks, the folks of Mountain View were preparing for a celebration—not only because of the holiday, but because of the wedding. Everybody knew Right John Webber and Alexis Juneau Smythe from Chicago were going to get married on the evening before Christmas Eve. Everybody knew because everybody was invited. And nobody would have missed it for the world.

On the day of the wedding, Almeda Webber was in her glory, for it was in her kitchen that most of the food was being prepared. That made her the boss. The only visitor to the kitchen she didn't order around was John's mother from Houston. Though it had seemed strange to Alexis not to meet her future mother-in-law until the last minute, the two had hit it off very well. Both sat together now at the kitchen table. Alexis was peeling potatoes, but Mrs. Webber apparently thought such a task beneath her, for she merely sat and watched. Unlike Alexis, who wore old jeans, John's mother was dressed rather formally. Alexis could see a farm kitchen was not Mrs. Webber's favorite place; nonetheless, she liked the woman despite her slight air of pretense.

"There's another peck out in the back kitchen

when you finish them," Almeda said to the bride, not waiting for an answer. Almeda was supervising a whole crew of neighborhood women, who were ranged at a long trestle table making fruit pies with an efficiency that would have put the best assembly-line workers to shame. One woman mixed the ingredients for the pastry. Another kneaded it lightly. Another rolled it. Two women had the task of cutting the dough and shaping it into the pie pans. There were several others who prepared the fillings. As they worked, the women talked nonstop, occasionally throwing out some homey bit of advice to Alexis, who as often as not blushed at their remarks. "You know what I always tell my husband, dear?" one woman shouted across the kitchen.

"No," Alexis answered with a smile. "What?"

" 'Opal,' I say, 'Once a king, always a king. But once a night is enough.' " All the women except John's mother laughed at this, but when Alexis smiled at her helplessly, her future mother-in-law smiled, too.

Countless pies had already been baked, and cobblers, and enough bread and biscuits to feed a three-day marching army. There was a roast of beef bigger than any Alexis had ever seen, even in restaurants, and a number of roasted chickens sat warming in a huge covered enamel pan on top of the stove. There was a pork roast, too, from one of the farm pigs— Jeremiah had been his name. It no longer made Alexis flinch to know she would eat something she'd previously been acquainted with!

Once she'd finished the potatoes she would gladly have helped with something else, but Almeda insisted she had done enough, seeing as it was her own wedding. The kindly woman suggested that Alexis take a nap, and indeed, she had every intention of going upstairs to lie down. She only made it as far as the front parlor, for there she found Patience and John putting the finishing touches on the Christmas tree. Alexis stood unnoticed for a moment, letting the deep warmth of her love swell up to fill her whole body as she watched the scene. By the fireplace, Patience knelt, her hair catching the light of the flames and shining back. It was afternoon and not very dark in the room. The girl was popping corn in an old-style metal popper held over the fire by a long handle. Alexis suspected the popcorn was for eating rather than stringing—the tree was already so laden with ornaments, all of them old-fashioned and most of them homemade, that she couldn't imagine where there would be room for another thing.

In fact, John was standing beside the tree with a crystal snowflake on a string dangling from one finger. He was so tall it was easy for him to reach most of the tree, and he was so handsome in the dim light of the afternoon that it was hard for Alexis to breathe when she looked at him. In his red-and-black flannel shirt and blue denims, he seemed every inch the farmer. Yet when he lifted his hand to a high branch and carefully balanced the ornament on a tiny twig, she recognized the delicate touch of the artist. He was so many things. He was hers, and she was determined that the love they shared would be nurtured between them so that it might grow deeper as all the years went by.

"That must be it," she said, laughing and walking toward him. "There isn't room for anything else."

"There's one more thing," he answered. And Alexis looked down at the boxes the ornaments had been stored in. In his methodical manner, John had folded every piece of tissue that had wrapped the fragile items. It looked as though every box had been emptied.

"I don't see any other ornaments," she commented.

"That's because you're looking in the wrong place." She could tell by the dancing light in his eyes that he was up to something. She glanced at him quizzically, and he lifted a finger to tap the upper left pocket of his shirt.

"In your pocket?" she asked, a little confused. He nodded. She reached toward the pocket, resting her hand for a moment on his broad chest. His shirt was warm from the heat of his body, and again her love for him rose to fill her with happiness and gratitude. She drew a sharp breath; he raised her chin with his finger, planting a deep kiss on her parted lips.

"Hey!" Patience quipped, "that's no fair. We haven't put up the mistletoe yet!" They all laughed at that, including Old John, who'd been in the room the whole time but not of it. He'd been asleep in a wing chair by the fire.

John drew Alexis out of the parlor into the front hallway, scented with pine from a huge Christmas wreath hanging there. In the soft winter sunlight falling through the window, his hair glowed golden, and when she looked up at him she noticed the light, or something else, made his blue eyes look a little hazy, a little misted. He drew from his pocket a small object wrapped in red tissue. Taking Alexis's hand, he placed the package in her palm.

Slowly she unfolded the tissue, and saw there a beautifully formed pendant in the shape of a bell. Made entirely of diamonds set in white gold, it was suspended from a white-gold chain. As she lifted the lovely piece of jewelry, it caught the sun and sent dazzling light shooting all over. "Oh, John, it's so beautiful, so very beautiful. Here, put it on for me. Is it a Christmas present?"

"In a way, love," he said, his hands fastening the chain, then settling on her slender shoulders. He bent forward so that his lips grazed her listening ear. "It's a Christmas present and a wedding present. It's a reminder that this season will always be doubly blessed for you and me. . . ."

ALEXIS'S MOTHER HAD proved to be more of a sport than Alexis had ever suspected she could be. She had made no fuss over the fact that her daughter was marrying a man she herself hadn't met, hundreds of miles from home—and with less than two months' notice. As for meeting the Webbers, Margaret had pretty much fallen in love with John, who had flown up to Chicago with Alexis and Patience for Thanksgiving. She seemed more strained in the presence of Old John and Almeda, and wasn't to meet the Roosevelt Webbers until the reception. But all in all, she managed very well, and Alexis had the feeling that after the wedding, future visits from her mother might just be a possibility.

The one thing Margaret had insisted on was that Alexis's gown be made by the same Chicago designer who had made her own mother's wedding dress, and her mother's before her. Now as she dressed for the ceremony, Alexis was helped by Lizzie Cabe and Margaret. Both women sighed in appreciation when they saw how perfectly the cream-colored creation in imported silk suited the bride. Despite the richness of the material, the dress cleverly achieved a casual air. It was ankle length with a ruffled yoke and stand-up collar that gave it a sort of country-pioneer look, perfectly appropriate to a wedding in Mountain View.

As she arranged Alexis's veil for her, Lizzie couldn't help shedding a tear or two. "It's been wonderful having you here in the house, Alexis," she said. "I'm going to miss you something awful...."

"Thank you, Lizzie," Alexis answered, kissing her friend on the cheek. "Thank you for everything. But I don't believe you'll miss me now that you've got a permanent boarder...." Both women giggled at that, then explained to Margaret that Lizzie had recently married George Fox, who had bought fifty acres nearby for an experimental farm. He farmed the land but didn't live on it, since he and Lizzie could live in the house in town. The arrangement suited everyone, including Roosevelt Webber, from whom George had bought the land. The purchase, plus a government contract to act as a consultant on George's project, had pretty much solved Roosevelt's financial problems. Alexis didn't tell her mother that. The less said the better.

When the three women agreed that Alexis was quite ready, and when Margaret and Lizzie had commented that she was the most beautiful bride they'd ever seen, Lizzie left mother and daughter alone for a final few minutes.

There was a moment's awkward silence, a pause filled with shared emotion that didn't easily find its way into words. Then Margaret stepped up to Alexis, took her hand and kissed her cheek. "My dear," she said, her even voice not entirely hiding her deep feeling. "You are a woman and have been for some time. You have your own way of doing things and of looking at things. In many ways, you have more experience of life than I have. So there is no advice I can offer you—"

"Mother, I—"

"But there is one thing I'd like to say on this very important occasion," Margaret went on. "Before the courage fails me. You have been a joy to me, my dear, all your life. Had you been my own flesh and blood, I couldn't have loved you more than I did, than I do. And I know that Wallace always felt the same. Perhaps that's why we never felt bad about not telling you what I'm about to tell you now...." She hesitated.

Alexis stood perfectly still, as beautiful as a Doulton figurine of a bride. She was afraid even to say, "What?" After a moment Margaret went on.

"Your father and I had to swear never to reveal what I am about to tell you as a condition of being able to adopt you. After careful thought, though, I have decided to let you know who your real parents are—were."

"You mean you know? You mean all this time you've known?" Alexis was shocked, so shocked she wasn't sure she wanted to hear the rest of what her mother had to say. But Margaret tenderly squeezed her daughter's hand and went on.

"There are two reasons why I feel justified in breaking the promise I made when you came to me. The first is that your real father has been dead for some years, and your real mother is no longer in any way associated with our family. The other reason is that I know that now you're married, you'll begin to give some thought to having a child—children—of your own, and I'm convinced you should know what their lineage will be. Alexis, you are the daughter of Wallace's brother, Stuart, your uncle Stuart whom you knew as a child...."

"Uncle Stuart?" He'd been a favorite, though she'd lost track of him as she'd grown older. Never had she suspected. It would take a long time for her to sort out her feelings. She couldn't even begin. "And my biological mother?" She didn't want to say "real mother." Margaret was her real mother.

"Your biological mother was the daughter of another very prominent Chicago family. You must remember that it was in the fifties that you were born. Things were different then. Some people felt certain things should be hidden...."

But Alexis wasn't listening to this part of Margaret's explanation; she was thinking about a different aspect of this shocking news. "Mother," she said. "Do you mean I'm a Smythe by blood?"

"Yes, dear, through and through. Though not a MacIntyre, I'm afraid."

Alexis kissed Margaret, and both women managed

a small laugh. "Does that surprise you so—being a Smythe by blood, I mean?"

"Yes," Alexis answered honestly. "I always thought I came from a different—oh, I don't know—a different sort of family."

"It doesn't really matter in the end, does it, dear?" Margaret asked. "You are you, no matter what, aren't you?"

"Yes, mother. Yes, indeed.. . ."

They talked for a few minutes longer, prolonging these special moments together, but soon it was time to go. Despite her jitters, which her mother told her were appropriate and traditional, Alexis walked calmly down the stairs into Lizzie's living room, where Lizzie, Patience and Almeda as well as several neighbor women had gathered to escort the bride the few steps down the street to the church, where the groom stood waiting. Though it was late December, it was quite mild. Over her gown Alexis wore only a cream-colored silk shawl, which was taken from her shoulders by one of the women as the bride entered the church. In the twilight, candles glowed from every corner of the small building, filled with relatives and friends. But Alexis had eyes only for one person. On the arm of Old John Webber, who was all spruced up for the honor of giving her away, she walked down the aisle toward him, her foot not faltering in its step.

As she approached the altar to the beautiful strains of a Bach violin piece played by one of Right John's students, her beloved turned to look at her, and she saw in his eyes love and the promise of love. She joined hands with him. She received his respectful kiss. She received his vow of devotion, and with joy in her heart, she pledged herself: his companion, his lover, his wife.

After the ceremony, it wasn't the violinists but the fiddlers who provided the music. Those who had been at the church made their way back to Old John's farm, where others awaited them, everything in readiness for the wedding feast.

The whole house was full of the happiness of what some jokingly called the best party since the banker's wake. Even Right John's parents from Houston seemed to enjoy themselves, and Margaret, fine lady that she was, acted as though this country party was as good as any she'd ever been to, which, of course, it was.

There were speeches; there were toasts. The eating and dancing went on for hours—all manner of drinks flowed like the river. Alexis had been to plenty of weddings where the bride and groom hadn't been able to spend one moment together during the reception. It wasn't that way at her reception. She and John danced as if nothing could tear them apart. It was a good portent, as all the neighbors pointed out teasingly every time the music stopped for the musicians to take a breather. It was a good portent, too, that Roosevelt Webber managed to pay his respects to Margaret MacIntyre Smythe as though nothing upsetting had ever happened between them. Another good omen: Mary Holmes came to the party with a handsome escort, and when she offered her best wishes to the bride and groom, it was clear she was sincere.

John and Alexis stayed at the party for a good long

time, but he warned her they'd have to escape without notice. He had even outlined a plan. He snuck away first; she followed, first changing into a pair of jeans and a thick sweater. The truck was parked out near the highway, but John himself was waiting behind one of the tool sheds. Together they ran to the truck. They climbed in and pulled away, both surprised the ruse had worked so well. John had told her about "shivaree," an Ozark ritual of such boisterous and vigorous pranks that some couples were terrified by the noise and general rowdiness. It was an old custom not much practiced anymore, but John didn't want to take a chance.

They drove for a while in silence, every now and then one of John's hands leaving the wheel to tenderly caress his wife's. Their destination was a small cabin on top of a hill overlooking a deep valley, a dark hollow in whose depths stood tall trees silvered by the moon.

He stopped the truck. Gently he embraced her, then sighed and got out, coming around to open her door and lift her down, into his arms. For a moment they stood in a clinch in the brisk moonlit air. Then they approached the cabin. Many years before, this log structure had been the Webber family "honeymoon cabin," where many a bride and groom had got their start on married life. In Old John's time it had fallen into disrepair, but Right John had hit upon the idea of fixing it up for their honeymoon. Only the two of them knew it was fit for use.

As Alexis walked up the path, it occurred to her that had anyone told her a year ago she would be spending her wedding night in a cabin in the hills, she would have laughed at them. But if she was laughing at the moment, it was out of pure happiness.

They entered, and after many kisses John decided he'd better stoke the stove. His sure motions at the work made Alexis confident about the future. Not only was she looking forward to her life with this man, who was as dear to her as breath itself, but she would also be at home in the hills, especially since she'd got a book contract. For when she had finally given up the Chicago project, another had come her way. After her honeymoon, she planned to embark on the most comprehensive in-depth study of the lives of Ozark women that had ever been done.

Alexis watched John move around the cabin by the light of kerosene lamps, making things ready for the night. To her, the little building was a haven, a mansion more wonderful than the houses of Kenwood— or anywhere else on earth. She moved toward John, toward his arms, arms strong enough to share work, gentle enough to share love. She wanted to tell him how happy she felt, how her heart was near to bursting with her love for him. But the minute he sensed her coming toward him, he turned and grabbed her, and the deep passion of his kiss extinguished any possibility of speech. For endless moments they were lost in the wonder of each other, until finally a giggle bubbled out of her, pushing them apart—but only inches apart.

"What is it, sugar?" he asked. "What's so funny?"

"I was just thinking about the advice someone gave me."

"You mean at the reception? Yeah, I got told a thing or two myself—as if I didn't know...."

"I wasn't thinking about that exactly," she said. "Though I certainly know what you mean. Funny, wasn't it?"

He nodded his head before his lips took hers again. After a little while she pulled away and went on, "The advice I was thinking about was this: once someone told me I should stick to my own kind."

"Oh?" John said, the tiniest bit of insecurity still evident in his voice. "What does that mean?"

"It means that *you're* stuck with me," she replied teasingly.

"Imagine that..." he murmured. And his deep laughter, his sweet melodious laugh filled the little log cabin. "Just imagine that...."

He captured her lips with his own. He captured her willing body in his arms. And he swept her off her feet and carried her toward the waiting quilt-covered brass bed....

ABOUT THE AUTHOR

"I love writing about handsome artists—musicians especially!" So says novelist, editor and prolific poet Lucy Snow. *A Red Bird in Winter*, like her first Superromance, features a musician with an unusual past that haunts him in the present. Only Alexis, an elusive yet deeply loving woman, has the power to shake Right John's world in the most exciting way....

There the similarity between the two stories ends. While some of Lucy's characters are based on people she has met, Alexis and John are pure fiction. With *Song of Eden* and *A Red Bird in Winter*, the author continues to hold her family's creative tradition: her sister is a painter; her mother, a talented craftswoman.

As a free-lancer Lucy enjoys immensely both "real" travel and armchair excursions from her cozy Toronto home. The romantic heart of Belgium is next on her itinerary.